D0846400

"STAY WITH ME IF YOU DARE."

Her words were both a surrender and a challenge. She let Patrick take her cold hands in his and bring them to his lips to warm her fingers. ''Come to me, Fenella,'' he whispered.

She obeyed without hesitation, slipping her arms about his and drawing him against her, so that her full breasts were crushed enticingly against his chest and her thigh was nestled against his own.

Fenella's sight was ragged with anticipation. Effortlessly, he swung her into his arms and walked over to the bed, gently setting her down as if she were his most precious possession. When he went to blow out the candle by her bedside, Fenella surprised him by staying his hand.

''Leave it on. . . .''

SO WILD A DREAM

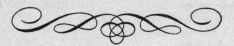

by

Leslie O'Grady

AN ONYX BOOK

NEW AMERICAN LIBRARY

NAL BOOKS ARE AVAILABLE AT QUANTITY DISCOUNTS WHEN USED TO PROMOTE
PRODUCTS OR SERVICES. FOR INFORMATION PLEASE WRITE TO PREMIUM MARKETING
DIVISION, NEW AMERICAN LIBRARY, 1633 BROADWAY, NEW YORK, NEW YORK 10019

Onyx is a trademark of New American Library.

SIGNET, SIGNET CLASSIC, MENTOR, ONYX, PLUME, MERIDIAN
and NAL BOOKS are published by NAL PENGUIN INC.,
1633 Broadway, New York, New York 10019

First Printing, October, 1988

1 2 3 4 5 6 7 8 9

PRINTED IN THE UNITED STATES OF AMERICA

1

FENELLA STOPPED PACING around the drawing room and listened for the hundredth time. All she heard was the steady ticking of the clock on the mantel keeping time with the thudding of her heart. There were no clopping hooves to herald her father's return, no sure footsteps in the hall to allay her fears for his safety on this black, windy night.

Suddenly the bonging of the clock chiming the hour startled Fenella. Could it be ten o'clock already? Eight hours had passed since her father had driven the dogcart off in the pouring rain to deliver the O'Hara baby. Surely it couldn't be taking the child this long to enter the world, since this was the mother's ninth pregnancy and should have been her easiest. But, as a doctor's daughter, Fenella knew any birth was apt to be long and unpredictable.

She shivered and drew her brown woolen shawl closely about her, more for reassurance than warmth. She hurried across the room and went to the window for yet another look.

"No one should be out on a night like this," Fenella grumbled as she cupped her hands against the cold glass and peered out into the gloom.

At least the driving rain had stopped and the moon was trying valiantly to appear. Fenella could see its ghostly, fitful reflection in the pool at the front of the house as shadowy storm clouds scudded across the inky sky, propelled by an ever-rising wind.

Fenella drew away from the window and listened again. First, the wind was nothing more than a breeze, soft and secret murmurings of lovers as it drifted past. Then it turned and gathered force, rattling windows as it moaned

and wailed like a banshee, warning of impending sorrow
and doom.

Fenella's heart seemed to stop. Was it only the wind
she heard, or the keening of the banshee, foretelling her
father's own demise this night?

Her wide brown eyes glazing with terror in anticipation
of what was to come, Fenella pushed up her left sleeve
and absently rubbed the puckered red mark encircling
her wrist like a shackle.

William, my love, please don't let me see the banshee
this time, she prayed in her mind when words wouldn't
pass her stiff, dry lips.

She squeezed her eyes shut, dreading what she would
see when she opened them again. But when Fenella finally gathered enough courage to do so, she saw only the
parlor as it usually was, cozy and prosaic by lamplight,
with nothing amiss. She looked around cautiously. The
pair of worn wing-backed chairs in front of the fireplace
were unoccupied, as was her father's favorite chair by one
window. The cheese, bannocks, and whiskey Fenella had
set out on the tea table for him were untouched. Nothing
was out of place.

And she was mercifully alone.

Fenella let out the breath she had been holding in a
shaky sigh of thanks to William, but she didn't bolster
her flagging courage with false reassurances that there
were no such baleful spirits as banshees. She knew better
now.

She turned and glanced out the window again. "He'll
be home soon," she said hopefully. "All I can do is
wait."

Then she seated herself in one of the wing-backed
chairs and continued her vigil. Soon the heat of the turf
fire and the lateness of the hour caused her head to fall
forward as she drifted off into a light, dreamless sleep.

Sometime later, Fenella awoke with a start, disturbed
by some vague, nameless noise. Although still groggy
with sleep, she sensed that she was not alone, and that
whoever was in the house was not her father, for he would
have announced his presence immediately by singing
some ancient Irish air off-key.

She sat rigidly in her chair, not daring to blink an eye or even take a deep breath. Then she heard the heavy, hesitant footsteps of someone entering the parlor.

Fenella's chair was positioned at an angle with its high back almost facing the entrance, so that whoever had come in couldn't see her sitting there. Yet all she had to do was glance up into the mirror over the fireplace, and she could see her unwelcome guest reflected quite clearly.

As Fenella raised her eyes to the mirror, she almost gasped aloud, for the intruder was a fearsome man dressed in unrelieved black from head to toe, tall and menacing as he stood in the shadows of the doorway and looked around furtively. Then, as Fenella watched, he took off his hat and strolled over to the tea table, where he boldly helped himself to one of her father's bannocks, wolfing it down as though he hadn't eaten in weeks. When that was devoured, he reached for another.

For one fanciful moment Fenella wondered if she were looking at a flesh-and-blood man or a spirit from Irish folklore. She knew that every November Eve, many an unmarried girl set a table with food in hopes that the *fetch*, or spirit twin, of her future lover would climb through the window and dine. But it was now mid-April, not November, and this intruder had used the door as any ordinary mortal would. Besides, Fenella had no desire to take a lover, now or ever.

She held her breath and waited, wondering what to do next. Perhaps if she just sat there quietly, the man would go away and leave her alone. But what if he were a robber and tried to harm her before ransacking the house? She glanced about wildly, searching for anything she could use as a weapon to defend herself.

There, just an arm's length away, was the fireplace poker.

Without so much as a second thought, Fenella sprang to her feet, grasped the poker, and pulled it from its holder with a loud clang. She heard the man curse in surprise as she swung around to confront him, the poker now grasped in both of her hands and wielded high like a club, ready to bash in his head if he dared make a threatening move toward her.

The moment her gaze flew to his face, however, she

faltered, suddenly unsure of herself, and could only stare speechlessly at the pitiful wretch before her. He had been handsome once, as his clean-shaven face attested. But he was now so gaunt that his high cheekbones were all knife-sharp edges greatly accentuated by sunken hollows below. Even by lamplight, his skin had an unhealthy paste-white pallor, and deep shadows underscored ice-blue eyes so devoid of emotion or spirit that it was as if some internal fire had died, leaving a shell of a man without a soul.

But what held Fenella's attention was his dark hair. It was cropped close to the scalp like a convict's, giving him the undignified look of a plucked chicken.

"Who are you and what do you want here?" Fenella demanded with false bravado to mask her fear.

Anger flared in those eyes for just a second, then died, but when the man spoke, his voice was strong, arrogant, and surprisingly cultured. "I am Patrick Quinn," he said, enunciating his name slowly, as if he had momentarily forgotten it.

Fenella stared in disbelief, the poker still raised high.

"Are you daft, woman?" he said, scowling in annoyance. "I said, I am Patrick Quinn." He sounded more sure of himself this time.

She lowered the poker at once, though she still did not feel safe in this man's presence. "So, you must be Cadogan Quinn's son."

"That I am."

Aside from sharing eyes of the same pale blue color, there was scant resemblance between the two men. One was a thoroughbred, the other a bull. The son was tall, long-limbed, and dark, obviously possessing the Spanish blood so often found in the men of Cork, while the father was of average height, stocky, and Viking fair. Even though he was emaciated, Patrick Quinn's features were fine and aristocratic, while Cadogan's were thick and broad, as though his face had been pummeled in one brawl too many.

"Why didn't you knock or at least announce your presence?" Fenella grumbled. "You frightened me half to death. I thought an escaped convict had broken into the house."

"But that is precisely what I was," he replied bitterly, "a convict."

Fenella gaped at him, then turned away, ostensibly to return the poker to its place by the fire, but in reality to hide her flushed cheeks. Cadogan rarely spoke of his son to her, but Fenella knew from her father and sundry village gossip that Patrick Quinn had been convicted of a crime four years ago, in 1876, and sentenced to an English prison.

When Fenella was more composed, she turned to face him. "Please forgive my poor manners, Mr. Quinn. I am Fenella Considine. My father, Dr. Liam Considine, is the dispensary doctor in Mallow."

He scowled. "Considine? Where's that charlatan Rourke?"

"He left to open a more profitable practice in Dublin," she replied. "My father replaced him a little over three years ago."

"That was after I was sent . . ." Patrick Quinn's face clouded over as the sentence trailed off. Then he snapped, "You know my father?"

Fenella nodded. "Who in all County Cork doesn't know the Quinns of Rookforest? My father and I are proud to count Cadogan a valued friend. We are often his guests for dinner."

"How is the old man?" Patrick Quinn asked, his voice softening for the first time with obvious affection.

Fenella looked at him for a moment. She would hardly call Cadogan Quinn, a hale and vigorous man of fifty, an "old man."

"He is well, but your mother—"

"Is dead," he snapped. "I know. At least they had the decency to tell me that. And is my cousin, Miss Atkinson, still living at Rookforest?"

"Yes, she is."

A wistful smile made him look less fierce and more appealing. "Ah, my wild Meggie-of-the-moor. . . . She must be such a beauty by now, breaking hearts right and left throughout all of Ireland."

Fenella felt a twinge of envy whenever she thought of the stunning Margaret with her fiery auburn mane, mischievous hazel eyes, and bold, flirtatious manner that all men found so utterly captivating. "That she has, as I'm sure you'll soon be seeing for yourself. I'm assuming you're bound for Rookforest?"

He bristled. "So quick to be rid of me, are you, Miss Considine?"

Fenella stiffened her spine and bit back the retort that was on the tip of her tongue. "I did not mean to imply that you are not welcome here, Mr. Quinn. We extend hospitality to all who come to our door. It's just that the hour is quite late, and my father was due home hours ago. You must forgive me if I place concern for him above your own welfare."

Then she walked over to the window and looked for any sign of her father. The drive was empty, save for Mr. Quinn's horse tied out front, its head down and its back to the wind.

Just as Fenella turned to ask her abrasive guest to leave, he began swaying unsteadily on his feet. Patrick Quinn turned quite ashen, his knees buckled, and he staggered, one hand outstretched in a desperate attempt to break his fall.

"Mr. Quinn!"

Fenella managed to catch his arm and steady him, surprised that he was so heavy for one so thin. By using all of her strength, she was able to ease him down into her father's chair before he collapsed. Once he was seated, Patrick Quinn's head lolled back as if he hadn't the strength to hold it up any longer, and Fenella was alarmed to see his face waxy with a thin sheen of sweat.

"When is the last time you ate a decent meal?" she demanded suspiciously.

"You needn't concern yourself, Miss Considine," he muttered. "You've made it quite clear I am a nuisance to you, so I won't impose upon your hospitality any longer."

Then he struggled to rise, but the exertion was too much for him. He fell back gasping and glaring at Fenella as if she were to blame for his weakened state.

She gritted her teeth and ignored his deliberate baiting. "I am going to the kitchen. I expect the bannocks and cheese to be gone when I return. However, I would advise against the whiskey on an empty stomach."

And without waiting to hear Mr. Quinn's reply to her

imperious command, Fenella gathered her skirts and strode out of the parlor.

In the kitchen, she hacked away at a joint of cold ham to expel some of her anger. Patrick Quinn had to be the most sullen, surly young man she had ever had the misfortune to meet! Why, he acted as though she were personally responsible for sending him to prison.

Suddenly Fenella was overwhelmed with shame and remorse for thinking such uncharitable thoughts of one less fortunate. The man had spent four years of his life in prison, a hellish experience, judging by the looks of him. Perhaps he had a right to be bitter and resentful of those who had remained free.

I mustn't judge him too hastily, she reminded herself.

When she returned to the parlor several minutes later, she was pleased to see the plate was clean, except for a few bits of cheese.

"Very good, Mr. Quinn," she said. "Now, if you'll just finish this plate of cold ham, I'll—"

Her sentence ended abruptly when she noticed the small gray mouse nestled in Patrick Quinn's cupped palm. Startled, Fenella bounded back with a shriek, the plate of ham teetering precariously in her hands. She managed to regain her balance just in time to keep the plate from crashing to the floor.

"Mr. Quinn!" Fenella cried, placing one hand over her racing heart as she watched the squeaking mouse dart up the man's sleeve and disappear beneath his coat's lapel. "That's a mouse!"

"Very astute of you, Miss Considine," he said. "And I'll thank you to refrain from frightening him half to death with your caterwauling."

"But . . . but whatever are you doing with such vermin on your person, Mr. Quinn?"

He gave her a cold, malevolent stare. "I'll have you know that Mr. O'Malley here is not vermin, Miss Considine. He has been my friend and boon companion for the past two years." His voice softened as he lifted his lapel and coaxed the wary mouse out into his hand once again. "Come out, O'Malley. There's nothing to be afraid of. This good lady has promised me she won't scream at you again. That's it.''

When the mouse reluctantly appeared and twitched its nose at Fenella, Patrick Quinn began stroking its head and back with one forefinger. "In fact, he has been my only friend, animal or human, in all that time."

Fenella could think of no response that wasn't fatuous or patronizing, so she set the plate of ham down and said nothing as she retreated to another chair.

She watched in silence as Patrick Quinn set Mr. O'Malley down on the tea table so he could partake of leftover scraps of cheese while his master devoured several slices of ham.

When they both finished, the mouse washed his whiskers fastidiously, then ran up his master's sleeve and returned to his hiding place.

Her guest looked over at Fenella. "A man will make a pet of anything in prison, Miss Considine, just to have a fellow creature to talk to and while away the interminable hours. Before Mr. O'Malley appeared in my cell, I had many pets. One was a brown, long-legged spider named Cynara." His voice became harsh when he said the unusual name. "I became her willing and adoring slave just for the pleasure of her company, catching flies for her to eat, and an occasional juicy ant for dessert. But she was fickle and eventually left me for another."

Fenella shuddered in revulsion at the gruesome image he presented.

He noticed her reaction and raised his dark brows mockingly. "Am I offending your delicate maidenly sensibilities with my frank speech, Miss Considine?"

"As a doctor's daughter, there is little that offends my sensibilities, Mr. Quinn," she retorted, "but I do believe you are deliberately trying to shock and provoke me."

He rose, and Fenella was pleased to see his gaunt cheeks had acquired a little color, and he looked stronger for having eaten. "You must forgive me, then. When a man is locked away for four years, denied the charming company of ladies such as yourself, he invariably loses any semblance of the social graces in the scramble to survive." He reached for his hat. "So I shall remove my boorish presence from your company and bid you good night."

Fenella rose, her lips pursed in exasperation. "I never said you were a boor, Mr. Quinn. Those are your words, not mine."

He set his hat on his head, his defiant gaze boring into her. "No, Miss Considine, but you were thinking it."

It took all of Fenella's self-control to keep from stamping her foot in vexation. "Are you telling me you are able to know what I am thinking before I speak?"

"One only has to look at your face to know what you are thinking, Miss Considine."

Fenella blushed, for she knew he spoke the truth. Hadn't William always said her expressive face was one of the attributes he most loved about her? Thinking of him made her eyes well up with tears, and Fenella bustled forward before Patrick Quinn could see them and wrongly assume he was the cause.

"If you are determined to leave, I'll show you out," she said, "but you are welcome to stay until my father returns."

When they reached the door, Patrick Quinn stopped and turned to her. For the first time, Fenella was aware of his great height, for the top of her head was about level with his shoulder, and she had to tilt her head back to look up at him. In the dim light of the hall, his face resembled a death's-head, his eyes as dull as two lumps of coal in their deeply shadowed sockets.

"On behalf of Mr. O'Malley and myself, I thank you for the excellent repast and delightful conversation," he said. "Since you are a frequent guest at Rookforest, I'm afraid you'll be doomed to endure more of my company in the future."

"I am sure my father and I shall manage somehow, Mr. Quinn," was her dry reply.

That elicited a smile from him, a mere drawing back of the lips as he sketched her a mocking bow and left.

Fenella stood in the doorway for a moment, not to see Patrick Quinn safely off, but to see if her father's dogcart was coming up the drive at long last. There was no sign of it. Disappointed, she glanced worriedly at the night sky. Already clouds were amassing on the horizon once again, heralding more rain. She prayed he would be home soon.

Shivering in the damp air, she turned and went back inside, the drumming of hoofbeats echoing in her ears as Quinn's horse galloped down the drive and into the night.

After taking the empty plates into the kitchen, where the maid-of-all-work would wash them in the morning, Fenella decided she couldn't battle her heavy, drooping eyelids any longer. Stifling a yawn, she took the lamp and went upstairs, where she undressed and got ready for bed.

No sooner had she finished plaiting her thick brown hair than she heard the familiar sound of her father's mare ambling up the drive. Slipping into her dressing gown and taking the lamp, Fenella hurried down the stairs to wait while her father unhitched the horse and rubbed her down for the night.

Fenella pounced on him the moment he walked in the door, humming some obscure Irish air under his breath. "Father, where have you been?" she admonished, and hugged him at the same time. "It's nearly midnight, and I've been worried half to death about you."

Liam Considine was a wiry man of average height who cared more about his patients than his personal appearance. His brown hair often went uncombed and his bushy beard untrimmed and flecked with bits of tobacco from his pipe. Fenella was fond of saying that if she didn't lay out his clothes every morning, he'd forget to dress and go out stark naked.

Now his merry blue eyes twinkled. "You worry about me too much, daughter, and that's a fact." He sighed wearily as he removed his coat and draped it over the back of his favorite chair. "The newest member of the O'Hara clan took his time making his grand entrance, that's all."

Fenella took the coat, inspected it for spots or tears, then folded it neatly over her arm. "The child is well? And Mrs. O'Hara?"

He nodded grimly as he walked into the parlor and poured himself his evening dram of whiskey. "Unlike the other four, this one survived and seems to be a fine and lusty lad. His mother is fit, considering the difficult birth.''

Liam lowered himself into the chair and stared at the empty tea table. "Where is my supper? Derelict in your duties, are you?"

Fenella scowled. "Forgive me, Father, but I'm afraid our unexpected guest ate all of the bannocks that Dierdre made this morning. There is still the ham, though, if you'd like that. I'll go slice it right away."

"Don't bother, daughter," he said with a wave of his hand that stopped Fenella in her tracks. "I shared buttermilk and potatoes with the O'Haras before I left." Liam was silent for a moment. Then he said, "You know, you should be fussing over a husband, not your old father."

Fenella's smile died, and she brushed an imaginary speck of lint from her father's coat as she turned away. "I like fussing over you just fine, Father."

Liam sipped his whiskey. "It's been over three years since your William left us," he said gently. "Time for you to stop grieving for him, to put the past behind you, where it belongs."

Fenella stared out into space at nothing in particular, her brow troubled. "I loved William so much, and when he died, a part of me died with him."

"I know. I felt the same when your dear mother departed this sweet green earth."

"And you've never found anyone to replace her, just as I'll never find anyone to replace William."

Liam drained his glass and rose. "But it's different for men, daughter. We have our life's work to fill our hours."

"And I have mine. You are my life's work."

He shook his head sadly. "Ah, Nella, Nella . . ."

She rubbed the mark on her wrist. "Even if I were to find another man to love me," she said bleakly, "how can I ask him to accept me, accursed as I am? He would have to be exceptional."

Liam took one look at his daughter's tormented face and his gaze slid down to her wrist. He could think of no words of comfort because there were none to be had. Instead, he turned the conversation around. "You said we had an unexpected guest this evening. Who would call on such a perisher of a night?''

Fenella hesitated for a moment. "Patrick Quinn."

Her father's eyes widened in surprise and he ran his fingers through his graying hair, mussing it and causing it to stand on end like the quills of a hedgehog. "Patrick here? Tonight? Cadogan said he was due home tomorrow."

Fenella sat down. "Well, he arrived sooner than expected." She hesitated a moment, then said, "Father, tell me about Patrick Quinn and why he was sent to prison. Oh, I've heard village gossip over the years, but I don't set any store in that. I'd like to hear the truth from you, if you please, for I am sure Cadogan has told you things he has never told me."

Liam glanced at the clock. "It's rather late, daughter. Can't it wait until tomorrow?"

"I've stayed up this late, Father. A few more minutes won't make any difference. Besides, my curiosity is aroused to an unbearable pitch. Please."

He surrendered with a sigh, then began filling his pipe. "Patrick is Cadogan's only son. Ever since he became a man some years ago, he's fancied himself in love with St. John Standon's sister."

St. John Standon, a member of the family known far and wide by the heavily ironic title of the "Saintly Standons" because they were far from it, was the Duke of Carbury's estate agent and lived in a magnificent Tudor-style house called Drumlow just north of Mallow.

Fenella frowned. "I thought Mr. Standon lived alone. I didn't know he had a sister."

But then why should she? Aside from bestowing a civil nod on the Considines after the church services every Sunday, the lofty St. John considered himself far above their common touch.

Liam nodded as he lit his pipe. "Well, he does have a sister and she goes by the unusual name of Cynara."

Cynara. . . . The same name as Patrick Quinn's pet spider. Now Fenella recalled how his voice had changed when he said that name with such coldness and loathing.

Her father continued. "We've never met her because she married an Englishman and moved away long before you and I left Cork city to come to Mallow. But before her marriage, Patrick Quinn began courting her. She's quite a beauty, I'm told, with raven hair and milk-white skin, like one of the ancient Irish queens, and the lad lost his heart to her. Well, her brother is an ambitious man and had higher things in mind for his sister than the son of a mere Anglo-Irish landowner, no matter how wealthy he be.

"So when the lady turned eighteen, she was packed off to London for a proper season in the hopes of attracting a wealthy, titled husband and advancing her family's social standing."

Fenella said, "So the lady didn't return Patrick Quinn's affections."

Her father shrugged. "Cadogan claims she did, but felt honor-bound to obey her brother, who had been responsible for her since the death of their parents. In any case, Patrick followed her to London in the hopes of making her change her mind and marry him."

"He evidently didn't succeed," Fenella said wryly, "in spite of his persistence."

"I'm afraid not. When the fair Cynara became betrothed to a blue-blooded marquess, our hothead Patrick abducted her in a friend's yacht and took her to Ostend, in Belgium, where he hoped to further his suit without distractions."

Fenella's eyes widened in shock. "He kidnapped her?"

"He most assuredly did. He lured her out into the garden during a ball, threw a sack over her to stifle her screams, and carried her to a waiting carriage. By the time anyone realized the lady was missing, she and Quinn were halfway to Dover."

"What arrogance!" Fenella thought of how she would have felt if someone had abducted her from her beloved William, and she shuddered. "Miss Standon must have been terrified out of her wits."

"She had enough of her wits about her to knock her abductor unconscious with an empty wine bottle and call the police."

"I applaud her courage! And then what happened?"

"Young Mr. Quinn was arrested and returned to England, where charges were brought against him by the

woman's finacé and her brother. He was sentenced to
four years in prison.''

"Serves him right," Fenella replied stoutly. "He committed a reprehensible crime and should have been punished for it.''

Her father shook his head sadly. "I'm surprised at you,
daughter. Usually you are more charitable to your fellowman. Aside from abducting the woman and frightening
her, young Quinn didn't harm her in any way.''

Fenella was silent for a moment as she weighed his
words. Finally she conceded, "Well, perhaps the sentence was unduly harsh, all things considered.''

Liam sucked on his pipe, sending a cloud of fragrant
gray smoke into the air. "Well, not physically harmed,
anyway. However, when word got out what had happened,
her reputation was almost ruined. The abduction was the
talk of London for months. Her fiancé had every right
to dissolve the engagement, but he was so in love with
her, he settled on avenging himself. That's why he insisted Quinn serve a prison term, to pay for the lady's
sullied reputation and to salvage his own pride.''

Fenella shook her head, suddenly overcome with pity
in spite of herself for the poor wretch that Patrick Quinn
had become.

"That certainly explains it," she said.

"Explains what?''

"Why he was so surly and sullen. To lose four years
of your life for something you consider to be no more
than a lapse of good judgment . . .'' Then she added
quickly, "Mind you, I'm not condoning what he did. His
actions were arrogant and unjust. But I can understand
why he is bitter and resentful.''

Liam nodded. "I don't envy any man a prison sentence. I know what goes on inside those walls, and it's
enough to crush the spirit out of the strongest man, especially one as proud as a Quinn.''

"That's exactly how Patrick Quinn looked tonight, Father, as if the spirit had been crushed out of him, leaving
nothing but a hollow shell.''

Liam took another deep puff. "Some men can bend
while others only break. We can only hope that he will

put the experience behind him and be the man he once was, now that he's home among family and friends.''

But later that night, as Fenella lay in her bed listening to the soft pattering of the rain on the roof, she found herself wondering if Patrick Quinn's dull, haunted blue eyes would ever blaze with spirit again.

Patrick halted his rented hack atop a nearby hill to get his bearings. Below him, the town of Mallow lay dark and quiet except for a sprinkling of lights here and there. The River Blackwater twisted and stretched like a silver snake in the moonlight, while the Nagles Mountains rose protectively beyond, their dark peaks cutting off the view and becoming one with the night sky whenever a cloud passed over the moon. Before him, the narrow limestone road lined with high hedgerows dipped, then veered off into a deep valley. Patrick knew that all he had to do was follow this road for several more miles and he would arrive at the great house of Rookforest.

He was home.

Home. . . . He savored the sound of it, repeating it over and over again in his mind as if he couldn't believe he was finally free. How many times during the past five days had he glanced furtively over his shoulder, certain he had been released by mistake and that they were coming to take him back and lock him up again? He broke out in a cold sweat just thinking about it.

Patrick felt Mr. O'Malley stir in his breast pocket, then settle down. He grinned as he recalled Miss Considine's reaction when she first saw the mouse, the high-pitched shriek, her eyes nearly popping out of her head. Well, at least she hadn't swooned, as any genteel young lady would. That was one point in her favor.

Touching his heel to his horse's ribs, Patrick started down the hill. He found himself thinking of Fenella Considine with frank distaste. She was certainly no beauty, with her wide, belligerent jaw and long, thin nose with its haughty tilt. And her coloring was so plain and relentlessly brown, from eyes and hair of a nondescript shade right down to her plain, unflattering dress, that she resembled nothing more than a drab woodhen. However, he grudgingly admitted she did have one redeeming attribute: attractive breasts, large and full above a waist so narrow he could have spanned it with his hands.

He chuckled to himself. At least he was still capable of being aroused by the sight of voluptuous feminine curves. He hadn't made love to a woman in so long, except in his vivid imagination, he feared ever responding to one again, even one as unappealing as the priggish Miss Considine.

How unfortunate for him that she should be the first woman he had spoken to since his release, for the doctor's daughter was a spinster from the top of her head to her prim little toes.

He smiled grimly to himself, for he could always tell. There was something about the way she carried herself, as if constantly on her guard, lest she accidentally brush against him and incite his masculine lust. And she felt sorry for him with a smug superiority. That above all made him dislike her heartily, a dislike that he was certain was reciprocated.

Tiring of thinking of prim Miss Considine, Patrick urged his horse into a slow canter, eager to make the most of the moonlight while he could. He didn't want to lose his way in the darkness, especially when the rains came again.

Patrick breathed deeply, savoring the scents of damp earth and grass, relishing the caress of the wind against his face. He had always taken such simple pleasures for granted—the sharp bite of the wind in his face, watching the day dwindle into the long Irish twilight, the company of good friends, freedom. And then he had lost them all.

The unfairness of it welled up in his throat like bile, and he felt himself quake with anger and bitterness for what had been taken from him. He dug his heels into his horse's soft belly, causing the animal to squeal in pain as he shot forward and galloped down the road.

No sooner did Patrick halt his lathered mount before the high iron grille gates of Rookforest than the benevolent moon slipped behind a cloud, plunging the landscape into darkness once again. But no matter, Patrick thought as he swiftly dismounted and pushed at the open gate. He knew the rest of the way by heart.

Like a blind man, he relied on the sound of the gravel

crunching beneath his shoes as he led his horse down
the long circular drive. The sighing of the wind through
the screen of large silver and russet beech trees told him
he was nearing the lawn, which gently sloped up toward
the house itself.

Within minutes he was standing before the vague
shadow, looking up at darkened windows. Not a welcoming lamp or candle shone in any of them. Both family
and servants were abed. Not one had waited up for the
prodigal's return.

A numbing feeling of rejection washed over him, min-
gling with bone-wearying fatigue, but he grimly ignored
it and began pounding on the door with the last of his
strength, demanding admittance. After what seemed like
an eternity, a light shone through the fanlight above the
door, and Patrick could hear someone on the other side
cursing roundly in Gaelic while she fumbled with the
lock.

Suddenly the door swung open to reveal a diminutive
figure standing there, lamp in hand, ready to do battle.
"Master Patrick!" she exclaimed in a voice breathless
with surprise and pleasure. "By the Holy, whatever are
ye doing here tonight instead of tomorrow, ye daft lad?"

Four years hadn't changed Mrs. Ryan much, Patrick
decided as he stepped into the foyer, whipped off his hat,
and tossed it onto the narrow hall table. The housekeeper
was a tiny white-haired woman with sharp berry-black
eyes that had caused the other servants to dub her "Ailagh
of the Hundred Eyes" behind her back.

But she was appalled by the change in him. "Arragh,
Master Patrick, Master Patrick . . ." she groaned with a
shake of her head as she set her lamp down. "By the
Holy, what have they done to ye?"

"Their worst, Mrs. Ryan," he replied. "But as you
can see, I have bested them. I have survived." But just
barely, he added to himself, shaking his head to clear it
of the strength-sapping weariness.

Then he took her in his arms and hugged her cautiously, lest Mr. O'Malley be crushed in the process.
Patrick wanted to pick the housekeeper right up off the
floor and whirl her around until she was dizzy, as had

been his custom in the old days, but he knew he didn't have the strength for it now. Soon, he promised himself.

Mrs. Ryan sensed this at once. "It's glad I am to see ye, Master Patrick, that I am." When he released her, she stepped back a pace and gave him a critical stare from head to toe. "Och, my darlin' lad, what a sorry state yer in! Your clothes are hangin' on ye like a scarecrow. Didn't they ever feed ye over there?"

His stomach turned at the memory and he shuddered. "Boiled potatoes and a bit of meat on Sunday. That's all I ever had."

"Well, don't give it another thought. Cook will put some meat on those bones soon enough, I'll see to that." Then Mrs. Ryan's face hardened. "How could they lock up the likes of you just like ye were a common criminal?"

"But it's over, Mrs. Ryan," he reminded her gently. "In the past and best forgotten." He would have to remember to take his own advice.

"The English . . . bah!" she sputtered with a shake of her head. "What do they know of justice? What have they ever known of justice?"

Patrick felt drained as vivid, unwanted memories engulfed him. He didn't want to think about prison anymore. All he wanted to do was sleep for a thousand years and forget the horror and the pain.

"Ye poor boy . . . here I am prattlin' away, and ye bein' perishin' on yer feet. Come. I'll have the old room ready for ye in less time than it takes a fairy to leave a changeling on the doorstep."

He thought of his old room, small and cramped, and a feeling of terror swept over him, leaving him shaken.

"I . . . I don't want to stay in my old room, Mrs. Ryan," he said, swallowing convulsively. "I want a larger one. One of the guest rooms will do nicely."

She looked at him sharply; then her face changed as comprehension dawned. "As ye wish, Master Patrick." She turned to go, hesitated and turned to face him again. "And yer father? Do you wish me to wake himself and tell him you've arrived?"

"There is no need," came a booming voice from the top of the stairs. "Himself is already awake."

As Patrick looked up to see his father in robe and slippers hurry down the curved staircase of Connemara marble, his throat constricted with deep emotion. The years had thickened Cadogan Quinn's broad shoulders and barrel chest, so that he looked as stocky and powerful as a red Kerry bull. And there were new lines of sadness scored in his cheeks. But his blue eyes, the same pale shade as his son's, were as sharp and clear as ever.

Patrick's mind was boiling over with things he wanted to say to his father, expressions of love and regret, but he found he could not. Finally, all he did was extend his arms wordlessly to the older man.

Cadogan was not demonstrative by nature, leaving such displays of emotion to the weaker sex. But now he stepped forward and clutched at his son in a quick embrace. When he stepped back, his eyes were unnaturally bright.

"Hang it, why didn't you let us know what time you were coming?" he demanded gruffly, to cover the deepness of his feelings. "I would have sent a man to Mallow station for you."

"I didn't come by train," Patrick replied, relieved to feel Mr. O'Malley stir. "I rented a horse in Cork and rode."

"All that way?"

Patrick nodded, "I thought the train would be too . . . confining."

Mrs. Ryan just shook her head.

"You needn't worry. I stayed at inns along the way."

His father, who had been studying him, said, "What happened to your hair? I thought they were supposed to let you grow it out before they released you, so you could blend in with the common herd?"

A wry smile touched Patrick's mouth: "They usually do, so no one will know you were in prison. But I'm afraid I was never an exemplary prisoner, Father. I bedeviled them all from the moment I entered the place until the moment I left. This was the warden's way of punishing me for all those gray hairs I gave him."

Cardogan nodded in approval even as anger flared in his eyes at the cruelty of it. "Never let it be said that a Quinn went down without a fight." Then he clapped Patrick on the shoulder. "We have much to talk about, son, but it can wait until morning. I know you've had a long journey and want to rest.''

Tomorrow would be soon enough to talk about his mother's death, and how he could repay St. John Standon for the monstrous wrong done to him.

Patrick stifled a yawn and nodded sleepily as Mrs. Ryan said, ''I'll have the Green Room ready for you in a moment, Master Patrick, and wake one of the men to tend to yer horse, poor creature.'' And she went bustling up the stairs, leading the way with customary efficiency.

''It's good to have you home again, son,'' his father said.

And together they followed Mrs. Ryan.

Fifteen minutes later, Patrick just stood in the middle of the wide, long Green Room and luxuriated in the sheer expansiveness of it. This was a veritable cavern, not a cage, with enough space to waltz in.

Still, in spite of the room's size, he was seized by the feeling that the walls were beginning to close in on him. In panic, he rushed over to the windows and flung back the curtains, letting the dark outdoors become an extension of the room, widening it out to the horizon and beyond. Then he strode back across the room to open the bedchamber door, noting with satisfaction that he could see down the upstairs hall. Finally the breathless feeling of being caged slowly evaporated.

Patrick vowed never to lock another door again.

After settling in Mr. O'Malley for the night, he peeled off the cheap suit he had been given when released and slid into bed. He had been looking forward to this moment for as long as he could remember. The freshly laundered sheets, fragrant with dried herbs and flowers instead of stinking with dirty straw and stale sweat, felt as cool and smooth as the finest silk against his dry, rough skin. Like a child, Patrick wallowed in the sensual luxury of it, slowly drawing first one leg, then the other back and forth across those heavenly smooth sheets. Then he rolled over on his side and rubbed his face against the embroidered case covering a pillow filled with soft goosedown rather than hard, rasping coconut husks.

With a sigh of contentment he closed his eyes and kept

telling himself over and over again that he was finally free.

But he slept fitfully at first, dreaming of shrinking cages that grew smaller and smaller and treadwheels that whirled faster and faster until he was spun off into nothingness and awoke gasping, bathed in a cold sweat.

Close to dawn, he finally fell into a deep, exhausted sleep.

2

PATRICK JOLTED AWAKE to the sound of screaming.

At first he thought it was the tantara made by hundreds of black rooks beginning their raucous morning exodus from the demesne trees, but as his senses returned one by one, he realized the sound was all too human.

"O'Malley!" he cried, sitting bolt upright in time to see one of the maids running for the door, the long tails of her starched white cap flying straight out behind her. Swinging his long legs over the side of the bed, Patrick wrapped the top sheet around his waist to cover his nakedness, and went in search of his pet.

He found O'Malley cowering behind a silver picture frame on the table. When Patrick extended his hand, the mouse scrambled into it, stood on his hind legs, and squeaked furiously in protest.

Patrick smiled in agreement. "Women can be so annoying, can't they? Imagine being afraid of one wee mouse . . ."

Hearing footsteps hurrying down the hall, Patrick turned to see the outraged Mrs. Ryan, an upraised broom in hand, followed by the maid, who gasped and averted her eyes at the sight of a half-naked man standing in the center of the room.

"Good mornin', Master Patrick," the housekeeper said. "It's sorry I am for disturbin' you, but Brigid here swears by the Blessed Virgin that she saw a mouse in your room." She glanced at the maid sharply. "A mouse in *my* house . . . I told her she must have imagined it."

"No need to call out the dragoons, Mrs. Ryan," Patrick said lightly, extending his hand to show her the culprit. "And Brigid wasn't imagining it. Mr. O'Malley here is a friend of mine, and he's not to be harmed."

The housekeeper looked as though Patrick had just asked her to sell her only child, while Brigid took a step back and stared goggle-eyed.

"Not to be harmed?" Mrs. Ryan moaned. "You don't know what yer askin' of me. I am responsible for keepin' this house clean and free of rodents, Master Patrick."

"Mr. O'Malley is not an ordinary rodent, Mrs. Ryan," was his stern reply. "I am very attached to him, and he shall remain unmolested. I expect you to warn all the servants that they are not to harm him, or they shall answer to me. Is that clear?"

"Surely ye can't expect us to control the cats, Master Patrick . . ."

"I expect the cats to be kept out of my room."

The housekeeper surrendered with a dismal sigh. "If that's how ye be wantin' it . . ."

"Those are my orders, Mrs. Ryan. See that they are obeyed. And, oh yes. I'll need a small tin and some straw to make accommodations for O'Malley. You needn't worry about supplying his meals. I'll do that from my own plate."

Mrs. Ryan gave him an odd look before she turned to the maid, a pretty, rosy-cheeked girl with a slightly vapid expression. "You heard Master Patrick, Brigid. From now on, when you clean the upstairs rooms, you'll take care to keep the cats away and not to harm the mouse, is that understood?"

"Aye, Mrs. Ryan," she replied, bobbing a curtsy and giving Patrick a fearful surreptitious glance that plainly told him she thought him quite mad.

"Now be off, ye witless lass, and go heat water for the young master's bath," Mrs. Ryan ordered. When the maid bobbed another curtsy and fled, the housekeeper turned back to Patrick. "Yer bath will be ready shortly, and then I'll send Summers to attend you."

Patrick nodded in approval. His father's valet would have to do until he could hire a man of his own.

"If ye won't be wantin' anything else, Master Patrick . . ."

He adjusted the sheet about his hips. "Is breakfast being served, Mrs. Ryan? All I've dreamed about for the last four years is a breakfast of Cook's currant bannocks dripping with butter and lashings of bacon to go with my eggs.''

That earned him her forgiveness for the matter of Mr. O'Malley, and she broke out in an approving grin. ''Breakfast was hours ago, and it's luncheon we'll be servin' by the time yer up and about. But I know yer fondness for Cook's bannocks, so I've had them leave some for ye.''

He grinned and planted a kiss atop her white head. ''You are a jewel among women, Mrs. Ryan.''

''Aye, that I am, if I do say so meself.''

''If I were thirty years older and you weren't already spoken for, I'd marry you myself.''

She chuckled as she shook her head and turned to leave. ''Aye, it's a young rogue ye are, Master Patrick.''

After thoroughly scrubbing out the scents of prison embedded in his body and being dressed in old clothes that no longer fit him, Patrick strolled through the house, taking time to reacquaint himself with the Georgian mansion his great-grandfather had built toward the end of the last century.

Rookforest hadn't changed at all, these elegant, graciously appointed rooms that opened into one another in the Palladian manner. But he had. He could see it reflected in the startled faces of old servants he passed in the hall, the pity and sorrow underlying their hearty words of loyalty and welcome, the uneasiness in their eyes. He might be the master's son, but he was a stranger to these people now, shaped and changed by circumstances he couldn't control.

On the way to luncheon, he walked down the short hallway that served as a portrait gallery for the Quinns and stopped before a life-size portrait of his late mother, still draped with black crepe after two years as a testament to her husband's devotion. Seeing the likeness of Moira Quinn, always referred to as ''The Beautiful Moira,'' caused a lump of regret to form in Patrick's throat. His mother's dark eyes sparkled back at him with laughter and life, silently pleading with him not to grieve for her.

He blinked quickly and walked away, silently cursing

those heartless men who wouldn't let him see her before she died.

By the time he reached the dining room, a black cloud had settled over him, spoiling the day before it had even begun.

When Patrick entered the room, he found his father seated at the head of the long Irish Chippendale table and inspecting the silverware to make sure his servants were fulfilling their duties.

Cadogan set down the fork with a satisfied nod, then rose. In the bright light of day, he looked older somehow, his face more creased and careworn than it had appeared last night.

"Good morning, son," he said. "I trust you slept well."

"Like a babe, Father," he lied, his gaze sliding hungrily over to the sideboard crowded with an assortment of covered silver dishes.

"Stop standing there like a stranger waiting for an invitation," his father said gruffly. "Take a plate and help yourself."

Patrick didn't need to be told twice. He took a plate, walked over to the sideboard, and began looking under one covered dish after another, his mouth watering at the tantalizing aromas of sizzling bacon, hot ham, and warm yeasty bannocks. Then he began filling his plate and felt compelled to keep going until it was piled high with more food than he could possibly eat in one sitting.

"You can always go back for seconds," his father said gently.

"I intend to." And he seated himself.

He had to fight the impulse to place his forearms on the table to guard his food like some wary wolf, for he knew his father would be shocked to witness how truly uncivilized he had become in prison. Instead, he forced himself to remember his manners by spreading his napkin across his lap and pouring himself a steaming cup of red tea. He savored the rich linen texture of the napkin and the cool heaviness of the silverware in his hand, sensory experiences that had to be relearned.

"What would you like to do today?" Cadogan asked.

His mouth too full to reply, Patrick just shrugged.

"I would suggest we ride around the estate this afternoon, if you're up to it."

Patrick swallowed his food before saying, "I'd like nothing better, Father, but I'm not sure I can handle one of your horses."

"Our horses."

"It's been a long time since I've ridden a horse with any mettle. The plowhorse I rode home last night could barely canter."

"Riding is something an Irishman never forgets, no matter how long he's been off a good horse. We'll start you off on a horse a child could ride."

Patrick smiled slightly as he continued eating. The hot bannocks, little buns overstuffed with currants, melted in his mouth, their sweetness contrasting sharply with the saltiness of the bacon. Ambrosia fit for the gods. Oh, how he had missed it!

Cadogan continued with, "I put Brian Boru out to stud after you . . . left. He wouldn't let anyone else near him, so I thought it best to retire the addlepated beast before he killed someone. And I kept his first colt for you. He's a fine three-year-old named Gallowglass."

Patrick thought of the spirited chestnut stallion that once only he could ride, and softened at the memory. "I'd like to see him and his colt."

Suddenly the dining-room door flew open and a lissome feminine figure in a bottle-green riding habit stood poised dramatically in the entrance.

"Patrick!" the sprite cried gleefully before running toward him, as uninhibited as a child. "Oh, it's so wonderful to have you home again!"

He barely had time to rise from his seat before the young hellion hurled herself into his arms, causing him to stagger from the force of her assault.

"Meggie . . ." he murmured, clasping her to him in a long embrace. "How is my wild Meggie-of-the-moor?"

"I'm just fine," she replied, backing away and clasping his hands so she could hold him at arm's length for her critical inspection, "but, Pat, you look absolutely dreadful."

It was a bald statement of fact uttered without a trace of pity, so Patrick didn't take offense at his cousin's im-

petuous words. "A prison term isn't exactly a pleasure
jaunt to the Continent, wild Meggie."

Then she uttered an outraged sound when she noticed
his broken nails and blackened fingertips. "And whatever happened to your poor hands?"

"The result of picking oakum, I'm afraid," he replied,
"a particularly nasty—"

"It sounds horrid and I don't want to hear about it!"
she cried, clapping her gloved hands over her ears.
"You're out of that terrible place now and we shan't discuss it."

"That suits me just fine because I don't wish to talk
about it."

Cadogan cleared his throat. "Will you be joining us
for luncheon, Margaret?"

"Of course," she replied with a toss of her curly russet
mane. "Riding always gives me an appetite." Then she
rounded the table to seat herself across from Patrick,
peeled off her black kidskin gloves, and took her plate to
the sideboard.

Seeing his vivacious, ebullient cousin raised Patrick's
spirits as nothing had since his return to Ireland. Margaret Atkinson, the only child of Cadogan's favorite sister, had come to Rookforest as a shy, gawky child of
twelve when her parents were drowned while yachting off
the coast of Galway. Once she was over the tragedy, the
youngster had brightened their lives like a comet streak-
ing across the night sky. She soon became the daughter
Patrick's mother, Moira, never had, and more like his
own sister than a cousin. Even the gruff Cadogan, usually
so objective about horses and people, had a blind spot
where Margaret was concerned and had always spoiled
her shamelessly.

Everyone loved Meggie.

As Patrick watched his cousin seat herself across from
him, he smiled and shook his head. "Miss Considine
was right. You have grown into a beautiful young woman,
Margaret."

Her eyes sparkled at the compliment even as her brows
rose in surprise. "Fenella Considine said that about me?
When did you meet her?"

"Last night, on the way home," Patrick replied, sopping up the last of the egg yolks with a crust of bread. "I was tired and hungry, so when I saw a light in the window of a small house outside Mallow, I stopped, hoping the inhabitants would let me rest and perhaps give me a bite to eat." He rose and took his plate over to the sideboard, talking as he helped himself to more food. "She thought I was an escaped convict and nearly attacked me with a poker."

"That doesn't sound like Fenella," Cadogan said, wrinkling his brow. "The Considines are hospitable folk."

"That may be," Patrick said as he returned to his seat, "but I could tell the lady disliked me on sight."

"Even when you told her who you were?" Cadogan's voice rose in surprise.

Patrick nodded. "Oh, she at least treated me civilly when I introduced myself, and offered me refreshment. But I could tell she still found me beneath contempt." The memory of Fenella Considine's pitying stare still rankled him.

Margaret's voice was serious when she said, "That's so unlike Fenella! She can be standoffish and moody at times, but once you come to know her, you'll find she's a kind, generous person who would give you her last shilling if you needed it."

"Perhaps . . ." was all Patrick said.

"Well, you'll have plenty of time to become acquainted with each other," his father said. "The Considines are often guests here a Rookforest. We're great friends, you know."

"So she told me." Tiring of hearing Miss Considine's virtues extolled, Patrick turned to Margaret and said, "You're eighteen now, Meggie, and I'm sure the suitors have been lining up outside the gates, vying for your hand. Tell me, will you be leaving us soon to marry?"

Suddenly all the laughter went out of Margaret's face, and she became uncharacteristically grave. "There is no one, Patrick."

Cadogan gave her a teasing smile. "Come now, lass. Surely you would count the Earl of Nayland as a suitor."

"You may count him as a suitor, Uncle, but I certainly

do not!'' Then Margaret turned her attention to her plate
and jabbed at a boiled potato in stony silence.

"And what, pray tell, is wrong with this Earl of Nayland?'' Patrick wanted to know. "Is he a hunchback with
two heads? Does he eat little children for breakfast?''

Margaret didn't laugh. "No, but he is so . . . old.''

"Old!'' Cadogan gave an exaggerated sigh and shook
his head. "He's only thirty years old, three years older
than your cousin here, and hardly in his dotage.''

"But he has thinning hair and weak eyes from keeping
his nose in a book all day, and he has no interest in
horses. Imagine!'' Margaret cried indignantly. "Me wed
to a man who has no interest in horses!'' Suddenly she
got a faraway look in her eye and murmured, "Besides,
he's got no fire in him.''

Cadogan chuckled at that. "No fire in him, eh? Well,
my headstrong niece, I wouldn't judge by appearances,
if I were you. The earl just may surprise you in that
area.''

"I don't intend to give him the opportunity,'' she replied. Then she finished eating and rose gracefully to her
feet. "If you'll excuse me, I have to go change my
clothes. Pat, it's wonderful to have you back home among
us again.'' Then she rounded the table to give him a
quick kiss on the cheek and left.

Patrick sat back in his chair, his voracious appetite
satisfied at last. Before he could ask about the object of
Margaret's scorn, his father said, "If you're finished, why
don't you change into riding clothes and we'll tour the
estate?''

Patrick nodded. If anything could make him feel less
like an outcast, it would be seeing Rookforest again.

Minutes later, Patrick joined his father in the stableyard, where two horses were saddled and waiting, a long-
limbed gelding for Cadogan and a small, gentle mare for
Patrick.

Patrick said nothing as they mounted and slowly
walked their horses, for he felt as though he had just
returned to earth after living on the moon. To eyes accustomed to the monotonous gray walls of prison, devoid

of any aesthetic pleasure, Rookforest was a veritable feast for the senses.

The great house itself was a perfectly proportioned rectangle of gray granite, with four bay windows on either side of the main entrance. The architectural symmetry was pleasing and comfortable.

Patrick could see part of the garden, his mother's pride and joy, where she would spend hours consulting with the head gardener. During different times of the year, flowers such as jonquils, parrot tulips, white and crimson peonies, and the ever-present snapdragons all bloomed for her delight.

As they rode through the wooded demesne, the sky darkened suddenly and a fine mist began to fall, causing Patrick to turn up the collar of his coat lest he catch one of the chills he was so susceptible to. Still they pressed on, and soon the woods thinned and gave way to open countryside. Cadogan finally reined in his mount when they came to the top of a hill.

Suddenly the sun came out again and Patrick squinted at the landscape before him, for even the soft, dreamy colors of Ireland seemed unnaturally bright after the pervasive grayness of prison walls. The fields were pockets of intense green in shades ranging from a pale yellow-green to a deep, rich blue-green, and all were crisscrossed by even stone walls like strands of black pearls. The bright whitewashed walls of the farmhouses dotting the landscape almost hurt Patrick's eyes, while in the distance, the dark blue of the mountains and the hazy, shifting blue of the sky then soothed them.

It was a beautiful land, and he had missed it.

"Look," Cadogan said, pointing to the horizon. "A rainbow to welcome you home."

Patrick turned to see the rainbow arch across threatening storm clouds, while the very air about them seemed to shimmer and vibrate with a golden haze.

But he did not remark upon it, for he wasn't sure he believed in good omens anymore.

"Looks peaceful, doesn't it?" Cadogan said.

Patrick nodded.

His father's face clouded and he tugged at his horse's

mane nervously. "Well, it isn't. I fear troubled times are coming to us once again, Patrick."

Patrick scowled. "What do you mean?"

"The last few summers have been unusually damp and cold," Cadogan replied, "and the harvests have been poor. The prices for cattle and butter were particularly low this year. Tenants everywhere can't pay their rents, and some have been demanding reductions."

Patrick stroked his horse's neck. "But you've always been a fair landlord, Father. Our tenants should have no complaints." His voice hardened. "You've never been like Saintly Standon, charging unreasonably high rents and evicting those who can't pay."

"There's a difference. I own this land. Standon is only a land agent for Lord Carbury. It's his job to make Drumlow show a profit."

"But at the expense of the people?" Patrick snapped.

"Hold on, son. I'm the last one who'd defend the man, especially after what the bastard did to you. But you have to remember that I'm in the minority. There's more like Standon than there are of me."

Patrick nodded reluctantly, for he knew his father spoke the truth. Many of the estates throughout Ireland were owned by landlords who lived in England and cared nothing for the country or its people save the profit their estates there generated. The Quinns not only owned Rookforest outright, they had always dealt fairly and directly with their tenants rather than through a land agent like Standon.

His father looked at him. "You've heard of Charles Stewart Parnell?"

Patrick smiled wryly. "They did allow us to read newspapers in prison, Father. I know who Parnell is, and what he stands for."

Cadogan sighed, his expression troubled. "I just don't know what's going to happen, Patrick. What with Parnell's Land League urging tenants not to pay rents they deem unfair, and landlords threatening evictions, I just don't know. . . . Some say we could see the return of the Ribbonmen."

A cold sliver of fear ran up Patrick's spine. He hadn't yet been born during the Great Famine of the late for-

ties—the "hungry forties," Mrs. Ryan called them—but
he had heard chilling tales of these secret gangs dedicated
to murdering landowners and their agents. In fact, his
old nurse's favorite admonition had been that the ghosts
of Ribbonmen would chop him into little pieces if he
wasn't a good boy.

"Let's hope it doesn't come to that, Father," he said.

"I'm not hopeful, son," was Cadogan's glum reply.
"I've heard of several farmers near Skibbereen who were
burned out in retaliation for trying to buy the land of an
evicted neighbor."

"That's because the farmers think land-grabbing is
reprehensible," Patrick said. "It's profiting from your
neighbor's misery."

"Still, it doesn't bode well for Ireland."

Without warning, a cloud passed over the sun, darkening the landscape ominously and sapping the vibrancy
out of the brilliant colors.

"Come," Cadogan said. "There is still much for you
to see."

An hour later they arrived at the farthest reaches of
Rookforest's twenty-five hundred acres, land that bordered Drumlow on its east side.

"I think we should return, Father," Patrick said tightly.
"I have no wish to meet Standon by accident today. I
fear I would murder the bastard with my bare hands."

Cadogan nodded, turned his horse around, and headed
for the road with Patrick not far behind. They hadn't
gone more than a half-mile when they arrived at the
crossroads and noticed a dogcart with two passengers
coming from the opposite direction.

"Why, it's Liam Considine and Fenella," Cadogan
said with such relish that Patrick looked askance at his
father. "Come, I'll introduce you to the doctor."

Before Patrick could object, Cadogan urged his horse
into a trot and started toward the cart. Patrick followed,
though he was in no mood to make polite conversation
with the standoffish Miss Considine.

And she was in no mood to make conversation with
him, judging by the way she stiffened and looked away
the moment her disapproving gaze lit upon him.

"Liam . . . Fenella," Cadogan greeted them as he reined in his horse. "I'd like you to meet my son, Patrick."

Patrick liked the doctor on sight, for Liam Considine radiated an easygoing warmth that his daughter, staring stonily off into space, sorely lacked.

"The pleasure is mine," Dr. Considine said, extending his hand to Patrick. "I believe you've already met my daughter."

Fenella looked over at Patrick, her dark eyes always judging him and finding him lacking. "Yes, we have."

He bowed from the waist. "So, Miss Considine, we meet again. And this time you have nothing to fear from me, good lady, since you are in the company of two able protectors."

The sarcasm in his voice was not lost on her, for she flinched and turned an unflattering shade of red. The doctor gave Patrick a surprised glance, but was not about to reproach one of his betters. Cadogan, however, had no such qualms.

He turned in the saddle, his eyes blazing with fury. "You must forgive my son for his rudeness. He has been out of polite society for so long that he has forgotten his manners."

The unexpected vehemence of his father's reaction stunned Patrick, and for a moment all he could do was gape in disbelief.

"You will apologize to the lady at once," Cadogan insisted.

Miss Considine shook her head. "Please, there is no need . . ."

"But there is," Patrick said, stung by his own father's betrayal. "I apologize for my churlishness, Miss Considine. My father is right. I have been out of polite society for far too long." Then he nodded briefly at the Considines, bid them good day, and started riding away.

Cadogan caught up with him moments later and stopped him.

"Whatever possessed you to be so rude to Miss Considine?" he demanded. "The poor girl has never done anything to you."

"Oh, but she has," was Patrick's sullen reply. "She

detests me. She thinks I am nothing but a criminal, below her touch. I can see the loathing in her eyes each time she looks at me, and I resent it.''

''You are imagining it. I've never met a woman less judgmental of others than Fenella Considine. This is all some silly misunderstanding on your part.''

''On my part!'' Patrick cried heatedly, clenching his fists on the reins and causing even his docile mare to dance in alarm. ''Well, thank you for your unswerving loyalty, Father!''

''You're not a child, Patrick, so stop behaving like one!'' His face was livid. ''Let me tell you something about the Considines that you are not aware of. When your poor mother was dying, half out of her mind from the pain, Dr. Considine gave her medicines that helped her. She died a painless death, thanks to him, and I will be forever in his debt. So I will not hear one unkind word about his daughter, do you hear me?''

That unexpected revelation took the wind out of Patrick's sails. ''I . . . I'm sorry, Father. I didn't know,'' he muttered, feeling every inch the fool.

''And now you do. I've invited the Considines to dinner tomorrow night, so I expect you to be friendly, is that clear?''

''Yes, Father.''

They rode back to the house in strained silence.

Pulling up the collar of her ulster against the mist, Fenella stared straight ahead as the cart rattled down the narrow road, her thoughts not on Patrick Quinn but on bittersweet memories of her beloved William and how her own life had changed since the night last year when he had appeared to her in a dream and turned her life upside down.

Almost every waking hour of her day was consumed by thoughts of that night and its devastating aftermath. Most people mistook her preoccupied air for a natural reserve or standoffishness, but she couldn't help what people thought. And she usually made no attempt to rectify their erroneous impressions, for that would mean offering explanations and possibly revealing her terrible secret.

She rubbed her wrist and inadvertently shuddered.

Liam, attuned to his daughter's every mood, stopped humming under his breath long enough to look over anxiously. "What is it, daughter? Another vision?"

Fenella shook her head and said nothing, her thoughts a hundred miles away.

Liam said, "Prison has certainly taken its toll of Patrick Quinn." When his daughter made no response, he stared at her. "Fenella? Did you hear what I said?"

She shook herself. "I'm sorry for drifting, Father. What did you say?"

He patiently repeated himself, and Fenella agreed with him before lapsing into brooding silence once again.

Liam tried again. "And what did you do to provoke that young man just now?"

"I honestly don't know," she replied. "I fear Mr. Quinn has prejudged me and made up his mind to dislike me. Perhaps it is because I nearly attacked him with the fireplace poker last night. Or perhaps he senses I disapprove of what he did to Miss Standon."

Liam nodded. "Perhaps." Then he added, "Since he is Cadogan's son, I would suggest you try to be civil to the lad from now on."

Fenella looked offended. "I try to be civil to everyone. But there is just something about Patrick Quinn that makes me want to shake him!"

"You have to remember he just spent the last four years of his life in prison. Give him time. Perhaps after he's had a few months to lose that bitterness he wears like a suit of armor, he'll become a more pleasant human being."

Somehow, Fenella doubted that, but before she could comment, she saw the telltale thin line of blue smoke rising above the hilltop, and she let thoughts of Mrs. O'Hara's new baby drive Patrick Quinn from her mind.

As the cart rounded a bend in the road, the cottage came into view, its whitewashed walls and honey-colored thatched roof contrasting sharply with the green fields surrounding it. Standing not far off was the ruin of another cottage, its walls crumbling and roof gone, its interior choked with weeds, tansy, and queen's wort.

Fenella frowned and shook her head. "Such waste . . .

Why build a new cottage when they could have repaired the old?''

Liam snorted. "Because it's cheaper for the landlord to build a new cottage for new tenants, that's why.''

Fenella still couldn't see the sense in putting the new building up right next to the ruin, but she realized full well that profits motivated landlords more than good sense.

The moment the cart pulled into the yard and stopped, several ragged, barefoot children with dirty faces appeared out of nowhere to gather round. Fenella called them by name and gave each one a sweet from the bag she carried; then she smiled as they thanked her and ran off to greedily devour the rare, unaccustomed treat. No sooner had the children disappeared than the cottage door swung open. A brown hen emerged and sauntered across the year, followed by a piglet squealing in protest at being thrown out. Then a tall, thin man stood in the doorway and stared at the Considines without saying a word.

Fenella stared back, for the man was not Tim O'Hara, the farm's tenant, and she found herself wondering why such an able-bodied man was visiting a neighbor in the middle of the day when he could have been working in his own fields.

"Good day to you, John," Liam said, stepping down from the cart and rounding it to assist his daughter down.

"Good day to you, Dr. Considine," the man called John replied. "You here to see O'Hara?"

Liam nodded. "And my daughter to see the missus and her new baby.'' Then he and Fenella walked toward the cottage.

The man called John mumbled something that could have been a greeting to Fenella, then stepped aside so they could enter.

"To all within, God's peace," Cadogan said, and Fenella echoed the Irish greeting.

The moment she crossed the threshold and stepped into the dim main room that also served as a kitchen, her eyes began to smart and water from the smoke of the turf fire that burned continuously in the fireplace to her right. She blinked several times, and as her eyes became accustomed to the dimness, she noticed that, besides John and

Tim O'Hara himself, there were two other men inside whom she didn't recognize.

But her father did, for he was smiling and introducing them all to her. Fenella just smiled and nodded politely as several pairs of dark eyes regarded her without expression.

Finally Tim O'Hara said, "I expect you're here to see the missus, Miss Considine."

"And your new son, if I may, Mr. O'Hara."

A grin split his homely face. "Another son to work the land with me," he said, grabbing a chair and leading the way across the hard dirt floor to a closed door at the opposite end of the room. He opened it and said, "Kate, look lively now. Miss Considine has come to call."

Fenella found herself in a tiny room she knew served as bedroom for both the parents and younger children, while the older children slept in the attic room beneath the roof.

Mrs. O'Hara, in spite of the fact that she had just given birth the night before, was sitting up on her straw mattress, her greedy baby feeding noisily at her breast. By the feeble light of the solitary small window, Fenella could see the woman looked pale and drawn, poverty, overwork, and childbearing leeching what little life there was out of her.

"Good day, Mrs. O'Hara," Fenella said, trying to sound cheerful as she set her parcel of clean old clothes next to the mattress. "And how are you feeling today?"

Kate O'Hara was almost pretty when she smiled. "It's fine I am, Miss Considine, thank ye for askin'. And I thank the good Lord for giving me such an easy birthin' this time." Then she looked down at her baby with such maternal pride and devotion that anyone would have thought this her firstborn.

Fenella scowled in puzzlement. She distinctly remembered her father saying Mrs. O'Hara had had a particularly difficult birth last night, that's why he had stayed out so late. But soon the aggrieved male voices drifting in from the main room claimed and held her attention.

"I don't know what Standon expects of me," one said. "I barely made enough to feed my family, and he wants to raise our rents."

Another added, "When I told him I couldn't pay, he threatened to evict me, the bastard. Told me there was plenty who would be willin' to take over my farm and make it pay if I couldn't."

"Filthy land grabbers!" someone sputtered. "I know what I'd like to do to the lot of 'em!"

Several voices rose in assent and Fenella strained to hear over Mrs. O'Hara's soft voice as she thanked Fenella repeatedly for the old clothes.

"We won't let them take our farms this time. By the Holy, we'll fight back."

Fenella felt her blood run cold. Then the men lapsed into Gaelic, and she couldn't understand what they were saying.

Suddenly Kate O'Hara startled her by handing her the baby and struggling to her feet.

"Please, Mrs. O'Hara!" Fenella admonished her. "You've only just had a baby and need your rest."

She shrugged as she pushed a greasy strand of hair out of her eyes with her free hand. "I've been lying here, useless like, since the lad here was born yesterday afternoon. I've got my Tim and the others to feed. Maeve don't know how yet, though she does try something fierce, poor little mite. Yesterday she burned the few potatoes we had. So dried out inside they was, it was like eatin' dust. She cried so when her da yelled at her."

Something Mrs. O'Hara said brought Fenella up short. "You say your baby was born yesterday afternoon?"

She nodded. "I remember the doctor looked at his big gold watch and told me 'twas three o'clock."

Then why had he told Fenella the O'Hara baby was born at ten o'clock at night?

Just at that moment the baby screwed up his face and wailed at the top of his lungs, and soon Fenella forgot all about her father's error as she tried to soothe and quiet the noisy infant.

Minutes later, her father called to her and they left the O'Hara cottage for home.

3

WHEN PATRICK WALKED into the drawing room on Friday evening, he noticed that at least one of their guests had already arrived.

A tall, languid young man was deep in conversation with Cadogan as they stood before the fireplace and sipped drinks. Judging by the stranger's steel-rimmed spectacles, Patrick assumed him to be none other than Meggie's unwanted suitor, the bookish Earl of Nayland.

Cadogan glanced up. "Ah, Patrick, do come in. There's someone I'd like you to meet."

As the other man turned to face him, Patrick was relieved to find that the earl was neither hunchbacked nor two-headed, though his fine, wispy blond hair was beginning to recede, giving him a high, domed forehead and making him look older than his thirty years. Still, he was such a fine figure of a man, with a good-looking face that even whiskers and a mustache couldn't conceal. Patrick wondered why any woman, especially the flirtatious Meggie, would have such an aversion to him.

"Son, I'd like to introduce you to Lionel Paige, Earl of Nayland," Cadogan said. "Nayland, this is my son, Patrick."

"Lord Nayland . . ." Patrick said, extending his hand almost warily, as if expecting to be rebuffed.

If the nobleman was startled by Patrick's unorthodox appearance, he had the grace and breeding not to show it. His forthright gaze held Patrick's without wavering, and his handshake was firm as he said, "The pleasure's mine, Mr. Quinn," in a clear, decisive voice.

"Let's not stand on ceremony," Patrick said, for he found himself warming to the earl in spite of Meggie's reservations. "Please call me Patrick."

The earl grinned, revealing even white teeth. "Patrick it is."

Cadogan went to pour another whiskey, and when he handed it to Patrick, he scowled at the door in annoyance. "I wonder what can be keeping Margaret? She should have been down hours ago." Then he turned to the earl. "I must apologize for my niece's behavior."

Nayland brushed the apology aside with a brief wave of his hand, and surprised Patrick by seeming more amused than angered by Meggie's rude tarrying. "It's a woman's sacred duty to keep us waiting, is it not, gentlemen?"

The men chuckled at that, then seated themselves and waited for the rest of the party to arrive.

"My father tells me you are new to the area," Patrick said as he settled himself in the comfortable chair.

The earl sipped his drink and nodded. "I come from Yorkshire, but I have summered in Ireland for several years now, and have always wanted to own an estate here. When I heard that Devinstown was up for sale, I couldn't resist offering for it."

Patrick was familiar with Devinstown, an estate of some five hundred acres to the east of Rookforest, though the Shea family had lived there since the time of Cromwell.

Patrick raised his glass in a salute. "You're to be commended for running the estate yourself."

"Oh, but I don't," Nayland said with an apologetic smile. "I let others do that for me. I'm afraid I'm rather a traitor to my class, you see. Farming, hunting, shooting—they have never held any appeal. I prefer a more quiet, contemplative existence amidst elegant surroundings. I purchased Devinstown with the intention of restoring it to its former grandeur. The house and gardens have been sadly neglected of late, as I'm sure you know, and it gives me great pleasure to plan what needs to be done and supervise the work."

And now Patrick understood why his cousin had such an aversion to this man. She was his complete antithesis. "Quiet" and "contemplative" were alien words to Meggie's vocabulary, she who lived to ride to the hounds and could outshoot half the men Patrick knew.

Still, Patrick mused, just because a man preferred a quiet, contemplative life of the intellect and appreciated beauty in all forms didn't mean he was weak or unmanly, but he suspected Meggie didn't share his opinion. Still, she was young yet and had led a sheltered life at Rook-forest. She had much to learn about men.

Suddenly, as if on cue, Meggie herself appeared in the doorway and the three men rose.

"Good evening," she said, sweeping into the room in a rustle of taffeta skirts. "So sorry to keep you gentlemen waiting."

"You are always worth waiting for, Miss Atkinson," the earl said with a slight bow from the waist.

"You are too kind, Lord Nayland," she replied, though her eyes glittered with hostility. Then she said, "I can see the Considines haven't arrived."

"It's early yet," Cadogan said. "Would you care for some sherry before dinner, Margaret?"

"Yes, thank you."

While Cadogan was pouring, Patrick let his gaze rake his cousin over. He smiled and shook his head. "Who would have thought that the little scapegrace who always had to win every race and be the first up every tree would turn into such a beauty?"

Margaret looked stunning and would have been a credit to any man. Her evening dress, while not as elaborate or of the first fashion as those worn in Dublin or London, was of a shimmering bronze taffeta that provided the perfect foil for Margaret's vivid coloring. A topaz necklace that her uncle had given her one Christmas sparkled softly at her throat, drawing the gaze downward to the low scoop neck of her gown, which exposed a modest amount of ivory bosom. Margaret's thick, lustrous hair had been tamed for the evening, swept away from her brow and gathered into an elaborate cascade of curls at the back.

She grinned impishly. "I may resemble a lady tonight, but I'll have you know I'm still that scapegrace inside. No one will ever change me."

Then she gave Nayland a challenging glance as if daring him to try.

Patrick just chuckled indulgently.

He glanced across at the earl to see what the nobleman's reaction would be. Instead of praising Meggie fulsomely and earning her contempt, he wordlessly raised his glass to her and complimented her with a look of undisguised admiration in his eyes.

But Margaret pointedly ignored him by turning to take the glass of sherry her uncle offered, then seating herself on a chair rather than the settee, where Lord Nayland could sit next to her. Then she began talking of horses with an enthusiasm the earl obviously didn't share, all in an attempt to demonstrate to him just how different they were and how pointless his suit would be.

Patrick was on the verge of rescuing the poor man with questions about his ongoing renovations of Devinstown, when the butler announced that the carriage had just returned with the Considines.

The moment Fenella appeared, Patrick felt his jovial mood sour and start to slip away. But he reminded himself that he had to try to be pleasant to her for his father's sake, for Cadogan was pleased to see her indeed.

"I trust we're not late," Dr. Considine said, smoothing his unkempt beard with his fingers.

"No, no, of course not!" Cadogan replied, walking forward and bringing them into the group's cozy circle. "You know everyone here."

"Of course," Fenella said with a bright smile. "Margaret . . . Lord Nayland." Her smile faltered ever so slightly when her gaze fell on Patrick, but she recovered herself beautifully. "How are you, Mr. Quinn?"

"Just fine, Miss Considine," he replied with a smile. "As always, it's a pleasure to see you again."

Then his father was offering the newcomers refreshment, and Margaret was urging Fenella to sit next to her on the settee, so Patrick quietly went to lean against the mantel, where he could observe those present.

The prim Miss Considine almost looked pretty tonight, he conceded, in a simple dress of some dark wine-colored material that added a little color to her pale cheeks and brought out the reddish glints in her dark hair. But mere prettiness faded into the background when placed next to Meggie's arresting, full-blown beauty. Yet Miss Considine seemed to accept her subordinate status without a hint of jealousy or resentment, a mark in her favor.

While the women talked of the O'Hara baby and Dr. Considine had the earl engaged in a discussion about books, Patrick noticed that his father was sitting there quietly, his rapt attention on Fenella. Cadogan's eyes never left her, and his expression now held a softness that had usually been reserved for Patrick's mother.

Patrick stiffened suddenly as a revelation hit him with the swiftness of an approaching thunderstorm. Was his father in love with the doctor's daughter? It would certainly explain his constant defense of her.

Suddenly the voices faded away, and as Patrick stared at his father, every gesture, every nuance of his expression took on a new, more ominous meaning. He was acting like a man in love, and Patrick cursed himself for not seeing it sooner.

He downed the rest of his drink in two searing gulps and his eyes narrowed in determination. Fenella Considine would never become Mrs. Cadogan Quinn if he had any said in the matter.

The sound of Margaret calling his name broke through his reverie. "Patrick, why don't you come join us?"

Just as he was about to reply, the butler announced that dinner was served. But it didn't escape his notice that his father escorted Fenella into the dining room.

Patrick accepted the brandy decanter Dr. Considine passed across the table and filled his glass.

He relaxed in his chair, feeling uncomfortably stuffed after the sumptuous meal they had just enjoyed. One day he would have to stop devouring each meal as though it were his last, but right now, feeling bloated was preferable to feeling ravenous. Now he settled down to enjoy the all-male after-dinner ritual of cigars and brandy, another of the amenities he had once taken for granted and had sorely missed in prison.

"So, Nayland," Patrick said, "have your tenants been clamoring for rent reductions as well?"

The earl relaxed, lit his cigar, and sent a puff of gray smoke into the air. "Oh, yes. I received their requests just yesterday."

"And what are you going to do about them?" Cadogan asked.

"I've agreed to their demands," he replied. "Since I don't rely on Devinstown solely for my income, I'm in a position where I can reduce my tenants' rents in poor economic times. At least for the time being."

"Well, I do what I can for my tenants," Cadogan said, "but I can only do so much. The farmers have a job to do, and I expect them to do it." He waved his hand, encompassing the large dining room with its magnificent crystal chandelier overhead. "We still have this house to maintain, and our own servants to feed and clothe." He leaned back in his chair. "I'll take each case separately. Those that need to have their rents reduced will get a reduction, but I have a feeling that some of my tenants are more well-off than they'd like me to believe."

Dr. Considine ran his hand through his hair before speaking up. "I disagree with you there, Cadogan. I've seen more hardship on my rounds and in the dispensary every day. And I must say it's getting worse."

Cadogan shifted in his seat. "That may be true, but I'm not running a relief organization. I rent out my land to make a profit. And if any farmer thinks I'm going to give him my land free and clear, he's sadly mistaken. I'll die first!"

"That's what Parnell and his followers are advocating," Patrick said. "Ireland for the Irish."

"Now, that will never happen. Besides, we Quinns are just as Irish as the next man."

Dr. Considine stared moodily into his glass. "I wonder what Saintly Standon will do?"

The earl flicked ashes from his cigar. "He'll do whatever his master tells him to do," he said contemptuously, earning Patrick's approval. "And the Duke of Carbury is a harsh master indeed."

"How so?" Patrick asked, his curiosity aroused.

Nayland looked across at him. "The duke is well-known in London society for foolishly squandering great sums of money on harebrained schemes. His current project is a very expensive one concerning the development of a horseless carriage because he can't tolerate the odor of horse droppings. He's already spent thousands of pounds on it."

Everyone laughed roundly, and Cadogan muttered, "A horseless carriage indeed!"

When the laughter faded, he continued. "Carbury just wants money—lots of it—from his Irish estate. He wouldn't care if Standon stole the money, just so his coffers are filled regularly. As far as I know, he's never even visited Ireland once to inspect his estate or see just how dire conditions are for the farmers. He's content to let Standon administer it as he sees fit as long as he gets results. And Carbury doesn't listen to excuses."

"And," Patrick said, "since Standon wants to remain in the duke's good graces, enjoying the life of a member of the gentry, he dances to the duke's tune." A slow smile of satisfaction lit up his features as he stared into the dark depths of his glass. "He's nothing but a whore."

"Very appropriate," the earl agreed with a chuckle. "So with the duke clamoring for money, I wouldn't be surprised if Standon tries to raise his tenants' rents."

Exclamations of outrage flew around the table.

Cadogan turned to Dr. Considine. "What have you heard on your rounds, Liam?"

The doctor hesitated, then drained his glass. "There is much talk of Captain Moonlight."

The earl scowled. "Captain Moonlight? Who is he?"

"He's not one person," the doctor replied. "Captain Moonlight refers to the members of a secret society dedicated to overthrowing landlords."

"Cowardly bastards masquerading as patriots, if you ask me," Cadogan muttered, his eyes glittering with aversion. "They terrorize the countryside and try to bend people to their will with violence."

"Such as?" Nayland prodded.

Dr. Considine replied, "If the moonlighters decree that no rents shall be paid, and a farmer defies them, they'll maim his cattle to teach him a lesson. If someone tries to grab his evicted neighbors' land, they'll dig a symbolic grave at his front door as a warning to him to back off."

Cadogan shook his head. "It's the Ribbonmen all over again, only by another name."

"Have they been known to murder estate agents?" the earl asked.

"Estate agents and landlords," Patrick added.

Nayland raised his brows. "I say! So I may be in danger from these moonlighters, then?"

"We are all in danger," Cadogan said heavily, reaching for the decanter to refill his glass.

Then they all fell silent, each man with his own thoughts.

While the men were discussing their tenants and moonlighters, the ladies were discussing the gentlemen over tea.

As Margaret poured the steaming brew into delicate procelain cups, she said, "I have always thought it most unfair that we ladies are always banished after dinner. What can they possibly have to discuss that's so important?"

Fenella took the proffered cup. "My father once told me all they do is relate ribald stories unfit for ladies' delicate ears."

"Like sniggering little boys," was Margaret's disdainful comment.

"I sometimes think the gentlemen would be quite astonished to learn just how much we really do know about matters they've deemed unfit for our ears."

Margaret's eyes narrowed. "Not that I would want to stay in Lord Nayland's presence any longer than necessary."

Fenella hesitated, for she sensed in Margaret's voice and manner that she wanted to share a confidence, something Fenella dreaded, for she knew Margaret and Cadogan were fiercely divided on the subject of Lord Nayland. And Fenella, who was loyal to them both, didn't want to take sides in a matter that could have such consequences for all involved.

With Margaret regarding her so expectantly, Fenella felt compelled to make a comment. "I find Lord Nayland to be an amiable, pleasant young man."

"I find him exceedingly tedious, with all his talk of books and gardening, and I wish my uncle wouldn't keep inviting him to dinner!"

"Perhaps your uncle enjoys his company."

Margaret shook her head. "That is not his only reason." She took a deep breath. "He is hoping that the earl will one day ask for my hand in marriage."

Fenella tried to look surprised, but in truth she knew all about Cadogan's wishes in that direction. He had told her as much on several occasions.

"I take it you would not welcome such a match?" Fenella said carefully.

"Of course not!" Margaret set her teacup into its saucer with an audible clink, rose to her feet in an agitated whisper of taffeta, and began pacing the room like a caged tigress. "Uncle Cadogan is always telling me what a fool I am for not encouraging the man. Granted, Lord Nayland is handsome, and wealthier than half the landlords in County Cork." She rested her hands on the back of her chair and leaned over to affix Fenella with a desperate stare. "But what no one seems willing to take into account is the fact that I don't love him and I never shall!"

Fenella's heart went out to her. She knew marriages among the landed gentry and aristocracy were often arranged for considerations other than love, but to Fenella, love surpassed wealth or titles.

Margaret was staring at her with an odd, intense expression on her face. "I can see you understand. I know you were in love once, but the man died."

Fenella looked at her sharply, shocked and upset by Margaret's unexpected blunt statement. "Yes, I was," she admitted. "He was a lawyer from Cork city, and I loved him very much." Odd how the words could still sear her. She tried to keep her voice from trembling and failed. "He caught pneumonia one cold rainy night and died before we had a chance to marry."

Margaret suddenly looked guilt-stricken and came around the chair to grasp Fenella's hands. "Do forgive me, Fenella! I didn't mean to bring up the past and hurt you. But you know how important love is to a woman, and perhaps you can help me to convince Uncle Cadogan that Nayland is not the right man for me."

So, the girl was after an ally.

Fenella gently withdrew her hands. "Margaret, you're placing me in a extremely awkward position. You are asking me to take your side against Cadogan, who has been a great friend to my father and me ever since we moved to Mallow.''

Margaret stiffened, her lovely face suddenly hardening. ''So you won't help me.''

''Margaret, you don't need me to champion your cause. No one is forcing you to marry the earl. Your uncle would never do that to you.''

''No,'' she admitted reluctantly, ''but I'm sure if Nayland asks for my hand, my uncle will expect me to accept. And I owe him so much, Fenella. He took me in after my parents died, gave me a home and enough love for three daughters. I would feel obligated to accept Nayland's suit, if that's what Uncle Cadogan really wanted.''

''Your uncle is not a monster, Margaret. I'm sure he would take your feelings into account if he knew you were really so set against such a match.''

''Perhaps not. But he respects and admires you, Fenella. He would listen to you if you took my side.''

Suddenly a startling thought popped into Fenella's head and she voiced her suspicions. ''Margaret, are you in love with someone else? Is that why you're so against Lord Nayland?''

She hesitated for a split second before replying, ''Of course not. I merely do not wish to marry the Earl of Nayland.''

Fenella was just about to press her further, when the men filed into the drawing room, ending all conversation.

Margaret swept away to go to her uncle and slip an arm through his. ''There you are. We thought you had abandoned us.''

Cadogan chuckled, but his gaze drifted toward Fenella. ''You know me, lass. I was never one to leave the ladies for very long.'' Then he turned to the earl. ''Will you honor us with a melody or two tonight?''

Nayland smiled. ''Only if Miss Atkinson turns the pages for me.''

Fenella watched as anger flared in Margaret's eyes, but in spite of her dislike of the earl, she agreed, and the two went over to the piano in the opposite corner of the room.

To Fenella's chagrin, Patrick Quinn seated himself beside her on the settee before anyone else could.

"Mr. Quinn . . ." she murmured, trying to resist the urge to slide away from him into the farthest corner.

He said nothing as the earl seated himself at the instrument and selected his music. "I see our young lord is a musician as well as a man of infinite patience."

"He is a man of many talents," Fenella replied, keeping her attention focused straight ahead.

The room fell silent as the earl began to play.

Even as the room filled with the melodic strains of Chopin and Mozart the earl played so effortlessly—except when Margaret neglected to turn a page fast enough— Fenella was acutely aware of the man sitting not two feet away. She sensed he didn't like her, so why was he insisting on forcing his disagreeable presence on her? Fenella fidgeted in her seat.

And then the musicale was over.

"Well done!" Patrick said, clapping enthusiastically. Then, without warning, he turned to Fenella and said, "Do you play the piano as well, Miss Considine?"

It was the first time he had spoken to her without that underlying tone of mockery in his voice, and his unexpected politeness caught Fenella off guard. "Why, yes, Mr. Quinn, but not as well as Lord Nayland, I'm afraid."

His pale, dispirited eyes regarded her solemnly. "Then we shall have to hear you play sometime. I'm afraid poor Meggie is not very accomplished at it."

Margaret, who had heard him, made a face, then went over to where the doctor was sitting and engaged him in conversation while Cadogan and Nayland strolled over to the fireplace. Fenella was paired off with Patrick and forced to talk with him whether she wanted to or not.

"Do you always accompany your father when he visits the sick?" Patrick asked.

"Upon occasion," Fenella replied. "Sometimes a woman's presence is reassuring, especially to another woman. They will tell me things they feel too shy to discuss with my father."

"Ah, what a veritable angel of mercy you must be!"

She looked at him sharply, but curbed her tongue. "I do what I can, Mr. Quinn," she said stiffly. "And what about you? I assume you will be helping your father to administer Rookforest now that you are here."

"Eventually . . ." he replied cryptically, as if he were dreading it.

Without warning, Fenella's wrist began to throb. Patrick's voice became fainter and fainter, and Fenella had to strain to hear him. Then the drawing room grew dim and shadowed, as if someone had turned down the lamps. Fenella tried to resist, but the feeling of light-headedness that she had come to dread was taking hold of her in its grip, imprisoning her senses. She blinked once, and when she opened her eyes, the drawing room and all of its occupants had disappeared.

In its place were the ruins of Ballymere Castle, now bathed in the clear light of midday. Fenella heard voices, the light trill of a woman's laughter followed by a deep, teasing masculine voice, but she could see no one yet. She watched as one dreaming, for she knew from past experience that she was powerless to return to the present until the vision had played itself out.

In seconds, a woman came running around a corner of crumbling stone wall, her skirts held up by both hands so she could evade her pursuer without tripping. Fenella couldn't see the woman clearly, for her face was averted as she looked back over her shoulder, but she obviously didn't fear whoever was chasing her, for she was breathless and laughing. Then she turned and Fenella saw her face.

It was Margaret.

No sooner did Margaret collapse against a nearby stone wall than a man came into view. He was tall and dark-haired, dressed in the plain homespun garb of a farmer, his shirt sleeves rolled up to expose muscular forearms. As he bore down on Margaret, Fenella could see that it was Terrence Sheely, the eldest son of one of Cadogan Quinn's most prosperous tenant farmers.

This time Margaret didn't try to evade him. When Terrence caught up with her, she boldly flung herself into his arms and greedily pulled his head down to her waiting mouth. Young Sheely responded by pressing her back against the wall with his body, his hands braced on either side of her shoulders as he met her fierce, passionate kiss with one of his own.

The vision ended in another blink of an eye. One moment Fenella was staring at the embracing couple, the next she was back at Rookforest's drawing room, seated next to a furious Patrick Quinn.

"Am I boring you, Miss Considine? Do forgive me for being such dull company that your mind wanders and you sit there like a statue."

"I . . . I beg your pardon. I didn't mean to—"

"That's quite all right," he said frostily as he rose. "I assure you I understand all too well." And without another word, he stormed over the whiskey decanter and poured himself such a generous drink that even his father looked at him askance.

But Fenella had no time to soothe Patrick's bruised feelings, and she didn't dare explain the truth to him. She nervously scanned the faces of those present, but everyone was oblivious of what had happened to her— everyone was oblivious except Patrick—but she doubted if he even understood the real significance of her trancelike state.

So Fenella's secret was safe.

Suddenly she noticed her father staring at her with a quizzical expression on his face. Nodding imperceptibly, Fenella signaled him that she wanted to leave.

Liam made a great pretense out of squinting at the clock on the mantel. "Good heavens! Ten o'clock already?" Then he rose slowly. "Well, Cadogan, as much as my daughter and I enjoy your hospitality, I'm afraid we must take our leave. It's getting late, and I have to be in the dispensary bright and early tomorrow, even though it is a Saturday."

"As much as I regret letting you go," Cadogan said, glancing at Fenella, "I realize that duty must come before pleasure."

Everyone rose, and Margaret said, "I'll have Bell send for the carriage and fetch your wraps."

As Fenella went to bid Cadogan and the earl good night, she noticed out of the corner of her eye that Patrick was still leaning against the mantel, making no attempt to join the rest of them as they drifted toward the door.

His father noticed as well, for Cadogan turned and glared at his son. "Our guests are leaving," he said.

Patrick straightened and crossed the room to Fenella's side. "Do forgive me for my lapse of good manners,

Miss Considine," he said, bowing over her hand. "I was just so lost in thought, I failed to notice you were leaving."

Fenella felt her cheeks grow warm at his reference to her own behavior. "There is no need to apologize, Mr. Quinn."

She was spared further comment when Bell, the butler, entered the room with their wraps, and after bidding everyone good night once again, Fenella and her father went outside to where Cadogan's carriage was waiting to take them home.

"You had another vision, didn't you?" Liam asked, once the carriage was on its way and he and Fenella were alone.

She shivered in the damp night air and drew her thick woolen wrap more closely about her. She was grateful for the darkness of the carriage so her father couldn't see how really distraught she was.

"Yes, I had another damned vision," she replied angrily, "right in Cadogan Quinn's parlor, just as I was conversing with his son!"

"Now, now, daughter . . ." Liam murmured, putting his arm around Fenella's shoulders and drawing her close to comfort her. "Don't be upset."

Fenella let hot tears of frustration fall. "What is wrong with me, Father!" she wailed. "Why do I—"

"Hush, or the coachman will hear you."

She lowered her voice, but the vehemence lingered. "Why do I keep having these visions? Am I going mad? If that's the case, I suggest you just lock me away in an asylum and forget that you ever had a daughter!"

"Now, Nella," Liam said, his voice surprisingly harsh. "By the Holy, I won't have any talk of locking you up in an asylum, do you hear me? You're as sane as I am."

"Then why have I been cursed with these visions?"

"I don't know, Nella. If I were a holy man, I'd say you have been given this gift of second sight for a reason, a reason that is not yet apparent to you."

"A gift, you say?" she scoffed. "I find it more a curse than a gift, a curse I would give anything to be rid of."

Needing to be alone with her tumultuous thoughts, Fenella drew away from the shelter of her father's arm, wedged herself into the corner of the seat, and stared out the window. It was a moonless night, and the impenetrable inky blackness matched the bleakness of her mood.

She hadn't been born with second sight. She had acquired it a year ago in an unbelievable, improbable way: William came to her in a dream. When she reached for him, he grasped her left wrist and told her without speaking that he was giving her a special gift. The following morning, Fenella awoke to find a puckered red mark like a burn scar encircling her wrist, a terrifying reminder that she might not have been dreaming after all.

A month later, she had her first vision, and her life changed forever.

Suddenly the carriage lurched forward, jostling Fenella out of her daydream and returning her to the present.

"What did you see this time?" Liam asked.

Fenella took a deep breath and told him.

Liam's surprised gasp filled the carriage. "By the Holy! Margaret and old Sheely's boy? You're certain?"

She nodded wearily. "I saw them as clearly as if they were sitting right here, but I pray what I saw is not true."

Fenella had never liked Terrence Sheely. Oh, he was so handsome he had half the farmer's daughters in love with him, with his sun-bronzed skin and a fine, strapping physique from working the land day in and day out. But his mist-gray eyes were too bold and presumptuous for Fenella's taste. Though he was always deferential to her whenever they passed on the street, she always had the uncomfortable feeling he was undressing her with his eyes.

Liam was silent for a moment, then nodded slowly in agreement. "If Margaret and young Sheely are romantically involved and meeting secretly, her uncle will be furious, especially seeing as how he's longing for a match between her and Nayland."

Fenella sighed and placed her fingertips to her forehead. "I pray I'm wrong. I do admire and respect Cadogan, and I know he would be hurt if his niece betrayed him."

Liam was silent for a moment. When he spoke, he spoke slowly, as if choosing his words carefully. "Is that all you feel for Cadogan Quinn, daughter, admiration and respect?''

Fenella turned, wishing she could read his expression in the semidarkness of the carriage. ''Yes. What else should I feel for the man?''

''Do you think you could ever feel the way a wife feels about her husband?''

''If you're asking me in a roundabout way if I could love and marry Cadogan Quinn, I'm afraid the answer is no,'' she replied.

''You could do worse. Cadogan's a fine man. Wealthy and highly respected too.''

Fenella regarded her father out of suspicious eyes. ''What is this all about, Father? Are you suddenly weary of my company and trying to marry me off?''

Liam made an indignant sputter in the darkness. ''I am not trying to marry you off to anyone. Cadogan confessed to me that he has tender feelings for you and asked me to find out if you were of like mind.''

She groaned in consternation. ''Well, I'm not, so you must discourage him with great kindness and delicacy. I enjoy the man's company, but I do not love him. Unlike Miss Standon, I would never marry a man I didn't love just for position or material gain.''

''I know that, daughter, and I wasn't implying that you should. It's just that . . . well, I'm not getting any younger, and I would die a happy man if I knew you were settled.''

''You're not going to die for a long, long time yet,'' Fenella snapped, ''so don't even upset me by talking about it.''

Chastened, Liam fell silent once again, and several minutes later the Quinn carriage slowed and drew to a halt. He and Fenella were home.

Fenella finished plaiting her hair, blew out the candle, and slipped into bed, where she lay wide-awake in the darkness, watching a square patch of moonbeam make its way across the floor.

Restless, she rolled over onto her left side. Her father's revelation about Cadogan's romantic interest in her disheartened Fenella. She had no illusions about herself.

She was a rather plain young woman cursed with visions and haunted by bitter memories of a tragic lost love. She should be honored that a man of Cadogan Quinn's stature desired her for his wife. Yet when she thought of the burdens she would bring to such a union, she knew she would never have the courage to go through with it, even for her own future security and her father's peace of mind.

Fenella smiled wryly to herself as a picture of the glowering, dour Patrick Quinn slipped unbidden to her mind. She could just imagine his reaction to such a match. And what of Margaret?

Fenella's smile died as she tossed and turned once more in her efforts to get comfortable. But her thoughts wouldn't let her. If she and Cadogan were an unsuitable pair, then Margaret and the Sheely boy were a disastrous combination that could lead only to heartbreak—that is, if they were indeed meeting secretly at the castle ruins.

There was only one way for her to find out.

Tomorrow she would go to Ballymere Castle.

The following afternoon found Fenella standing before the ruins and catching her breath from the long, arduous walk up the steep hill.

The castle must have been truly magnificent when it was first built in the sixteenth century, but was now nothing more than a crumbling ruin choked with nettles and dock, and inhabited by a few wild birds. One section of battlements was still standing, its crenellated edge like square jagged teeth against the blue sky, while a section of well-trodden stairs against another wall led to nowhere.

Fenella glanced around and felt uneasiness well up in her, for the scene before her was exactly as her vision had shown her. The sky was clear blue, with clouds gathering to the west. The castle's stones were the precise shade of warm sun-washed gray. There was only one difference: Margaret was nowhere to be seen.

Fenella waited for several minutes, listening, but there was nothing but the gentle sighing of the breeze through the ancient stones. After several minutes more, she almost collapsed with relief. The vision had been false this time.

She was about to turn and start back to the dogcart when the first faint trill of laughter reached her ears.

"Oh, no!" she murmured in defeat, slowly turning to witness the inevitable.

Fenella felt as though she were reliving last night. She saw the giddy, breathless Margaret come running around a corner with the Sheely lad in hot pursuit. When Margaret reached the wall and turned to the man, Fenella already knew with a sinking heart that they were going to embrace.

Before Fenella could leave quietly without being noticed, Margaret turned her head abruptly and saw her. She froze at once as their gazes locked, her hazel eyes wide with disbelief, her flushed complexion draining of all color.

"Meg, alanna, what's wrong?" Terrence Sheely said, bewildered by the sudden change in her and not noticing the cause.

"We have a spy in our midst," Margaret replied, never taking her eyes off Fenella.

Young Sheely turned, his handsome face registering first surprise, then alarm as he realized the ramifications of discovery. When his presumptuous eyes narrowed menacingly, Fenella found herself wishing she had stayed home.

"I was not spying," she insisted. "I merely came here to enjoy the view from the castle, I apologize for disturbing you."

And she turned on her heel and started back down the slope. Behind her, she heard Margaret and Sheely talking between themselves in low, hurried voices.

"Fenella, wait!"

She stopped and turned to see Margaret running after her, while Sheely started walking away after one final sharp, assessing glance at Fenella.

Margaret made no attempt to prevaricate or make excuses. "You saw us kissing, didn't you?"

Fenella didn't deny it. "Yes, I did."

Margaret swallowed hard. "I know this may sound odd, but Terrence and I love each other. We want to be married one day."

"Then why not bring him home to your uncle and declare your intentions? Why must you meet in secret?"

Margaret tossed her head defiantly. "You know as well as I that Uncle Cadogan would never accept him. Terrence is the son of one of Uncle's tenant farmers, far beneath the touch of an Atkinson. He wants me to marry a man like Nayland, someone he considers more suitable, not the man I love."

Fenella sighed. "It is not my place to lecture you on the propriety of this, Margaret."

Hope suffused her face. "Then you won't tell Uncle Cadogan?"

"He is my friend, Margaret. Keeping silent about something like this is tantamount to lying."

Margaret grasped her arm. "Please, Fenella. All I'm asking for is a little time. I know I can convince Uncle that Terrence and I belong together, but I must have time. What can be the harm in it?"

"What can be the harm in meeting a man alone, in such a deserted place?" Fenella asked incredulously. "You're old enough to know the answer to that, Margaret Atkinson."

"He would never seduce me!" Margaret retorted hotly, hazel eyes flashing. "Terrence may be a farmer, but he's too much of a gentleman."

"No man is too much of a gentleman."

"Oh, and I suppose you know so much more about men than I."

"I never claimed to be an expert on the subject," Fenella said. "But a woman should always be wary of compromising situations, because the world will deal much more harshly with her than any man, no matter how guilty."

Margaret's lips tightened stubbornly. "Terrence would never do that to me. I'll have you know our meetings are quite harmless. We exchange a few kisses and talk about our future together, that is all."

Fenella just shook her head. "Margaret . . ."

"Won't you give me the benefit of the doubt? Please, Fenella! I swear nothing will happen."

Fenella hesitated, then relented. What could be the harm in keeping silent and letting the girl have her flirtation? Obviously the danger and illicitness of the situation were what had attracted Margaret to Sheely in the first place. No doubt she would soon grow tired of the novelty of it and seek a man of her own class.

Reluctantly she nodded. "All right. I'll promise not to say anything to your uncle, but you must promise me that you'll tell him yourself."

Margaret's face broke out in a relieved smile and she hugged Fenella. "I will! Oh, thank you, Fenella! You won't regret it."

Then she went rushing off down the hill to where her horse was tethered among the trees.

As Fenella watched Margaret hurry off, she was already beginning to regret making such a rash promise.

4

ON THE FIRST sunny day a week later, Fenella accompanied her father into the nearby town of Mallow. After leaving him at the dispensary, which was already crowded with patients at eleven o'clock in the morning, she proceeded to go shopping.

As the dogcart jounced over the main street's rough cobblestones, past shopfronts with their upstairs lodgings for their proprietors, Fenella wondered what Mallow had been like nearly a century ago in its heyday as the "Bath of Ireland."

In those days, people from all over Ireland had flocked here to socialize and partake of the healthful mineral waters flowing from the base of a limestone hill on the northeastern side of town. The gentry stayed in their dignified gray-fronted town houses for the Mallow season that began in May, while the inns were filled to overflowing with people who came to see and be seen. During the day everyone congregated at the Spa House, with its pump room for taking the waters, consultation room, and baths. But when the sun went down, wild young bucks would expend their high spirits by racing their horses through the town at breakneck speed, cursing noisily, and breaking windows.

Today, the town was as sedate as an old dowager in her twilight years. The once-glorious Spa House now stood hiding quietly behind its row of tall poplars, and the streets of Mallow observed the leisurely ebb and flow of farmers and gentry going about the daily business of living.

There was much to be said for peace and quiet, Fenella decided. With all the talk of unrest and bad times coming, she wondered how long Mallow was going to remain a peaceful and tranquil country town.

When she reached almost the end of the main street, she halted the mare, got down from the dogcart, and paid a child a ha'penny to hold her horse while she went shopping.

A half-hour later, Fenella had made all of her purchases and was ready to go home.

As she started back to the dogcart, she found herself thinking of Margaret and Cadogan again and became so preoccupied with her own thoughts that she failed to respond when someone called her name.

It wasn't until a man blocked her path and a deep mocking voice said, "Are you once again determined to ignore me, Miss Considine?" that she came out of her fog to find the tall figure of Patrick Quinn standing before her.

He looked better since she had first seen him a week ago, she thought, even though that haunted air persisted. Although his clothes still hung on him like a scarecrow, his complexion had lost its unhealthy prison pallor and regained some color. With a tall silk hat concealing most of his cropped hair from curious stares, Patrick Quinn could have passed for any gentleman, if one didn't examine him too closely.

As usual, his surliness annoyed her, but she resolutely decided that she was not going to lower herself to his level by verbally sparring with him in front of half the town.

"I beg your pardon," Fenella said, shifting her parcels in her arms. "I was lost in thought and didn't notice you standing there."

"No offense taken," he replied lightly, the sarcasm gone. "Actually, it's rather refreshing not to be noticed by someone today."

Fenella found his words puzzling at first, until she glanced around. Then she noticed that Patrick Quinn was the center of attention, however subtle. Some passersby barely glanced in his direction, while others blatantly stared. Many faces brightened briefly with the light of recognition, but no one approached him or acknowledged him in any way. Fenella observed more than one gentleman duck his head and pretend not to see Patrick before hurrying across the street.

But he noticed. His eyes darkened with cold, hard fury, while white lines of strain formed on either side of his mouth.

"Well, Miss Considine," he muttered between clenched teeth, "it would appear I have mastered the art of becoming invisible. Or do you suppose I have managed to contract leprosy without my being aware of it?"

Fenella didn't know what to say. It was obvious that the good citizens of Mallow were either embarrassed to have a former convict in their midst or afraid of him. In either case, they didn't know quite how to approach Patrick. So they said nothing and ignored him.

"Will you walk with me, Mr. Quinn?" she asked. "My dogcart is not far from here."

He gave her an ironic look. "I'm surprised someone of your sterling reputation would lower herself to be seen in the company of Ireland's master criminal."

His bitter, cutting words angered her, but Fenella willed herself to ignore them as he took her parcels and fell into step beside her.

"Ireland's master criminal, are you?" she said. "My, you have a grand opinion of yourself!"

"I only speak the truth," he said. "I was imprisoned unjustly, and when I return to my homeland, I find myself shunned by my peers and so-called friends."

Privately Fenella thought that abducting a woman hardly qualified as a minor offense, but all she said was, "They will come around, in time, if they are truly your friends."

"You are so sure . . ."

"I am. True friends don't desert each other in time of need."

Patrick inclined his head. "I bow to your superior knowledge of human nature."

She kept her eyes on the street ahead and decided to risk saying what was on her mind. "You'd catch more flies with honey than vinegar, you know."

Patrick gave her an arrogant stare. "Are you implying that my personality lacks warmth, Miss Considine? That

I am bitter, mocking, and rude, not to mention surly and sullen?''

Fenella blushed to the roots of her hair. "Mr. Quinn, I—''

"It's so easy to judge others, to say we know how they feel. But I should like to know what you would do, Miss Considine,'' he said quietly, without rancor, "if you had been locked away for as long as I was.''

Fenella was spared the necessity of replying, for without warning, Patrick stopped in his tracks and muttered, "Standon!''

There, dismounting from his white horse across the street, was none other than St. John Standon himself.

Even though Fenella had only a nodding acquaintance with the man she saw every Sunday in church, occupying a prominent front pew, she, like every other woman there, had done her share of peeking at Lord Carbury's estate agent, for St. John Standon was the type of man who invited stares and caused heads to turn. He was not as tall as Patrick, but as lithe and graceful as a dancer, with thick, dark, wavy hair and heavily lidded blue eyes that gave him a sensual air. And his face . . . If ever a man's face could be termed beautiful, it was St. John Standon's, clean-shaven to give the world an unobstructed view of his strong jaw, lean cheeks, and full lips.

As Fenella watched him cross the street and come toward them, apparently unaware of Patrick standing there, glowering at him, she found herself wondering how such a physically perfect man could act so vengefully toward another human being.

She glanced up at Patrick standing stock-still beside her, and the look of frigid, implacable hatred in his eyes made her shiver. His nostrils flared and his lip curled disdainfully, making him resemble a wolf about to tear its victim to pieces.

"Look at him," Patrick growled. "He struts as though he were the uncrowned king of Ireland.''

Fenella said, "Mr. Quinn, if you would be so kind as to return my parcels to me . . . You are holding them so tightly, I fear you are about to crush them.''

He shook his head slightly as if to clear it, then murmured, "Yes, of course," before handing the parcels back to her. Then his attention went right back to the man now approaching them.

Patrick balled his hands into fists at his sides and moved to plant himself right in the man's path. "Standon!"

Standon stopped. Not the barest hint of recognition flickered in his eyes. "Yes?" he inquired with exaggerated politeness. Then he noticed Fenella, so he flashed her a winning smile as he tipped his hat. "Good day, Miss Considine. I trust you and your father are keeping well?"

His good looks were so intimidating that for a moment Fenella just stared at him stupidly, astounded that he even knew her name.

When she regained her wits, she replied, "Good day, Mr. Standon. We are fine, thank you."

"And what about me, Standon?" Patrick's voice was low and deadly. "Don't you want to know how I've been keeping for the last four years?"

Standon looked at him again, more intently this time, letting his gaze insolently rake him up and down. "Well, I'll be bound! It's none other than Patrick Quinn himself. Has it been four years since they put you away? My, how quickly time passes!"

"It seemed like an eternity to me."

Standon insouciantly flicked an imaginary speck of lint off the sleeve of his superbly cut coat. "Well, Quinn, I must say prison appears to have done you a world of good."

"Mr. Standon!" Fenella cried, appalled, for a crowd was beginning to gather.

He sketched her a bow. "I did not mean to offend you, good lady. But Quinn besmirched my family honor and broke the law, so you cannot expect me to feel much sympathy for the man."

"Family honor!" Patrick scoffed, trembling. "What do you know of honor? You're nothing but a whore, Standon, who'll sleep with whichever man pays the most."

Patrick saw Standon respond with a scowl. Then without warning his arm drew back and his fist shot out with lightning speed. The moment bare knuckles connected to Patrick's jaw with a dull crack, snapping his head back with the force, his whole face exploded with pain and twinkling colored lights danced before his eyes. The street tilted and whirled, and before Patrick could catch himself, the cobblestones came rushing up to meet him as he fell.

Dazed, Patrick heard several feminine shrieks from a great distance, and several voices in the crowd.

"Look! His hair is all cut off!"

"Didn't take much to knock him down, did it?"

"He's done for now."

The warm salty taste of iron filled his mouth as red-hot rage coursed through him. He fought with all his might to get up, but all he could manage was to flounder on his back helplessly, like a turtle turned on its shell. He was aware of Fenella kneeling beside him, an expression of shock and concern on the face floating above him, but he didn't want or need her solicitude. All Patrick wanted to do was rise and beat St. John Standon's perfect face to an unrecognizable bloody pulp.

Meanwhile, St. John Standon had whipped off his hat and coat and stood with fists upraised. "On your feet, Quinn! If it's a fight you want, I'll give you one you'll never forget."

Patrick groaned and rolled over on his side, managing to hoist himself onto all fours with superhuman effort. He shook his head to clear it. Then he struggled to his knees, cursing his prison-weakened body for failing him just when he needed strength.

"Will you stop it!" Fenella railed at Standon as she took Patrick's arm and began hauling him to his feet, her touch firm but curiously gentle.

He thought he would die of humiliation, but since no one else was coming forward to help him, he needed her strength and support.

"I'll kill the bastard!" he muttered as he fought for breath and spit out blood onto the cobblestones.

"You're in no condition to kill anyone, Patrick Quinn," she snapped as his legs buckled and she braced herself to bear his weight.

But he was determined to try. The moment Patrick regained his balance, he was just about to launch himself at Standon. But he was saved from his own folly by the sudden appearance of a uniformed constable elbowing his way through the crowd.

"All right, break it up. Break it up, boys. Time to go about your business."

As the crowd began to disperse reluctantly, the young constable glared at the two men. "Now, would one of you gentlemen care to tell me what happened?"

Standon began slipping on his coat, all the while keeping a watchful eye on Patrick lest he unexpectedly attack. "It's quite simple, constable. Quinn here insulted me, and I responded as only a gentleman would."

"Are you sayin' he provoked you, sir?"

"I am." Standon flashed a warm, conspiratorial smile at Fenella. "You can ask the lady, if you don't believe me."

The constable turned to Fenella. "Is that true, Miss Considine? Did Mr. Quinn provoke Mr. Standon into hitting him?"

Fenella glanced at Patrick's stony face, then reluctantly nodded.

"Do you wish to press charges, sir?" the constable asked Standon.

Patrick felt panic rising like gorge when he saw the slow smile of malice spread across his adversary's face.

But Standon only shook his head. "I think Quinn has spent enough time behind bars," he said magnanimously. "I'll not press charges this time. But be warned, Quinn," he added. "If you ever threaten me again, I'll see that you rot in prison for the rest of your miserable life."

"I'm quaking in my boots, Standon."

"Good day to you, Miss Considine," Standon said, tipping his hat. Then he turned on his heel and sauntered down the street as if he didn't have a care in the world.

After delivering a short, stern lecture to Patrick on the consequences of breaking the law in Mallow, the constable also went about his business.

When Patrick and Fenella were alone again, save for a few curious bystanders drifting past, he watched as she reached into her purse, took out a clean white handkerchief, and wordlessly handed it to him. Then she knelt

down and retrieved her parcels that she had dropped when
she went to his aid.

"What, Miss Considine?" he said, gingerly dabbing
the blood off his chin. "No angry recriminations from
you?"

"If you want to get your face bashed in, it's no concern
of mine, Mr. Quinn." She handed him his hat. "But I
would make sure I was in fighting shape before I provoked a man like St. John Standon again. He's very good
with his fists, as you've just experienced firsthand."

"I could kill that bastard with my bare hands for what
he did to me!"

"And what good would that do?" Fenella retorted, her
dark eyes flashing. "You'd only be sent back to prison
for your pains."

"It would be well worth the satisfaction."

"Would it really, Mr. Quinn? Somehow, I doubt it."

He made no reply.

Fenella gave him a reproachful look, then proceeded
to walk toward her dogcart. Patrick followed her.

She set her parcels inside the cart, then turned to him,
her expression softer than he had ever seen it. "Would
you care to stop at the dispensary, Mr. Quinn, so my
father can tend to your jaw?"

Patrick managed a feeble smile despite the pain. "Your
concern for me is touching, Miss Considine, but you
needn't go out of your way. The blow didn't loosen any
teeth, and aside from having a sore, bruised jaw, I am
quite all right. My pride is injured more than my body."

The woman hesitated, then faced him squarely. "May
I give you some advice, Mr. Quinn?"

"I don't need advice from anyone, least of all you,
Miss Considine."

Her cheeks became suffused with color, and she pursed
her lips into a thin, angry line, much as an outraged
governess would when confronted by a fractious charge.
"Very well, then. I'll not give you any!"

And without so much as a "good day," she took the
reins and climbed into her dogcart.

But it soon became apparent that Fenella wasn't going
anywhere.

While she and Patrick were arguing, they had failed to

notice that Mallow's main street was gradually filling with people. Many were on foot, while others filled farmers' wagons and carts. Some hurried out of shops. There was even a tinker or two leading their donkeys. Now, as Fenella tried to turn her dogcart around and return up the street for home, she found her way blocked by a moving wave of humanity. Fighting that crowd would have been a task as torturous as a salmon swimming upstream, so she gave up.

She turned to Patrick, who looked just as puzzled as she. "Where is everyone going? It isn't market day today."

He stopped a barefoot lad hurrying by. "Where is everyone going?"

"To the bridge, to hear the man from the Land League," the boy replied, then melted back into the throng.

Fenella looked at Patrick. "So, they've come again to stir up more trouble."

"The Land Leaguers were here before?"

She nodded. "Last year. They say about twenty thousand people came from miles around to listen."

Patrick extended his hand to her. "Shall we join the crowd and hear what these Land Leaguers have to say?"

When Fenella hesitated, he added, "Unless, of course, you're ashamed to be seen with the likes of a ruffian like myself."

With a look of consternation, she resolutely placed her hand in his and stepped down. Patrick placed a steadying hand beneath her elbow and together they eased themselves into the crowd.

As Fenella was swept down Mallow's humpbacked main street with Patrick and the others, she could see the boy had spoken the truth. The crowd's ultimate destination was the bridge that spanned the River Blackwater, and here they gathered, stopping traffic in all directions so they could hear the man who must have been standing on a platform made of several boxes so he could be seen by everyone.

As the Land Leaguer began addressing the crowd, his fist raised in the air to punctuate every utterance, Fenella was not really interested in hearing what he had to say, for she had heard it all before and was sick unto death of such rhetoric. She was more interested in the reactions of the people around her.

Most of the women, such as herself, appeared skeptical and apprehensive, as they thought of how rebellion and its subsequent violence would disrupt their homes and leave their husbands and sons maimed or dead. The men, however, those same husbands and sons, appeared to eagerly embrace the Land Leaguer's message, often shouting, "Irish lands in Irish hands!" and "Down with the land robbers!" after the speaker made a particular point that struck a responsive chord.

Glancing at Patrick standing beside her, Fenella noticed that, as a member of the landlord class, he did not appear to be impressed. But he listened intently anyway, his brow furrowed in thought.

Finally he said to her, "I have heard enough. Do you wish to stay?"

Fenella shook her head, and he escorted her through the crowd and back to her cart.

That evening, Fenella had her father's supper on the table by the time he came whistling through the door. After giving his clothes a cursory once-over to see if there were any small tears to be mended or spots to be cleaned before morning, she let him go upstairs to wash.

When he returned, they sat down to dine on a meal of smoked ham and potato cakes that Fenella's maid-of-all-work had prepared before leaving.

Fenella treasured these quiet times alone with her father, when the problems of the world were kept at bay at least for a little while. Judging by Liam's worried expression and the way his shoulders sagged, Fenella had the feeling he was bearing more of the world's woes than he ought.

"And how was your day today?" she asked, as she always did before they began eating at the kitchen table.

Fenella listened attentively while her father told her of setting a farmer's broken leg, tending a child's cat scratch that had become infected, and stitching up a gash on the O'Gorman boy's head.

When he finished, she said, "And I myself had quite an exciting day."

Liam's eyes twinkled. "Mrs. Burrage didn't have the thread you wanted?"

Fenella gave him an exasperated look. "I know a woman's life is rather dull compared to that of a dispensary doctor, but it occasionally has its exciting moments. And today was one of them."

"Well, daughter, don't keep me in suspense. What happened to you today?"

She dabbed at her lips with her napkin. "Patrick Quinn got into a fistfight with St. John Standon."

Liam stared at her, then shook his head. "It was bound to happen. Who won?"

"I suppose one could say Mr. Standon. Patrick insulted him, and Standon hit him." Fenella shook her head. "I felt so sorry for Patrick. He just didn't have the strength to fight back, though he tried valiantly. I think if the constable hadn't intervened when he did, Patrick would have tried to fight Standon and gotten beaten even worse for his pains."

Liam looked thoughtful as he took a bite of ham. "It would be best if young Quinn just put the past behind him and ignored Standon."

"I doubt if he'll do that. You should have seen him when he first laid eyes on the man." She shivered. "The hatred and rage in his eyes . . ."

"Young Quinn will never forgive Standon for sending him to prison, and I can't say that I blame him."

"Do you think he would try to harm him?"

Liam shrugged. "He'd be a fool if he did. We're not living in the days of Strongbow, when the clans retaliated for such offenses by wiping out their enemies. We have laws. If young Quinn harmed Standon, he'd find himself back in prison for the rest of his days, if not swinging from the gallows. But he may just be hotheaded enough to risk it."

"Let's hope not," Fenella replied, moving quickly to refill her father's empty teacup. "Cadogan would be heartbroken if that happened."

Liam's face brightened. "Concerned for Cadogan, are you?"

"Concern is not the same as love," she retorted, "and well you know it. So you can just stop your matchmaking right this minute, Liam Considine."

He always knew when he had pushed his daughter too far, and he always had the good sense to retreat. They finished the rest of their meal in silence.

As Fenella rose to clear the table, Liam said, "I hear there was a meeting in town today."

"Yes," she replied. "A Land Leaguer spoke by the bridge. Patrick and I went to listen."

"And what did he have to say?"

Fenella turned. "He was frightening. He said if the landlords didn't reduce their rents, there could be violence." Her voice trembled. "Is that true, Father?"

He smiled benignly as he rose and put his arm around her. "You needn't worry yourself over such matters, daughter. Your old father will protect you from harm."

Fenella scowled at him. "But we women do need to worry ourselves over such matters. Men may govern, but it is women who will be required to care for those affected by any violence. May I remind you that I do have a brain, Father, and I am fully capable of reasoning."

"Now, now, daughter. No need to get huffy with your old father. I didn't mean to patronize you."

"See that you don't." Mollified, she left the dishes and headed for the parlor.

Liam followed her, and together they seated themselves before the fire, which they always did every evening after supper. Fenella worked on her embroidery during this comfortable ritual, while her father poured himself some whiskey and lit his pipe.

"I fear the Land Leaguer was right. Troubled times are coming once again," Liam said softly, staring into the fire.

Fenella's needle moved slowly and steadily. "I've been hearing whispers of that for months."

"There's talk that we'll be seeing times as hard as we had during the Famine."

Her needle stopped, poised in midair. "Really, Father?"

Liam nodded solemnly as he sucked on his pipe. "I was only a lad of twelve in 1847, but I remember those were horrible times. A blight destroyed the potato crop, you see, and the people who depended on it for their main source of food had nothing to eat. People were starving to death, daughter.

"I remember going with my father to Skibbereen one day. En route, we saw children nine or ten years old who looked like wizened old men, their faces as wrinkled as prunes and their bodies bent and twisted with pain. Men and women were lying right where they died, on the side of the road, with no one burying them in a decent grave." He shook his head. "It was horror on top of horror in those days."

"Couldn't anything be done to help them?" Fenella said indignantly.

Liam shrugged. "There are those who insist the British government was responsible. They wouldn't let Ireland sell her wheat abroad because of the Corn Laws. And the landlords didn't care. As always, all they were concerned about was getting their rents. But if the crop failed, how could their tenants get any money to pay them?"

"So what did the people do?"

"They emigrated by the hundreds of thousands," her father replied, "many going to America, and others to Australia. You had to see it to believe it, Nella. The boats lined up in Queenstown, all the people saying farewell to those who were staying behind. And most of them knew they wouldn't see their families or friends again."

"It must have been a very sad time."

"Oh, it was heartbreaking. And, unfortunately, it seems that history is about to repeat itself."

Fenella looked up in alarm. "Do you really think so, Father?"

He lifted one shoulder in a shrug. "I don't think it will be as bad, but bad enough. The potato crop has failed again because of the weather, and there's great unrest among the tenants once again. I'm hearing the same blathering I heard all those years ago when I was a child, and I don't think it bodes well for Holy Ireland."

She set her embroidery aside, suddenly tiring of it. "If these secret fraternities appear once again to kill landlords, that means our friends the Quinns and Lord Nayland could be in danger."

"Perhaps not. Quinn and Nayland have an advantage over men like Saintly Standon. They live here, not in England, and they have a greater stake in making a success of their estates."

Somehow, that didn't comfort Fenella. She thought of the men in the O'Hara cottage that day when she had gone to see the new baby, the desperate anger in their voices and the frustration in their eyes. She thought of the crowd gathered in Mallow today. All they were concerned about was feeding their families and farming their plots of land. Each served his own interest. When their survival was the issue, they were not apt to be objective and see matters from the landlords' point of view.

She sighed and tried to remain optimistic. "Well, let's pray it doesn't come to that."

Feeling suddenly drained, Fenella excused herself and went upstairs to bed, but it was a long time before her tumultuous thoughts about the day's happenings quieted enough to allow her to fall into a fitful sleep.

Fenella awoke with a start.

Something had disturbed her sleep. She sat up in bed and listened. Then she heard the voices. They were muffled, as though someone were making a great effort to keep from being heard. Just as Fenella swung her legs over the edge of her bed and rose, she heard the familiar sound of a door slamming. Rushing over to the window, she saw the shadowy shapes of two men hurrying down the path to the road.

After lighting a candle, Fenella padded on bare feet to her father's room. She was not surprised to find his bed empty, the covers thrown back and the clothes she had set out for tomorrow missing from the back of the chair.

But his black medical bag was still there.

Fenella frowned in bewilderment. She was used to her father being summoned from his bed at all hours of the night to attend some medical emergency, but he always took his bag. Yet this time he hadn't.

Fenella grasped the bag, turned, and flew down the stairs in the darkness, calling for her father at the top of her lungs. But when she flung open the front door, he and his companion were nowhere to be seen.

She stood there shivering from a combination of consternation and cold, and when she realized she was not going to catch her father, she turned and went back inside.

The following morning, when Fenella asked him where he had gone off to in the middle of the night without his bag, her father replied that it was to tend a woman with an illness that luckily didn't require the use of his medical instruments. But he avoided looking at her as he made his excuses, and Fenella suddenly felt uneasy.

But as the day wore on, Fenella put such thoughts behind her. If her father wanted her to know something, he would certainly tell her.

Months later, she would regret not asking.

5

MARGARET STOOD BEFORE the imposing mahogany door to her uncle's study and took several slow deep breaths to quiet the butterflies fluttering in her stomach.

Why, she wondered as she raised her hand to knock, had he summoned her to his study today? The last time he had done so was when she was thirteen, and Ailagh of the Hundred Eyes had caught her behind the stables lifting her riding habit skirts on a dare, so the handsome new undergroom could see her pretty, neatly booted ankles.

When Uncle Cadogan was through applying his riding crop to her tender backside, she had hobbled out of his study much wiser than when she had first gone in.

"What have I done this time?" she muttered under her breath.

Suddenly it dawned on her. Margaret's hand trembled, then fell away: Fenella had told Cadogan about seeing her with Terrence up at Ballymere Castle.

Margaret's heart stopped, then started with a rush, the sound pounding like a drum in her ears. She had been on tenterhooks for the past two weeks, wondering when Fenella would break her promise and inform on her. Well, Margaret was prepared to charm Uncle Cadogan as she had never charmed him in her life. She would deal with the traitorous Miss Considine later.

Tossing her head defiantly, Margaret took a moment to smooth the front of her leaf-green dress and straighten the skirt. Then she took another deep breath to make herself appear composed and rapped her knuckles smartly against the door.

"Come in!" came Cadogan's booming voice from within.

Margaret threw open the door and swept inside. "You wished to see me, Uncle?"

Cadogan, seated behind a large pedimented oak desk that seemed to fill the opposite end of the room, looked up. "Yes, Margaret, I did. Please close the door behind you and come in."

The small, well-lit room was Cadogan's private domain, as neat and orderly as the man himself, with everything in its proper place. Books and ledgers were stacked with mathematical precision, so they could be retrieved at a moment's notice, while Cadogan's desktop was devoid of papers, except for a small pile of them to one corner. In addition to Cadogan's swivel chair, there was only one other chair in the room because Cadogan saw only one person at a time in his study.

When Margaret seated herself, she feigned innocence. "Now, Uncle, what have I done to be summoned to your private sanctuary? Am I to be chastised for being too rude to the earl? Or going riding without a groom once too often?"

Then she held her breath and waited for the explosion.

Cadogan chuckled indulgently. "No, my girl, this time you're not here for a scolding. I merely wanted to ask your opinion of your cousin Patrick, that's all."

Margaret almost fainted from relief. Fenella had kept her promise after all. Cadogan didn't know about Terrence—yet. She still had time.

"Patrick?" she said with a dazzling smile. "What do you wish to know?"

Her uncle leaned back in his chair, his brow furrowed. "I want to know about his mental state. Has he fully recovered from his imprisonment, do you think?"

"Perhaps you should consult Dr. Considine," she suggested.

"I'm not interested in a medical opinion. I want to know what you think."

Margaret stared at the framed hunt prints on the opposite wall while she collected her thoughts. Finally she looked at Cadogan and said, "In many ways, he's like the old Patrick I remember. When we go riding every day, he pushes himself so hard to excel, I fear for his safety. And he delights in teasing me just as he always did. But his moods are as changeable as Irish weather, Uncle Cadogan. One moment he'll be laughing with me at some shared joke, and the next he'll become so melancholy, locked away within himself. He was never like that before. And his behavior can be so odd at times . . .''

Cadogan nodded sadly. ''I agree. His obsession with that mouse is unnerving, especially when he brings it to breakfast. A mouse doesn't belong at the breakfast table. I'd kill it if I could, but I don't have the heart to insist he give up the creature, if it brings him some measure of comfort.''

''Mrs. Ryan tells me he still can't bear to sleep with the bedroom door closed. One night, she accidentally closed it after Patrick had gone to bed. He awoke instantly and opened it again. She said he looked terrified.''

Cadogan smiled dryly. ''After spending all that time confined to a cell, I couldn't blame him for that.''

''And he has nightmares,'' Margaret added.

''How do you know that?''

''One night I was having difficulty sleeping, so I went down to the kitchen for a biscuit. As I passed Patrick's room, I heard him moaning and muttering in his sleep, so I looked in. He was thrashing about, but I thought it best not to wake him.''

Cadogan shook his head. ''He still refuses to go to church or to call on people he's known from childhood.''

''Perhaps he feels humiliated after the drubbing he took from Saintly Standon in Mallow,'' Margaret suggested. ''He also told me those 'people he's known from childhood' cut him in the street, so I can see why he doesn't wish to force himself on them''

''They dared snub my son?'' Cadogan growled, his eyes flashing. ''Pompous asses, the lot of them!''

''And in case you hadn't noticed, Uncle Cadogan,'' Margaret added, ''you and I haven't received any invitations from our neighbors since Patrick returned home.''

''Who needs to go to yet another boring dinner or ball anyway!'' he muttered. ''I've never gone where I'm not wanted and neither has Patrick.''

''I don't miss them either,'' Margaret said. All those

boring, shallow young men trying to steal a kiss . . . Then she looked out the window at the russet beech trees swaying in the wind. "There's something else I find odd. Patrick never talks about what prison was like. Whenever I ask, he becomes very short with me and says he doesn't wish to talk about it. Then he starts discussing something else."

Cadogan sighed heavily and rubbed his eyes with thumb and forefinger. "An experience like that surely must leave its mark on a man."

"But if only he would share it. That's too great a burden for anyone to bear alone!"

"I agree. But we can't force Patrick to confide in us, my girl. All we can do is be patient and pray that our old Patrick will return to us one day."

"We may have a long wait, Uncle."

"Perhaps not." When Margaret raised her brows, a question in her eyes, Cadogan smiled mysteriously. "Thank you, Margaret. You've been most helpful."

Realizing she had been dismissed, Margaret rose and crossed the study. When she reached the door, her uncle called out, "Send Patrick to me, will you?"

"Of course, Uncle."

The moment the study door closed behind her, Margaret leaned heavily against it and let out a long sigh of relief at her escape. Her trysts with Terrence were still a secret. As long as Fenella kept her promise, Margaret would be able to buy herself some time, time to find a way to make Uncle Cadogan accept her love for a farmer's son.

As she went in search of Patrick, Margaret upbraided herself for her selfishness. Here she was thinking only of herself and Terrence, when her poor lost cousin was in such dire need of understanding.

She had been appalled at the change in him, even though she did her best to hide it behind an audacious air. There were times when she just wanted to weep for the man he had once been, and the one he had become. She wished there were something she could say to him, but each time she tried, she stopped herself, afraid she would say the wrong thing and offend him. These days, one tended to walk on eggs when around Patrick.

She searched all of Rookforest for him, and finally found him strolling in the yew walk near the garden, his hands clasped behind him and his head deeply bowed, a man whose thoughts were so far away, they might have dwelt in America.

Margaret told Patrick his father wanted to see him, and offered to walk with him as far as the study. But when Patrick curtly told her that wasn't necessary, she whirled around to hide her hurt and headed for the stables instead.

Cadogan stared at his son seated before him and tried to avoid looking at the mouse perched on Patrick's shoulder.

In spite of his bruised jaw, Patrick was looking much healthier than that night he had arrived a month ago. Those huge meals he ate so voraciously were beginning to fill him out so his face was losing that gaunt, skeletal look. His hair was growing out thick and black, so by the time several more months passed, no one would be able to look at him and tell he had served a prison sentence.

But the look in his eyes still worried Cadogan. The spark from within hadn't yet been ignited, leaving his gaze as lifeless as blue glass.

"I would like you to start helping me run Rookforest," he said.

Patrick looked panic-stricken. "I . . . I don't know if I'm ready for it yet, Father."

This took Cadogan aback. "Why not? You've run the estate before. It's nothing new to you."

Patrick rose and went to the window. "I don't know if I can face the tenants."

Cadogan burst out laughing. "Afraid of the tenants! We rule them, they don't rule us, my boy. What they think of you is of no consequence. Besides, the best way to conquer your fears is to face them head-on. Running away from them won't do you any good."

Patrick's head snapped around and he glared at his father. "Are you calling me a coward?"

"No, son. I'm merely asking you to try. It may be difficult the first time, but it will get easier as time passes.

You need to build up your confidence, and what better way than by helping me with the estate?''

Patrick's sigh was resigned. ''You're right, of course. What do you wish me to do?''

Cadogan rummaged through the papers on his desk, found the ones he wanted, and collected them together. ''Tomorrow is Tuesday, which is my office day. I would like you to take my place, if you are agreeable.''

The mouse scampered down Patrick's sleeve and into his cupped hand. Cadogan had all he could do to refrain from speaking his mind.

Instead, he said, ''Several tenants are overdue with their rents, so hopefully, they will pay tomorrow. And several short-term leases are coming up for renewal next month. I would like you to study them and make recommendations to me concerning their renewal.''

''You would evict them, even when popular sentiment is running so strongly against such action?'' Patrick asked, absently stroking the mouse with his forefinger.

Cadogan nodded. ''I consider myself a fair landlord. If a tenant is hardworking and honestly tries to pay his rent, I'll give him the benefit of the doubt. But several who have leases expiring are shiftless no-accounts. They want the land given to them outright.''

Patrick slipped the mouse into his breast pocket, then reached for the papers his father handed him. ''I'll study these and let you know what I think.''

Cadogan nodded. ''I'm sure we'll be of like mind, so I'll stand behind whatever decision you make during office days.''

Patrick smiled wryly as he rose. ''You have such faith in me.''

''Of course I do. You're my son.''

The following morning Patrick went to the Quinns' estate office in Mallow. No sooner did he settle himself behind the desk than three men barged into the office.

He recognized two of his tenants, but their ringleader, a burly, thick-necked youth with flaming red hair, was someone new. He had the look of a rabble-rouser about him.

Patrick rose and tried to appear confident, for he knew

if these men sensed his nervousness, they would have the
upper hand and press him ruthlessly to grant their demands.

"Finnerty . . . Mullray," he said, nodding in acknowledgment of the two men he knew, who mumbled
something in turn. Then he looked at the redheaded
youth. "And who are you?"

"Jamser Garroty," he replied, assuming a belligerent
stance with feet planted slightly apart, "son of Galty
Garroty. An' where is the squire?"

"My father couldn't be here this morning, so he sent
me in his place. I am Patrick Quinn."

The moment he identified himself, Patrick saw a crafty
look of recognition flare up in Jamser Garroty's face, but
luckily, he made no comment.

"I shall be collecting your rents and determining what
improvements need to be made in your farms," Patrick
said.

Young Garroty didn't back down. "We come about our
rents." He added, "Yer honor," as an afterthought.

The slight sneer in Garroty's voice was not lost on
Patrick, who said nothing, merely indicated chairs.
"Won't you gentlemen sit down, and we'll discuss
them?"

Finnerty and Mullray meekly slid into the seats, but
Garroty remained standing. He was their ringleader and
he wasn't about to back down in front of his friends.

"The fact of the matter is . . . yer honor," Garroty
began, "we can't pay our rents. We had a poor harvest
last year, but I'm sure you wouldn't be knowin' that,
since ye were . . . away, yer honor."

"I'm fully aware of the situation, Garroty," Patrick
replied, his face as impassive as stone. "Proceed."

"We lost a dozen of our cows. On top o' that, there's
no profit in butter."

"An' my wife an' two of my sons been dreadful sick,"
Finnerty added in a halting voice. He had shifty eyes and
wouldn't look directly at Patrick. "An' me not havin' a
penny to pay the doctor."

"Talk to Dr. Considine," Patrick said. "I'm sure he
wouldn't ask for payment until you could afford it."

"An' when will we be able to afford it . . . yer honor?"

Garroty demanded, thrusting his jaw out. "If we don't pay our rents, himself will evict us. Then it'll be the workhouse, or the boat for sure."

Refusing to be intimidated, Patrick rose to his full height and stared long and hard at Garroty until the man's gaze faltered, then fell away. Then he looked from Finnerty to Mullray and back to Garroty.

"My father and I have decided to study each tenant's case before making a decision," Patrick said. "So your rents won't have to be paid for another two months. At that time, we'll decide whether or not to reduce rents. We don't want to have to evict anyone."

"Ye'd best think twice before ye evict anyone . . . yer honor," Garroty said. "That land is our land an' there are people who will see to it we keep it."

Patrick smiled slowly. "Are you threatening me, Mr. Garroty?"

"Not threatenin'. I'm warnin' ye . . . yer honor."

Then he whirled on his heel and stormed out, followed by his timid friends.

After the three men left, Patrick laced his fingers behind his head and relaxed, feeling triumphant. That hadn't been so hard after all. He smiled as he felt his confidence returning; then he made a mental note to discuss the Garroty farm with his father when he returned to Rookforest. He suspected that this Galty and his belligerent son were not among his father's best tenants. He found himself wondering why the shiftless were often the first to think the world owed them a living.

As the day progressed, matters greatly improved.

Although the majority of the tenants who came to the office had the same woeful tale of failed crops and falling prices for cattle and butter at market, none of them were as threatening as Garroty. After Patrick reassured them that everything would be done to see that no one lost his farm, and agreed to make certain improvements, they left satisfied for the time being.

By three o'clock Patrick was ready to go home, so he locked the office, got on his horse, and started back to Rookforest.

* * *

The Considine house looked so restful, so serene in the diffused golden light of later afternoon, that Patrick was tempted to stop as he had his first night in Mallow.

Hidden from view by a bend in the road, the small dwelling suddenly appeared as if by magic as soon as one rounded the corner, once again making Patrick think he had happened upon an enchanted cottage. By daylight, a still pool nearby threw up its reflection, the water's image somehow gentling the soft gray walls and slate roof, making it welcoming. The tall lime and oak trees surrounding it blocked any view of Mallow.

It was the perfect house for a doctor, Patrick thought as he halted his horse before the gently curving drive, near enough to town to serve his patients, yet secluded for privacy.

Suddenly he knew he had to stop. Finnerty's family needed medical attention, and Patrick had promised Dr. Considine would look after them. It might be a gesture of goodwill to tell the doctor what he had done.

Yet the doctor didn't appear to be at home.

After knocking repeatedly on the front door and getting no response, Patrick quietly walked around the back, where he found Fenella.

She was kneeling in the dirt, assiduously weeding her small well-tended flower garden. Her back was toward him, so she didn't realize someone was watching her as she attacked a weed with dirty bare hands and a trowel.

"I'll teach you to spoil my garden," she muttered aloud, yanking out a weed by its roots and contemptuously flinging it aside.

Patrick couldn't help himself. He burst out laughing.

Startled by the unexpected sound, Fenella rose to her knees and twisted toward him, her eyes huge and her lips slightly parted. The moment she saw who it was, her pale cheeks flushed a delicate pink.

"Mr. Quinn . . ." she murmured, flustered as she stood up. "I didn't hear you come up the drive."

She glanced down, saw that her hands were filthy, and blushed even harder.

"I knocked, but no one answered," Patrick replied, carefully picking his way along the narrow garden path.

"So I thought I'd come around back to see if anyone was home."

"Just me," she said lightly, brushing her hands together in an effort to shake most of the dirt off. When she reached up to push an escaped tendril of hair out of her face, she accidentally left a smudge on her cheek. "Do forgive me. I must look a sight."

Actually, Patrick found himself thinking she looked quite appealing, all mussed and flustered as she was. Gone was her guarded air, the starchiness that usually irritated him. In its place was an inviting approachability.

He surprised himself by saying, "One cannot tend a garden so lovingly without getting dirt on one's hands."

He must have surprised her, too, for she just stared at him speechlessly. When she regained her voice, she said, "Would you care to come in for a cup of tea and some bannocks?" She flashed him a shy smile. "I seem to recall you have a particular fondness for them."

"That I do, but I'm afraid I can't tarry. I only stopped by to talk to your father, but since he is not here . . ."

"I'll have you know I am perfectly capable of giving him a message, Mr. Quinn," she said.

"No need to get prickly. I didn't mean to imply that you couldn't."

To mollify her, he proceeded to tell her what had transpired during his office day, and how some members of the Finnerty family needed medical attention.

Fenella looked aggrieved and shook her head. "The Finnertys would have all the medical care they require if my father knew they were in need of it."

This took Patrick aback. "So they haven't been to the dispensary?"

She shook her head. "I've never heard my father mention their coming to the dispensary or asking him to ride out to their farm."

Patrick scowled. "Perhaps Finnerty was lying to win my sympathy."

"That sounds like a fair assessment of Francis Finnerty to me. He's a sly, shifty one. He'd sell his own brother if he could profit from it."

Patrick studied her for a moment. "You seem quite knowledgeable about these people."

"And why shouldn't I be? I've come to know many of them quite well since moving to Mallow. And those I don't know, my father does."

"Tell me . . . what is your opinion of Galty Garroty's son?"

She surprised him by saying, "Jamser's all fire and brimstone when he's got his cronies to back him up, but get him alone and he's a tabby cat."

Patrick raised one brow. "When he came charging into my office today, I had him pegged as a rabble-rouser."

"He could be, but not on his own," she replied. "He lacks the wherewithal up here"—she tapped her temple with a forefinger—"to be a true leader of men."

The action of raising her arm caused the sleeve of Fenella's dress to pull back, exposing her wrist.

The moment he saw the puckered red scar, Patrick blurted out, "Miss Considine . . . whatever happened to your wrist?"

He regretted the thoughtless words the moment they popped out of his mouth.

Suddenly she changed right before his startled eyes. All the warmth drained out of her face, to be replaced by icy dislike. Fenella dropped her hand and hastily pulled down the cuff to conceal the scar.

"It's nothing, Mr. Quinn," she said flatly. "I burned myself once a long time ago, that's all. You needn't concern yourself."

Before he could apologize, she said, "Thank you for stopping by," as she knelt to retrieve her trowel. Without so much as sparing him another glance, Fenella began striding toward the back door of the house, her head held high. "I'll tell my father you called and give him your message concerning the Finnertys."

"Miss Considine, I—"

But he was too late. The loud bang of the back door slamming shut cut him off in mid-sentence as surely as if Fenella Considine had slapped him across the face.

For a moment Patrick just stood there, stunned. Then he became livid. Her rejection of his apology was tantamount to rejecting him.

"Miss Considine!" he shouted, running to the closed

door and pounding it with his fist. "Please open this door. I wish to speak to you."

No answer. He tried the latch, but she had locked the door from inside. He called her name again and waited. No one peered out a window, no one came to the door. The house was so still it might as well have been empty.

Tiring of standing there like a prize idiot, Patrick strode around to the front of the house and mounted his horse.

He would be damned if he was going to beg Fenella Considine to accept his apology. Surely she knew he hadn't meant to hurt her feelings with his careless statement. Yet by the way she had acted, one would think her face had been scarred, not her wrist.

Without so much as a backward glance, Patrick dug his heels into his horse's side and galloped for home.

From her bedroom window Fenella watched him tear down the drive as if the hounds of hell were snapping at his horse's heels.

When Patrick Quinn disappeared from view without so much as a backward glance, Fenella turned away and cursed herself for her stupidity.

Why had she run like a frightened rabbit? All the man had wanted to do was apologize. She had seen the stricken expression on his face when he realized he had embarrassed and hurt her by calling attention to her scar. And she in turn had angered him by refusing to give him the opportunity to make amends.

"Fenella Considine, you are the world's biggest fool!" she muttered as she swept down the stairs into the kitchen, where she poured some water into a basin and began scrubbing her dirty hands. "You made much too much of it. You should have dismissed it and talked about something else. He soon would have forgotten all about it."

But as she stared at the mark that no amount of washing would remove, she knew why she had run. She couldn't risk Patrick asking more questions about it, questions she couldn't answer without revealing the accursed power it gave her.

Fenella rinsed her hands and dried them on a coarse towel.

"You only called attention to yourself, my girl," she said aloud. "Now Patrick Quinn probably thinks you're a hysterical spinster. And you're still going to have to apologize to him for your odd behavior. Cadogan has been good to us, and I don't want to lose his friendship because of some silly misunderstanding with his son.''

Tomorrow, she decided. She would go to Rookforest and apologize to Patrick tomorrow.

But the following day, Wednesday, dawned cold and dank, with the rain slanting down in sheets across the gray landscape, so Fenella decided Patrick could wait another day for his apology. Thursday's weather was not much better, and on Friday Liam rode off in the dogcart at daybreak and didn't return until late afternoon, too late for Fenella to drive herself to Rookforest.

It was Saturday before she finally ran out of excuses. She had to go to Rookforest and face Patrick.

So she dressed in her best dress of dark gray wool, for its collar of exquisite Limerick lace always made her feel pretty and gave her courage. Then she left for Rookforest in the dogcart.

The moment Fenella arrived, Mrs. Ryan ushered her into the drawing room while she went to fetch master Patrick.

He kept her waiting just to punish her, as she knew he would, so she walked over to the tall, narrow windows overloooking the front lawn and watched as two herons soared gracefully into the air and disappeared over the treetops.

The sound of doors opening alerted Fenella, and she turned around in time to see Patrick enter the room. He looked distinguished today in a coat of brown tweed homespun that fit him well, but there was no mistaking the air of icy reserve emanating from him.

He raised his brows in surprise. ''Why, Miss Considine . . . I had wondered when we would be seeing you again, if ever.''

Fenella nervously moistened her dry lips with the tip of her tongue. ''I came to apologize to you, Mr. Quinn, for my inexcusable rudeness to you on Tuesday.''

''I have forgotten it,'' he said with a dismissive wave of his hand.

But judging from the implacable look in his eyes, Fenella had a feeling he remembered the slight all too well. Further explanation would be necessary before he forgave her unconditionally.

She stood there for a moment, staring at the intricate pattern in the wine-colored Turkish carpet as she groped for just the right words to express herself.

"I . . . I know I behaved very badly, but I am very sensitive about my . . . my disfigurement," she began softly, without raising her eyes, "and I try to hide it as best I can. When you noticed my scar and called attention to it, I became embarrassed and ashamed. That's why I locked myself in the house and wouldn't come out."

When she looked up, she was startled to find that Patrick was walking toward her in his long stride. He stopped a few feet away and looked down at her, his features composed and inscrutable.

"You needn't be embarrassed or ashamed, Miss Considine," he said with surprising gentleness. "I am the one who should be ashamed of myself for my callousness that day. And I do apologize to you."

To Fenella's astonishment, he took her hand and bowed over it with courtly grace. His fingers were warm and strong, and the force of his touch made shivers travel all the way up her arm, leaving Fenella shaken.

When Patrick brought his head up, Fenella found herself gazing into his pale blue eyes. She had never known ice-blue eyes could project such warmth and compassion.

She smiled ruefully as she withdrew her hand from his disconcerting grasp. "You did try, but if I remember correctly, I wouldn't let you."

He shrugged. "Well, now I have, so why don't we let bygones be bygones?"

Fenella felt as though a cloud had lifted. "Agreed."

Suddenly Patrick walked over to one of the tall windows and stared moodily out at the trees tossing in the wind. "Take comfort from the fact that many have scars that go much deeper than yours."

She inferred at once that he was speaking of himself and the invisible emotional scars his imprisonment had inflicted on his very being. For the first time, Fenella felt a tug of sympathy toward this bitter, withdrawn young man so at odds with the world. She wished she could say something to comfort him, but she knew he would neither welcome nor want her sympathy.

Her face must have betrayed her, for Patrick's eyes narrowed and that air of remoteness descended upon him once more like a cloak.

He bowed. "Thank you for calling today, Miss Considine. If you will excuse me, there are pressing matters I must attend to."

Then he turned on his heel and left.

As Fenella slowly crossed the drawing room into the hall and was handed her wrap by the butler, she found herself thinking inadvertently of Cynara Standon, now leading the grand life as a peeress in England. Did the marchioness ever give a thought to this man who had suffered so much because of his love, however misguided, for her? Did she ever regret what her brother and fiancé had done to Patrick Quinn?

She wondered.

Little did Fenella realize she would find out the answer the following morning when she attended church services.

6

ON SUNDAY MORNING Patrick shifted in the Quinn pew and glared at Margaret, who was trying to suppress the self-satisfied smile of a woman who has gotten her own way. That morning, she had stubbornly refused to go to church unless Patrick accompanied them, and after hearing his father rant and rave for the better part of an hour about their immortal souls, he decided there could be no harm in capitulating.

He regretted it the moment he stepped inside and felt all those surprised, curious eyes following his progress down the aisle. Patrick had stared straight ahead, except for one fleeting moment when he happened to glance down and saw Fenella Considine. She had given him a tremulous smile, and he acknowledged her with the barest of nods.

Now, as he waited for the services to begin, he thought about their meeting yesterday afternoon.

For the first time since he had met her, Patrick's dislike of Fenella Considine had wavered somewhat. Perhaps her sensitivity about her scar made her so preoccupied and withdrawn.

So deep in thought was Patrick that he failed to notice the flurry of whispers beginning at the back of the church and spreading through the congregation like wildfire. It wasn't until Margaret uttered a hoarse, "Oh, no!" and gripped his arm that he turned to see what was causing all the commotion.

The impeccably dressed, graceful figure of St. John Standon started down the aisle, oblivious of the astonished eyes and craned necks. Yet it was not the man who caught Patrick's attention, but the woman on his arm.

His eyes widened in disbelief even as his mind formed the word "Cynara!"

At first, all he saw was a tall, willowy figure gliding regally along as she clung to her brother's arm. She was dressed entirely in black, but the significance of her attire didn't register at once. All he could see was her face, that beautiful face that had tormented and haunted him every night in prison for the last four years.

As Cynara drew closer with every step, Patrick saw that she was even more beautiful than he remembered. Maturity had softened her oval face, giving her white skin the translucent glow of fine porcelain and making her soft mouth with its plump lower lip even more sensual.

When Standon reached his family's pew, which was directly across from the Quinns', he stood aside to open the door for his sister, giving Patrick an unobstructed view. Just at that moment, she looked over at him. When those violet eyes gazed into his, Patrick felt as though Standon had hit him in the jaw again, knocking the wind out of him.

He stared at her, but she quickly looked away before he had a chance to read what she was thinking. Then she entered the pew and sat down, facing straight ahead, giving him only her perfect profile to stare at.

Patrick sat there, his thoughts roiling, but his body numb with shock. What was she doing here in Ireland? he wondered. Why wasn't she in England with her husband?

He felt hot all over, followed by perishing cold that robbed his limbs of all sensation. His heart began racing, then seemed to stop, while thoughts raced faster and faster, splintering into disjointed fragments before spinning out of control.

He had to get away from her. He had to be alone.

Ignoring his father's hand on his arm, Patrick rose unsteadily to his feet like a drunkard, pushed open the pew door with such violence that it slammed shut with a crash when he was halfway down the aisle.

No one dared follow.

* * *

The moment Fenella stepped out of the church, the buzzing was so thick around her that she felt as though she were standing near a beehive.

"So that is Cynara Standon," her father murmured as the lady and her brother emerged and walked over to Reverend Black.

"Father, don't stare!" Fenella hissed under her breath, grasping his arm and steering him toward a group of people.

"And why shouldn't I, daughter?" he retorted. "Every other man here is staring. She is a beautiful woman, as ravishing as Dervorgilla herself, I'll be bound. The kind of woman a man would give his kingdom for in the old days."

"Father, please . . ." She snorted derisively. "This is no time for a history lesson."

But even Fenella couldn't resist another peek herself, and had to admit that her father was right. Cynara Standon possessed the same dark, dusky beauty as the legendary queen of ancient Ireland. And, like Dervorgilla, she undoubtedly inspired envy in the hearts of other women and desire in men. No wonder Patrick Quinn had fallen so hard for her.

Fenella couldn't help but think of Patrick as she and her father acknowledged the greetings of people they knew gathered outside the church for a few minutes of gossip. The return of Cynara had obviously come as a great shock to him. Fenella had seen his white, blank face with its glazed eyes as he fled down the aisle, and her heart had gone out to him.

Cadogan and Margaret had stayed, but disappeared through the side door the moment the service was over, successfully avoiding prying questions.

Now the Standons were leaving as well. St. John took his sister's arm with a proprietary air, and the two of them hurried to their waiting carriage, taking time only to smile and nod at those who happened to greet them. The moment the carriage moved away, speculation flowed as freely as wine from an uncorked bottle.

"I wonder what she's doing back in Ireland," Fenella blurted out, her curiosity getting the better of her.

Liam glanced disapprovingly at a group of women obviously discussing just that. "She's probably just visiting her brother."

"Then why isn't her husband with her?"

"Perhaps he decided to stay in England, or perhaps he's back at Drumlow, though why he would let such a woman out of his sight is beyond my ken."

"And why was she dressed all in black? One would think she was in mourning."

Liam gave her an exasperated look. "Who knows why women choose the attire they do? But whatever the reason, I'm sure we'll find out all in good time, daughter."

But whatever Cynara Standon's reasons were for being in church today, Fenella had the uneasy feeling the woman's reappearance did not bode well for Patrick Quinn.

The library was bathed in the rare rich gold of a blazing sunset, but Patrick was in no condition to appreciate the vivid blue sky or the dancing light filtering through the trees.

He sat sprawled in a button-back chair of rich oxblood leather, one hand reaching to pour the last of the whiskey into his glass, the other tenderly cradling Mr. O'Malley. Patrick had been conversing with the mouse since late that morning, when he had locked himself in the library after returning from that debacle in church.

For once, being locked up in a room made him feel safe and secure.

"She's boo'ful, O'Malley," he said for the thousandth time, raising the glass in a toast and draining it in one swallow. "Ev'n after all this time, shtill as boo'ful as ever."

Mr. O'Malley sat curled in the palm of Patrick's hand, staring intently out of tiny black eyes as though he could understand.

"Thought I h-hated her for what she did to me. She broke me, that's wha' she did. Never thought a woman could break Patrick Quinn, but she did. T-took away my freedom. T-took away my life. T-took away my soul. Know what that does to a man, O'Malley? Leaves 'im a half a man. Now she's come back for the rest of it."

With a low sob of anguish, Patrick flung his head back and let the tears stream down his cheeks.

"An' ye know what, my fine fr-friend? I shtill love 'er, in spite o' it."

He reached an unsteady hand toward the bottle on the table, and when he saw that it was empty, he swore and flung it across the room, where it crashed against the floor and broke with a resonant tinkle. The noise made O'Malley flee up the sleeve of Patrick's coat.

Suddenly there came a loud knock at the door.

"Patrick Quinn, open that door!" came his father's booming voice.

"Go to hell!"

His tormentors refused to oblige him. They unlocked the door from the outside and strode in, an army of them, wavering marching figures.

Through the drunken haze fogging his mind and vision, Patrick saw two Cadogans and three Margarets approach him.

"I think we've let him indulge himself long enough, don't you?" the twin Cadogans asked.

"Oh, Patrick . . ." the three Margarets said in unison, their voices shrill and ringing.

"Well, let's get him to bed," Cadogan said, reaching for his son.

"Love 'er shtill," Patrick muttered as he felt himself hauled to his feet, where he swayed unsteadily.

"Margaret, get one of the footmen to help me," someone said. "I'll never manage him on my own."

A frightened female voice said, "What about his mouse? I can't bring myself to touch it."

"I never thought I'd live to see the day Margaret Atkinson was afraid of one wee mouse. You needn't be. It just ran up his sleeve and is hiding behind his lapel."

Patrick had time to grin at that just before his world dissolved into a warm, comforting fog. Then he remembered nothing else.

When Patrick awoke the next morning, his skull felt as though it had been pierced with a spike, and his mouth tasted like the stable floor. Groaning in agony, he rolled over and pulled the sheet over his head, seeking the warm oblivion of sleep, but the pain wouldn't let him. It relentlessly throbbed all the way down to the roots of his hair.

He managed to haul himself into a sitting position, prepared to take the consequences of yesterday's excesses. But when he pried open his bleary eyes, the dazzling light nearly blinded him, and his resolve failed. He fell back into bed with a moan and remained there for the rest of the morning and part of the afternoon, trying not to think of yesterday and his reason for getting falling-down drunk.

Sometime later, Mrs. Ryan came by to ask, in a voice thick with disapproval, how he was feeling and if he would like something to eat. But the very thought of food caused Patrick's stomach to churn and growl in warning, so he dismissed the housekeeper with a few unintelligible grunts.

Finally, when the pain in his head subsided a few hours later, Patrick rang for tea and bannocks. Once the food had revived him somewhat, he rang for his father's valet to dress him. Then he went downstairs.

He found his father in his study.

"Father . . ." Patrick greeted him, squinting against the light from the windows as he entered the neat room and seated himself. "If you laugh, I swear I'll—"

"I'm not laughing, son," Cadogan said as he leaned back in his chair, his expression troubled. "Seeing Cynara Standon walk into church yesterday was a shock for us all, but for you it must have been sheer hell."

"It was." Patrick rose and went to the windows, staring out at the gray landscape that matched his bleak mood. "But at least I can be consoled by the fact that, once her visit to her brother is over, she'll return to England."

Cadogan cleared his throat uneasily. "Son, I hate to be the one to tell you this, but Cynara isn't returning to England."

He whirled around, his eyes wide with disbelief. "What?"

"I said, Cynara isn't returning to England. She's come back to Ireland to live with her brother. For good."

When Patrick just stood there and stared, stupefied,

Cadogan rose and led him back to his chair as if he hadn't a will of his own. "I think you'd better sit down."

Patrick's mind was in turmoil, and his head began to throb. Cynara back for good? Impossible! "B-but what about her husband?" he blurted out.

Back behind his desk, Cadogan said, "Her husband is dead. That's why she was dressed all in black in church yesterday. The Marquess of Eastbrook was accidentally shot in a hunting accident last month."

Patrick was silent while he took it all in. "Where did you hear this?"

"Your cousin Margaret found out." A wry smile twisted Cadogan's mouth. "Don't ask me how, but this morning she drove off bright and early for parts unknown, and when she returned, she knew all about the marchioness's return to Mallow."

"Village gossip, nothing more."

"Don't turn up your nose at village gossip, son. Nine times out of ten, it's more truth than lies."

Patrick felt cold all over. "Don't spare me. I want to know everything."

His father nodded. "According to your cousin's sources, the marquess died before Cynara could give him a male heir. Since their daughter can't inherit—"

"Cynara has a child?"

Cadogan nodded. "A little girl, eighteen months old. The spitting image of her mother, I'm told, except that her hair is blond." He gave Patrick a minute to take in that bit of news, then continued. "Everything passed to the marquess's younger brother, who generously offered a home to Cynara and her child, plus a small living allowance."

"Then why isn't she still in England, where she belongs?" Patrick demanded, his voice rising.

"If you'll stop interrupting me, I'll tell you!" Cadogan snapped. "It appears the man's wife is a vain, greedy woman, jealous of Cynara's beauty and fearful of her influence. She pressured her husband into withdrawing his offer of support, so Cynara had nowhere else to go but back to Drumlow."

Patrick stared at the bare, polished expanse of his father's desk, flexing the fingers of his right hand as if it

were clasped around Standon's throat. "And how does
St. John feel about having his ambitions thwarted?"

Cadogan shrugged. "Margaret didn't say anything
about that. But you know St. John isn't one to let anything get in the way of his ambition. He'll find another
way to use his sister to get what he wants."

"Perhaps this time he can sell her to a duke," Patrick
muttered between clenched teeth. "Much more presti-
gious than a mere marquess."

Then he rose to his feet and started for the door.

"Where are you going?" Cadogan asked.

"Out riding," Patrick replied without turning around.
"I need some fresh air to clear my head."

Then he was gone.

Cadogan threw down the papers in disgust, unable to
concentrate, and leaned back in his chair. He was worried about his only son.

His thoughts kept going back to yesterday evening,
when he and Margaret had found Patrick locked in the
library in a drunken stupor. Cadogan couldn't forget his
son's slurred words: "Love her still."

He rose, went over to the windows, and jammed his
hands into his pockets. He could see Patrick, now dressed
for riding, striding down the path toward the stables, his
head bowed into the wind. Cadogan wished he knew what
his son was thinking.

He suspected Patrick was thinking of Cynara.

What was he going to do now that the woman who had
obsessed him was back in Mallow, her situation changed?
A married woman living in England with her devoted
husband was blessedly inaccessible, but now that she was
a widow and living practically next door . . . Would he
forgive her for the hell she had put him through and begin
courting her again?

Cadogan fervently hoped not. There was trouble coming for the Irish landlords, and the last thing any of them
needed was to have Patrick embroiled in trouble of a
different sort with Cynara Standon. No, Cadogan needed
a son with a clear head to be his ally.

As he watched Patrick disappear behind a line of silver

beeches, Cadogan shook his head. "Patrick, Patrick . . . Whatever am I going to do with you?"

Well, if Patrick was unsettled, at least Margaret's future was promising. As soon as Cadogan could make her see the wisdom of marrying Nayland, her future would be secure indeed.

Margaret was late for her Tuesday meeting, and that made her careless.

Instead of tethering her mare, Bramble, in the woods and climbing the rest of the way on foot, she boldly rode up the hillside, not bothering to check if anyone were watching her. When she reached the ruins, she could see no sign of Terrence, so she called his name.

When no one answered, she patted Bramble's lathered neck and said, "I'm just too late. He's gone."

Just as Margaret was about to admit defeat and return home, Terrence himself materialized out of nowhere, stepping out from behind a bit of ruined wall.

"Terrence!" she cried in delight.

But he made no move toward her and actually seemed displeased. "Are ye daft, woman," he growled, "riding up here where anyone could see ye?"

"Don't be angry with me. No one's going to see us," she replied, sliding off her mount's back and running to the man she loved.

"Fenella Considine did," he reminded her, his dark gray eyes furious.

"And she promised me she would never betray us," Margaret replied, flinging herself at him and entwining her arms around his neck. She knew just how to cajole Terrence out of one of his moods.

Much to her chagrin, he grasped her wrists and untangled himself from her eager embrace.

Stung by his rebuff, Margaret tossed her head. "Well, I certainly expected a warmer welcome than that from you, Terrence Sheely."

He squinted as he ignored her to scan the woods and valleys below. When he was satisfied that no one was watching them, he turned his attention back to her, and gave her a wide, radiant smile before pulling her into his arms.

"If it's a warm welcome you want, alanna . . ." he growled before his lips met hers.

With a small groan, Margaret surrendered to him, pressing her slender body to his, reveling in the feel of his hard chest crushing her breasts as she raised her arms to his neck once again. And when his mouth came down on hers possessively, she closed her eyes and gave herself up to the sheer pleasure of his touch.

When they finally parted, breathless, Terrence gave her a reproachful look. "Ye can't blame a man for being too cautious, my dear. Mind ye, it wouldn't do to have your uncle find out about us. Or me own father, for that matter."

"I know we have to be careful," she admitted, "but I was just so afraid I was too late, and you had already left."

His eyes danced. "As much as I burn for ye, I don't like being kept waitin', alanna."

"I had a good reason for being late." And Margaret told Terrence about Cynara Standon's return and its effect on Patrick.

Terrence smiled diabolically. "So, Saintly Standon's grand plans have come topplin' down around his ears." He spat. "Someday he'll get what he deserves, a prime place in hell."

Margaret placed her fingertips against his lips. "Hush. Let's not waste time discussing the Standons, shall we?"

Terrence grinned and took her in his arms.

Later, after watching Terrence set off across the fields at his jaunty walk, Margaret mounted Bramble and started back to Rookforest, taking great pains to avoid open spaces and keeping to the woods.

She glowed with happiness and her love for Terrence. Oh, she knew most people would consider them a mismatch, the rough, uncouth farmer and the fine lady, but that's what had attracted Margaret to him in the first place. She loved the wildness about him, and the sensations he evoked when his callused hands stroked her face so tenderly, and the strength of those arms around her. Just listening to his lilting voice, as melodious as a harp, caused shivers to run up and down her spine. And Terrence Sheely was a man of passion, unlike Lord Nayland, who reminded her of a rarefied hothouse flower.

Margaret ran her tongue over her lips, still bruised from Terrence's insistent kisses, and she smiled to herself. Oh, yes, he certainly was a man of passion.

It was unfortunate that Terrence's father, a tyrant if ever there was one, expected him to marry a wealthy farmer's daughter so her dowry would be used to support Terrence's eight younger brothers and sisters. Such was usually the fate of the eldest son, but it was not one Margaret intended for her Terrence.

"Well, my dowry from Uncle Cadogan can support them all just as well as some farmer's daughter's," Margaret said to herself.

Suddenly the sound of someone calling her name jostled Margaret out of her blissful daydream. She looked up to see Patrick riding toward her.

"What are you doing out riding alone, without a groom?" he demanded as he drew his horse alongside hers. "It's nearly four o'clock."

She tossed her head defiantly. "I often go out riding alone. I am wild Meggie-of-the-moor, remember? I do as I please."

He didn't smile. "Well, you shouldn't. With these moonlighters stirring up rebellion among the tenants, it's not safe for a young woman to be out alone, especially a landlord's niece. Father needs to use a firm hand with you, and he hasn't."

"You needn't go biting my head off just because Cynara Standon is back in Mallow," she said.

Patrick glanced at her sharply, his dark brows scowling. "That was a low blow, cousin."

"Sorry, but it was justified and you know it."

He smiled dryly. "I suppose it was."

They rode in silence for a few minutes, each absorbed in his own thoughts.

Finally Margaret said, "This must be terrible for you, Pat."

The bitterness and spite came pouring out of him. "To know that the woman who rejected me and sent me to prison is now living not seven miles away? To know that I risk seeing her again every time I go into Mallow, or to church on Sunday? Yes, cousin, one could say that this is terrible for me.''

Margaret said, ''Did Uncle Cadogan tell you why she is here?''

Patrick nodded. ''Yes, he did. And he said you were instrumental in finding out.''

''My dressmaker's daughter is a maid at Drumlow, and she is a notorious gossip. Apparently not even the servants knew that Cynara had been widowed until she arrived on Friday with her little girl in tow. The Saintly Standons are a closemouthed pair. They don't want anyone knowing of their affairs.''

They rode together past the gardens.

Margaret looked at Patrick's tight, pinched face and prayed for the courage to ask him a question that had been burning in her mind.

''Patrick, what are you going to do now that Cynara is free?''

He twisted in the saddle, his face a dark mask. ''What do you mean?''

He looked so fierce that Margaret had to look away. ''Are you going to court her again?''

Patrick threw back his head and roared mirthlessly, causing the horses to shy in alarm. ''Court that woman?'' He sneered. ''After what she did to me? My dear Meggie, what kind of fool do you take me for?''

A fool who doesn't realize he's still in love, Margaret thought to herself.

But she said, ''I don't take you for any kind of fool at all, Pat. I was just wondering, that's all.''

''Well, you can put your mind at ease. Cynara Standon—excuse me, the dowager Marchioness of Spite—could throw herself naked at my feet and I wouldn't have her.''

''Patrick Augustus Quinn, such language in front of a lady!'' Margaret said, feigning shock. ''In any case, I'm happy to hear you have sense enough not to get caught in her web again. And I'm sure Uncle Cadogan will be too.''

Suddenly he surprised her by saying, ''And speaking of my father, has he said anything to you about his feelings for Fenella Considine?''

Margaret's eyes widened in astonishment. "I didn't know Uncle Cadogan had any feelings for her." This bit of news shook her down to her boots, and she had to halt Bramble so she could gather her wits about her. "Oh Patrick, you can't be serious!"

He stopped his horse and regarded her solemnly. "Oh, but I am."

"But . . . but she's nearly thirty years younger than he is. And besides, Aunt Moira was the love of his life. He would never desecrate her memory by marrying again."

Patrick raised one shoulder in an eloquent shrug. "Think about it. He invites the Considines to dinner regularly, and one time when I was most rude to the lady, he gave me such a dressing-down—"

"That's because Uncle Cadogan is kind and generous by nature." She scowled at him. "You don't think he would actually ask her to marry him, do you?"

"Who knows what my father will do? He has always been his own man."

"And even if he did ask, Fenella could refuse him."

Patrick gave her skeptical look. "What woman in her right mind would refuse a wealthy landlord such as Cadogan Quinn?"

"A woman who didn't love him."

"Some women marry for gain, not love," he replied, and they both knew he was speaking of Cynara.

"But not Fenella Considine," Margaret insisted. "She would marry for love."

"You know the lady so well?"

"I know she was once betrothed to a man, but he died tragically. She must have loved him very much, because I've never heard her name coupled with another man's."

Patrick snorted in derision. "What man would want her? She is rather plain, or haven't you noticed?"

"Looks aren't everything, Pat, as well you know. Fenella Considine may not be beautiful, like Cynara Standon, but she has a good heart, like Aunt Moira, and she's steadfast."

He reddened. "Touché once again, Meggie."

"What are cousins for, if not to remind us of our failings?"

Her teasing tone made him laugh.

They fell silent and began walking their horses, for the stables had come into view behind the trees.

Margaret needed time to absorb what Patrick had just told her, and the more she thought about it, the more she didn't like the idea of a possible liaison between Fenella Considine and her uncle. That would spoil everything. Once married to Cadogan, Fenella would surely feel compelled to tell him about Margaret and Terrence.

That evening, Fenella found dinner at the Quinns' to be awkward and strained. Patrick was in a surly, sullen mood, saying little to anyone unless spoken to, and while Margaret was scrupulously polite, she was plainly not as friendly toward Fenella as before. Only Cadogan was as attentive as ever.

Fenella was relieved when the interminable evening was finally over and she and her father went home.

No sooner did Fenella turn out the lamp and go to bed than there came a loud, insistent pounding on the front door. She threw on her dressing gown and rushed to see who it was, but her father was already at the door, talking in a low voice to another man who was only a shadow.

"What is it, Father?" she asked in a hushed voice as he closed the door and started up the stairs.

"Moonlighters," he tersely replied as he brushed past her into his room and closed the door.

Fenella waited patiently, and when her father emerged fully dressed, his medical bag in hand, she said, "Someone has been hurt this time."

"I'm afraid so, daughter," he said grimly, hurrying past her and offering no other explanation. "Don't wait up for me. I may be out all night."

He was down the stairs and out the door before Fenella could say another word.

She had to wait until the following morning at the breakfast table before she found out what had happened.

"It was a farmer near Ballyclogh," her father said wearily, his eyes bleary and red from lack of sleep. "One of his neighbors was evicted, so he tried to grab the land. The moonlighters maimed several of his cows as a warning, but he defied them by complaining to the local constabulary."

Liam took a sip of strong red tea and kept his gaze affixed on the table. "So last night the moonlighters carded him and his wife."

Fenella frowned. "Carded? What is that?"

"By the Holy, girl!" her father snapped. "Haven't you ever seen a sheep carded?"

She felt sick. "You don't mean . . . ?"

He nodded and sighed. "They pound nails through a board to make a carding tool, then they hammer it into their victims' back and drag it down." Liam pushed his cup away in disgust. "It wasn't a pretty sight, Nella. Luckily I got to them before they bled to death."

Fenella was shocked into speechlessness for what seemed like an eternity. When she regained her voice, she said, "How can these moonlighters call themselves men? They're nothing but animals!"

"They feel their cause is just, and that the end justifies the means."

Fenella shuddered as she rose to clear the table. "Their methods are loathsome."

Liam said nothing.

She turned. "Doesn't anyone know the identity of these moonlighters?"

He shook his head. "If anyone does, they won't come forward. They're afraid for themselves and their families. I can't say that I blame them."

Fenella said nothing as she stared out the kitchen window. Everything looked so deceptively peaceful this morning. The sun was shining for once, and the blue sky clear, without a cloud on the horizon. Her little garden was filled with colorful blossoms swaying in the breeze that had just sprung up.

But Fenella knew that fragile peace would soon be shattered forever, and for the first time she wondered what horrors her second sight would reveal to her in the weeks and months to come.

7

THE EMPTY BARN was dark and quiet, smelling pungently of cattle, hay, and conspiracy.

The expectant silence was broken by the sound of a door creaking open in protest, and the darkness banished by bright, bobbing light from a lantern held by a man, the first of eight to file into the barn and gather around.

Once all were assembled and satisfied no one had observed them enter the building, the man with the lantern set it down in the center of the packed earth floor and regarded each man with a stern expression.

"Ye all will be noticin' that one of our number is missing," he began.

The rest of the men looked at one another and their faces registered surprise when they counted heads and realized he had spoken the truth.

One of them said, "Where is—?"

"He isn't here with us tonight because he wasn't asked," their leader said, cutting him off. "And he wasn't asked because he is a traitor."

The hush that fell in the barn was as thick as the gray winter mists that rolled off the mountains. Then, when the full enormity of their leader's accusation penetrated, protestations flew thick and fast.

"Who told ye such a lie?"

"He's as loyal as I am!"

"Me own mother would inform on us before he would!"

Their leader held up his large callused hands for silence. "One at a time, boys. Ye'll all have a chance to defend 'im, though he doesn't deserve yer loyalty."

One man stepped forward into the circle of light. "Why

do ye claim he's a traitor? He's one of us! He's always joined us whenever we called 'im.''

A ripple of assent filled the barn.

"Now, that is a fact," the leader agreed. "But ye can't say he's one of us. He's not a farmer, is he? He's never paid English landlords high rents for the privilege of farmin' his own land. He's never worked from dawn till dusk, tillin' the soil. He's never seen his crops wither and die at the whim o' the weather, or his cattle starve. He's never heard his children wailin' from hunger, now, has he?''

The men fell silent, for they knew he spoke the truth. Still they persisted in their absent member's defense.

"But he's always joined us whenever we called 'im, an' done his share.''

"Aye, that he has," the leader agreed. "But I wonder if he's really committed to the cause we all hold dearer than life itself, to free Ireland from the shackles of the English.''

"What makes ye say that?'' another asked.

The leader began strolling around the barn with the confidence of a born orator, addressing each individual man as though he were the only one in the room. "Do ye agree that the Heany himself and his wife deserved to be carded?''

Seven heads bobbed in unison, followed by a chorus of "Aye!''

"Well, one of us didn't agree, that's why he wasn't invited to accompany us when we paid old Heany a visit. An' when he heard what we did behind his back, he was none too pleased with the likes of Captain Moonlight. By the time he was through letting me feel the edge of his scaldin' tongue, I felt like I had been carded meself.''

The men exchanged uneasy glances.

"A man who doesn't share our convictions," the leader continued, "is a danger to us. He knows who you are''— he pointed to one man, then another and another—"and you . . . you . . . and you, not to mention meself. And what do ye suppose he could do with such information?'' When no one said anything, he put the unthinkable into words for them: "He could inform on us. He could tell the constabulary who we are and everything we've done, and where would that leave us?''

"Hangin' high from the gallows," another muttered reluctantly.

"It's right you are."

The accused's stauchest defender said, "But if he did that, wouldn't he swing himself? He's just as guilty as the rest of us."

The leader scoffed at that. "He's one of the gentry, me boy. He hobnobs with the likes of Cadogan Quinn. Goes to dine in the landlord's great house every week an' drinks his fine claret. Ye think they're going to let one of their own swing? Arragh, they'll find some way to get him off. They'll pat 'im on the back and say he just pretended to be one of us so he could get the goods on us. Then they'll give him a pardon for turnin' informer, see if they don't." He fell silent for a moment. Then he said, "Think on it, boys, and think on it hard. Our lives depend on your decision."

He scanned their faces as they muttered among themselves, and was satisfied to see shock and disillusionment written there. He had presented his case forcefully, striking at them where he knew them to be most vulnerable, and they had reacted as he knew they would.

But that same one man refused to be convinced.

"He would never inform on us," the dissenter grumbled stubbornly.

The leader looked at his men. "And the rest of ye? Do ye agree with that? Do ye honestly think in yer hearts that he wouldn't inform on ye, if he had the chance?"

"I think he would," another said.

Slowly, six more heads nodded in assent.

Their leader smiled grimly. "It's a sensible lot ye are, boys."

The lone dissenter spread his hands in appeal. "Are you all so quick to forget what he's done for us? Are you so quick to condemn the man without lettin' him speak for himself? Are ye just goin' to condemn him without a trial?" He looked around again. "He'd give us a chance to defend ourselves."

"No matter what he's done for us," another man said,

"we can't risk havin' an informer in our midst. We've all got too much at stake."

The others all agreed reluctantly.

Satisfied that he had won them over at last, the leader took a deep breath and let it out. "Now that we're all in agreement on that score, we've got to decide what's to be done about him."

When no suggestions were forthcoming, he said it himself: "We've got to make an example of him so others will think twice about betraying Captain Moonlight." The leader paused for effect. "He will have to be executed, and swiftly."

The shocked silence hung thickly in the air.

Only one man sprang forward and cried, "No! Ye'll not be murderin' him! We never agreed to be a party to murder."

The leader strode over to him and grasped his collar in a stranglehold. "Mind ye, if we're all in agreement, that's what we'll do, make no mistake about it!" His chilling voice dripped with menace. "An' if ye have thoughts about informin' on Captain Moonlight yerself, me boy, drive 'em out of yer mind this minute. You wouldn't want yer pretty new bride to suffer Mrs. Heany's fate, now, would ye? Carding's mighty hard on a woman's soft skin. I'm told the scars last until they put 'er in 'er grave."

The young man turned chalk white and swallowed convulsively several times, he eyes bulging in panic and fear as beads of sweat rose on his brow. He laughed nervously. "Ye wouldn't do that to me."

"Oh, wouldn't I, me boy? And every man here, make no mistake about it."

The leader gave him a full ten seconds to consider the import of his threat, then released him.

"So, are ye with us?"

The young man thought of his pretty, delicate wife with her gently curved back, so velvety to the touch when he came to her at night. He nodded reluctantly, cowed at last.

The leader smiled slowly as he clapped him on the shoulder and said, "Good lad," for he knew the surest way to win a man's compliance in anything was to threaten those he held near and dear.

"Now, let us discuss the fate of our traitor," he said.

Someone brought out a jug and began passing it around. After numerous toasts to Captain Moonlight, they got down to the business of discussing the fate of Dr. Liam Considine.

A month later, Fenella was sitting before the cold fireplace, darning her father's socks, when she happened to glance up at the clock and notice how late it was.

She set down her sewing and rose, stretching her arms high over her head to ease the stiffness in her shoulders, for she had been working at her sewing for half the afternoon. Then she went over to the window to see if her father was coming up the drive.

The last vestiges of the long summer twilight were about to fade from a sky rapidly turning from a deep, dark blue to black. Even at this point, the trees were dark enough to form silhouettes against the sky. A sprinkling of stars was beginning to appear, and if Fenella craned her neck, she could just make out the moon beginning to rise.

Before leaving late that afternoon, her father had promised her that he would be home before darkness fell.

"You've got fifteen minutes to make good on that promise, Father," she muttered before returning to her chair and her sewing.

But fifteen minutes later, he still wasn't home.

Frowning now, Fenella rose and reached for her woolen shawl. It might be early July, but the weather was unseasonably cool, a carryover from the wet spring hanging on tenaciously. She put on her shawl, went to the door, and opened it.

As she stood there letting the cool, night-scented breeze caress her cheeks, she scanned the drive and road beyond for any sign of her father, a ritual she often performed. But lately, due to all the talk of agrarian unrest, Fenella found herself worrying constantly about her father's safety when he went out alone.

Just that morning over breakfast, she had expressed her fears and concerns to him.

"Father, I worry about your going out so late at night. With these moonlighters terrorizing the countryside . . ."

She couldn't finish her sentence and looked away help-lessly.

"Now, Nella, don't worry yourself into a fret over me," he said, placing a comforting hand on hers. "I'm a doctor, and I have a responsibility to go to my patients whenever they need me. I can't let some band of rene-gade farmers frighten me into not doing my duty. You know that."

"Those 'renegade farmers' are ruthless savages who maim innocent people, Father," she said. "Who knows what would happen to you if you happened upon them committing some crime while you were visiting the sick? They might even kill you."

"They're not murderers, Nella," he said. "No one is going to harm me, daughter. All the farmers for miles around know me and the good I do. By the Holy, I heal their wives and children when they're sick, don't I? So why should their menfolk harm me?"

Fenella had reluctantly agreed, and they finished their breakfast in silence.

But now, as the night drew black as a peat bog and there was no sign of the dogcart coming down the drive, she felt her fears returning in full force.

Finally she decided there was nothing she could do but wait, so she shut the door and returned to her sewing.

An hour later, she started when she heard the front door open.

"Father, is that you?" she called, rising and flinging down the last of the socks. "You are as quiet as a mouse. What, no songs for me tonight? I didn't even hear the cart come up the drive."

He was standing in the foyer like one in a trance, and as Fenella crossed the parlor to welcome him home, her father said not one word of greeting to her, just stared straight ahead as if she didn't exist. His unblinking gaze was curiously leaden, and the twinkle gone from his eyes as he started up the stairs before she could even reach him.

"Father, what's wrong?" Fenella demanded, stopping at the foot of the stairs to stare in bewilderment at his retreating form.

Liam said nothing, just began climbing the stairs

slowly without even the aid of a lamp, one heavy step at
a time, like a man burdened with the weight of the world
on his shoulders.

"Father, what has happened?" Her voice rose to an
urgent wail. "Did you lose a patient? Did someone die?"

When her father still refused to answer as he reached
the top of the stairs and started down the hall to his room,
Fenella knew that something was dreadfully wrong. She
ran for the lamp; then, gathering her skirts out of the
way, she raced up the stairs as though Satan himself were
on her heels. She reached the top just in time to see her
father disappear into his room.

"Father, please say something. You're frightening me.
I . . ."

What she saw frightened her into silence: her father's
room was empty.

There was no one there.

Fenella stood in the doorway, one upraised hand
against the jamb to support herself, the other holding the
lamp aloft. Her disbelieving eyes desperately scanned
every corner of the bedroom and back again, but no force
of her will could conjure her father. He was simply not
there. The room was empty.

"Where is he? He's got to be here!" she babbled,
lurching crazily around the room, peering behind the bed
and around the wardrobe, any place where he might hide.
"I saw him climb up those stairs with my own eyes. I
saw him come into this room with my own eyes. He's got
to be here somewhere. He couldn't have just disappeared
into thin air like some . . . ghost."

Just at that moment, the scar on her wrist began to
throb as if in warning, and suddenly Fenella knew the
significance behind what she had seen tonight.

Her father was dead.

"No, he can't be."

But even as she uttered those words of denial, she knew
there could be only one explanation for what she had
seen—or hadn't seen—tonight, and it was not a rational
one.

She had seen her father's *fetch*.

Fenella felt a soothing calmness radiate from her wrist
to engulf her. She set the lamp down on a nightstand,

then seated herself in the chair where she usually laid out her father's clothes for the next day.

Now it was all so clear why her father hadn't looked at her or spoken to her tonight. What she had seen wasn't her father at all, but an eerie apparition that was the mirror image of Liam Considine.

She recalled a second, more sinister old Irish legend of the *fetch*. According to that version, if you saw someone's *fetch* in the morning, that person would face great danger but ultimately come to no harm. But if you saw someone's *fetch* at night, the same specter that revealed a young maid's lover on November's Eve could foretell a person's death.

And since Fenella had been cursed with the ability to see into the future, she had been warned of her father's untimely death.

Suddenly Fenella shook herself out of the lethargy that bound her and jumped to her feet. Perhaps the *fetch* had been sent to her as a warning. Perhaps her father was still alive and there was time for her to save him.

Heedless for her own safety, she ran down the stairs and out into the night.

Half an hour later, Fenella was in Mallow, pounding on the constable's door loud enough to wake the dead.

"Miss Considine!" he said, leading the half-fainting Fenella into the tiny foyer. "What's wrong?"

"It's my father, Constable Treherne," she said, gasping for breath after her long run into town, and nearly doubled over from the aching stitch in her side. "I know he's in danger. You must find him before it's too late!"

Constable Treherne said, "And how do you know that, Miss Considine?"

"He drove off late this afternoon, and he promised me he'd be home before nightfall. He hasn't come back yet, and I'm worried that something has happened to him."

The constable exchanged looks with his wife hovering in the background. "Your father is a doctor, miss. Doesn't he often stay out late visiting the sick?"

Fenella shook her head wildly. "Yes, but not this time. You don't understand. I just have a feeling that something dreadful has happened to him."

When the constable hesitated, Fenella said, "Please. I'm begging you. Please find my father before it's too late!"

Treherne studied her for a moment, then nodded reluctantly. "All right, Miss Considine, if you insist. . . . I'll get some men together and go look for your father."

Fenella managed a heartfelt smile. "Thank you, constable. You'll be saving my father's life."

The constable gathered his men, as promised, and one of them escorted Fenella home while the others went to search for Liam Considine.

All she could do was wait patiently for her father to walk through the door.

An hour later, it was not her father, but Constable Treherne who first walked through the door, followed by several townsmen from Mallow, their hats in their hands.

Fenella needed just one look at their somber, grim faces and downcast eyes to know the worst had happened. She slowly rose from her chair and gripped the back of it for support.

"Y-you've found my father?" she asked, her voice breaking.

The constable nodded solemnly. "I'm sorry to have to be the one to bring you the bad news, Miss Considine, but your father is dead."

Fenella felt as though she had been shot through the heart. The room began spinning crazily, but she took a deep breath and willed herself to be strong, for her father's sake. Fainting would not accomplish anything. There were things she had to know.

"Where did you find him? How did he die?"

"Are you sure you wish to hear this, miss? You've had a terrible shock."

"Yes, constable. Spare me nothing. I must know the truth."

Constable Treherne took a deep breath. "We found his dogcart and horse standing by the side of the road not two miles from here, near the bridge. He was in the stream below. Near as we could tell, he must have fallen into the stream and hit his head against the rocks. That's what he died from, a blow to the head."

Fenella scowled at him. "Why would my father get out of his cart on the bridge when he was so close to home? Did his horse go lame?"

"Not that we could see, miss."

Rapidly losing patience, Fenella snapped, "I find it difficult to believe he would leave the cart for no reason at all and just topple into the stream."

The constable shifted his weight and cleared his throat. "Er, there were some signs that the doctor had been drinking, miss."

"That's preposterous, constable! My father never drank a drop when he went to call on his patients."

"All I know is what I saw. Or smelled, in this case," Constable Treherne said.

"What do you mean?"

"His shirtfront was soaked with whiskey, Miss Considine. He reeked of it."

The men who had been there all nodded silently in agreement.

Fenella's shrill voice rang throughout the small parlor, "My father was not drunk!" Then she collapsed into her chair and sat there in stunned silence, trying to assimilate what she had been told.

"We know this has come as a cruel blow to you," she heard the constable say from far away, "but I'm afraid I've got to ask you some questions."

Fenella looked up. "Before I answer any questions, would you be so kind as to send a man to Cadogan Quinn and ask him to come at once?"

The constable turned and said something to one of the men, who nodded and left for Rookforest.

Fenella sat there and stared out into space, feeling as though her entire body were wrapped in cotton batting, insulating her senses and emotions from the horror of this night. She was vaguely aware of people moving about around her and she heard hushed voices, but nothing really penetrated her benumbed brain.

But the moment she saw Cadogan come charging into the parlor, his disheveled hair at odds with his neat dinner attire, something inside her broke, like a dam bursting.

"Oh Cadogan, Cadogan! My father's dead!" she wailed, rising to her feet and staggering toward her friend's outstretched arms, where she broke down, sobbing uncontrollably.

"I know, Fenella, and I'm so very sorry," he crooned, enfolding her in his embrace and pressing her head into his shoulder.

She abandoned herself to the comfort he was offering as though she were a child of six crying over some hurt, and he her father. Cadogan's arms were so strong, yet he held her so tenderly as she cried her eyes out.

Finally, when no more tears would fall, Fenella pulled away. "I can't believe it. I just can't believe my father's dead. I feel as though I'm dreaming, and at any moment I'm going to wake up and see him come right through that door."

Cadogan's eyes were glazed with tears. "Neither can I. Liam Considine was always a good friend to me. It's hard to believe he's gone, and so . . . so senselessly."

Fenella's face crumpled. "Oh, Cadogan . . . what am I going to do?"

He led her back to her chair and pressed a handkerchief into her hand. "You're not going to worry about a single thing, that's what you're going to do. I shall make all of the funeral arrangements myself, so you needn't concern yourself on that account." He hesitated for a moment, then added, "And I want you to pack some things and return to Rookforest with us."

Fenella dabbed at her eyes and shook her head emphatically. "Thank you for your generous offer, but I can't leave this house. Not now."

"Fenella . . ."

"No, Cadogan! I couldn't possibly leave this house tonight. It comforts me to stay here, among my father's things. Please do not argue."

She was so adamant, all he could do was capitulate. "As you wish, my dear. But I'll send Mrs. Ryan or Margaret to stay with you tonight. You've just suffered a tremendous blow and mustn't be alone at a time like this."

For the first time, Fenella noticed Patrick standing quietly in the background with a strange expression that was neither sadness nor pity.

"Thank you for coming," she said to him.

Patrick stepped out of the shadowy hallway and into the warm light of the parlor. Fenella found herself thinking quite irrationally that this Patrick differed radically from the man who had first walked into this cottage that stormy night. His hair had finally grown out to what must have been its normal thick black thatch, and all these weeks of dining well had filled out his tall, solid form to its former strength and size. Patrick Quinn had become an imposing man.

"I'm sorry about your father," he said. "I didn't know him well, but I liked him."

The words were simple, but sincerely spoken.

After thanking Patrick again, Fenella bit her lower lip to keep it from trembling, but she failed. Fresh tears spilled helplessly, and as she dabbed them away, she realized she would probably burst into tears whenever she thought of her father and the way he had died.

Cadogan patted her on the shoulder. "If you'll excuse me for a few moments, my dear, I must speak with the good constable."

Fenella suspected he wished to garner further details concerning her father's death, so she just smiled slightly and nodded, then closed her eyes and rested her head against her chair's high wing back. She didn't want to think, she didn't want to feel such pain. She just wanted this ordeal to be over.

After days of grim, raw weather, the sun came out in time for Liam Considine's funeral and spread its offensively cheerful light throughout every corner of the small, crowded churchyard, making the many black-clad mourners stand out among the gravestones like rooks in a cornfield.

Rain would have been more in keeping with her feelings of sadness and loss, Fenella decided as she stood at the graveside with Cadogan at her elbow. But at the same time, the warmth of the sun on her shoulders was like a reassuring arm or a benediction. That thought forced a smile to her lips behind her heavy black veil.

Finally the service was over. The last bit of earth was

thrown on the coffin, and the mourners began moving away to resume their lives. Finally only Fenella and Cadogan remained.

"Fenella . . ." Cadogan said softly, touching her elbow to tell her they should be leaving.

She nodded. "Good-bye, Father," she murmured, then turned and began walking away from the grave with reluctant, measured steps. Behind her, she heard the heavy thuds of earth being shoveled atop her father's simple casket, and the grim finality of the sound almost made her turn back. But Cadogan had drawn her arm through his and was resolutely leading her forward, guiding her toward the gate where Patrick and Margaret waited solemnly, and out of the past.

Cadogan said, "Your father was well-loved by many people, rich and poor alike. I think half of Cork must have come to pay their respects today."

"He tried his best to help people, especially the farmers," Fenella said. "It's gratifying to see his selfless efforts on their behalf were appreciated."

Cadogan fell silent for a moment; then he cleared his throat. "Fenella, what are you going to do now?"

She lifted one shoulder in a shrug. "I haven't really thought about it."

"Will you . . . ? I mean, are you . . . ?" Cadogan made an exasperated noise and turned beet red. "Curse it, Fenella, I'm a plain-speaking man who's never been good at flowery words. What I mean to say is, how are you going to live now that your father's gone?"

"If you're referring to my financial situation, please don't concern yourself for another minute. Both my former fiancé and my father left me provided for." But just barely. If she were careful and lived frugally, she could get by.

"Oh."

Fenella looked at him in surprise. "Why, Cadogan, you sound almost disappointed."

"I am, in a manner of speaking. You see, I was going to invite you to come live with us at Rookforest if you were in straitened circumstances. We certainly have enough room for you."

"I . . . I'm honored, Cadogan, and I thank you for your most generous offer."

"It's the least I could do," he replied. "I owed your father a debt I can never hope to repay for his kindness to my Moira during her illness. But if helping you would repay that debt in some little measure . . ."

"You are too kind. But as I said, I have been provided for."

For a moment he looked chagrined, as though he couldn't put his thoughts into words. Finally he blurted out, "But what will you do, Fenella? You're a comely young woman with her whole life ahead of her. Damme, are you going to live alone for the rest of your days, burying yourself in good works?"

Fenella didn't know how to respond to Cadogan's impassioned plea. In light of what her father had once told her about the landowner's romantic intentions toward her, Fenella feared in his gruff, oblique way, the man was proposing to her.

Visibly upset, she withdrew her arm from his. "I . . . I don't know what I'm going to do. I have just lost my father, and I'm afraid I haven't been able to give a thought to my future. It's just too soon."

He sighed dismally. "I understand. Do forgive me for my blunt tongue."

Fenella was spared from replying as they reached Patrick and Margaret standing at the gate along with a waiting carriage pulled by four black horses decked out in somber mourning regalia, with black plumes attached to their bridles. Patrick handed Margaret in, then waited while his father assisted Fenella. Then the men got in and all spoke little during the interminable drive back to Fenella's house.

Later, after the Quinns departed, leaving Fenella truly alone for the first time since her father's death, the full realization of her loss hit her.

But as she slowly walked through rooms that would be forever empty of her father's personality, Fenella realized that once again she had lost her sense of purpose along with a loved one.

When she had become engaged to William, she had planned a life as his devoted wife and helpmate, who would make a comfortable home for him and raise their children with love and understanding. Then he had died, shattering her dreams into dust.

So she assumed a new purpose in life, that of the dutiful daughter selflessly caring for her father. And now, even that had been taken from her, leaving her bereft once again.

"How much grief must I bear?" she cried out to the empty house.

She fought back tears as she returned to the parlor and noticed her father's pipe on the table near his favorite chair. Never would she sit up for him with his pipe and whiskey waiting. Never would she darn his clothes. Never would she feel so useful again.

She was twenty-three years old and a spinster without prospects, with the long, lonely years of uselessness stretching out before her like a road leading nowhere.

Then she thought of Cadogan, and what he had said to her that morning. All she had to do was encourage him a little, and he would fill her life with such purpose as she had never known, as his wife and the mistress of his domain.

"But you don't love him, Fenella," she said aloud to herself, rubbing the scar on her wrist. "And besides, would he even want you once he knew the truth about you and your accursed talent?"

She smiled dryly. If only her second sight could predict her own future, but she knew that was impossible. She had tried often enough to summon her powers for her own benefit, but they displayed a remarkable propensity to do as they pleased. So it appeared her future was destined to be what she made of it.

Shoulders bowed with sadness, Fenella slowly walked up the stairs to her room. She was bone-weary now and needed the oblivion of sleep. She would think of her future tomorrow.

The following afternoon found Patrick riding Gallowglass hard across Rookforest's rolling green hills.

To his chagrin, Patrick found that no matter how hard he tried to concentrate on the changeable terrain with its cross-hatching of high hedges and wide ditches, he could not erase the persistent picture of his father and Fenella together. All during Liam Considine's wake, and later at the church and graveside, Cadogan was Fenella's shadow. His hand was always at her elbow, his head bent to catch her every word, like an attentive suitor.

Patrick was almost certain his father was on the verge of asking Fenella to marry him.

That unappealing thought distracted him, breaking his concentration, and he was forced to turn Gallowglass away from the high hedge looming before them.

He swore under his breath. "One would think you cared for the lady yourself, Patrick Quinn."

Although he and the prickly Miss Considine had been getting along better lately, theirs was an uneasy truce at best. And he had no desire whatsoever to have her for a stepmother. But what could he do if his father was determined to marry her?

Scowling, Patrick reined in his horse for a moment atop a high hill. As he sat there, he noticed another horse and rider cantering slowly across the field below. Even from the distance he could see it was a woman riding sidesaddle, with the long veil of her top hat streaming out behind her. He squinted in an endeavor to see her face, but she was too far away for him to discern her identity.

Suddenly, without warning, the woman's horse shied. The unexpected sideways movement caught its rider by surprise and she went flying over the animal's left shoulder. She hit the ground hard and lay still.

Patrick sprang into action, galloping down the hill at breakneck speed and was out of the saddle before Gallowglass could even come to a complete stop.

Patrick hurried over to where the woman was lying facedown, her right arm flung up to conceal her face. Her hat had fallen off, and her dark hair was somewhat disheveled where a few hairpins had been shaken free. Patrick's eyes scanned the area impatiently for any sign of the groom who usually followed a gentlewoman at a discreet distance. There was no one. The foolish woman had gone riding alone.

He knelt down on one knee beside her, placed a hand

on her shoulder, and gently shook her. "Miss, are you hurt?"

Suddenly she moaned and stirred beneath his hand. Thus encouraged, Patrick sought to gently turn her over onto her back.

"There, there, miss. I'll have you . . ."

Thick lashes fluttered and startled violet eyes stared up into his.

Patrick's hand sprang back as if it had touched a viper lying in the grass, and he jumped to his feet. "You!"

"Patrick . . ." Cynara Standon murmured.

Just hearing her utter his name in that deep, throaty voice that had haunted his endless, solitary nights in prison, Patrick felt himself shudder, but this time in revulsion. At least he told himself it was revulsion. But he could not tear his gaze away from those melancholy eyes or that lovely face, so perfect in its classical beauty.

"Don't expect me to help you to your feet, Cynara," he said coldly, with utter contempt. "You see, any gentlemanly instincts I once possessed were ground out of me in prison."

"I don't expect anything from you, Patrick," she replied, then managed to struggle into a sitting position. She buried her face in her hands for a moment, and took several deep, quivering breaths to compose herself. "My horse shied at a rabbit."

"You should have taken a groom with you."

"I prefer riding alone."

She tried to rise, but failed. Cynara looked up at him, her eyes unnaturally bright. "P-please help me. I . . . I feel so weak."

The appeal in her voice brought Patrick's gentlemanly instincts rushing back, and he found himself extending a helping hand toward her, however grudgingly.

The moment his fingers tightened around hers, Patrick felt the force of her touch right through the leather of their gloves. He remembered her touch all too well. The intimate shock traveled all the way up his arm with a swift and growing heat that almost caused him to lose his grip, but he steeled himself against it, and hauled her to her feet as if she weighed no more than a sparrow.

"Thank you," she said breathlessly, swaying against him.

Patrick did the only thing he could do to keep her from collapsing: he instinctively slid his arm around her waist, still narrow in spite of her having borne a child. As Cynara fell against him in a semiswoon, her intoxicating perfume filled Patrick's nostrils, almost making him dizzy with its spicy, exotic scent and evoking powerful memories of long summer twilights when he and Cynara would sit so close together in the little riverside folly at Drumlow.

Patrick stiffened, fighting against those seductive memories with all the strength of his will, but Cynara's soft, silken hair was brushing his cheek as her head lolled against his shoulder. Except for the stiff whalebone stays of her corset protecting her like armor, Cynara felt so soft she appeared to melt into his arms. Patrick gritted his teeth as he felt a urgent tightening in his loins, a sensation that had long gone unfulfilled and was almost excruciating in its intensity.

"Are you hurt?" he demanded gruffly, putting her away from him before she could detect the tangible physical effect she was having on him.

Cynara blinked and snapped out of her swoon. "I . . . I don't know what came over me. I felt a little faint just then. Thank you for your concern."

"You mistake mere politeness for concern, madam," he said stiffly. "I merely was ensuring that your brother wouldn't blame me for any injury you might sustain."

Without another word, Patrick whirled on his heel and strode across the field to where Cynara's bay gelding was grazing, oblivious of all the excitement his behavior had caused. Patrick gathered the reins, then led the now-docile animal over to where its mistress stood. He took a moment to collect her hat and dusted it off before thrusting it at her.

He looked at Cynara's tall, rangy horse distastefully. "I suppose I shall have to help you mount as well."

Cynara's full lower lip quivered as she set her hat back on her head. "I would appreciate it. I . . . I still feel a little shaky, and couldn't possibly manage on my own."

"Very well. Come over here and I'll give you a leg up, though Lord knows why I should bother."

Cynara hesitated, then took a step toward him and boldly placed her hand on his arm. "Patrick, please don't be this way."

Her touch again. . . . He wouldn't look at her. "What way?"

"So cold. So bitter. We used to be friends once."

He threw back his head and laughed, a harsh, cynical sound that echoed through the valley. "How else am I supposed to feel, Cynara? Need I remind you that I spent four years of my life rotting in prison all because of you and that bastard brother of yours, and you expect me to act as if nothing happened?"

She stepped before him so he would be forced to look down at her, and she spread her hands beseechingly. "I begged them not to press charges against you, but they wouldn't listen to me. I had nothing to do with sending you to prison. It was all St. John's doing, and . . . and my fiancé's. You must believe me. I wouldn't have hurt you for the world."

"And I suppose you were helpless to prevent it?"

Her gaze slid away and her expression became troubled. "You know St. John. He's just like our father. He has never listened to me. He thinks my sole purpose in life is to serve as a pawn for his own lofty social ambitions."

Patrick stood there watching an errant breeze tug at her loose hair, and he had the overwhelming desire to catch at the strands and feel their silkiness between his fingers. He would like to pull out her hairpins one by one until . . . He mentally shook himself. He must not fall under Cynara's compelling spell again, he must not! He shouldn't even be standing here talking to her as easily as if all the wasted years and pain hadn't existed between them.

Despite his best intentions, he couldn't resist saying, "You didn't have to strike me with the bottle that night on the yacht in Ostend. You didn't have to summon the police and have me arrested."

Those magnificent violet eyes pleaded with him to understand. "You kidnapped me, and I was frightened half out of my mind. I had no desire to be . . . be ravished by any man, even you!''

"There was no need to do what you did," he insisted stubbornly. "You knew how I felt about you. I would have listened to reason, if you had but taken the time to reason with me."

"You say that now, but you were far from rational that night. If you could have just seen yourself! You were wild, unyielding . . . a Patrick I had never known before. You were determined to have me, and nothing I could have said would have stopped you!"

"Even so, you could have interceded to keep me from being sent to prison." He took a deep breath, and his voice shook with emotion. "You ruined my life, Cynara. You consigned me to a living hell. I'll never forgive you for that. Never."

She bowed her head, and when she spoke, her voice was so soft, Patrick had to strain to hear her. "I . . . I know. When I first saw you in church that Sunday, when I saw how much you must have suffered in prison . . ." Her voice ended on a choked sob and she shrugged helplessly. "God, if I could only take it all back . . ."

Then she rallied enough to grasp his hand in both of hers and hold it tightly. "But it wasn't my fault, Patrick. St. John was adamant. He wanted his revenge, and he promised I would suffer if I didn't do exactly what he told me to." Cynara released him and her eyes filled with tears. "You know I have never been able to stand up to my brother. He is just like my father—cruel, unfeeling . . ."

"Then why have you returned to live under his domination once again?"

"Because I am destitute! And I have nowhere else to go!" she cried. "Would you rather that my child and I wore rags and starved?"

Patrick said nothing, just stared down at the tops of his boots.

When she became calmer, Cynara said, "I don't know how much you have heard about my . . . my life as the Marchioness of Eastbrook."

"Precious little," Patrick said carelessly, to wound her. "I'm afraid all the petty goings-on of London society are not our chief concern here in Mallow. So boring and shallow, you know.''

Cynara ignored his barbs and went on to tell him what he already knew about her husband's death, leaving a daughter, not an heir, and how his brother had inherited the title and fortune.

"His family would not provide for you and your daughter?'' he inquired with raised brows. "They sound like a cold, heartless lot to me, each concerned with himself. I would say that you all deserved one another.''

Cynara uttered a soft sigh of reproach. Then she told him what he also already knew, that her brother-in-law had made improper advances, and his jealous wife had forced Cynara out.

"She had no cause to think me a threat,'' Cynara insisted. "I didn't want her fool of a husband for a lover. All I wanted was a home for my little Louisa and myself.''

At the mention of her child, Cynara's face softened with maternal radiance, making her even more beautiful. Patrick turned away and busied himself checking the saddle's girth.

Cynara said, "So here I am, back in Ireland, at my brother's mercy once again.''

"I wish you and your brother all the happiness you both deserve.''

Cynara's ivory skin blushed a pale rose at the heavy sarcasm in his voice. "That was unworthy of you, Patrick,'' she said softly.

He silently cursed her for her ability to make him feel as though he were to blame for the troubles she had caused. He wanted to remove himself from her presence as quickly as possible. "Now, if you'd be so kind as to mount, I'll be on my way.''

Cynara hesitated, then took a step closer. "If it's any consolation,'' she said, "I suffered as well in a sort of prison of my own. You see, the joke was at my expense. My handsome, attentive bridegroom turned out to be a wicked, depraved man.''

Her color deepened and she stumbled over her words. "S-soon after I was married, I discovered he . . . he occasionally enjoyed the favors of men as well.'' She

ignored Patrick's shocked stare and hurried on. "And
. . . and when he died, it was not in a hunting accident
on the North York moors as was reported in all the newspapers."

She took a deep breath and closed her eyes. "He . . .
he was murdered in a part of London where no respectable gentleman would dare be seen. But because his family was so wealthy and powerful, they had the means to
hide the truth and keep scandal at bay." She opened her
eyes and managed a wry smile. "So you see, Patrick,
you are not the only one to suffer at St. John's hands. I
have paid a high price as well."

Patrick stood there in dumbfounded silence.

Then he resolutely laced his fingers together, held out
his cupped hands, and waited for Cynara to place her
foot in his makeshift stirrup.

With one final curious glance at Patrick, Cynara gathered the reins and accepted his assistance. Once she had
struggled into the saddle, she just sat there for a moment,
swaying slightly, her eyes closed, as if the weakness had
suddenly assailed her again.

"Are you sure you can ride back to Drumlow alone?"
he asked, not unkindly.

"I'll be fine."

Then, without another word, Cynara urged her horse
into a slow walk and they disappeared across the field,
leaving Patrick to stare after her.

8

FENELLA HAD JUST come from her garden and happened to glance out the parlor window, when she noticed a dog-cart rattling up the drive. As the cart drew closer, she saw that its driver was a stranger, a rather large, robust woman who seemed to fill the small vehicle to overflowing.

When the cart reached the front door, the woman bellowed, "Whoa!" and hauled back on the reins with such force that she nearly pulled her poor pony's head into its chest. When the cart came to a halt, she disembarked with all the finesse of an elephant backing out of a stall.

Fenella darted away from the window and was debating whether to pretend she was not at home, when there came a thunderous pounding on her front door.

"If you don't want her to knock your door down, I would suggest you answer it," Fenella said to herself.

She opened the door and found herself staring up at a woman who must have been all of six feet tall, with generous bosom and hips encased in a traveling dress of gray serge that matched the color of her hair and eyes. "Yes?"

"Miss Considine?" the woman inquired, advancing across the threshold so Fenella was forced to step back or be knocked aside. "Miss Fenella Considine?"

"I am she," Fenella replied, suppressing her annoyance at the stranger's rudeness. "I am afraid I have not had the pleasure of making your acquaintance, Miss . . . ?"

"Mrs.," she said in her booming voice, grasping Fenella's hand in a crushing grip and pumping it. "Mrs. Edith Janeaway."

"Well, Mrs. Janeaway," Fenella began, "you must forgive me if I seem a bit puzzled by your sudden appearance. If I may be so bold, why have you come to call on me? We are virtual strangers, madam.''

Mrs. Janeaway grinned, revealing strong yellowish teeth. ''Oh, but we shan't be strangers for long, my dear Miss Considine.'' Without so much as a by-your-leave, the woman headed for the parlor, where she turned and stopped. ''In fact, after you've heard what I've come all the way from Cork to say to you, I'm sure we shall become the best of friends.''

Somehow, Fenella doubted that, but she held her tongue as she closed the door and invited the woman to sit down, since she was bound to help herself to a seat anyway. Fenella felt a surge of irritation when Mrs. Janeaway lowered herself into the doctor's favorite chair, which creaked and groaned in protest under her considerable weight.

''Would you like a cup of tea, Mrs. Janeaway?'' Fenella asked. ''And some freshly baked bannocks as well?''

''That sounds splendid, Miss Considine. I must confess a bit of refreshment always assists my intellectual processes.''

Fenella turned without comment and went into the kitchen. She emerged a few minutes later bearing a tray, which she set down on the tea table.

As Fenella poured, Mrs. Janeaway helped herself to a bannock. ''First of all, I must offer my sincerest condolences to you on the recent loss of your father. He was a fine, fine man.''

Fenella nodded her head in acknowledgment, but inside, she was seething with impatience. What did this coarse woman want? But somehow she sensed Mrs. Edith Janeaway would not be rushed.

''These bannocks are delicious,'' she murmured, dabbing at her lips with a napkin in a curious dainty gesture for one so large. Her protuberant gray eyes were always moving, and now they scanned the parlor with lively curiosity. ''Charming little place you have here, absolutely charming.''

''Please forgive my rudeness, Mrs. Janeaway, but why have you honored me with your presence this morning? If you don't tell me, I shall expire of curiosity.''

Edith Janeaway chuckled at that. "You're just like my Harold—that's my husband. He's always saying to me, 'The point, Edith, make your point!' "

Fenella felt an odd sympathy with the man.

Suddenly Mrs. Janeaway became all seriousness. She set down her half-eaten bannock and leaned forward in her chair, causing it to creak with every little shift of her weight. "You have, of course, heard of the Land League?"

Fenella sensed danger, set down her teacup, and laced her fingers together primly in her lap. "Everyone in Ireland has heard of the Land League."

"And you are familiar with its noble aims?"

"Of course." She thought she ought to say no more than that.

"And, as a loyal Irishwoman, I am certain you support those noble aims."

Fenella was on her guard now. There was just something about the way the Janeaway woman was looking at her, with a crafty, expectant expression on her fleshy face.

"I am not opposed to anything that will better the lives of the farmers," she began.

Edith Janeaway grinned triumphantly. "I knew it! I knew I would find a kindred spirit in you, Miss Considine!"

"But," Fenella added emphatically, "I do not condone violence for any reason, Mrs. Janeaway."

The woman's smile vanished, and she looked affronted. "Neither does the Land League condone violence, Miss Considine."

Fenella raised one brow. "Perhaps not publicly, but I believe the League is not averse to violence occurring, if that is what it takes to further its aims."

Mrs. Janeaway shook her head, causing her double chin to shake. "That is a vile slander spread by our enemies. It is simply not true."

Fenella felt the blood rush to her cheeks. "Oh, but it is, Mrs. Janeaway, though you may deny it till Doomsday! Captain Moonlight has committed the most appalling atrocities here in Mallow, maiming animals, frightening innocent people half to death . . . The list is endless."

"I will concede that there has been violence, but desperate times demand desperate measures, Miss Considine. But don't you see? It's only because farmers are desperate that they resort to such deplorable means. If the Land League succeeds in its aims, there will no longer be any need for brigands to take the law into their own hands."

"I'm sorry," Fenella said obstinately. "I don't believe the end ever justifies the means."

Mrs. Janeaway was silent for a moment, like a soldier taking time to reload with more ammunition. Then she said, "Would you be willing to do anything to stop the violence?"

"Of course," Fenella replied without hesitation. The moment she saw the triumph flare up in the other woman's eyes, she realized she had fallen into a neatly set trap.

"Splendid! I knew you wouldn't fail me, Miss Considine."

Fenella drummed her fingernails against the saucer. "To the point, Mrs. Janeaway, if you please."

The woman leaned forward, nearly knocking over her teacup with her shelf of a bosom. But even this near-catastrophe didn't distract her. "I have come to enlist your aid in a cause that Irish womanhood is uniquely qualified for—that of aiding and supporting our menfolk."

Fenella scowled. "Forgive me for being obtuse, Mrs. Janeaway, but how can I—?"

She held up her hand. "If you will be so kind as to refrain from interrupting me, I shall explain. Just from our short acquaintance, I can tell you are a young woman of considerable intelligence and strong convictions." Edith Janeaway paused as if waiting for Fenella to acknowledge the compliment. When Fenella didn't, Mrs. Janeaway continued.

"The leaders of the Land League are in danger of being imprisoned. We suspect the government intends to prosecute them for conspiracy in preventing the payment of rents and with interfering with evictions." Mrs. Janeaway's eyes grew cold and hard. "And if that happens, we women may be called upon to take their place."

Fenella just stared at her.

A dry smile played across the other woman's mouth. "Does it astound you to think members of your own sex could contemplate such activities?"

"No, Mrs. Janeaway, it does not. I know full well my own sex is capable of anything, given the opportunities now denied us. I am merely astounded that you could wish me to be a part of it."

"Why not? You are intelligent and articulate, from what I've heard. Your father was well-known in Mallow and its environs as a champion of the people. Why shouldn't his daughter follow in his footsteps?"

"Because his daughter isn't sure she wants to."

That angered Mrs. Janeaway. She reared back, her eyes popping, her pale skin mottled with red spots. "How any loyal Irishwoman could refuse to aid us in our cause . . ." She shook her head.

"As I said before, I have my doubts about the justness of your cause, Mrs. Janeaway. And I also find myself torn. Although I have great sympathy for the farmers, especially since the harvests have been so poor, I also count several of the landowning class as good and dear friends."

The other woman's lip curled back in a sneer. "You mean the likes of Cadogan Quinn and that fop Nayland?"

Fenella raised her chin defiantly. "Yes, I do. Both of them are honorable men, and both have done much good for their tenants."

"Perhaps they have," she conceded, "but what about men like St. John Standon? Don't you want to help put a stop to their rule of greed and misery?"

"Not at the expense of my old and cherished friendships," Fenella said stoutly.

Mrs. Janeaway shook her head in disgust. "You disappoint me greatly, Miss Considine."

"I'm sorry I cannot help you, Mrs. Janeaway," she replied, rising to let the other woman know their interview was at an end. "But Cadogan Quinn and his family have been most kind to me. I cannot betray that kindness."

"Such loyalty . . ." She sneered.

Fenella felt her temper rise, but she held it in check.

Arguing with this woman would be fruitless, because the redoubtable Edith Janeaway would always have an answer to any objection Fenella posed.

Mrs. Janeaway hauled herself to her feet and had the effrontery to wag one fat finger at Fenella. "There's going to come a time when you have to choose sides, Miss Considine, either landlord or tenant. I hope for your sake that you choose the right one."

Then she turned on her heel and sailed through the parlor, her head held high.

"I'll see you out," Fenella said.

"There is no need," Edith Janeaway replied without a backward glance as she opened the door.

"Oh, but I insist."

Just as Fenella reached the stoop, she saw Patrick Quinn come cantering down the drive on his huge black horse. She saw the expression of astonishment on his face as he watched the formidable Mrs. Janeaway maneuver herself into the dogcart, and Fenella had to suppress a smile.

As Patrick slowed his horse to a walk and approached the dogcart, Fenella was seized with an irrepressible spirit of mischief.

"Good day to you, Patrick," she greeted him.

"Fenella . . ." he said, glancing curiously at Mrs. Janeaway, who was trying to turn her recalcitrant pony around in the drive.

"Mrs. Janeaway, I would like you to meet Patrick Quinn," Fenella said. "His father is none other than Cadogan Quinn, who owns Rookforest. And, Patrick, this is Mrs. Harold Janeaway, an acquaintance who came to call."

Both acknowledged the introduction with all the civilities, but Fenella thought Mrs. Janeaway's responses were rather garbled, and she did glare at Patrick before making her excuses and setting her cart back down the drive.

Fenella watched her leave, and as the cart turned a corner, she couldn't resist waving. Mrs. Janeaway, however, did not wave back.

Fenella looked up at Patrick, who was staring at the departing woman as though she were a visitor from the moon.

He said, "I have never seen anyone quite so . . . so . . . ." Words failed him.

"Redoubtable?" Fenella said. "Formidable?"

"The word 'elephantine' came to mind." He scowled in bewilderment. "Janeaway . . . That name is not familiar to me. Is she from around here?"

"Nor to me. In fact, I've never even seen her before today." While Patrick listened, she quickly told him of the reason for Mrs. Janeaway's visit.

Patrick raised his brows at that.

"So she was trying to recruit you for a Ladies' Land League. And did you refuse her request?" he asked.

"Of course," Fenella replied. "I would never do anything to harm your family, or Lord Nayland." Then she had to look away because Patrick was regarding her with an unnerving intensity.

When she looked back up at him, she noticed how much more Patrick had changed with the passage of another month. Now that his luxuriant raven hair had grown back, he had let it grow even longer than convention dictated, so that it grew over the tops of his ears and curled about his collar, as if in defiance for its once being cropped so short. He had even grown an impressive set of side whiskers, but still disdained a beard. While still lean, his face had filled out nicely, and his body was now strong and conditioned, with an easy feline grace of its own.

But there was still something remote and haunting about his eyes, Fenella decided, a deep abiding sadness that might take years to erase.

"Would you care to dismount and have a cup of tea?" she asked.

He shook his head. "Thank you, but I can't stay. I'm on my way to Mallow on business for my father. He asked me to stop by here to invite you to dinner on Friday night."

When Fenella hesitated, Patrick said, "My father told me to remind you that you haven't called at Rookforest since your father died a month ago."

Fenella's gaze fell away. "But I'm in mourning. And I'm sure he can understand that I haven't felt like socializing."

"He anticipated that response, and he also told me to tell you that he understands. But he still wishes you would accept his invitation. 'Hang the conventions' were his precise words on that subject, and you know how conventional my father is."

Fenella noticed he didn't say he and Margaret would enjoy her company as well, but she smiled anyway. "Thank you. Please tell Cadogan I would be delighted to hang the conventions and come."

Patrick nodded gravely. "I'll give him your message. The carriage will call for you at the usual time."

Then he nodded, touched his heels to his horse's sides, and cantered off down the drive.

No sooner did Patrick turn away from Fenella than he forgot about her and an enticing image of Cynara filled his mind. He swore under his breath and urged his horse to go faster and faster, as if he could leave the memory of her far behind, but he realized it was useless.

Ever since he had helped Cynara when she was thrown, Patrick found himself obsessed by her. From the time he awoke in the morning, he could think of nothing else except Cynara, Cynara, Cynara. His haunted, fevered brain conjured her when she wasn't there, all limpid violet eyes and breathless, dusky voice tempting him, destroying his concentration until he feared he was going mad.

The only time she left him in peace was at night. As he had so many nights in prison, Patrick would imagine her lying naked beside him, her rook-black hair spread out like a dark wave on the pillow, her perfect ivory body open and inviting, ready to be pleasured and feasted upon. Only when that fantasy helped him achieve his own release with its attendant shame and self-loathing did she disappear like some wraith, freeing him from her bondage until the new dawn.

As Patrick turned left at the crossroads and headed for Finnerty's farm, he shook his head in disgust. "It's daft I am," he said to Gallowglass, who cocked one ear back to hear what his master was saying. "I can't love the woman—not after all I've suffered at her hands. Yet I

can't stop thinking of her day in and day out. It's mad I
am, I tell you. That's the only explanation.''

Within minutes, Francis Finnerty's farm came into
view, and Patrick was able to put Cynara out of his mind
and concentrate on the upcoming unpleasant estate business his father wanted him to handle.

Finnerty's farm was like all the others on the Rookforest lands except that it was larger. The main dwelling
was no simple three-room thatched cottage, but a comfortable two-story farmhouse complete with a new slate
roof, thanks to Cadogan's generosity and commitment to
improvements. The barn a short distance away was sturdy
and cavernous, the pride of the estate.

No, Patrick thought as he rode around the house toward the back, the Finnertys certainly had nothing to
complain about in his estimation, but then, the tenants
were apt to view their individual situations differently.

He knew he was being watched. Out of the corner of
his eye he caught the briefest movement of a curtain being pushed aside in one of the downstairs windows. But
he paid no attention. He was, after all, the landlord's son,
here to do the landlord's business. He could ride wherever he liked on his father's land without being chal-
lenged as a trespasser.

Patrick rode through the fields, and when the house
and barn finally disappeared behind a hill, he found what
he had been seeking.

There, at the end of a field, stood a newly erected
cottage trying its best to be inconspicuous, a dwelling
that had no right to be there at all. Patrick scowled as he
sat back in the saddle. He knew at once what Francis
Finnerty had done and why, and while Patrick could understand it, he also knew that Finnerty could not be allowed to get away with such a flagrant violation of his
rental agreement.

Suddenly Patrick heard someone call his name, and
when he turned in the saddle, he saw the shifty-eyed Finnerty himself, with one of his healthy, strapping sons on
either side, come walking toward him. The father carried
a pitchfork, but his sons were unarmed. All three wore
wary, righteous expressions, and the air around them was
thick with tension.

"Good afternoon, gentlemen," Patrick said without dismounting.

"Mr. Quinn," Finnerty said, and his sons mumbled something unintelligible.

Patrick looked at the cottage, then back at the men. "Why has a cottage been built on this land, Mr. Finnerty?"

Finnerty's fingers tightened on his pitchfork, and he looked Patrick straight in the eye for once. "It's for me eldest son, Joseph, here. He just got married, and needed a home and bit o' land o' his own."

"And what happens when Joseph has a son of his own, Mr. Finnerty?" Patrick asked. "Will that little plot of land be divided once more when that child weds and needs a home and bit of land of his own?"

Finnerty's jaw tightened stubbornly. "You can't expect a man and his young wife to live with their parents. A man needs a home of his own and land to farm. I have enough land, so I gave it to my son."

"But it's not yours to give," Patrick reminded him. "You only rent this land from my father, and according to the terms of your rental agreement, you are not allowed to subdivide this land among any of your children."

The one called Joseph glared at Patrick. "This land belonged to us before the English—"

"Enough!" his father snapped, cutting him off before he could get himself into trouble. Then Finnerty looked up at Patrick. "What would your father do if he couldn't leave his land to his son?"

Patrick wanted to tell them that he understood their need to pass on something to future generations of their family, but he knew if he expressed sympathy, they would mistake it for weakness and try to wheedle him into allowing the subdivision to remain. And, as Patrick knew from previous years, this would be disastrous for future farmers and for the ultimate survival of Rookforest itself.

So he was purposely heartless. "You can't compare them. My father owns the land, and can do whatever he pleases with it. You only rent the land and must abide by our agreement."

"It's not right!" Finnerty grumbled, his florid face turning white with frustration and rage.

"It's the law," Patrick replied, scowling. He shortened the reins, causing Gallowglass to toss his head and dance in place. "You have two weeks to take the cottage down."

Suddenly Patrick saw the two sons exchange glances as if passing a signal between them. "I would think twice before doing anything rash, gentlemen," he said coldly. "You harm me, and my father will see that you swing for it."

The men glowered at him, their anger barely contained. Patrick could read the white-hot rage in their eyes, and he knew they would've liked nothing better than to drag him from his saddle and beat him to jelly. But something restrained them. And then he learned what it was.

Unable to contain himself any longer, Joseph blurted out, "You just wait, yer honor. Yer time will come. Captain Moonlight will see to it."

And without another word or a backward glance, the three of them turned and walked away.

When Patrick returned to Rookforest, he found his father in his study, seated behind his neat desk.

"Well?" Cadogan said, looking up.

Patrick seated himself across from his father's desk and took Mr. O'Malley out of his pocket, ignoring Cadogan's look of disapproval. "You were right, Father. The Finnertys—"

"Hang the Finnertys. Did Fenella agree to come to dinner?"

Patrick felt his eyes widen in surprise. One of his father's tenants was blithely disregarding his rental agreement and Cadogan Quinn's major concern was Fenella Considine's presence at dinner?

"Yes, she has agreed to come."

A look of profound relief passed across Cadogan's features, and he rose. "Glad to hear it. How did she look?"

Patrick caught the mouse's eye and shrugged. He said to Cadogan, "She looked sad, though she tried her best to be cheerful. I would suspect she misses her father very much."

Cadogan clasped his hands behind his back and stared

out the window. "She needs to be with people. Can't stay cooped up in the house all by herself."

"She is in mourning. As you know, people usually don't accept social invitations at such times."

His father shot him a look that plainly said he was beyond such meaningless conventions.

Patrick stroked Mr. O'Malley's back gently with his forefinger, trying to choose his next words carefully, lest he infuriate his father. But in the end, all he could blurt out was, "Are you in love with Fenella?"

Cadogan cleared his throat, then turned back to his desk, where he straightened out some papers that were already in order before seating himself. He looked as embarrassed and uncomfortable as Patrick felt for asking such a personal question.

"You know me, son. I'm a plain-speaking man. I'm not a poet full of fancy words. But yes, I . . . I love Fenella." Then he turned beet red and looked away, as though there were something unseemly about a man discussing the softer emotions with his son.

"And does she love you?" Patrick asked, and held his breath.

Mr. O'Malley scampered up his sleeve and stood attentively on his shoulder as if absorbed in this conversation as well.

Cadogan said, "I don't know. I haven't told her I love her."

Patrick breathed an inaudible sigh of relief. He still had time to stop this folly before it went too far.

"Surely she must sense how you feel about her."

His father shrugged. "I never was any good at reading a lady's thoughts, you know that. Except your mother. She knew we were going to get married without my even asking her."

Patrick smiled wryly. "Somehow, I don't think Miss Considine is like that. You'll have to tell her you love her, Father, and find out if she loves you before you ask her to marry you." Then he waited, and held his breath, half-fearing his father's reply.

"Well, I do want to marry her."

Patrick tried to hide his disappointment. "Do you think she will accept you?"

"Don't know. I am old enough to be her father. I'm not the dashing, romantic sort most women like, but Fenella is a practical girl. She knows I'd be a good husband to her. I'm a wealthy man, so she'd never have to want. Besides," he added, "I'm not as young as I once was. I need a companion for my old age."

Patrick, who had once been romantic enough to throw away four years of his life for the woman he loved, found his father's pragmatism on the matters of love and marriage distasteful and cold-blooded.

Now Cadogan was eyeing him strangely. "You don't have to worry about Fenella taking your mother's place. Moira will always be my first love and hold a special place in my heart. What I feel for the girl is different. And you're still my heir. Any children that may follow will not be entitled to Rookforest."

Children! Patrick hadn't even thought of that possibility, and he found the thought of stepbrothers and sisters oddly disturbing. But he hid his emotions behind a quick smile. "You rogue, Father."

Cadogan grinned.

"I wish you all the luck with the lady. When do you intend to ask her to marry you?"

Cadogan leaned back in his chair, laced his fingers behind his head, and stared at the ceiling. "She just lost her beloved papa, so I don't want to rush her. She'll want to observe a year of mourning. But when that's over . . ."

"I'll have a stepmama," Patrick said lightly, though he was seething inside. A new young stepmama to bear a brood of sniveling, envious stepbrothers.

"Hopefully." Suddenly his father was all business. "Enough talk of weddings and stepmamas. What did you find out at Finnerty's farm today? Is it true he subdivided his land?"

Patrick nodded, relieved to be off the topic of Fenella, and related all that had happened that afternoon, while Cadogan listened attentively. When Patrick finished, his father rose to his feet and began pacing the study.

"Hang 'em!" he swore. "I can't allow Finnerty to get away with it."

Patrick sighed. "I can almost sympathize with him. He wants to hand down something to his sons."

"Hmph. If they have their way, every estate in Ireland will be divided and subdivided and subdivided again until we'll all be living on the head of a pin." He shook his head emphatically. "Can't let that happen."

Patrick nodded ruefully. "It would be just like the eighteenth century all over again."

"Exactly. That's why rental agreements today prohibit subdividing. Took my father years to get rid of all the middlemen and farmers with their long-term leases. Now we're going to go back to that?"

Patrick took Mr. O'Malley and put the mouse back in his breast pocket. Then he looked at his father. "There's something else you should know. Old Francis and his two sons were most defiant toward me today."

Cadogan turned a furious shade of red. "They attacked you?"

"Nothing like that. But I sensed the boys would have liked to pound me into the dirt."

"Insolent dogs!"

"I sensed a change in their manner, Father, and I think you should be aware of it. With the Land League's talk of giving back the land to the Irish, and Captain Moonlight terrorizing the countryside, I think we could have a fight on our hands. The farmers aren't deferential to us anymore. They're becoming bold."

"Don't know their place. Well, if they want a fight from Cadogan Quinn, they'll get one."

Patrick stared at his father. "What do you intend to do?"

Cadogan leaned over his desk. "If the cottage isn't down in two weeks, I'm going to evict the Finnertys. Make an example of them."

Patrick said nothing.

9

FENELLA WAS AWAKENED by the sound of screaming.

Bolting out of bed, she flew to the window and looked down. There was Dierdre, her maid-of-all-work, slowly backing away from the front door as if she had seen a ghost.

Opening the window, Fenella called down, "Dierdre! Whatever is the matter?"

The maid looked up, and Fenella started at the abject terror she saw written on that pale, round face. "Oh, miss!" Dierdre wailed, wringing her hands in her apron. "It's horrible! Ye must come down and see."

"I'll be right down."

Slipping on her dressing gown as she hurried downstairs, Fenella wondered what on earth could have frightened Dierdre so. She found out the moment she opened the front door and almost stepped onto the stoop. Fenella stopped herself just in time.

There lay the body of what had been a large black rook before its head was severed. That was lying a foot away in a pool of its own blood.

Fenella grimaced as she swept the skirt of her dressing gown aside. "Dear Lord, how disgusting!" Then her disgust rapidly turned to anger as she considered the full ramifications of the dead bird.

"Dierdre, don't stand there quaking in your shoes. A strapping country girl like you has certainly seen a dead bird before."

Dierdre began to wring her hands nervously. "Sure 'n I've seen dead birds before, miss, but never like this, with their heads cut off on purpose and left on somebody's doorstep."

"It was probably put there by some of the village boys

who think it's amusing to frighten a woman living alone."
But even as she dismissed the incident with such a glib
excuse, Fenella felt a small shiver of fear skitter up her
arms.

Dierdre wasn't fooled either. "Oh miss," she said,
gathering her skirts to step daintily around the stoop as
she came inside, "what if it wasn't village boys who done
this? What if"—she lowered her voice to a whisper and
glanced nervously around—"it was moonlighters, sent as
a warning like?"

Fenella closed the door behind her. "And what would
the moonlighters be warning me of, Dierdre? I am a simple woman who minds her own affairs, and I am certainly
no threat to them."

The maid looked decidedly uncomfortable. "They
know yer friendly with the Quinns, miss."

"And this displeases them, does it?"

"So I've heard, miss."

Fenella's eyes narrowed suspiciously. "What exactly
have you heard, Dierdre?"

The maid shrugged and shuffled her feet. "Oh, a bit
here and a bit there, miss. Just village gossip, nothin'
more."

Fenella put her hand on the girl's shoulder, forcing her
to look up and meet her gaze. "Dierdre, you've worked
for me ever since my . . . my father and I came to Mallow. We've always treated you well, haven't we?"

The girl nodded. "Oh, yes, miss. You 'n the doctor
have always been kindness itself to me, kindness itself."

"Well, then, you could return that kindness by telling
me what you have heard."

Dierdre's eyes darted around the parlor as if she suspected the furniture of spying for the moonlighters. "Ye
know how much regard I have for ye, miss," she began,
"but I can't tell ye more than that. All I know is the
moonlighters don't take kindly to those that are too
friendly with the landlords and estate agents. That's anyone, not just yerself, miss."

Fenella's hand fell away. "I see."

"No, miss, I don't think ye do!" Dierdre cried desperately, her voice rising with fear. "Captain Moonlight
is everywhere. If he was to find out I talked to ye, said

anything at all, I'd be carded, or worse.'' She clapped her hand over her mouth and mumbled, ''I said too much as it is.''

Fenella knew she wasn't going to get any more out of the recalcitrant and frightened Dierdre, so she sighed and said, ''I understand, Dierdre, truly I do. Why don't you put that poor bird in a sack and bury it somewhere, then wash off the stoop.''

''Yes, miss.'' Dierdre bobbed her head in relief and rushed off toward the kitchen, evidently finding disposing of a dead bird preferable to enduring Fenella's questions.

As Fenella went back upstairs to wash and dress, she thought about what Dierdre had said and the terror in her eyes when she spoke of Captain Moonlight as if he were some omnipotent being rather than a band of mere mortals. But that's exactly what these men wanted. By striking terror into the hearts of the common folk, like Dierdre, no one would dream of defying them.

No one except Fenella Considine.

''How dare they think they can intimidate me!'' she muttered as she sat before the mirror and twisted her heavy hair into a simple knot. ''I shall be friends with whomever I please.''

But in spite of her defiant attitude, Fenella realized she was in a very vulnerable position. Her father was gone. She lived alone now, with no man around to protect her, and her nearest neighbor three miles away. Last night, she hadn't even heard a sound when the dead rook was deposited on her doorstep. Not a sound. How simple it would be for the band of moonlighters to break into her house one night and . . .

She snapped her eyes shut and banished the thought from her mind. She wouldn't give them the satisfaction of frightening her.

Later, as Fenella sat in the kitchen and ate her breakfast of hot buttered bannocks and strong red tea, she recalled Mrs. Janeaway's visit and something that obnoxious woman had said about everyone being called upon to choose sides.

Was Fenella being singled out because her father was once so prominent in the community? After all, if the doctor's daughter suddenly had nothing to do with the Quinns, perhaps others would follow her lead.

Her smile was hard and determined as she drained her teacup. Fenella Considine was not going to be a pawn in anyone's game.

As she rose and got ready to go into Mallow, little did she realize that remaining neutral was going to be more difficult than she imagined.

Anyone in Mallow could have been a moonlighter.

As Fenella walked down the main street, farmers and their sons who knew her wished her a good day as they tipped their caps respectfully. She looked deeply into their eyes each time, hoping to see any sign of guilt written there, but if any of them were responsible for trying to frighten her into submission, they had schooled their faces well not to betray them.

It sickened her to think that people who had known her and her father for three years—people he had healed and cared for without asking a shilling in return—could turn upon her now. Well, all she could do was show them that Fenella Considine would not submit to their bullying tactics.

An hour later, Fenella had finished making all of her purchases and was about to climb into her dogcart, when a deep masculine voice called her name. Turning, she came face-to-face with St. John Standon and his sister.

They were a beautiful pair, as well-matched as the spirited, high-stepping blacks that pulled their carriage. St. John looked dashing and suave in a finely tailored black frock coat that fitted his form to perfection and accented his masculine beauty. His sister had put away mourning and was attired in a walking ensemble that could have only come from Paris, the blue-violet material matching her unusual eyes.

"Mr. Standon," Fenella murmured politely, though a trifle coolly.

"Ah," he said contritely as he swept off his silk top hat, "you still have not forgiven me for the drubbing I gave Quinn." But his eyes betrayed his true feelings by sparkling with mirth.

She caught the sharp glance his sister gave him at the

mention of a fight. Fenella said, "I'm sure my opinion of your conduct is of scant importance, Mr. Standon."

He spared himself from commenting further by saying, "Do forgive me for my rudeness, Miss Considine. I don't believe you have ever met my sister, Lady Eastbrook."

"I have seen you in church, of course," Fenella said, "but no, we have never met."

"Then allow me to present Cynara Eastbrook. Cynara, this is Fenella Considine, the late Dr. Considine's daughter."

"How do you do, Miss Considine?" Cynara said in her low, breathy voice.

"Lady Eastbrook," Fenella responded with a brief nod of her head. "I trust you are enjoying your stay in Ireland?"

With another glance at her brother, she said, "It is most . . . agreeable."

Fenella was just about to make her excuses and leave, for she felt ill-at-ease in the company of the Standons, when Cynara said, "Would you mind accompanying me into Mrs. Burrage's dress shop, Miss Considine?" She glanced up at her brother again. "I need several items of an intimate nature and St. John does so detest sitting there while I shop."

Fenella was so taken by surprise at the request that she couldn't very well refuse gracefully. "Very well, Lady Eastbrook."

St. John swooped down and claimed Fenella's hand, bowing extravagantly over it. "Thank you, Miss Considine. You have just spared me from a fate worse than death." Then he turned to his sister. "I shall give you one-half hour, and then I'm leaving. You shall have to walk back to Drumlow."

"I promise I shan't tarry," Cynara said with a smile; then she adjusted her frilly parasol and started down the street.

As Fenella fell into step beside the other woman, she found herself wondering why she, a mere doctor's daughter with no social pretensions, had been singled out for the pleasure of Cynara Eastbrook's elegant company. She found out at once.

Cynara glanced at her from beneath a thick fringe of

sooty black eyelashes. "I suspect you are wondering why I have sought your company, Miss Considine."

"The thought had occurred to me, Lady Eastbrook."

"To put it simply, I need a friend."

That confession took Fenella aback, and her brows arched in surprise. "But a woman of your position must have many friends, Lady Eastbrook."

"Ah, acquaintances, yes, but true friends, no," Cynara replied with a tragic smile. "When one is beautiful and wealthy, Miss Considine, one inspires envy more than friendship, and I'm afraid this is especially true of me." She sighed then, a small, heartrending sound.

"When I became the Marchioness of Eastbrook, everyone courted me. But when my . . . my fortunes changed and I had to return to Ireland . . . well, people court me now only to gloat at my misfortune."

"Surely that can't be true," Fenella said.

Cynara shook her head. "Oh, yes, it can, Miss Considine. The few invitations that I did accept were disastrous. All people wanted to do was gossip and stare at me. As a result, I no longer accept invitations, though my brother has urged me to do so." She sighed again. "I am very lonely for female companionship, Miss Considine. I long to chatter with another woman about, oh, all those things our sex enjoys chatting about."

Fenella felt her cheeks grow pink. "But, Lady Eastbrook, I am a doctor's daughter. We hardly move in the same social circles."

"That may be true, Miss Considine, but believe me when I tell you that it does not matter one iota to me. I have heard many fine testaments to your character. You have been praised for your honesty, kindness, and generosity. I am extending the hand of friendship, and hope that you will accept it."

Fenella cleared her throat. "You have placed me in an awkward position, Lady Eastbrook. If you have heard anything about me at all, then you know that I am very good friends with the Quinns."

Something like disappointment flashed in the violet depths of her eyes. "Ah, I see. You are afraid that a friendship with me would strain the loyalty you feel toward the Quinns."

"Quite frankly, yes."

Her exquisite voice quavered as she said, "Well, I can certainly understand that. The Quinns bear my family a great deal of ill will, much of it justified, I'm afraid."

That surprised Fenella. She hadn't expected Cynara to take the blame for what had happened between her and Patrick.

By this time, they had arrived at Mrs. Burrage's. Cynara stopped and turned a brave face toward Fenella. "I can certainly understand your reluctance to form any sort of *parti* with me, Miss Considine." Suddenly she reached into her handbag, pulled out her card, and handed it to Fenella. "I have no desire to come between you and the Quinns. However, should you change your mind, please feel free to call upon me at Drumlow at any time. I would be most grateful of the company."

Then she bade Fenella good day with one of her sad, lost smiles, and disappeared into the dress shop, leaving a subtle trace of her exotic perfume lingering in the air.

When Fenella was back in her cozy parlor, she took Cynara's card out of her own handbag and stared at its embossed lettering for the longest time, wondering what she would do.

The following morning, Fenella awoke to find each and every flower in her garden with its blossoms cut off, their colorful heads scattered crazily on the ground.

When the initial shock had worn off, she muttered, "Cowards," and fought back tears of anger and frustration as she picked up the blossoms and threw them away, leaving a garden of only bald stems and leaves.

The day after that, a tearful Dierdre told Fenella that she could no longer come to work for her. She gave no reason, but she didn't have to. Fenella already knew why: her friendship with the Quinns had offended the almighty Captain Moonlight, and she was being made an example of to those who would defy him.

Fenella eased Dierdre's conscience by telling her she couldn't have afforded her services much longer anyway, and the moment the maid left, Fenella harnessed the pony herself and headed for Rookforest.

* * *

When Fenella stepped into the foyer, Mrs. Ryan took one look at her and said, "Arragh, Miss Considine, what has happened? Yer as pale as a ghost and shakin' like a sapling in a gale."

"Where is Master Cadogan, Mrs. Ryan?" Fenella asked, twisting her fingers together to keep them from trembling. "I know these aren't exactly calling hours, but it's most important that I see him at once."

"Don't ye worry none about callin' hours," the old lady replied warmly, patting Fenella on the hand. "The master would receive ye anytime, day or night, he's that fond of ye. Right now, they be all havin' breakfast, so if ye'll just follow me . . ." She started off down the corridor in her long, sure stride.

When the diminutive housekeeper reached the dining room, she flung open the double mahogany doors and nodded to Fenella to go inside.

Cadogan, Patrick, and Margaret were all seated around the table, having their breakfast, and all three started with surprise when Fenella strode into the room.

"Please forgive me for intruding at such an ungodly hour . . ." Fenella began.

Cadogan was on his feet in an instant. "Don't apologize. You're always welcome here."

Patrick, who had also risen, was the first to notice her distress. "Fenella, what's wrong?"

She gratefully slipped into the chair that Cadogan held out for her. "I . . . I think I am being threatened by moonlighters."

Margaret gasped in surprise and exchanged looks with Patrick, while Cadogan's thick brows came together in an implacable scowl and he barked, "Hang it, what have they done to you?"

In a halting voice Fenella told them about the dead rook on her doorstep and the wanton vandalism that had been done to her garden just yesterday.

"Cowards!" Cadogan muttered savagely under his breath as he flung himself down in his chair. "Picking on a defenseless woman . . ."

Margaret made no comment, and Fenella was outraged to see the corners of Patrick's mouth quiver with suppressed laughter.

"I'm afraid I fail to see the humor in my situation," Fenella said stiffly, glaring at him.

Patrick dabbed at his lips with his napkin and his voice was patronizing. "Judging from the types of atrocities committed by these moonlighters in the past, killing a rook and vandalizing flowers seem mere childish pranks by comparison." He leaned back in his seat. "Are you sure some rude boys aren't your culprits?"

"I must admit that the thought had occurred to me," Fenella said. "Since my father died, I do live alone, and am fair game for the more rowdy village boys who might think it amusing to harass me.

"But I find it rather a coincidence that these outrages occurred right after I was visited by Mrs. Janeaway of the Land League, who tried to recruit me for her cause, but failed. And I also find it rather a coincidence that my maid-of-all-work, who has worked without complaint for the past three years, informed me just an hour ago that she is leaving my employ."

Margaret shrugged. "There are many reasons why servants leave a particular position. Perhaps she is going to work for higher wages for someone else."

Fenella turned to her. "Then why didn't she tell me so? Dierdre was most evasive when I pressed her, and seemed frightened."

"You think the moonlighters warned her off," Cadogan said, passing her a cup of tea.

Fenella nodded.

"But what reason would they have for singling you out?" Patrick demanded, his expression skeptical. "The moonlighters have attacked land grabbers and farmers, not defenseless women living alone."

"Yes," Margaret agreed. "It doesn't seem logical to me. Your father was well-loved in Mallow. Everyone respected him. Why should they want to harm his daughter?"

Fenella shook her head. "I have racked my brain, and I cannot resolve it either. None of this makes any sense."

Cadogan cleared his throat. "Hang it, Fenella, you can't stay there alone. It's too dangerous. I want you to move here to Rookforest."

She smiled at him. "Thank you for offering, Cadogan, but I'm afraid I can't accept."

"Why not?"

She lifted her chin resolutely. "I'll not give the moon-lighters the satisfaction of driving me out of my home."

"Courage is an admirable quality," Cadogan said, "but in this case, I think you're being foolhardy."

Fenella gave him a gentle smile. "We've had this discussion once before, my friend, and my answer is still the same."

"Damn if you aren't the stubbornest woman I've ever met," Cadogan said, but there was a glint of admiration in his eyes as he said it. He added, "At least let me send one of our girls to replace the maid you lost."

"That would be greatly appreciated," Fenella said.

"Perhaps she could live in," Margaret suggested, "so you wouldn't be alone."

"And I'm sure Constable Treherne could provide you with police protection," Patrick added, "or at least a man to watch your house at night."

Fenella smiled wanly as she looked around the table. "Thank you all. I feel better already, having talked to you."

As she rose to leave, Cadogan rose with her. "Hang it, we're friends, aren't we? Friends help each other in troubled times." He crooked his arm and extended it to Fenella. "May I walk with you?"

"Of course," Fenella replied, and after bidding Patrick and Margaret good day, she departed with Cadogan.

Patrick stared moodily after them, his eyes narrowing in speculation as Fenella and his father disappeared through the double doors.

"Well, Pat," Margaret began, tossing her hair over her shoulder, "I can tell by that dark scowl clouding your brow that you doubt Miss Considine's story."

His crooked grin was cynical and dry. "Ah, perceptive as always, Meggie-of-the-moor."

She raised one thin brow. "So you don't think moon-lighters are terrorizing her?"

"Why? Why would they choose a harmless spinster living alone, especially the daughter of a man who was practically a saint to these farmers?" Patrick leaned back in his chair and folded his arms. "Wasn't she a picture, Meggie, bursting in here all teary-eyed and distraught? And didn't Father just rush to comfort her?"

"You think this was all an act on Fenella's part to ensnare Uncle Cadogan?" Her voice rose in mild surprise.

"Don't you?"

Margaret shook her head. "My jaded, cynical cousin, you think all women are as devious as Cynara Standon, don't you?"

The truth hurt, but he hid it easily behind an uncaring facade. "Jaded? Cynical? No, dear cousin. Merely realistic."

Then he rose and bade her good day.

Outside Rookforest's gates, half-hidden by a long row of thick, concealing shrubbery, a lone figure watched and waited.

Suddenly his patience was rewarded. The wrought-iron gates swung silently open and a dogcart driven by a woman moved through and turned right. She kept her eyes straight ahead, never seeing him, never even suspecting him of being only ten feet away.

He watched until the dogcart disappeared around a bend in the road, then cursed roundly under his breath and stepped boldly from his cover. So, she persisted in defying them, even though she had been warned and warned again.

The time for generosity and warnings had passed. Fenella Considine had to be taught a hard lesson she would never forget. And Captain Moonlight would be her teacher.

He turned and went striding down the road.

When Fenella returned to Rookforest that Friday evening for dinner, she sensed an air of ambivalence at once. Only Cadogan and Lord Nayland seemed genuinely pleased to see her.

As she entered the drawing room, Lord Nayland rose at once and bowed over her hand. "It's delightful to see you again, Miss Considine," he said, his smile warm and welcoming. "I know it's been a difficult time for you, since the loss of your father, but I think it'll do you a world of good to be out among friends.''

"I'll drink to that," Cadogan said, and went to pour Fenella a sherry.

Margaret, who looked lovely in a low-cut gown of peach-colored shot silk dripping with Carrickmacross lace, seemed unusually dour and didn't even smile when Fenella greeted her, though her words were politeness itself.

And as for Patrick . . . He was standing before one of the long windows, one hand parting the curtains so he could look out at something that absorbed his interest more than Fenella's entrance. The dying daylight brought out the blue-black sheen of his dark hair and illuminated his closed, brooding expression. He looked the epitome of elegance tonight in his black evening attire, with its snowy expanse of shirtfront. But Fenella sensed a distinct chill emanating from his distinguished personage, and she shivered in spite of the room's warmth when Patrick simply nodded to acknowledge her presence.

What have I done to offend him this time? she wondered to herself as she sat down on the divan. She could feel his hard blue eyes boring into her back.

But she had little time to spare for Patrick or Margaret because Cadogan was handing her a glass of sherry and asking, "No more rooks on your doorstep?"

Fenella shook her head. "No, thank God. And thank you for sending Lily to keep me company."

Not only did the large, tall maid ease Fenella's fears, Lily was surprisingly adept as a lady's maid, her thick, blunt fingers agilely coaxing Fenella's heavy, unruly hair into the dignified coronet she wore tonight.

"My pleasure," Cadogan said, beaming.

Lord Nayland shook his head. "These moonlighters . . .''

"Doesn't anyone know who they are?" Fenella asked.

Patrick let the curtain drop and sauntered over to his favorite place by the mantel. "If we knew that," he drawled, "they'd all be in jail or swinging from a rope."

After giving his son an odd look, Cadogan said, "Had any trouble yourself, Nayland?"

The young lord removed his spectacles and rubbed his

eyes. "I've been able to reduce all of my tenants' rents, but now some of them are refusing to pay them altogether. I can hold out for a while because my English estates are profitable, but sooner or later I am going to have to evict some tenants."

"I'm sure I'll have to evict Francis Finnerty," Cadogan announced.

Margaret's eyes widened and she turned pale. "Oh, Uncle Cadogan! The Finnertys have farmed that land for as long as I can remember. You wouldn't evict them now, not when the harvests have been so bad."

"Can't be helped, niece. Finnerty subdivided his land against our agreement, and he's refused to put it to rights. I have to evict and make an example of him."

Now high color infused Margaret's pale cheeks. "Have you ever stopped to consider what your tenants are going through? Do you ever think that perhaps they are only trying to do what they can to survive?"

This little speech took everyone aback, especially Cadogan.

"Just whose side are you on, niece?" he growled.

She rose and tossed her head, her eyes flashing the bright fires of rebellion. "I'm on the side of fairness and justice, Uncle Cadogan. I know we are landlords and depend on the rents for our livelihood—"

"Amen to that!"

"—but I think we should make an attempt to put ourselves in our tenants' shoes."

Cadogan tossed down his whiskey in one swallow and glared at her. "What foolishness is this, Margaret? What Irish rebel have you been listening to?"

"Am I not allowed to have any opinions of my own?" she demanded hotly. "Must I only parrot whatever you and Lord Nayland say?"

Fenella decided it was time to intervene before matters worsened. Rising and fanning her face with one hand, she said, "I'm feeling a trifle warm. Margaret, perhaps you'd like to show me the gardens. It's such a lovely evening for a stroll."

"Yes," Margaret agreed. "The air has become quite stifling in here."

She went flouncing off in a rustle of peach silk, leaving Fenella hurrying to keep up.

Outside, the late-summer twilight was beginning to surrender to the encroaching darkness, the sky a pale blue over the treetops. Overhead, rooks by the hundreds filled the sky as they returned home to roost, their raucous cries dwindling as they settled themselves in the branches for the night.

Strolling silently by Margaret's side through the garden, Fenella noticed that while the flowers were closed tightly for the night, their faint perfume lingered pleasantly, underscoring the stronger scents of damp earth and newly mown grass.

She breathed deeply, feeling utterly content for the first time since her father had died. Here, behind Rookforest's high walls, she felt safe. Rooks filled the trees, not lying dead on her doorstep, and the flowers weren't mutilated. Captain Moonlight and the wanton destruction he spread couldn't touch her here.

Suddenly Margaret said, "You're going to tell my uncle about Terrence, aren't you?"

"I was hoping I wouldn't have to," Fenella replied. "I thought you yourself would have told him by now."

Relief shone in the younger woman's eyes. "Thank you, Fenella. You don't know how much your silence means to me."

So, Margaret had no intention of telling Cadogan after all.

Dismayed, Fenella said, "I don't know how long I can keep silent about it, Margaret. Every moment that goes by, I feel as though I'm being disloyal to your uncle. He has been kindness itself to me, and I owe him more than I can ever hope to repay. Keeping silent is tantamount to lying."

Margaret, however, was concerned only with herself. "But you promised!"

Fenella decided to try to reason with this headstrong young woman who was making her feel so old.

"Margaret, have you ever stopped to consider how dangerous this liaison of yours is?"

"Dangerous? Don't be preposterous! Terrence loves me. He wouldn't hurt me for the world!"

"Good God, are you blind?" Fenella snapped, losing all patience at last. "Haven't you seen what has been happening around you? The farmers are preparing to war with the landlords. You and your Terrence are on opposite sides, my dear, in case you hadn't noticed."

No one outside her family had ever spoken to Margaret so sharply before, and she showed her displeasure by looking down her slim, aristocratic nose at Fenella. "Patrick was right about you. You're just a priggish spinster who couldn't possibly understand a love like the one Terrence and I share."

The words stung Fenella as sharply as if Margaret had slapped her in the face. Patrick had said that about her? And she had thought he was beginning to like her. Fenella felt absurd tears prick the backs of her eyes, but she fought them down, for she would not give Margaret the satisfaction of knowing she had wounded her pride.

Margaret went on with, "Our love is so great it can overcome any obstacles."

Oh, you poor spoiled darling, Fenella thought. She said, "Ah, I see. You intend to trade all this"—she swept her arm in a wide arch that encompassed the house and grounds—"for Terrence's three-room cottage, and your fine silks for rough homespun?"

"Perhaps in the beginning, once we marry," Margaret conceded, "but then we shall immigrate to America or Australia, where there are more opportunities for a man like Terrence to make his fortune. And he will, you know. Terrence is intelligent and very ambitious. And one day, we will return to Ireland in triumph."

"I see."

Actually, Fenella saw all too clearly. Terrence would seduce Margaret, if he hadn't already, then demand more land from Cadogan or a handsome bribe to leave Ireland forever, without the millstone of a spoiled, pregnant wife around his neck. And Margaret was too blind to see it.

Fenella sighed. She shouldn't be too quick to judge the girl, for she herself had once known such all-consuming passion with her own William. And look what that had led to. . . .

Margaret stopped and clutched at Fenella's arm. "So you won't tell Uncle Cadogan?"

"Margaret, I can't make any more promises."

Something like hatred flared in the depths of her eyes, and her lips tightened into a thin, hard line. "I wouldn't tell him, if I were you. You could be very, very sorry."

The threat was so unexpected and so casually uttered that it took Fenella by surprise and hung heavily in the air like the dampness rising from the ground. Fenella thought of the dead rook, her mutilated garden, and her own vulnerability, and she shivered.

Because it was not in her nature to capitulate so easily, she squared her shoulders and said, "I don't take kindly to threats, Margaret."

The girl just smiled and started to glide away down the garden path, her smug, self-satisfied voice floating back. "Well, I would take this one seriously, if I were you."

Suddenly Rookforest didn't seem like such a safe haven from the outside world. The rooks were silent, as if watching and listening, and the shadows had lengthened and fallen heavily on the lawn.

Fenella followed Margaret's rapidly retreating figure back inside.

Dinner was an unpleasant, uncomfortable meal for everyone, and Fenella was glad when it was finally over.

By pleading a headache, she successfully avoided having to be alone with Margaret while the men were served their brandy and cigars.

To Fenella's astonishment, when they were all assembled in the foyer and Cadogan was just about to send for the carriage to take her home, Patrick said, "I'll escort Fenella home tonight, if you don't mind, Father."

" 'Course not," Cadogan replied, and he sent the butler for Fenella's wrap.

She could hardly refuse Patrick's offer, even if she were still smarting with the new knowledge of what he really thought of her. So, after saying good night to everyone, she just smiled politely when he slipped the wool shawl around her shoulders and escorted her outside to where a dogcart was waiting.

It was a clear and cloudless night, complete with a spattering of shining stars and a pale full moon hanging low like a great wheel of cheese in the sky. But to Fe-

nella, seated beside Patrick as the dogcart made its way
down the drive, such a night was more menacing than
beautiful. She found herself shaking uncontrollably.

"Cold?"

The sound of his voice made her jump. "No," she
replied honestly. "Afraid."

Patrick turned his head toward her, and she could see
his teeth flash white in the moonlight as he grinned.
"With such a brave specimen as myself to escort you? I
should be offended that you doubt my ability to protect
you. I'm not the same weakling who was just released
from prison, you know."

The words "priggish spinster" still rankled, and Fenella ignored his easy bantering tone. She sighed. "I
used to enjoy a moonlit night once. My fiancé and I used
to go strolling in the moonlight on a warm summer's
night. Sometimes we'd even go down to the ocean and
walk along the shore, listening to the waves break against
the rocks. So peaceful. But now, a moonlit night means
Captain Moonlight will be abroad, spreading terror in his
wake."

Patrick stared straight ahead. "What was he like, your
fiancé?"

She had only mentioned William to let Patrick Quinn
know that a man had once found a priggish spinster attractive enough to want to marry her. His subsequent
interest startled her, all the more because it seemed genuine.

"He was the most wonderful man in the world," she
said simply. "He was strong and just and loved to laugh.
An honorable man."

"How did he die?"

It was my fault. If I hadn't desired him so much, if
I hadn't succumbed so willingly to pleasures of the
flesh . . .

When Patrick said nothing, she realized she had only
thought those damning words, not spoken them aloud.

"He . . . he died of pneumonia three years ago."

"I'm sorry."

"So am I. William was a good man, and intelligent,
one of the finest lawyers in the city of Cork. He had so

much to offer the world. He shouldn't have had his life cut off at such a young age.''

She rubbed the scar on her wrist. And he shouldn't have come back to curse her with the terrible burden of second sight.

"Life is often unfair, but you're still a young woman," Patrick said, keeping his eyes on the winding road ahead. "You'll find someone else."

"No," she replied with great finality.

Now he did turn to look at her, his pale blue eyes glittering in the moonlight, an air of tension about him. "No? There is no one whose suit you would accept?"

There was something in Patrick's voice that warned her, a note of desperation perhaps. And she saw with blinding clarity the direction this conversation was taking and why.

"You needn't worry, Patrick," she said coldly, moving perceptibly away from him so her sleeve no longer touched his. "I would not accept your father's proposal of marriage, even if he were to offer it to me tomorrow."

He started, as if she had somehow surprised him. Then he had the grace to look embarrassed. "Forgive me for insulting you, but I had to be certain."

"Be certain of what? That I am not the fortune hunter you think me?"

"I had to know your intentions," he said.

After all that had happened to her, being thought of as a fortune hunter by the insufferable Patrick Quinn was just too much for Fenella.

She twisted in her seat and glared at him. "And who are you to choose your father's wife, Mr. Quinn? As I recall, no one stopped you from making a fool of yourself over the woman of your choice."

Even in the moonlight, she could see his face darken with anger. But his voice was controlled as he said, "Eloquently put, Miss Considine. I most humbly offer my apologies for having misjudged you."

"I may be a priggish spinster, sir, but I am not without scruples, and marrying a wonderful, kind, decent man for his money is not anything I'd stoop to."

Patrick's eyes widened as he heard his own words hurled back at him and he caught the underlying pain in her voice. He suddenly felt miserable and ashamed for the things he had said about her.

"I've been wrong about you, Fenella," he said. When she made no comment, he added, "Can you find it in your heart to forgive me?"

At first, she only stared straight ahead, still filled with righteous anger and indignation. Then she thawed, and reluctantly nodded. "I think we can let bygones be bygones."

He grinned and shifted the reins to his left hand so he could extend his right to her. "Friends?"

Fenella shook it solemnly. "Friends."

Then she sat back and enjoyed the steady clopping of the horse's hooves and the sounds of the night. In a few minutes, her house would appear around the bend in the road and she would be home.

Just as they reached the widest part of the bend, she felt the scar on her wrist begin to grow warm and throb. Fenella sucked in her breath and clenched her hands together, desperately fighting down the waves of panic sweeping over her as she recognized the beginnings of yet another vision.

Why here? Why now? her frantic brain cried.

She looked at Patrick. His attention was focused on the road ahead as it turned. As soon as the dogcart rounded the bend, Fenella would be home.

She felt that queer dizziness, so she closed her eyes. What she saw when she opened them again almost caused her heart to stop.

Her house was on fire.

Bright tongues of orange flame came shooting out of all the windows, while a wall of it leapt to the sky and consumed the roof. Only the outer stone walls remained standing, like a shell whose insides had been gutted and devoured.

Fenella saw several shadowy figures running away.

It was a nightmare. She could hear the fire's greedy crackle and hiss, followed by the crashing of beams. She could feel the unbearable blistering heat, even from this distance, as the cart drew closer and closer. The acrid smell of smoke filled her nostrils, choking her. But she couldn't close her eyes or turn away from the horror of it. Not until the vision had run its course.

The end came quickly. Her lids came down, her head drooped. When she raised it again, her house was just as she had left it hours ago, quiet and dark. The flames were gone.

But this time, it had been all too real to Fenella. Without thinking, she grasped Patrick's arm. "Look! My house is on fire!"

Alarmed by her expression of wild-eyed terror as well as by her viselike grip on his arm, Patrick halted the horse in the middle of the road. He stared at the house. It stood there, dark and undisturbed in the moonlight. No smoke came billowing out of the windows, no flames shot into the air.

He looked at Fenella as though she had gone mad. "What are you saying? Your house is not on fire."

Her blank, unblinking stare didn't waver. Her lips twitched and she mumbled something that sounded suspiciously like, "But it will be."

Suddenly Patrick thought he heard the sound of glass breaking somewhere at the back of the house. He brought the reins down on the horse's rump, and the animal bolted forward with a snort. Within seconds they were at Fenella's front door.

Patrick looked at the upstairs windows, where flickering orange light now danced crazily. Fenella had been right: her house was on fire.

Patrick was on the verge of leaping out of the dogcart when he felt himself restrained by Fenella. "You mustn't go in there," she cried, her fingers biting into his arm. "You can't possibly fight it yourself. You will be killed."

"But what about Lily? She could be trapped in there."

"She's not there. I gave her the night off."

"Then we'll drive to Mallow for help," he said, "and pray we're not too late."

"Hang it, Fenella," Cadogan said as he rested his hand on her shoulder, "you've got to come to Rookforest now. There's nowhere else for you to go."

He was right. The dozens of men that had rushed from their nearby farms had worked valiantly for hours carrying buckets of water from the pond to save her house, but it was no use. The raging fire had had too great a head start. By the time Fenella and Patrick had arrived with help, the entire upper story had burned and caved in.

Now there was nothing left but a burnt-out shell beneath rising wisps of smoke as it smoldered in the moonlight.

Though Fenella's eyes and nose were smarting from the acrid smoke fouling the air, she was too numb to cry. She just stood there staring out of unblinking eyes, her arms crossed and her shawl pulled protectively around her like a cocoon, as one man after another gave up the fight and trudged home.

She stared at what had once been her home. "Gone . . ." she muttered. "Everything is gone. I've lost everything."

Patrick crossed the lawn, rolling down his shirtsleeves as he came. He looked exhausted, his face streaked and smudged with sweat and soot, for he had fought the fire as bravely as the others.

"We may as well go," he said wearily to his father. "There's nothing more we can do here."

Cadogan, who had come as soon as he had seen the brilliant orange sky, said, "You have to return to Rookforest this time, Fenella."

The moonlighters had won.

She was defeated, and she knew it. She acquiesced without argument and allowed him to lead her over to the carriage and assist her inside.

Fenella didn't so much as glance back as the carriage started on its way.

10

PATRICK AWOKE with the acrid smell of smoke still stinging his nostrils and the bitter taste of it coating his tongue. His eyes felt as raw as if someone had peeled them, and he had to squint against the feeble daylight trickling into his room.

He sat up in bed with a groan, his sore, aching muscles protesting every little movement. He felt bone-tired, as though he hadn't slept at all, and he knew why.

There was something very strange about the fire last night, odds and ends that just didn't fit together to form a satisfactory whole. It had been preying upon him with all the tenacity of a dog worrying a bone.

He shook his head to clear it, then rose to shut his bedroom door for privacy. After opening the curtains, he checked O'Malley's nest, and when he saw his compatriot was missing, the fire was momentarily forgotten in the ensuing panic.

Patrick whistled a few frantic low notes, then stood very still and waited. Within seconds, he was relieved to hear an answering squeak, and when he looked down, there was the mouse sitting at the big toe of his right foot.

He knelt down and scooped up O'Malley, feeling the familiar tug of kinship with his pet. "You mustn't go wandering off like that, my friend," he admonished him, "unless you want to become cats' meat."

The mouse retorted with a squeak of disbelief.

As Patrick washed and dressed under the benevolent eye of O'Malley, he kept running the sequence of last night's events over and over in his mind, trying to justify his reasons for thinking something had been amiss. But the answer danced beguilingly just out of reach, eluding him.

Just when he was about to give up, everything slid into place.

He could have sworn Fenella had said the house was on fire before there had been any sign of flames.

Patrick's hands stopped in the midst of buttoning his waistcoat, and he stared at his stunned reflection in the mirror. It was true. When she had gripped his arm and warned him about the fire, he distinctly remembered looking at the house. At that time, he could have sworn it was not in flames, but dark and empty. When he expressed his confusion and incredulity to Fenella, she mumbled some response, but for the life of him, he couldn't remember what she had said.

It wasn't until they raced up to the house that they saw the first faint dull orange glow of fire coming from the back rooms.

Patrick slowly buttoned the rest of his waistcoat, his shocked mind refusing to believe what logic told him to be true: Fenella had known all along that her house was going to burn down.

When Fenella awoke to find herself in a strange bed, in a strange room, she knew with a sinking heart that she had not dreamed the horrible events of the previous night.

She lay there as one dead, her limbs cold and wooden, her crushed, beaten spirit oblivious of the feminine elegance of her bedchamber, with its offensively cheerful pale yellow walls and delicate gilt-edged French furnishings. She had lost everything that had ever been dear to her—William, her father, and now her home—and for the first time in her life she had nothing left to live for. She was even too hollow inside for the blessed release of tears.

There came a soft knock on the door, but she was beyond caring who wanted to see her. When she didn't answer, the door opened of its own volition and Mrs. Ryan came tiptoeing in carrying a breakfast tray.

The housekeeper's kind, motherly face brightened when she saw Fenella lying there. "It's awake ye are," she said.

Even the woman's soft, lilting voice grated on Fenella's nerves, threatening to swell her self-pity into an ocean. She averted her face and said, "Please go away, Mrs. Ryan. I wish to be alone."

Ailagh of the Hundred Eyes saw much, so she was not offended by Fenella's brusqueness. She merely bustled right over and set the breakfast tray on the bedside table.

"It's a good breakfast ye need, Miss Considine," she said. "Good food always cures what ails ye. Some of Cook's currant bannocks straight from the oven, eggs, a lashing of bacon, and a pot o' tea. Food for the soul."

Then she swept around the room with hearty determination, drawing the curtains aside to let in the sunlight. "It's a beautiful day, that it is. Ye better be up and about to enjoy it. Ye never know when the clouds are goin' to come rollin' in again."

Fenella said, "Lately, my life has been filled with nothing but clouds, Mrs. Ryan, smothering black ones."

The housekeeper's face fell into more somber lines, and she came to stand by Fenella's bedside. "I know the pain yer feelin', miss, believe me, I do. When I was about yer age, I lost three of me children when our cottage burned down. Just babies, they were. But the Lord blessed us and gave us four more, only to have this lot of 'em die during the Great Hunger. Then, just when I thought it was all over, the good Lord sent me my Seamus." The berry-black eyes sparkled with sympathy. "So ye see, ye just never know what the Lord has planned for ye."

This was the first Fenella had ever heard of Mrs. Ryan's tragic past. She shook her head sadly. "However did you go on?"

"Mind ye, I'm not sayin' it wasn't hard, 'cause it was. Brutally hard. There were times I wanted to give up and die. But then I reminded meself that there are people on God's great earth that have more sufferin' heaped upon 'em than I, and I should count me blessings and get on with me life. Just be thankful ye or Lily weren't in that building when it burned."

Fenella took a great shuddering breath. "You shame me, Mrs. Ryan."

"Arragh, that was not my intention, miss," the house-keeper replied softly, "in tellin' ye me own tale of woe."

"I know what your intentions were, Mrs. Ryan, and I thank you for them." She smiled tremulously. "I think I'm ready for breakfast now."

Fenella sat up, while Mrs. Ryan arranged the pillows to support her back. Then the housekeeper stood back and said, "I've taken the liberty of havin' yer dress washed and ironed, so whenever ye're ready to see Master Cadogan, I'll send it up."

"Thank you, Mrs. Ryan."

The housekeeper smiled, then left.

When she was alone again, Fenella bravely tackled the food on the tray, but despite Mrs. Ryan's inspirational story, she found she lacked the inner strength to put her heartbreak behind her just yet. Tears scalded her eyes and blurred her vision, so that she finally had to put the tray aside.

But soon she found her tears of sorrow giving way to tears of fury. Who had done this to her, and why? The same people who had left the dead rook on her doorstep and ruined her garden, that's who. But why? That was the answer that kept eluding her.

And why hadn't the sight warned her of this catastrophe sooner? Perhaps she could have prevented it from ever happening.

Fenella rubbed her wrist, weary of searching for explanations that she was never going to find. After nibbling a bannock and drinking a cup of tea, she rose and rang for Mrs. Ryan.

Fenella found Cadogan in his study talking with Patrick.

Both men rose as she entered, but Cadogan came forward to take both her hands in his, fussing over her like a mother hen. "How are you this morning? Did you sleep well?"

She smiled wanly. "As well as can be expected, under the circumstances."

When she looked over at Patrick and bade him good morning, he returned her greeting somewhat distantly, then averted his eyes and fell silent. Disconcerted by his abrupt turnabout, Fenella turned to Cadogan and asked, "Do the police have any idea who could have done this?"

"Constable Treherne was here just a few minutes ago," he replied, leading her over to the solitary chair, "and he is of the opinion that the moonlighters were responsible."

Fenella's knees turned to water and she sank into the chair. "Moonlighters? But why?"

"Perhaps you could tell us," Patrick said.

There was something about the way he said it, his sonorous voice silky with underlying menace, that caused Fenella to look over at him in alarm. His stance might have been casual as he stood before the window with his hands clasped behind his back, but the air about him crackled with a certain predatory tension as he returned her look from beneath half-lowered lids.

Evidently Cadogan was oblivious of such undercurrents. "Have you done anything to anger the moonlighters?"

Fenella shrugged helplessly. "If I have, I'm unaware of it. My father always helped the farmers of Mallow. I can't understand why they are persecuting me."

"They shan't any longer," Cadogan said. "You're staying at Rookforest now."

For the first time since Cadogan had broached the subject of her coming to live at Rookforest, Fenella did not even offer a token resistance to the idea. He was right. She had nowhere else to go, except to an uncle in London she hadn't seen since childhood, and he would not welcome being burdened by some charity case of a strange relative. Now that she had lost her house, her meager savings wouldn't stretch far. Under the circumstances, all she could do was swallow her pride and accept Cadogan's generous offer gracefully.

Suddenly Patrick flicked an appraising glance at Fenella. "Since she will be staying at Rookforest, Father, she'll need new clothes. After all, everything she owned burned with the house last night."

Such a blatant reminder of her new status caused Fenella to turn crimson, but she would not give Patrick the satisfaction of humiliating her.

"I could wear Margaret's castoffs, if she has any old

clothes she can bear to part with," she said. "They can be altered to fit me."

Cadogan opened his mouth as if to say something, then changed his mind when he saw the martial glint in Fenella's eye. "What a splendid idea. I'll speak to Margaret about it."

After thanking Cadogan yet again for his generosity, Fenella pleaded a headache and asked to be excused. Much to her chagrin, Patrick followed her.

No sooner did the study door close behind them than he said, "There is something that has been puzzling me all morning, Fenella."

"Oh? And what is that?"

He looked down at her, his expression veiled and guarded. "If I remember the events of last night correctly, you told me your house was on fire some minutes before I actually saw a blaze." He drew closer, until the buttons on his frock coat almost brushed against her bodice. "Could you tell me why that was so?"

Fenella felt the fear uncoil like a viper in the pit of her stomach. He knew!

"You . . . you must be mistaken," she stammered, taking a step back. "I told you the house was on fire the moment I saw the flames."

"Far be it from me to contradict a lady, but I know what I saw. Your house was not on fire when you first told me it was. I distinctly remember accusing you of imagining it. In fact, I was quite mystified by your behavior at the time." He took a step forward. "So, my dear Miss Considine, it would appear that we have two conflicting stories here. And it brings up an interesting point. If you saw the fire before it was set, you must have known it was going to happen."

Fenella stared at him, dumbfounded. "That's preposterous! Why would I allow someone to burn down my own house?"

"I don't know," Patrick said, his voice flat and cold. "But I intend to find out."

Then he whirled on his heel and left her standing there, gaping after him.

* * *

Fenella closed her book, and watched the raindrops go skittering down the window glass. She sighed contentedly, feeling at peace for the first time in days.

During her first week at Rookforest, Fenella had felt like a guest who had overstayed her welcome. She was only really at ease with Cadogan, for Patrick had suddenly become her enemy and Margaret had ceased to be her friend, though she had willingly given Fenella many of her castoffs.

But during her second week, she put aside her pride and made up her mind that Patrick and Margaret weren't going to make her feel uncomfortable and awkward during her stay. She accepted Cadogan's offer for what it was, an attempt to help a friend in need and repay the debt he felt he owed her father.

She scowled as she watched the trees toss in the wind. Patrick worried her. He avoided her in private and only wore a mask of politeness in the presence of others, and Fenella sensed he was determined to learn her secret at all costs, the secret that could destroy her.

"He thinks I'm a fortune hunter," she murmured sadly. "If only I were merely that . . ."

Hearing the library door open, Fenella leaned forward to look around the wing of her chair, and was dismayed to see Patrick himself standing in the doorway as if her thoughts had conjured him. The black expression on his face didn't bode well for her.

"Patrick . . ." she murmured.

He glanced around the room to make sure they were alone, then closed the door with a decisive click and crossed the room with the easy gait of a panther stalking its prey. He stopped before her chair and looked down at her out of narrowed, menacing eyes.

"My, my, aren't we all cozy, the lady of the manor sitting in the library on a rainy day. It doesn't take much getting used to, does it, living in a house such as this, with servants at your beck and call to do those annoying domestic tasks you once had to do yourself?"

She took a deep breath to keep her hands from trembling as she looked up at him. "I don't know what I have done to offend you, but—"

"Don't insult my intelligence by feigning innocence,

my dear Miss Considine. You and I both know you have designs on my father. You want to marry him and live a life of luxury forevermore.''

"I have no intentions of marrying your father," Fenella said as calmly as she could, trying to keep her temper in check.

Patrick's smile was cold. " 'Methinks the lady doth protest too much,' as they say. No, my dear Miss Considine, I think you want very much to snare my father. In fact, I wouldn't be surprised if you paid someone to burn down your house. How fitting. My father always did have a weakness for a woman in distress.''

Fenella felt her jaw drop at the outrageousness of what Patrick was implying, and for a moment she was just too stunned to speak. But not for long. She felt the blood rush to her face as a red mist of fury gathered before her eyes.

She jumped to her feet. "I don't have to stay here and listen to your insults!''

"Sit down!" Patrick barked, taking a threatening step toward her. "You'll stay here until I'm finished speaking to you!''

Fenella obeyed reluctantly and sank back down into her chair, but she leaned forward on the edge, her hands grasping the arms, her curled fingers digging into the soft leather as though she were poised for flight.

"How dare you accuse me of such a heinous act!" she snapped. "I would never do such a thing. Never!''

Patrick placed his right hand on one of the chair's wings and leaned forward until his angry face was only inches from Fenella's. "Then how did you have advance knowledge that your house would burn?''

So it all came back to that. Even if Fenella told him the truth about her accursed second sight, she knew he would never believe her.

She looked him in the eye and lied glibly from long practice. "I did not have advance knowledge of the fire.''

Patrick flung himself away from her. "Liar!''

"I am telling the truth!''

"I know what I saw!" The vehemence of it was an affront to the quiet library. Then he became calmer, enunciating every word carefully, as if Fenella were a child. "That house was not on fire when you told me it was, so you must have had advance knowledge. And you had that knowledge because you yourself hired someone to burn it, knowing that if you were destitute, my father would offer you a home at Rookforest. Once here, you—"

"That's not true," Fenella insisted with a shake of her head.

But Patrick continued to badger her, and Fenella continued to deny his accusations as calmly as she could, though her resistance was weakening under the harsh verbal onslaught. Finally, when he saw he wasn't going to sway or break her, he gave up.

"Very well, Miss Considine, maintain your posture of innocence all you like. But I shall find out the truth eventually, never fear."

"I've told you the truth," she replied coldly, rising, and praying her knocking knees would support her weight. "You just choose not to believe it."

As she swept past Patrick, her head held high, his hand suddenly shot out and grasped her wrist. Fenella gasped in surprise and tried to pull away, but his long, strong fingers held her as securely as a manacle.

"Let go of me this instant!" Her heart was pounding so loudly, it equaled the ticking of the clock on the mantel.

"Not until I'm ready," he replied. Then he studied her raptly. "I don't know what my father sees in you. Oh, you've certainly got the abundant charms of a tavern wench," he said, his gaze lingering on her heaving breasts before returning to her face. "But you're as plain as a pikestaff, my dear Miss Considine, and my father has always had a weakness for pretty, lively women, not priggish spinsters."

Fenella raised her head. "Such an attack is unworthy of even you, Patrick."

A pale flush of color raced up his lean cheeks. Without warning, he jerked her arm, catching Fenella off balance and causing her to stumble forward. Before she had a chance to check herself and back away, Patrick had deftly caught her other wrist and swung both her hands behind her back, pulling her against him in a captive embrace.

It all happened so fast, Fenella didn't have time to react. She just stood there speechless, staring up into Patrick's eyes, wondering how their cool blue color could appear so hot. Fenella was standing so close to him, she could see her own frightened face reflected in their shifting, shimmering depths, and feel the warm sweetness of his breath against her cheek.

Before she could take another breath or even think another thought, that cruel, mocking mouth was on hers, his bold lips warm, smooth, and insistent.

Fenella exploded at his touch, her senses leaping to life so that she became all too aware of the man who held her helpless against him, kissing her so shamelessly. She could feel the hard muscles of his arms through his frock coat as they restrained her so securely, and she was all too aware of the way he had expertly fitted his lean body to hers, crushing her breasts against his chest and insinuating one knee against hers through her skirts. And her nostrils were filled with the masculine scent of him, an intoxicating combination of heather, spice, and musky arousal.

His smooth, pliant lips were so sweet, his kiss so expert and seductive, that for a moment Fenella almost succumbed to it. She hadn't been kissed this way since William died, and she had almost forgotten how pleasurable a sensation it was, that urge to surrender in the face of masculine domination. But just in time she remembered who was kissing her and why, and she stiffened and tried to pull away, whimpering in fear and indignation.

The heartless Patrick only chuckled and tightened his hold as she struggled in his arms, plainly telling Fenella that he wouldn't release her until he had what he wanted from her.

Fenella squeezed her eyes shut and resisted with every fiber of her being, even when his lips parted and she felt the tip of his tongue demand entrance. And since William had often kissed her in just that way, and because of what usually resulted, Fenella knew she mustn't let Patrick take such liberties any further, or she would be lost. She purposely pursed her lips, denying him.

In desperation, she drew back her left foot and kicked him smartly in the shins.

Patrick grunted in pain and surprise and released her as if she were a white-hot poker. Fenella bounded back several steps, then sought to run around him for the door. But Patrick was too quick for her and sidestepped to block her escape.

"If you lay a finger on me again, I swear I'll scream this house down," she said, trembling from head to toe with a mixture of fear and fury. "And you can explain yourself to your father."

He just crossed his arms over his chest nonchalantly and smiled, but made no attempt to touch her. "Such outrage, such moral indignation . . . May I congratulate you on such a fine performance, my dear Miss Considine. You should contemplate a career on the stage after my father finally sees through you and sends you packing."

Eager to repay him for his churlish remarks, she blurted, "And what if I were to tell your father that you've been harassing me? I don't think he would take too kindly to such behavior."

Patrick's face hardened into marble. "I can be an implacable enemy, Miss Considine, so don't threaten me. You'll regret it."

"Then leave me alone."

"I'm warning you. I love my father and will not stand idly by while he falls into the clutches of a fortune hunter."

"If you'll excuse me, I don't think there's anything else we have to say to each other." With that, Fenella started for the door.

Just as she reached it, Patrick turned around. "Oh, yes, there is just one more thing." When Fenella hesitated, he said, "You won't have to worry about my kissing you ever again, Miss Considine. Your kisses are as insipid as the rest of you, and I don't care to repeat the experience."

Fenella wouldn't even dignify that remark with a reply. She merely opened the library door and left before Patrick could see the shadow of pain cross her face.

When she reached her bedchamber, Fenella locked her door and leaned heavily against it until her racing heart slowed down to normal and her breathing became steady once again. Then she went over to the washstand, poured water into the porcelain basin, and proceeded to wash her face and neck to rid herself of Patrick's touch. Then she studied herself in the mirror.

She might not be a beauty like Cynara Standon, or even striking-looking like Margaret, but William had always admired her looks, often remarking that her brown eyes were as large and soft as a doe's. And he had certainly appreciated her "tavern-wench" attributes.

"He liked my looks well enough to want to marry me," she reminded herself.

Even so, Patrick's cruel, hurtful remarks about her appearance had cut Fenella to the quick. They made her feel shunted and overlooked, less worthy as a person somehow just because her appearance didn't meet his standards of feminine beauty.

Fighting back tears, she kicked off her slippers and lay on the bed. She closed her eyes and tried to sleep, but she kept thinking of Patrick and his bold advances in the library.

His behavior had shocked her, but her own response to him had shocked her even more.

She rolled over on her side and tried to forget those ardent caresses, but it was pointless. She could still feel his mouth on hers, so hot, so insistent, urging her to surrender to him as she had always surrendered to William. She had almost forgotten what it felt like to be held and kissed by a man so passionately, even if it were in anger rather than love.

Fenella propped herself up on her elbows and listened to the rain beat even harder against the window. She had always thought of Patrick as a man deeply scarred by his imprisonment. Today she had been given another glimpse of him, a single-minded man capable of great passion. She was intrigued, yet repulsed, because, after all, he was her sworn enemy and she had to be very careful lest she betray herself.

Sighing, she lay back down and finally slept.

The following afternoon, Patrick's insulting behavior was momentarily forgotten as Fenella joined Cadogan for a ride around the estate.

"Keep your head up and don't look at the ground," he advised as they crossed the stable's cobbled courtyard and passed beneath the wide, leafy branches of the stately beech trees. "And you're sitting there like a sack of potatoes. Just relax and move with the horse."

Fenella forced herself to do as she was told, for Cadogan strove for perfection in anything he did, and he expected everyone to do likewise. Surprisingly enough, she felt herself in tune with old Shamrock, the gentle mare she was learning to ride.

"Fine," Cadogan said, beaming at her like a tutor with his prize pupil. "I'll make a horsewoman out of you yet, Fenella."

She smiled at that. "Well, it won't be for lack of trying, Cadogan."

Fenella's experience with horses had been limited to driving them in the dogcart, since a doctor's daughter of limited means had so few opportunities to ride the spirited blood horses the gentry favored. But ever since she had come to live at Rookforest, Cadogan had insisted she learn to ride, and he himself gave her lessons almost daily, whenever the weather permitted. Fenella suspected he did it as an excuse to be in her company.

"Nonsense. You'll be riding to the hounds before you know it," he said. "All it takes is practice."

"I don't know if I'll ever become that proficient, but I am beginning to enjoy riding."

Indeed she was. In Margaret's old black riding habit that had been altered to fit her, and with its elegant silk top hat and spotted veil, Fenella felt as though she could leap over the highest hurdles with ease.

"Let me see how you trot," Cadogan said, urging his mount to go faster.

Fenella did likewise, and this time, she was surprised to find she wasn't bouncing about as much in the saddle. When Cadogan nodded his approval, she smiled back in delight. Then they slowed their horses and walked around the house.

As they passed through the demesne and veered left, heading for open country, Fenella noticed that Cadogan hadn't said a word to her in what seemed like hours.

Glancing over, she noticed he had his head down and was frowning pensively.

"Cadogan?" she inquired gently. "Is something the matter?"

He looked at her. "It's Patrick. I'm worried about him."

"Why?" She held her breath as she waited for his answer.

Cadogan frowned as though confronted by a puzzle he couldn't solve. "He's been out of prison for five months now, and he still isn't himself. He's quiet and he keeps to himself too much."

"But I thought he was helping you to manage Rookforest."

"He has, and doing a fine job of it, too, as I would expect of any son of mine. But . . ." He shrugged helplessly. "I just don't know . . ."

"Have you talked to him? Asked him what's the matter?"

After her confrontation of a week ago with Patrick, Fenella felt she knew all too well what was gnawing at him: his resentment of her and the obsession with proving her a fortune hunter.

Cadogan looked uncomfortable and shook his head. "No, I haven't. I've always found it difficult to talk to Patrick about certain matters. Oh, we're closer than most fathers and sons, but there are just some things we can't discuss. We wind up embarrassing each other."

"You have to remember he did spend four years of his life in prison. An experience like that can't help but change a man. Perhaps you expect too much of him. Perhaps it's going to take more time to become the man he once was."

Cadogan halted his horse on a hilltop. "I suspect it's more than prison that's eating at him." He looked over at Fenella, his blue eyes clouded and troubled. "I think he's still in love with the Standon witch."

Fenella's eyes widened. "Cynara? After what she did to him?"

Cadogan nodded. "Even after the nightmare she made of his life. He's always lu . . . er, wanted her ever since he became a man. Oh, there were other women in his life, but they never meant anything to him. It was always Cynara.''

Then he gave Fenella a long, significant look that made her look away. ''Some men are fools. They waste their lives chasing women who will do nothing but bring them grief, when there are good decent women right under their noses. I'd like to think myself incapable of siring a fool, but I'm beginning to wonder.''

''But he's made no attempt to see her since she's returned. Surely if he were still in love with her . . .''

''Hang it, I wish he would. At the risk of making you think I'm an uncouth old man, Fenella, I have to say I wish my son would bed the witch once and for all, then maybe he'd be able to forget her.''

''You are not an old man, Cadogan,'' she said, fighting back the blush that rose to her cheeks, ''and you're certainly not uncouth. You're just concerned for your son.''

He gave her an appreciative smile. Then he added, ''And for that niece of mine as well.''

''Why are you worried about Margaret?''

As Cadogan urged his horse down the hill and Fenella followed, he said, ''I want her to marry Nayland, and she'll have none of it.''

''Would you really be disappointed if she didn't marry him?'' she asked.

''Of course I would. Nayland would give her the moon if she asked him for it. My Margaret deserves that much. Besides, a woman ought to marry, to care for a husband and children.''

Judging by the hopeful way Cadogan was looking at her, Fenella suspected he was referring to her as well, and expected some sort of response. But she remained purposely obtuse. She knew him well enough to know that Cadogan would never declare his intentions unless she gave him more encouragement than she had been. For he was the type of man who moved slowly where women were concerned, as if he were a soldier in enemy territory, and then only when very sure of himself. He would not tell a woman he loved her in so many words, he would show her by his actions. And he would keep on doing for her until she saw the light and reciprocated his interest. But come right out and say he loved her? Never.

So as long as Fenella did not encourage him, they would remain friends and never cross that boundary where friends became lovers.

Fenella was distracted when she noticed a horse and rider coming toward them, galloping at breakneck speed across the field. She recognized Margaret at once, coming from the direction of the tower and another assignation with Terrence Sheely, no doubt.

"What are you doing, riding about the countryside without a groom, Meggie?" Cadogan asked her as she reined in Bramble next to them.

Margaret tossed her head defiantly, causing her auburn tresses to catch the sun's highlights, hair that had no doubt been loosened by Terrence Sheely's eager fingers.

"You know I like to ride alone, Uncle Cadogan," she replied breathlessly.

"Well, see that you take one of the boys with you from now on," he growled. "With these moonlighters running about, decent women aren't safe."

"Captain Moonlight only rides by night," Margaret reminded him.

"You'll do as I say, Margaret Atkinson."

The warning tone in his voice even took his niece aback, for she was stunned into silence.

Then she looked at Fenella with a critical eye. "You're progressing rather nicely with your riding."

"Why, thank you," Fenella replied, startled by the compliment.

They turned their horses and rode back slowly through the demesne, and as they neared the front entrance to the house, they noticed a half-dozen men at the front door, talking to Patrick.

"Uncle," Margaret said, "is something wrong?"

"Stay here in case there's trouble," he said. "I'll ride on ahead."

Fenella and Margaret halted their horses, watching in curiosity as Cadogan rode to meet the men.

Since they were alone, Fenella said, "You were out at the tower again with Terrence Sheely, weren't you?"

"Yes!" she hissed, her hazel eyes furious.

"Margaret . . ."

"Don't lecture me again, Fenella! You are not my mother!"

"But I do care about you, Margaret."

"If you're so concerned, then leave me alone!"

Fenella just shook her head in frustration. "You just don't realize the danger you're in. Terrence could seduce you, he—"

"I almost wish he would!" Margaret snapped. "At least then I would know what it feels like to be a woman."

Losing all patience at last, Fenella retorted, "Go ahead, Margaret, disregard all of my attempts to guide you. Present your Uncle Cadogan with Terrence Sheely's bastard, and see what he thinks of you then."

Margaret stared at her. "How dare you speak to me that way! You are a guest in this house."

"I'm only trying to advise you and spare you heartache."

"You're a fine one to dispense advice, Fenella Considine. You never even saw your own wedding day. Or night, for that matter."

Stung, Fenella fell silent. There was nothing more she could say to Margaret.

They were interrupted when Cadogan suddenly came riding back to them, his expression grave. "My process server was attacked this morning, trying to serve the Finnertys their eviction notice." He looked from Margaret to Fenella. "I'm afraid this means war."

11

It was past midnight, and Fenella couldn't sleep.

Her thoughts kept returning to that afternoon, when the shocking news had come that the Quinns' process server was attacked, beaten, and tarred by three masked men as he went to serve an eviction notice on the Finnertys. Luckily, he escaped with his life. But the incident had infuriated Cadogan, who had taken his man's assault as a personal affront.

"I'll not tolerate it!" he bellowed, as Fenella, Margaret, and Patrick hurried into the house after him. "I've been more than fair with my tenants, and this is the way they repay me? Insolent dogs. It's time to take action. Time to show these people they can't take advantage of Cadogan Quinn's generosity."

"What are you going to do, Uncle?" Margaret asked, trying to keep up with him as he stormed through the hall like an enraged bull.

Cadogan stopped so suddenly, Margaret almost plowed into him. "Why, evict the lot of 'em tomorrow, Finnerty, his wife, and their turnip-brained sons. Turn them out and tumble their house to rubble."

"Be calm, Father," Patrick said. "You're going to need a level head if this eviction is to be successful."

Cadogan turned beet red for a second as he glared at his son; then the color receded along with his anger. "Calm? I am calm. Now, what do you suggest we do?"

"First of all, we'll need assistance," Patrick said. "Even the two of us and all of our men put together won't be enough, not if the Finnertys plan some sort of resistance, as they surely will."

"I wasn't intending to go alone," Cadogan said. "What do you take me for, a fool? I am going to the constabulary right now, and demand an escort for the eviction. If that's not enough, I'll call in the dragoons from Fermoy if I have to."

"I'll go with you," Patrick said, and the two men left, leaving Fenella and Margaret to worry and speculate.

Now, hours later, Fenella was still worrying about what would happen when the Quinns and their small army of constables confronted the recalcitrant Finnertys.

With a restless sigh, she rose and lit a candle, then put on her dressing gown. She felt odd tonight, her emotions as tightly wound as a spring. There was an electricity in the atmosphere, as though something monumental were about to happen. She could sense it. She rubbed her wrist absently, but the scar was absent of all sensation.

Suddenly the September wind rose, rattling the windows and sighing through the eaves, agitating Fenella further, heightening her restlessness and sense of foreboding. She grasped the silver candlestick and went sweeping out of the room in a wild flickering of light.

Minutes later, after wandering the empty corridors aimlessly, she found herself at the library entrance. Someone had left the door open as if in invitation.

Perhaps something to read will help me sleep, she thought, so she went inside and set her candlestick down on the reading table.

"Couldn't sleep?"

Fenella jumped with a squeak of surprise.

There was Patrick, lounging in one of the leather wing chairs just beyond the range of her candle's feeble light.

"Wh-what are you doing here?" she stammered. "You startled me."

"Just sitting here by myself in the dark, thinking."

And drinking, Fenella added, noticing the glass in his hand and the cut-crystal decanter of whiskey within reach. To her relief, it looked almost full, so Patrick hadn't been imbibing for very long.

He looked disheveled and bleary-eyed, not drunk, as though he had just come in from a long, hard ride. To make himself comfortable, he had removed his coat and unbuttoned his waistcoat and the top buttons of his white lawn shirt, the sleeves of which were rolled up to his elbows, exposing lean, strong forearms. His long booted legs were stretched out before him and crossed at the ankle.

Fenella could almost taste it, his dangerous, quixotic mood, and her inner voice urged her to leave before it was too late.

She fumbled for the candlestick. "It's late and I really should get back to bed. If you'll excuse me . . ."

She had forgotten how quickly Patrick could move when one least expected it. He sprang out of his chair with the grace and agility of a cat, and before Fenella had even turned around, he materialized at the door, barring her escape.

One corner of his mouth lifted in an ironic smile. "We always seem to choose the library for our little . . . discussions. But then, it's quiet and secluded at this time of night, so we won't wake Father or Meggie or the servants."

Fenella took a tentative step backward, only to be brought up short by the reading table. "What do you wish to discuss with me, Patrick?"

"Aren't you going to ask me what I've been thinking about all evening?"

She gripped the edge of the table as hard as she could to keep her rising panic at bay. "I'm sure it has something to do with me."

"You're right. It does." He stared at her in silence, his eyes hard and glittering as diamonds in the softly shifting light. "I have given this matter a great deal of thought, and I have finally deduced your real reason for being here at Rookforest."

Her nervousness made her bold. "Ah, so you've decided that I'm not a fortune hunter after all. I'm gratified to hear it."

Patrick's brows rose. "So, the little spinster has a sharp tongue . . ."

He's deliberately toying with me, Fenella thought as she watched Patrick slowly raise the glass he still held and drink deeply as he peered at her over the rim.

"I think you're in league with the moonlighters."

He said it so calmly, so conversationally, that for a moment Fenella thought she hadn't heard him correctly. "What?"

"You heard me. I think you're working with the moon-lighters to bring about my family's destruction. That's why that Mrs. Janeaway was visiting you, to enlist your aid."

Suddenly, as Fenella stared dumbfounded at him, Patrick changed. His light, conversational mood vanished, to be replaced by one of cold, calculating rage.

"You've had it planned all along. Your friends burned down your house deliberately because you knew my father was so besotted with you that he'd take pity on you and offer you refuge with us."

"No! That's not—"

"How perfect," he went on relentlessly, setting down his empty glass and slowly, inexorably coming toward her, "and how blind we all were not to see it sooner! With you installed here as my father's . . . confidante, all you have to do is listen and report back to your moon-lighter friends. They'll know every move we're going to make against them."

He was towering over her now, his lithe, muscular body taut with fury so palpable that Fenella could feel it as a physical presence, pressing her back.

"Have you already warned them of our plans to evict the Finnertys tomorrow, my dear Miss Considine? Will we find them ready and waiting for us? What, Miss Considine? At a loss for words, are we?"

"That's absurd," she retorted. "I am not in league with the moonlighters. I never have been. They are nothing but barbarians. I despise them and their methods."

A sarcastic smile twisted his face and his nostrils flared, making him look as diabolical as Satan himself. "How righteously you defend yourself."

"Because it's true!"

She tried to whirl away from him, but he deftly caught her wrist, twisting it savagely so that she winced and cried out in pain.

"Then how did you know your house would burn down before even I saw the flames?" he snarled between clenched teeth, his whiskey-scented breath hot in her face. "Tell me, damn you!"

Fenella never had the opportunity to answer him.

The scar on her wrist began throbbing like an aching

tooth, and she suddenly felt the all-too-familiar light-headedness sweep over her, leeching all strength and feeling from her limbs. She tried to resist the overpowering sensation by sheer force of her will, but the giddiness was too overpowering. Patrick's strident voice faded away into a whisper, then vanished altogether, and the library disappeared as her heavy lids drooped of their own volition.

When Fenella opened her eyes, it was no longer night and she wasn't in the library. She was outside at midday, an impartial spectator floating high in the sky, as free as a cloud over the open countryside.

She could see the large two-story farmhouse clearly, a makeshift red flannel flag hoisted high and unfurled over its slate roof. A ring of grim armed policemen encircled the house, keeping a crowd of unruly farmers at bay. Both Cadogan and Patrick were there seated on horseback and oblivious of the taunts and threats welling up and receding around them.

Suddenly a portly woman wearing a light blue tweed shawl shouted, "Go back to prison where ye belong, Patrick Quinn, and take yer father with ye!"

Patrick blanched, but ignored her with supreme arrogance.

As Fenella watched, Cadogan swung down from his horse. With the straining crowd physically held back, he marched right up to the farmhouse door and banged on it with his fist.

"Come out, Finnerty," he said. "Don't make it harder on yourself."

Suddenly the door swung open. A woman stood there, a basin in her hands. In the blink of an eye, she determinedly flung its steaming contents right at a startled Cadogan. He saw what was coming and managed to jump back and twist away, but not fast enough to evade the stream of scalding water.

The crowd cheered as he put his hands to his face and screamed, staggering back as if blinded.

Horror-stricken, Patrick was off his horse in an instant, rushing to his father's side. But it was not Cadogan's name he called.

"Fenella!"

She blinked. When she opened her eyes, she blurted out, "Cadogan . . . Got to warn him," before she remembered where she really was and that she was not among friends.

Fenella realized her mistake the moment she saw Patrick's livid face hovering above hers and felt his cruel fingers biting into her shoulders as he roughly hauled her to her feet.

"Did you think a fake swoon would deter me, Miss Considine?" He flung her contemptuously into a nearby chair. "Warn Cadogan about what? And you'd damn well better tell me the truth this time, or so help me God, I'll beat it out of you."

She cowered against the soft leather, realizing Patrick had every intention of making good his threat. She had to tell him the truth.

Fenella swallowed convulsively. "Tomorrow, when you go to evict the Finnertys, your father will be burned with scalding water."

"What!" he bellowed.

Patrick pulled her back to her feet, his touch purposely cruel. "Now, how could you possibly know that unless you're in league with the moonlighters?" He shook her until she was as limp as a rag doll and her neck felt as though it would snap from the force of the shaking. "The truth now, damn you! I'm sick unto death of your lies."

Exhausted from all the verbal and physical abuse that Patrick had heaped upon her this night, Fenella cracked.

"I saw it in a vision," she whimpered.

Patrick stopped shaking her. "A vision?"

Fenella's head bobbed up and down.

"You expect me to believe that?"

He was about to tighten his hold and shake her again when Fenella's own temper exploded. Gathering all of her strength born of anger and desperation, she shoved at his chest with all her might, breaking his hold and causing Patrick to go staggering back against the table. The candle jumped, its flame flickering wildly, casting long eerie shadows along the rows of books.

"I don't expect you to believe anything," she cried, scurrying behind the chair and positioning it as a shield between them, "but it's true. I have the power to . . .

see into the future. Sometimes. The tinkers call it second sight.''

His lip curled in a sneer as he recovered himself and faced her. "Second sight? Preposterous! I don't believe one single word of it.''

"I don't expect you to. But how do you think I knew about the fire?'' she cried in exasperation. "Not because I'm in league with the moonlighters, as you so stubbornly believe, but because I had a vision just before we arrived. I swear it on my father's grave!''

Her words tumbled out faster and faster as a thin sheen of sweat rose on her upper lip. "I saw men surrounding the house, and then I saw it burning as surely as I see you standing right here before me.''

"A likely story.''

He was not going to be easy to convince.

"Well, how do you explain what happened to me just a few moments ago?''

"As I said, a fake swoon to buy yourself some time.''

"Shall I tell you what I saw in the vision I just had?''

"Not that I'll believe you, but do proceed. I find your pitiful efforts amusing and inventive, even if they are all lies.''

He folded his arms across his chest in an attitude of patience and leaned against the table.

So Fenella told him what she had seen in her vision, omitting no detail great or small, telling him things she could not have possibly known in advance, such as the number of constables there. Then she told Patrick about the woman in the blue shawl and repeated her exact words.

For the first time, she saw that look of smug superiority wiped off his face and just a shadow of a doubt fill his eyes.

She added, "When you go to evict the Finnertys tomorrow, look around. I challenge you to keep an open mind. Count the constables. Watch for the woman in the blue shawl. You'll see I'm telling the truth. And whatever you do, don't let Cadogan or anyone else go to the door or they will be burned.''

Patrick said nothing, just stared at her for what seemed

like hours. In the quiet of the library, Fenella could almost hear him thinking, choosing and discarding theories.

"Not that I believe your unlikely tale for an instant—"

"Oh, for heaven's sake, Patrick! Why would I lie? You'll know after the eviction whether I'm telling the truth. And then if you're still convinced I'm lying, I'll leave Rookforest of my own volition, and you'll never have to see me again."

"If you are helping the moonlighters, you could have easily made arrangements for a woman in a blue shawl to be there tomorrow."

Fenella wanted to shake some sense into him herself. "How could I keep such an assignation if I have not left this house in the last three days? Ask anyone. And your father didn't decide when he was going to evict the Finnertys until today."

"You could have sent a note to your fellow conspirators telling them to have a woman with a blue shawl there, and telling her what to say."

Fenella made a derisive sound. "There wasn't enough time for such correspondence, and you know it. Besides, I doubt if half the moonlighters can read."

Patrick was silent again. "Who else knows about this . . . gift of yours?"

"It's not a gift, it's a curse," she retorted bitterly, "and only my father knew."

"And he's dead. How convenient for you that no one can corroborate your story. Why have you told no one else?"

"Why do you think? Because anyone else would believe me mad, or once word got out, people from all over Ireland would come to me in droves to have their futures foretold, as if I were some freak in a circus sideshow or a Gypsy with a crystal ball." She shot him a challenging look. "Much the same way everyone stared at you when you first went into Mallow after being released from prison."

Patrick's eyes widened and he turned livid at her comparison. For one horrifying moment Fenella feared she had pushed him too far. Then his expression softened, as if she had touched some responsive chord in him with her last statement. But any sympathy he might have felt for her was fleeting.

"I will concede it is possible you have the sight. I suppose you were born with it?"

Fenella shook her head. "I acquired it about a year ago," she began, then proceeded to tell Patrick the bizarre tale of how William had come to her in a dream and what had ensued.

He stared at her hard.

"And you really expect me to believe such folderol? I'm not an idiot, Miss Considine."

"I'm telling the truth, incredible as it may seem. Examine the mark for yourself."

She came around the chair and pushed up the sleeve of her dressing gown, defiantly baring her wrist so that the scar showed an angry red against her white skin.

"That day in my garden, you got only a glimpse of it. Notice how even the scar is, and how it encircles my wrist as perfectly as a bracelet. If I had burned myself on a hot stove, or spilled scalding tea on myself, the mark would be on the top of my wrist or the bottom. Not both."

He scowled as he slowly turned her wrist, examining it from every angle. "I will concede that it is a most unusual mark, but the result of a dream? You strain the bounds of credulity, my girl. This is something some Irish peasant would concoct, with fanciful tales of banshees and fairies."

His words were blunt and skeptical, but at least all the cold, mindless rage had gone out of him, and for that Fenella was thankful.

She passed her hand before her eyes, feeling suddenly drained and bone-weary from the futility of trying to convince him. "I don't know what else I can say, except to watch carefully when you evict the Finnertys tomorrow."

"I will. Like my father, I'm a fair man, and I'll give you the benefit of the doubt. But if you're lying . . ."

"I'm not. My claim is easily verifiable. If the woman in the blue shawl says what I claim she said in my vision, you'll know I am telling the truth. If she doesn't, you'll know that I am lying. But I'm not."

He frowned, still unconvinced. "You sound so sure of yourself."

He himself was sounding less and less sure of himself by the second.

"I am," she said with heartfelt intensity. "Now, if you'll excuse me, I'm tired and would like to return to my room."

"I'll escort you."

As he reached for his coat, Fenella said, "Patrick, I'd appreciate it if you'd not tell anyone else what I've told you tonight. I don't want anyone else to know about my strange . . . abilities."

"Throwing yourself on my mercy, are you?"

"Yes. Please. I'm begging you."

"You don't wish my father to know, to take the credit for saving him from injury tomorrow? My, my. How selfless of you."

She ignored the heavy sarcasm in his voice. "Especially Cadogan. Not yet." If ever, she added to herself.

He was silent for a moment as he considered her request.

"Your secret is safe with me, if indeed you are telling the truth," he said finally.

Fenella thanked him, and they walked upstairs together.

When Patrick returned to his own room, he set the candle down on the bedside table and began undressing. The bed creaked as he sat on its edge and struggled to pull off his boots, but the noise didn't awaken O'Malley, curled into a tight little ball in his straw-filled tin.

"Well, O'Malley," he said as he tugged off one boot, "now she expects me to believe she has second sight. Second sight . . ." He shook his head. "Have you ever heard of anything so absurd?"

But as Patrick started on the other boot, he paused.

Fenella certainly had been convincing, especially when she slumped to the floor and lay there as if in some sort of trance, her muscles rigid and her eyes wide open and staring vacantly at something only she could see. And that odd scar on her wrist was too perfect to be formed by a random burn. He accepted that. But to claim that it had been put there by her dead fiancé in a dream?

"Folderol," Patrick muttered, working off his other boot and letting it drop. "Peasant superstition."

His English blood made him logical and skeptical. He didn't believe in fairies or banshees or second sight. But the part of him that belonged to the imaginative Celt told him otherwise.

Patrick rose, feeling suddenly unsure of himself as he padded over to the window and drew back the curtain. It was a wild night tonight, with the wind blowing and dark clouds racing across an even darker sky. He shivered.

He remembered the stories his Irish mother often told him when he was just a boy. The beautiful Moira would come to his room just before he went to bed and regale him with fanciful, imaginative tales of fairies and goblins. He believed her absolutely because he was a child and his mother never lied to him, but as he grew older and saw no physical evidence of their existence, he realized they existed only in a nation's imagination.

His mother and Mrs. Ryan thought differently, however.

"Just because you can't see something, Patrick, or touch it, doesn't mean it doesn't exist," his mother would always say to him.

"Aye," Mrs. Ryan would chime in somberly. "There's much on God's great earth that can't be explained by mere man."

Moira and Mrs. Ryan would have believed Fenella possessed the sight. They would not have doubted her for an instant.

Patrick let the curtain fall back into place and he walked to his bed. Tomorrow he would find out if she were telling the truth.

And God help her if she were lying.

"If Fenella Considine has second sight, then I'm the Queen of England," Patrick muttered under his breath as he sat astride a restive Gallowglass at the Finnerty's eviction.

The scene before him was typical of any eviction. A makeshift red flannel flag was flying from the roof to warn all the neighboring farmers that an eviction was taking place. Farmers had left their fields and joined their wives and children to gather round in the hopes of putting pressure on the landlord—in this case, Patrick and his father—to desist. Since tenants were known to use rocks, clubs, pitchforks, and other forceful means of persuasion against their persecutors, a ring of armed constables surrounded the house to see that no one came to harm.

Patrick shifted in the saddle and drew his collar more closely about his chin, for it was chilly, and he smelled rain in the air. Then he scanned the crowd, looking for the woman wearing a light blue shawl. She was nowhere to be found among that sea of despondent, angry faces.

He snorted. "You'll have to do better than that, my girl."

Patrick was momentarily distracted as his father dismounted and went to talk with Constable Treherne. Around them, disgruntled mutterings rippled through the crowd, then rose into a collective wail of outrage as they saw the eviction was going to take place after all. The policemen didn't flinch even though they faced the wrath of neighbors and even relatives.

Out of the corner of his eye Patrick caught a blur of movement, and he turned his head to see the new arrival. There, standing not three yards away from him, was a heavy woman wearing a light blue tweed shawl.

He straightened in the saddle, unable to believe his eyes, but there she was just as Fenella had predicted. Then he shook his head to clear it, but the woman was not a figment of his imagination and didn't disappear.

He held his breath and waited.

She said nothing, just stood there before one of the constables and regarded the proceedings out of narrowed, resentful eyes, occasionally muttering something to the neighbor on her left. But she never called out to Patrick or even looked in his direction.

After a while, Patrick turned his attention back to his father, a scornful smile playing about his lips. "A lucky guess, Fenella," he muttered.

As Cadogan started toward the front door to confront Finnerty and get the eviction under way, the crowd erupted. Voices and fists raised, they surged forward in a wave of humanity, only to be repulsed by the policemen.

Then, rising above the howls of protest, came one clear, vehement voice: "Go back to prison where ye belong, Patrick Quinn, and take yer father with ye!"

Patrick twisted in the saddle again, pulling Gallowglass's head around, and his searching gaze met the hostile face of the woman in the blue shawl.

"What did you say?" he demanded, dreading her answer.

"Ye heard me," she shouted back brazenly, her double chin quivering. "I said go back to prison where ye belong and take yer miserable father with ye!"

Breaking out in a cold sweat, Patrick turned again in time to see Cadogan approaching the doorstep. The moment he knocked and the door opened, Fenella's dire premonition would come true, with tragic consequences.

"Wait, Father!" he shouted, and spurred his horse forward.

His fist upraised to knock, Cadogan stopped and turned back just in time, an expression of inquiry on his face.

"What is it, son?"

Patrick looked across at the house and chose his words. "I don't think you should be the first to go inside," he said, keeping his voice low. "Let the police do their jobs. It's been entirely too quiet in there. You don't know what kind of reception Finnerty is planning. He could be waiting to shoot you the moment you open the door."

Cadogan studied the house, then nodded. "That Finnerty is a sly old fox. I'd best be prudent."

He joined Patrick as they moved back and warned Constable Treherne to have his men proceed carefully in case of violent resistance.

Thus forewarned, the first man to demand entrance to Francis Finnerty's house agilely stepped aside when the door flew open. The crowd groaned in disappointment when the steaming basin of scalding water that Mrs. Finnerty flung at him missed its target and splashed on the ground with an impotent hiss.

As the police surged forward into the house to drive out the Finnertys, Patrick sat there removed from it all as if carved from stone, unable to believe what he had just witnessed with his own eyes. Around him, voices rose and fell like waves crashing against rocks, making noise, not words. A cold, heartless drizzle began to fall against his face.

"I just don't believe it," he muttered. "I saw it with my own eyes, but I still don't believe it."

Yet he must. He had seen her prediction come true with his own eyes. To deny it meant he denied himself.

Acceptance came slowly, grudgingly. Fenella had been telling the truth after all. She did possess the second sight.

The full ramifications of that simple acknowledgment caused Patrick to break out in a cold shuddering sweat. Suddenly he saw Fenella in a different light. She was no longer a simple doctor's daughter, ordinary and commonplace, but mythical somehow, an awe-inspiring figure endowed with great power many would envy, the power to see into the future, the ability to foretell a man's destiny.

At first, he felt sick with horror and revulsion at the magnitude of it. He wanted to drive her out of Rookforest. He never wanted to go near her again. He feared her because she was different.

And then he remembered what it felt like to be shunned because he had served time in prison, and abruptly his feelings changed, swinging in the opposite direction, like a pendulum. The desire to repudiate her was replaced by a growing desire to protect her, to shield her from those who would not understand, as one would hide a rare unicorn.

"God help me," he said, turned his horse, and rode back to Rookforest.

Fenella stood at one of the drawing-room windows, half out of her mind with worry.

The clock on the mantel somberly chimed two in the afternoon. Cadogan and Patrick had ridden off at nine o'clock that morning and still hadn't returned.

Outside, a fine drizzle was beginning to fall from a darkened sky of gray, low-hanging clouds, blurring the scene's hard edges and turning it into a soft watercolor sketch. Fenella shivered, though the drawing room was warm from the fire that burned cheerfully in the grate.

Just as she was turning away from the window, the sound of booted footsteps hurrying down the hall caused her to pause.

Patrick appeared in the doorway and hesitated for a moment. He was in such haste that he hadn't bothered to remove his coat, which was dark and soaked with rain, and his long black hair was wet and glossy. Then he closed the door behind him and came striding toward her. Fenella hurried to meet him halfway.

"What happened? Is Cadogan . . . ?"

"Unharmed," Patrick replied.

"Thank God!" Trembling and weak-kneed with relief, Fenella collapsed into the nearest chair.

"The eviction was successful," he said, "and neither the police nor any Finnertys were hurt badly, though one of the sons got a cracked skull for attacking Treherne. My father is still there overseeing the finishing of it. I thought it best if I returned here first, so you and I could talk without being interrupted."

When Fenella looked up at Patrick, she noticed the change in him at once. He was no longer hostile, but quiet and subdued, regarding her without mockery.

She smiled sadly. "It was just as I said, wasn't it? I can tell that you believe me now."

He nodded, visibly shaken. "Oh, I didn't at first. And then I saw the woman in the blue shawl. She said exactly what you said she would. I managed to stop my father just in time." Grateful eyes held hers. "Mrs. Finnerty was waiting for him with her basin of boiling water. He would have been scalded, perhaps blinded, if he had gone to that door."

Fenella put a shaky hand to her forehead. "Thank God he's all right." She looked up at Patrick fearfully. "You didn't tell him how you knew that would happen?"

"Don't worry, I didn't betray you. I merely warned him to expect resistance. A cautious policeman went in his place, and he must have been accustomed to such work, for he had the presence of mind to step aside just in time." He regarded her oddly. "You saved my father from serious injury. Thank you."

"Thanks aren't necessary. I'm glad my dubious gift could save someone," Fenella said bitterly, her voice breaking as she rose. "It didn't save my own father."

Surprise registered on his face. "You mean you foresaw your own father's death?"

She nodded miserably. "In a sense. The night he died, I saw his *fetch*. Do you know what that is?"

Patrick slowly ran his hand through his wet hair. "Yes, I do. The Germans call it a *doppelgänger,* I believe." He stared at her hard. "You actually saw this . . . spirit?"

"As clearly as I see you right now." Fenella told him about that night when she followed what she thought was her father returning home. "At the time, I thought it odd when he went upstairs without even looking at me or speaking to me, but when I entered his bedchamber and found no one there . . ." She shuddered at the vivid memory, then fought to compose herself. "That's when I ran all the way to Mallow for the constable, and they later found my father's body in the brook."

Patrick was silent as he took off his wet coat, folded it inside out, and draped it over the back of a chair. "That's an incredible story."

"And you don't believe it either."

"I don't want to," he said heavily, "but after what I witnessed today, I have no choice."

Fenella walked over to the window and watched the drizzle gather force and turn into a downpour. "Last night, you said you didn't believe in ghosts or banshees or fairies. Well, I do because I sometimes see such spiritual entities in my visions. It's as though my second sight is a window on another world." She ran her hands up her arms, wondering why she was bothering to confide in him, yet feeling compelled to share her burden with someone.

"Do you know what a waterhorse is?"

Patrick replied, "Of course. It's a spirit that lives in the sea. If one is lucky enough to capture it, it makes a superior mount. But if a captured waterhorse is allowed a glimpse of the sea, it will return to its watery land, dashing its rider to his death on the ocean floor."

Fenella nodded. "After my father and I moved to Mallow, we returned to Cork to visit some friends. One day, we went strolling along the shore, and I had a vision of a waterhorse rising from the depths of the sea and galloping on land. Then the vision disappeared, and I didn't think anything of it''—she turned to face Patrick—''until I saw Squire Lawson riding that exact same horse, a black brute with a mean rolling eye and a wide twisted blaze down his face. A horse he claimed he had found running free along the beach.''

''What happened?''

''The day after I saw the squire, his body was found on the beach. They said he had drowned. And his horse just disappeared into thin air. It was never found.''

Patrick walked over to her. ''It could have been an accident, you know,'' he said gently. ''Someone could have murdered him and stolen the horse.''

Fenella sighed, a long, drawn-out sound of misery in the quiet room. ''Ah, Patrick, so logical . . . I'd give anything if I could believe that.''

He was silent and reflective for a moment. Then he said, ''Have you had other . . . visions?''

''Oh, yes. Right after I acquired my so-called 'gift,' I had my first vision. It was a rather frightening one of a little girl being run down by a carriage as she raced after her ball into the street.''

''You must have been terrified.''

''I was. I couldn't understand what was happening to me. I became so hysterical and incoherent that my father feared for my sanity. But when the event actually occurred the following day in Mallow, I was able to warn the child in time to save her life. That's when I realized that William had indeed given me the ability to see into the future.'' She shook her head and said bitterly, ''And I thought he loved me.''

When Patrick made no comment, she added, ''I also had a vision the night my father and I came here to dine after you had returned home.''

''Ah,'' he said. ''I recall it now. You looked so bored I accused you of ignoring me. But all that time, you were in a trance.''

Fenella nodded, and prayed he wouldn't ask her what that vision was.

But instead, he asked, "Do you ever have visions of your own future?"

"Never. And I can only pray that I never do, because I surely would go mad."

"Can you have a vision whenever you wish?"

Fenella shook her head. "Oh, no, I don't control them, they control me. I wish I could, though. Then I would use my sight to predict when Captain Moonlight would next strike, or prevent someone I love from coming to harm. But I can't, and that is my greatest frustration."

Patrick then asked, "How do you know when you're about to have a vision? What does it feel like?"

"The scar on my wrist usually begins throbbing in warning," she replied, "and then I feel lightheaded and weak, sometimes dizzy. All sound fades away. When I blink and open my eyes again, I find myself in a different place witnessing an episode from someone's future. When the vision is over, I blink again and return to reality."

"It must be terrifying."

She smiled wanly. "It was at first, but not any longer. I am resigned to it."

"You're a brave woman."

Fenella turned to him and was startled to find him standing very close. Her frayed nerves already stretched to the limit, she stepped away with a high-pitched, nervous laugh. "You're quite right. It sounds even more preposterous in the retelling. I wouldn't blame you if you thought me mad and had me committed to a lunatic asylum."

Patrick's face darkened. "You are not mad, and there will be no more talk of lunatic asylums. You and your secret are safe here at Rookforest. No one will dare harm you."

Fenella twisted her fingers together nervously. She searched Patrick's face, but it showed no sign of revulsion or rejection, merely a gentleness she had once doubted he possessed.

"Why do you believe me?" she demanded. "Why aren't you treating me as though I were some . . . some freak to be laughed at and shunned? Anyone else would."

He looked away. "I'm ashamed to say I was going to

at first. The knowledge that you possessed such power made me fear you.''

Fenella was taken aback. ''Oh, Patrick, you have nothing to fear from me. I would never harm you.''

''I know that. Then I remembered what it is like to be an outcast,'' he said simply. ''And I rather suspect having second sight is like being in a prison.''

His sympathy was too much for Fenella to bear. Something long denied welled up and broke inside her, and she dissolved into tears.

Humiliated, she tried to brush past him, but Patrick was too quick for her, catching her and enfolding her in his arms before she could draw another breath. She struggled briefly, then surrendered, burying her face in his broad shoulder that smelled of wet wool and heather. Her arms went around his waist of their own volition, and she clung to him unashamedly.

He said nothing, just held her as William often had, with his cheek resting against the top of her head as he held her in the warm, comforting circle of his arms, anchoring her to reality. Patrick felt solid and unyielding, making Fenella feel cherished and protected once again, if only for a little while.

''Feel better?'' he asked when her tears finally subsided.

Fenella nodded as she clung to him, reluctant to part just yet. To her astonishment, Patrick seemed just as reluctant to let her go.

''You've borne that burden far too long,'' he said. ''It was time to share it with someone.''

Fenella sniffed. ''I've lived in fear of the day when someone would finally discover my secret and expose me as a witch or a madwoman.''

''I give you my word that I won't tell another soul.''

''Not even Cadogan or Margaret?''

''Not even my father or Meggie.''

Now Fenella did pull away, puzzled. ''Why are you being so . . . so kind to me, Patrick? You've disliked me from the first moment we met.''

Her candor caused a faint flush to stain his high cheekbones, and his gaze slid down to the floor. ''I misjudged you, Fenella, perhaps more than I have ever misjudged another human being." Then he looked up at her and she read the sincerity in the depths of his eyes. "At first I disliked you for the simple reason I thought you disliked me. Now I realize you were standoffish because of your secret. You couldn't let anyone get close to you for fear of discovery, could you?

"Later, after your father died, I thought you were merely a fortune hunter after my father's wealth. Now I know differently."

That admission gratified her. "I've never disliked you, Patrick," she said.

A smile as warm and playful as the sun dancing on water split his somber visage. "Not even when I called you a priggish spinster?"

Fenella smiled back shyly. "Well, perhaps then."

Suddenly Patrick grew somber once again. Before Fenella could stop him, he reached for her hand and brought it to his warm, smooth lips. "I have much to apologize to you for, Fenella," he said, his voice low. "Perhaps by keeping your secret safe, I can somehow make amends for my shabby treatment of you."

"Thank you, Patrick," she said, suddenly feeling as though she weren't all alone in the world anymore.

He glanced over her shoulder out the window. "Ah, there's my father now, riding down the drive. Let's go to meet him, shall we?"

Fenella nodded.

They had entered the room as enemies, but now they left it as friends.

12

TWO WEEKS LATER, Fenella was sitting in the drawing room embroidering when the butler entered and approached her.

"A letter just came for you, miss," he said, extending a small silver salver to her.

Fenella's brows rose in surprise as she set her embroidery hoop aside. "For me?"

"Yes, miss."

As she took the envelope, Fenella noticed it was of expensive ivory vellum and she savored the smooth, rich texture of it as the butler turned and left the room.

"Now, whoever could be writing to me?" she wondered aloud as she slit open the envelope with her finger and eagerly pulled out a heavy sheet of paper. When she caught a faint whiff of spice perfume, Fenella knew exactly who had written to her and why.

She began reading.

Dear Miss Considine,

Since it has been several weeks since our meeting in Mallow and I have not heard from you, I am taking the liberty of writing.

It would give me great pleasure if you would call upon me between the hours of 1 and 4 P.M. on Thursday, September 25.

I shall be looking forward to your visit.

As Fenella suspected, it was signed "Lady Cynara Eastbrook" with a flourish.

Rereading the letter, Fenella was amazed at the woman's presumptive tone. Of course she assumed that Fenella would jump to do her bidding, but then, weren't the plain always expected to serve the beautiful?

September 25. . . . That was tomorrow.

Fenella scowled as she refolded the letter and slid it back into its envelope. She didn't know whether to accept the invitation or send her regrets.

Part of her felt sorry for Cynara. She might be beautiful and she might have made a brilliant match with the Marquess of Eastbrook, but that day she had sought Fenella's company in Mallow, Cynara had seemed lonely and in dire need of a friend.

Fenella set the letter aside and returned to her embroidery. There were also Patrick's feelings to consider. Ever since he had discovered Fenella possessed second sight, his attitude toward her had changed markedly. He no longer vacillated between friendliness and enmity. In fact, he was always so solicitous of her welfare now, so quick to be her champion, that Fenella wondered where the rude, surly young man had gone.

She knew why he had altered his opinion of her. It was because they shared the bond all social outcasts shared, the opprobrium of their fellowman. The good people of Mallow had ostracized him because of his prison term, and they would surely do the same to her if news of her second sight ever became public knowledge. That shared bond eased all enmity between them, and his acceptance made her stay at Rookforest so much more pleasant.

Whatever Patrick's reasons, Fenella was grateful for his friendship. And with friendship came loyalty.

Fenella took up the letter again and stared at the envelope. Would she be betraying Patrick if she called upon Cynara? Yet if she did call, perhaps she could glean some information about St. John Standon that could be useful to the Quinns.

She smiled to herself. She could become a spy in the enemy camp.

The following afternoon found Fenella in the dogcart, driving off alone to Drumlow.

Fortunately, everyone from Patrick to Margaret had been out when she went down to the stables and requested the cart, thus saving her from having to lie about

her destination. She had never been to the Standons'
home, of course, for they were gentry and too fine to
entertain a mere dispensary doctor and his daughter, but
she had driven past Drumlow's imposing iron grille gates
often enough to know where the great house was located.

As she turned left at the crossroads, she began to have
second thoughts about her duplicity. Perhaps she should
have just showed the letter to Patrick and abided by his
decision.

Well, Fenella thought as she spied the many high chim-
neys of Drumlow rising over the treetops in the distance,
it was too late to turn back now.

The moment she arrived at the gates, however, she regretted not having turned back. Two burly, fierce-looking
men armed with rifles stood guard and regarded her suspiciously as she drove up and stopped.

"Miss Considine to see Lady Eastbrook," she called
out bravely.

"Is the mistress expecting you?" one of the men
growled.

"I wouldn't be here if she hadn't invited me," Fenella replied indignantly.

The other man grinned as he raised his rifle and moved
to unlock the gates. "Just obeying the master's orders,
miss. Can't be too sure of anybody these days, with
moonlighters about."

Fenella said nothing as she drove through and down
the long straight drive.

There was nothing warm or welcoming about St. John
Standon's house, built some forty years ago in the grand
Tudor style. Made of somber dark brown stone, Drumlow squatted untidily, its mullioned windows so narrow
they seemed incapable of admitting much light. The huge
front door, hinged in heavy wrought iron, looked mas-
sive enough to repel an army, let alone a few unwelcome
visitors.

Fenella disembarked from the dogcart and knocked on
that huge door. Seconds later, it swung open to reveal a
tall, gaunt butler with a sour face and small suspicious
eyes.

He quickly raked her over from head to toe as though
he knew her new dress was a castoff, then gave an almost

imperceptible sniff of disapproval before saying, "Yes?" in a haughty voice.

Fenella refused to be intimidated. "Miss Considine to see Lady Eastbrook. I believe she is expecting me."

"Of course. Follow me, please."

Fenella followed that rigid back into a darkly paneled foyer complete with vaulted ceilings she had to tilt her head back to fully appreciate. Then they entered a long corridor, also paneled, guarded at its entrance by a gleaming suit of armor. Finally the butler stopped before double doors that must have led to the drawing room.

Much too pretentious a residence for a mere land agent, she thought to herself.

"Wait here while I announce you to the marchioness."

He disappeared inside for a moment, and when he returned he said, "The marchioness will receive you," as though he were granting Fenella an audience with the queen herself.

She thanked him and entered yet another gloomy paneled room, where she encountered an astonishing sight: the beautiful, elegant Cynara Eastbrook was down on her knees in her fine silk gown, playing with the most beautiful little girl Fenella had ever seen.

Flushed and laughing merrily, Cynara rose to her feet without a trace of awkwardness and settled her skirts around her with one quick motion. "Do forgive me for receiving you in such an ill-mannered fashion, Miss Considine, but I do so enjoy playing with my daughter."

Enchanted, Fenella came forward, unable to take her eyes off the child seated with legs akimbo in the middle of the carpet, surrounded by toy blocks, wooden animals, and several dolls with bisque porcelain heads. Cynara's little daughter was as fair as her mother was dark, with gentle flaxen curls framing a rosy-cheeked face of extraordinary beauty. The only feature they shared was the eyes, for the child's were as wide and as violet as her mother's, with long silky lashes. Otherwise, she must have resembled her deceased father.

The child stared at Fenella somberly for a moment, then grinned before popping one small fist into her mouth.

"And how do we do, my precious poppet?" Fenella crooned.

The little girl giggled over her fist, then babbled something unintelligible.

Cynara beamed. "You are fortunate indeed, Miss Considine. Lou-Lou doesn't usually take to strangers right away."

"Lou-Lou . . . what a pretty name for such a pretty girl."

"Actually, her name is Louisa, but she prefers 'Lou-Lou,' so that is what we call her."

"Lou-Lou," Louisa said forcefully still staring at Fenella.

Cynara laughed, clearly delighted and amused by her daughter. She glided over to the bell pull and tugged it once.

"As much as I regret it, I shall have to send Louisa to the nursery now, otherwise we shall never be able to converse in peace," Cynara said. "This little lady would insist upon claiming all of our attention."

"And rightly so," Fenella said. "She is a delightful child. You must be very proud of her."

"I am, and I'm afraid I spoil her mercilessly. But I am not one of those mothers who surrender their children to nurses and never sees them until suppertime. No, I intend to enjoy my little Lou-Lou."

"You are to be commended, Lady Eastbrook."

"Cynara, please."

"As you wish."

Just at that moment, a harried-looking maid entered and jerked up and down in a parody of a curtsy. Cynara gave her a frosty glance and ordered her to fetch the nursemaid for Louisa and refreshments for them.

"Come to Mama, darling," Cynara said, extending her arms to her daughter. Louisa obediently reached out and allowed her mother to lift her up.

"Would you like to meet someone, Lou-Lou?" Cynara asked. "This is Fenella. Say how do you do to Fenella, Lou-Lou."

Louisa managed, "El-la."

"How do you do, Lou-Lou?" Fenella said with a big smile.

Louisa giggled, then turned to hide her face shyly against her mother's neck.

They were interrupted by another knock at the door. This time it was the nursemaid, a large, big-boned girl with a pinched face and no warmth about her. As she lumbered in and lunged for Louisa, she didn't even smile, just gathered her charge into her arms as if she were a sack of grain.

Sensing that she was about to be separated from her mother, Louisa crumpled her face and let out a heart-rending wail.

Distress registered on Cynara's face, and she took a step forward as if she would snatch her child back. But she restrained herself and just stood there as the doors closed behind nursemaid and charge, and the child's cries grew fainter and fainter.

"Now you can see why I spend so much time with my daughter," Cynara said ruefully. "I rather doubt that girl is competent to care for a canary, let alone a child."

"Then why don't you hire someone else?" Fenella asked.

Cynara shrugged. "Her first nurse—a veritable treasure of a woman—refused to accompany us to Ireland, thinking it a barbaric place, so I had to find a local girl." A wry smile touched her mouth. "There are not many people who will work for my brother, Fenella. Eilis is the best nursemaid I could find, and that's not saying much, I'm afraid."

An unhappy house filled with unhappy servants as well as masters.

Fenella could think of nothing suitable to say, and she stood there awkwardly.

She was rescued by the maid pushing a tea cart, so she and Cynara sat down closer to the windows and prepared to have tea.

Cynara began pouring, and Fenella admired her grace, every movement smooth and subtle.

"I'm so pleased you accepted my invitation," Cynara said, handing Fenella a delicate porcelain cup.

I could hardly refuse such an imperious request, Fenella thought, but she said only, "Thank you for inviting me."

"Are you enjoying your stay at Rookforest?"

"It's hardly a social visit, but yes, I am enjoying it." Especially since Patrick was now her ally. "The Quinns have done everything in their power to make me feel comfortable and welcome."

Cynara was silent as she nibbled daintily on a biscuit. After she dabbed at her lips with a napkin, she regarded Fenella oddly. Then she said, "I don't know how to broach this subject delicately, Fenella, and I know of no other way to tell you this than to be frank."

Overcome with curiosity, Fenella said, "Please do."

Cynara took a deep breath. "I'm afraid you are the subject of rather vile village gossip."

Fenella's eyes widened in surprise. "Me? Now, that is news, because I lead the dullest life imaginable, not at all the stuff gossip is made of. And what, pray tell, are people saying about me?"

"There is much speculation about your relationship with the Quinn men." When Fenella shot her a frozen look of indignation, Cynara became flustered and tried to soothe her. "Well, you are, after all, an unmarried woman living in a house with two very attractive and eligible men. People are bound to speculate."

"Those same people are forgetting Margaret Atkinson," Fenella said coldly, setting down her half-eaten biscuit. "She hardly qualifies as a chaperon at her age, but she is another female presence in the house nonetheless."

"Oh, now I can see that I have offended you, Fenella, and I didn't mean to. I know how fragile a woman's reputation is, and I was merely repeating village gossip as a precaution."

Fenella, however, was beginning to wonder if Cynara's motives were truly so noble.

"Thank you for your concern, Cynara, but I'm afraid I'm in no position to let anyone dictate my actions. If it weren't for the kindness and generosity of Cadogan Quinn, I'd be destitute today. Rather than indulge in idle gossip, the people of Mallow should be praising him for giving me a roof over my head."

"You are right, of course," she murmured, chastened. Then she poured on charm as thick as cream, hurriedly seeking to divert the conversation with amusing anecdotes of her life in England and her little daughter's antics.

By the time they had finished tea, Fenella was smiling and laughing with her, Cynara's previous tactlessness forgotten.

Later, after the same harried-looking maid noisily cleared away the cups and plates, Cynara rose and motioned for Fenella to join her on the divan. Fenella noticed her radiant hostess's lighthearted mood was rapidly vanishing, replaced by one of urgency.

Cynara glanced furtively at the door, then turned to Fenella. "Please don't think too harshly of me, Fenella, but I must confess I had an ulterior motive in inviting you today."

Fenella was not, in truth, surprised. "Oh?"

"Yes," Cynara said softly, looking away. "I was hoping you would agree to champion my cause to Patrick."

Fenella just sat there, stunned. "I beg your pardon?"

"I love him. I always have. Now that I am free, I want to marry him. But since my brother won't let me anywhere near him, I was hoping that you would plead my case for me."

Fenella rose and averted her face, lest it reveal her anger. "I thought it was over between you and Patrick."

"It will never be over between us. We belong together."

Now Fenella turned to face her. "Then why didn't you marry when you had the opportunity?"

"You know why. My brother wouldn't allow it, and my brother's word is always law. I had no other choice than but to obey him. This time, I shall find a way to defy him and be with Patrick."

Fenella bit back the retort that was on the tip of her tongue and tried to keep her temper in check. When she was more in control, she said, "And what makes you think that Patrick will marry you now?"

"Because he still loves me in spite of everything," the other woman said confidently. "Yes, Fenella, in spite of all those years lost to prison, he still loves me."

Fenella smiled. "Do forgive me for being blunt, Lady

Eastbrook, but I have never heard Patrick once speak of you in other than spiteful terms. It's impossible for me to conceive that he still loves you.''

Cynara's look was supercilious and knowing. ''Ah, now it is my turn to beg your forgiveness for being blunt. But I think I know men better than you do, my dear. And Patrick may not be aware of his own feelings just yet, but he does still love me.''

''So you presume to know his mind better than he himself does?''

''I do. You see, I met him riding one day. I had been thrown, and the dashing Patrick came to my rescue. Oh, he pretended to be impervious to me, but I could tell the old attraction hadn't died.''

Fenella felt her contempt for Cynara growing by the second. ''I see. And you would like me to sing your praises to Patrick and help him to recognize where his heart lies, is that it?''

Cynara smiled radiantly. ''Exactly. How astute of you to understand me so well. And perhaps later, when matters are further along, you could take him my *billets-doux.*'' When Fenella said nothing, Cynara became uneasy and uncertain of herself. A frown line marred the smooth perfection of her forehead. ''You will agree to this, Fenella? For our friendship's sake?''

Fenella stiffened her spine. ''No, Cynara, I will not. For Patrick's sake.''

The other woman's eyes narrowed and darkened with anger, turning into hard amethysts. Her full pouting lips tightened, making her soft, voluptuous mouth a slash. Then she rose as regally as a queen and looked down her nose at Fenella, as if she were an impertinent scullery maid.

''For Patrick's sake? What are you talking about?''

''I mean, Lady Eastbrook,'' Fenella began, her heart pounding loudly in her ears, ''that you have hurt him enough. If the two of you choose to rekindle your relationship, that is your affair. But don't expect me to be a party to it.''

All of the color drained from Cynara's face, which set in a mask of displeasure at being denied. She studied

Fenella coldly for a moment, then smiled, a self-satisfied grimace.

"I can't help but wonder why you won't help me with this one small request." She paused. "Is it perhaps because you want Patrick for yourself?"

That assertion caught Fenella unawares, and she found herself blushing as hotly as if she were guilty.

"Ah!" Cynara exclaimed in triumph. "I have hit upon the truth at last."

Fenella regained her composure and smiled. "You would think that, but no, I have no designs on him. He's just my friend, Lady Eastbrook, but a very good one. And I am loyal to my friends. I don't like to see them hurt."

"How noble of you."

"One of my few virtues, I'm afraid." Fenella retrieved her gloves and slipped them on. "Thank you for your hospitality, Lady Eastbrook. I enjoyed meeting Louisa. She is a charming child. Good day. I rather doubt that I shall come here again, so please, no more summonses."

And I pray your daughter doesn't grow up to be as shallow and self-centered as you are, Fenella added silently to herself as she started for the door.

Cynara's next words brought her up short.

"You'll never win him, you know. You're far too plain and provincial for a hot-blooded rogue like my Patrick."

Fenella said nothing. She didn't even spare Cynara a backward glance as she quietly let herself out of the drawing room and proceeded to her waiting dogcart.

She fumed in silence as she drove away. The audacity of the woman to think that she would agree to such a scheme!

Fenella had certainly been given another glimpse of Cynara Eastbrook's character. She was certainly beautiful, but she was a vain, selfish woman. Fenella found it most gratifying to deny her the one thing she wanted.

She found herself wondering how Patrick could have ever been attracted to her in the first place. But what had Cadogan once said to her about some men spending their lives desiring women who would only bring them heartache? Cynara was certainly one of those, but Fenella hoped Patrick had more common sense. He was too good for Cynara.

Just as Fenella drove her cart between the two armed guards and out the gate, she spied St. John Standon trotting toward her on his white stallion.

She prayed he would just tip his hat and ride on, but as luck would have it, he halted his horse, indicating that he intended to converse with her.

"Good day to you, Miss Considine," he said, sweeping off his hat and bowing low in the saddle.

He looked even more imposing on horseback, like some medieval knight out searching for dragons to slay. His impeccably tailored riding clothes did wonders for his broad-shouldered, slim-hipped physique, but he reminded Fenella of his house, impressive on the outside, but cold and shadowed within.

"Mr. Standon," she acknowledged with a frigid smile as she halted her pony.

He oozed charm as he flashed her a dazzling smile. "Am I to assume you've just come from visiting my sister?"

"Yes, I have."

St. John sighed. "Then I have come too late to enjoy your company as well."

"I'm afraid so."

"A pity," he murmured, his sapphire eyes sparkling flirtatiously. Then he said, "I understand Cadogan Quinn evicted the Finnertys recently."

"It's common knowledge."

"I am surprised. He's always been such a paragon of a landlord, so concerned for his tenants, so determined to cast the rest of us in a poor light. Now we'll see how he fares when they turn their wrath against him."

The spiteful diatribe didn't surprise Fenella.

"Mr. Standon, may I ask you a personal question?"

That ready smile spread across his face like melting butter. "Of course, Miss Considine."

"Why do you hate the Quinns so much?"

The smile faded and he stared at her for what seemed like an eternity. Finally he shrugged. "What can be the harm in telling you? I hate them, Miss Considine, because they always try to take what doesn't belong to them.

Cadogan Quinn stole the woman my father was to marry, the beautiful but faithless Moira. He was a grand landowner, you see, and my father nothing more than an estate agent.''

"I don't understand. Why should that make you hate the Quinns? After all, your father married someone else.''

"Ah, but my father never forgave us for not being the children of the woman he really loved, the woman he would love to his dying day, as he reminded us every day of his miserable life.''

His face darkened, turning ugly. "If Cadogan Quinn hadn't stolen Moira, she would have been our mother, and our father wouldn't have been so cruel to us. Then, when Patrick tried to steal my sister . . .'' He shrugged again.

"But Patrick loved her.''

"I know. That's what made denying him all the sweeter.'' St. John stared off into the horizon. "I know village gossip would have you believe I forced my sister to marry Eastbrook to advance us socially, but that is not true. I did it just to deny Patrick Quinn what he wanted. His prison sentence was an unexpected pleasure.''

You're a vile, disturbed man, St. John Standon, Fenella said to herself.

Now his eyes were on her again. "Spare me your pitying looks, Miss Considine. I don't need them.''

Without another word, he spurred his white stallion forward without so much as a by-your-leave and disappeared through the gates.

"You need much more than my pity," Fenella murmured.

As she continued her journey, she failed to notice the solitary horseman watching her so intently from the top of a nearby hill.

Patrick sat on Gallowglass and quietly surveyed the scene below.

He couldn't believe his eyes: Fenella had betrayed his trust by consorting with his enemy. Though he couldn't see her face, he recognized her pony pulling the Rookforest dogcart. And he certainly recognized St. John

Standon, sitting there so arrogantly on his white horse as he conversed with Fenella.

Patrick's fingers tightened convulsively on the reins, causing his horse to shake his head and whistle in alarm. Then he turned the animal's head around and rode in the opposite direction, intent on catching up with the dogcart down the road.

Then he would find out just what Fenella had been doing at Drumlow, and what she and St. John had been talking about.

Fenella had ridden about two miles when she heard a familiar voice call her name. Halting the pony, she turned to see Patrick waving to her from the top of a nearby hill. When she waved back, he started toward her.

As Fenella watched him skillfully maneuver his sure-footed horse down the steep incline, sending clumps of sod flying into the air, she studied him with admiration. He seemed more content now, more at ease with himself. Gone was that haunted look he would get in his eyes sometimes when he thought no one was looking.

And Cynara Eastbrook wanted to change all that, to ensnare him in her web once again.

Fenella felt a sudden fierce protectiveness toward Patrick well up inside of her. She would let no harm come to him.

Now he reached the bottom of the hill and was walking his horse toward her. Patrick's hair was windblown and his cheeks ruddy from the chill in the late-September air.

He smiled down at her much as St. John Standon had done moments before. "And where have you been on such a fine fall day?"

At first Fenella debated whether she should tell him the truth. But why should she try to protect Cynara Eastbrook? Let Patrick know just the kind of woman she was, and if he was fool enough to still want her . . .

So she looked at him squarely in the eye and said, "I've been at Drumlow, calling on Lady Eastbrook."

Patrick's smile died. "And may I ask why?" he said coldly.

"If you'll climb inside and drive, I shall tell you."

He dismounted, tied his horse to the back of the cart, and climbed inside, taking the reins from Fenella.

"I'm listening," he said.

So as they drove, Fenella told him of meeting Cynara Eastbrook in Mallow one day and how the lady had expressed an interest in a mutual friendship.

"Yesterday I received a letter from her asking if I would call upon her this afternoon. Actually, it was more like a royal command."

Patrick stared straight ahead, a muscle twitching in his jaw. "And why didn't you tell me about this letter?"

"I thought if I told you about it, you would prohibit me from going to see Lady Eastbrook. And I was curious. I did want to see her."

He turned to her now. "Why would you want to do that? You know how my family feels about the Standons."

"I know. But at the time, I felt sorry for her."

Patrick's eyes widened and he burst out laughing. "You felt sorry for Cynara? In God's name, why?"

"You may laugh all you like, but when I met her in Mallow, she struck me as being very lonely, so desperate for a friend. And we are very much alike. Oh, we don't look alike," Fenella amended hastily, "for she is beautiful and I am not. But our situations are similar."

Patrick shook his head. "I'm sorry, but I fail to see any similarities."

"We are both women at the mercy of fate, Patrick, with no control over our lives. Others control our destinies for us. When Cynara's husband died, she was forced to return to Ireland. When my father died, I had to accept your father's kind offer to live at Rookforest."

He looked bemused. "We've treated you that badly, have we?"

"You know that's not what I mean."

"Just teasing, Fenella. So you thought this would give you something in common with Cynara."

"Exactly."

"And did it?"

Fenella shook her head regretfully. "No, I'm afraid it didn't."

Patrick drove in silence for a moment, gathering courage for what he had to ask. "Then what did you and the lady talk about this afternoon, if you have nothing in common?"

"We talked about her daughter, Louisa, whom she calls 'Lou-Lou,' the most beautiful, sweet-tempered little thing that God ever created. I must say Lady Eastbrook is the most devoted of mothers, giving her daughter much attention when anyone else would have turned her over to the nursemaid."

Patrick stared stonily ahead. "And what else did you discuss? Me, perhaps?"

Oh, Patrick, I am so sorry, Fenella said to herself.

"We did," she said aloud. "In fact, as it turned out, you were the chief reason she wanted to see me." Then Fenella took a deep breath before blurting out, "She wants you back, and she wanted me to act as her go-between, singing her praises to you and carrying love letters."

Patrick's head jerked around, and there was such a look of yearning mixed with incredulity that for one horrifying instant Fenella feared Cynara had been right about him after all.

As he stared at Fenella, the color fled from his face, leaving it chalk-white and devoid of warmth. His eyes glazed and his lips twitched but no words of affirmation or denial came out. Finally he jerked on the reins and brought the cart to a halt by the roadside. He just sat there in silence, the heel of one hand pressed against his forehead.

Fenella almost reached out to place a comforting hand on his sleeve, then thought better of it and drew her hand away. She just sat there quietly, letting him get control of the emotions warring with each other across his face. She kept waiting for him to express the elation a man in love would feel, but Patrick just sat there, breathing heavily through his nose and shuddering with every breath.

When he did finally speak, it was not abut Cynara, surprisingly enough.

"Do you know the worst part about being in prison?" he asked.

"No," Fenella said softly. "Why don't you tell me?"

"It's not the treadwheel or picking oakum, although those were backbreaking and demoralizing. It's not the endless sleepless nights listening to the heartrending sobs of the other prisoners or the stench of urine every morning or the black beetles in the food." He laced his fingers together so hard his knuckles turned white. "It's the fact that you cease to be a human being."

Patrick groaned, an agonized sound that touched Fenella's heart. When she placed her hand on his, he reached for her, his fingers enclosing hers tightly, as if he would never let them go. Fenella winced at the strength in those fingers, but she did not pull away.

"It starts when you first enter prison." He spoke dispassionately, as though he were merely a spectator watching from a great distance. "They take away any personal articles you may have with you, as well as your clothes. Any little thing—a pen, your calling cards—that would remind you of home and who you are. Then they take you to the communal bath and bathe you in dirty, scummy water that resembles mutton broth to remove the last traces of your former self."

As Patrick droned on, telling Fenella about the indignity of having his hair cropped, his words came faster and faster, his sonorous voice becoming infused with raw emotion, rising and falling, registering incredible anger, bitterness, and pain.

"There were spyholes actually shaped and painted to look like eyes in the doors of our cells so we could be seen at all times, day or night, by the guards or the prison officials. There was always someone watching, watching, watching. Even our bodies weren't our own because we were constantly being searched and stripped and searched again in places so private, even the strongest of us trembled at the prospect of such violation. You talk of madness . . .

"But the greatest indignity was being called by the number on the back of my prison uniform. I was no longer Patrick Quinn, I was Convict Number Twenty-six."

He looked at Fenella, his eyes red-rimmed from the effort of restraining himself. "I had to keep reminding myself who I was, because to them I was no longer a man. I was nothing more than a bloody number!''

He took one great shuddering breath, flung Fenella's hand away, jumped down from the cart, and went marching off. She sat there silently, undecided. Should she go after him?

But Patrick didn't go far. He stopped several yards away from the cart, his feet spread apart, his hands balled into fists at his sides.

Suddenly, he whirled around, his face a twisted mask of anguish as tears streamed down his face. ''And after all I endured, she says she wants me back?''

Fenella was out of the cart in an instant, running, tripping over her skirts in her haste. When she faced Patrick, she grasped him by the shoulders, then enfolded him in her arms as he had done to her that day in the drawing room. He sobbed as he clung to her, his broad back shaking, but then the moment was over almost as soon as it had begun, for tears were unmanly and had to be controlled.

Patrick stood up straight, wiping at his eyes with the back of his hand. ''I'm sorry for the outburst.''

Fenella caught his hand. ''You had to talk about it with someone, but it's all in the past, Patrick. You've got to let it go,'' she said earnestly, ''and get on with your life.''

''Prison changed me, Fenella. I don't know if I ever will be able to forget it and become the man I once was.''

''No one is the same person he was four years ago,'' she said. ''I certainly haven't been the same since I acquired the sight. But I've learned to adapt, and so will you.''

''You sound so confident of that.''

''I am. Because I've come to know you, Patrick Quinn. You're stubborn and hardheaded. You're not the kind of man who lets adverse circumstances get the better of him. You survived prison, didn't you? You fight back. You persevere.''

Patrick looked at Fenella, her dark eyes alive with conviction and passion, and he really saw her for the first time. He noticed dancing golden highlights in hair that he had once dismissed as drab, and though her face would never inspire sonnets as Cynara's had, Fenella's features weren't as plain as he had once supposed. In fact, the longer he looked at her and the more familiar her features became to his eye, the more attractive she seemed. There was a warm inner glow that gave her clear skin a translucent quality and animated her expression in a way that superficial beauty could not.

And in spite of all the adversity life had handed her, she endured with great courage and strength.

Bemused, he lifted her chin with his fingers, and kissed her.

It was a quick, light kiss, a mere brushing of the lips. Then it was over almost before it had begun. But it was totally unexpected, and left Fenella shaken.

She stared at him as she tried to gather her scattered wits. "If I remember correctly, Mr. Quinn, you once told me my kisses were insipid and that you would never repeat the experience."

"I am often cutting and cruel, saying things I really don't mean," he replied, his voice heavy with regret. "I'm sorry I ever said that to you, Fenella. It was churlish of me."

"Apology accepted." Now she became somber. "What do you intend to do about Cynara?"

He turned from her and made a great pretense of returning to the cart. "Why, nothing at all. I care nothing for her." He extended his hand at her. "Come. We had best get home before Mrs. Ryan serves tea and we're not there."

Fenella let him hand her into the cart and they drove away.

On the way back to Rookforest, Fenella was glancing at Patrick sitting there, staring straight ahead moodily, when a startling thought popped into her brain.

Why, I love him. I'm in love with Patrick Quinn.

She sat back, momentarily disconcerted by such an unexpected revelation. It had been so different with William. The moment she had first seen him, when she and her father had gone to consult him on a legal matter, she knew that she loved him. That love for him had been sudden, a blinding flash of a Roman candle that had rocked her off her feet in the ensuing rush of emotion. Her newfound love for Patrick, she realized now, had been a gradual thing, rather like a rock rolling down a mountain, starting slowly, then gaining momentum until nothing could stop it and everything in its path was swept away.

But she did love him. The warm feeling in her heart could be nothing else.

True, they had started by disliking each other. Yet as the weeks and months passed, and Fenella got to know Patrick, he displayed many qualities she respected and admired—strength, loyalty, and integrity. Perhaps what she admired most of all was his acceptance of her second sight, when most men would have pulled away in fear and disgust. He was not afraid. And he was a man who could keep a secret. Her secret.

Seated next to him, their sleeves touching, Fenella glanced at him out of the corner of her eye. How did he feel about her? she wondered. She was flattered that he trusted her enough to share his shocking prison experiences with her, but did he feel a stronger emotion for her other than friendship?

She would have given anything to know what Patrick was thinking right now.

Patrick was thinking of Cynara.

So, she had attempted to enlist Fenella's aid in winning him back. A feeling of masculine triumph flowed through his veins. He almost wished Fenella hadn't refused to help her. It might have been interesting to watch the lengths Cynara was willing to go to.

Suddenly the old ambivalence returned in full force, throwing him off balance. Part of him wanted to spurn the perfidious Cynara, but another part of him still wanted her. He had his chance to finally win her. The lady was willing, even eager.

Yet he just couldn't bring himself to put the past behind him and take the first step toward a reconciliation. Horrors of prison life he couldn't bring himself to reveal to Fenella rose up like malevolent spirits to torment him.

No matter how much he wanted to possess Cynara, he just couldn't forget the past.

13

SEVERAL DAYS LATER, Fenella joined the Quinns on their way to Devinstown, for Lord Nayland had invited them all to spend the afternoon at his home to see the many improvements he had made in the dilapidated manor house since buying it.

Seated across from Fenella, Cadogan was still sputtering about Parnell's latest speech given in Ennis just that Sunday.

"Listen to this," he said, shaking the paper he held before him. Then he began reading: " 'When a man takes a farm from which another has been evicted, you must shun him on the roadside when you meet him, you must shun him in the streets of the town, you must shun him in the shop, you must shun him in the fair green and in the marketplace, and even in the place of worship. By leaving him severely alone, by putting him into a moral convent, by isolating him from the rest of his countrymen as if he were a leper of old, you must show him your detestation of the crime he had committed.' "

Cadogan's face was red with indignation as he looked from Fenella to Margaret, then to Patrick. "The fool's advocating anarchy!"

Patrick shrugged. "Social ostracism is preferable to moonlighter violence, I suppose."

His father glared at him. "Whose side are you on?"

"Our side, of course. I was merely making a comment, Father. Besides, Parnell was referring to land grabbers, not landlords."

Since Margaret had not wanted to go to Devinstown in the first place, she had been sitting there quietly sulking since they had left Rookforest. Now she said, "The farmers despise land grabbers as traitors who profit from their neighbors' misery. That's why Captain Moonlight singles them out for retribution.''

''Ah, so you've decided to join us after all,'' Cadogan muttered. ''And how, pray tell, do you know so much about the subject?''

Fenella thought of Terrence and held her breath.

But Margaret was quite adept at deception. She merely smiled benignly. ''Common knowledge, Uncle Cadogan.''

That mollified him, and Fenella gave an imperceptible sigh of relief. But she knew it was only a matter of time before Margaret's tongue slipped and she revealed her illicit relationship with the farmer's son.

Patrick folded his arms across his chest and looked out the window. ''Since Galty Garroty is now trying to grab Finnerty's land, it should be interesting to see if his neighbors take Parnell's advice to heart and shun him.''

Margaret said, ''I thought Garroty and Finnerty were friends.''

''They were,'' Patrick replied with a dry smile. ''I remember the first time I went to the office, Finnerty and Garroty's son came together to plead their case for lower rents. They pledged to stick together like wallpaper paste.''

''Ah, the Irish farmers . . .'' Cadogan shook his head. ''They all stick together until one of them can profit for himself, and then all loyalty goes out the window.''

''That's not true!'' Margaret said hotly.

Now Cadogan's suspicions were aroused. He cocked his head to one side and stared at her out of narrowed eyes. ''What did you just say, Margaret Atkinson?''

''I said not all farmers are disloyal.''

''And how would you know that, pray tell? I didn't know you numbered them in your social circle.''

''She learned it from me,'' Fenella piped up. ''I have often told Margaret about the farmers I know, and they are loyal for the most part.''

Margaret added, ''I was merely echoing Fenella's sentiments.''

Seeing that Fenella was responsible, Cadogan backed off immediately. ''Of course Fenella is right. Not all farmers are disloyal. But there are a few who would sell their fellowman for a few acres.''

The matter was dropped as the carriage moved through the gates of Devinstown and down the circular drive paved with crushed oyster shells that crunched under the horses' hooves.

When the carriage rolled to a halt and everyone disembarked, they all stopped and stared at the house before them.

Fenella, who had once visited Devinstown with her father long before Lord Nayland had bought it from the bankrupt Shea family, was amazed at the changes. The earl had obviously spared no expense and had invested a great deal of time as well into restoration. The outside of the small Georgian house had been freshly cleaned so that the bricks were restored to their original warm reddish hue, and it now boasted a new roof as well. The white trim around the windows looked freshly painted, and the age-old broken glass in the fanlight above the door finally had been replaced.

"It's beautiful," Fenella said to Patrick, standing at her side.

He nodded. "I have to give Nayland credit. He's done wonders with this place."

Margaret sniffed. "Well, I don't give him credit at all. This had been the Sheas' home for generations, and he took advantage of their misfortune to buy it right out from under them. He's a land grabber of the worst sort."

"Margaret, Margaret . . ." Cadogan muttered with a shake of his head. "You just won't let up on the lad, will you? For your information, the Sheas had been borrowing heavily for years to pay off Paul's gambling debts. They were up to their eyeballs in debt and had no choice but to sell. And I happen to know Nayland gave them more money than anyone else was willing to pay for a run-down wreck of a house. If he hadn't bought it, someone else would have. And I doubt if they would have restored it to its former glory. Torn it down, most likely, and just used the land."

Margaret glared at her uncle and opened her mouth as if to refute his defense of Lord Nayland, but she was distracted by the thunder of hoofbeats.

They all turned in time to see none other than Lord Nayland himself come sailing over a high stone wall on a rawboned gray hunter. As the horse landed, the shock of impact caused Nayland's spectacles to slip down his nose, giving him a comical appearance as he came cantering toward his assembled guests. But there was nothing comical about his superb horsemanship.

Fenella glanced at Margaret to see what effect Nayland's demonstration was having on her. Margaret looked as if she had just been bowled over by a feather.

"Good day to you all," Nayland said, grinning as he transferred the reins to his left hand so he could push up his spectacles with his right. It was no easy task, for his mount was as mettlesome as any Margaret had ever ridden, bobbing his head and dancing in place, eager to be off. Yet the earl handled him as if he were seated on a rocking horse.

"Nice bit of riding, Nayland," Cadogan said, taking care to keep a good distance away from the horse's iron-shod hooves.

Fenella and Patrick echoed his sentiments, but Margaret was curiously reticent as the earl looked at her expectantly.

Finally he said, "Well, Miss Atkinson, what is your opinion of my horsemanship? As an expert horsewoman yourself, I am anxious to hear what you think."

Her opinion was almost an accusation. "You never told me you enjoyed riding."

He grinned. "I don't enjoy it. But that's not to say I can't do it, or even excel at it, when called upon." His point made, the earl added, "Please go inside. I'll be right with you as soon as I get Greystone here back to the stables."

When he rejoined his guests in the drawing room, Nayland said, "I know you're all impatient for a tour of Devinstown, so let's begin, shall we?"

As they walked down long corridors and through beautifully appointed rooms, Fenella sensed Nayland was displaying his home solely for Margaret's benefit. Rather than going into complex discussions of drainage and rot that the men would have found interesting, he dwelt on the more decorative aspects that would appeal to a woman. He pointed out delicate decorative plasterwork along the walls and ceiling that had been repaired, as well as new wallpapers, draperies, and plush carpets underfoot.

Yet Margaret's only comment throughout the entire time was, "Have you really read all of these books?" when they entered Lord Nayland's extensive library.

As always, he seemed more amused than offended by her insulting questions. "Yes, Miss Atkinson, all five thousand volumes at one time or another. Not all at once, of course," he added with a teasing grin.

"No wonder you need spectacles," she muttered under her breath, but Nayland must have heard her, for he just smiled tolerantly.

After the house came the gardens. Margaret stifled a yawn of boredom when Nayland pointed out terraces, balustrades, and newly dug beds filled with colorful autumnal flowers, but her interest picked up again when he asked if anyone would like to see his stables.

"You keep horses?" she inquired.

"Twenty, as a matter of fact," he replied.

Margaret just stared at him in disbelief.

Cadogan shivered. "Hmph. It's too chilly for me. I'm going inside. Anyone else coming?"

"I am," Fenella said, catching Patrick's eye.

He cleared his throat and said, "I'll join you. I've seen enough horses for one day."

"Well, I would like to see if these twenty horses of yours even exist," Margaret said. "They're probably all donkeys, or so old and decrepit they're ready for the knacker."

"The lady disbelieves me," Nayland replied, grinning as he offered her his arm. "Come along, Miss Atkinson, and I shall show you that I can tell a horse from a donkey."

Margaret ignored his proffered arm and went flouncing past, while Nayland just grinned impishly and shrugged his shoulders in resignation and the rest of his guests went inside to the warm comfort of the drawing room. Later, when Margaret and the earl returned from the stables, everyone else was astounded to hear them conversing civilly, with nary a sarcastic word from Margaret as she discussed bloodlines with Nayland.

But horses and bloodlines were the furthest thing from Cadogan's mind.

Later, after dinner, when the ladies had withdrawn to leave the men to their port and cigars, he turned the conversation toward their estates, as always.

"So, Nayland," he said, "have you been able to hold your rents steady?"

The earl nodded. "When I informed my tenants that I would not be raising their rents, they then demanded that I reduce them."

"The ungrateful dogs are never satisfied," Cadogan muttered.

"And have you reduced your rents?" Patrick asked, helping himself to another glass of brandy.

"Yes, I have," Nayland said. "But then they came back and said they wanted even further reductions, which I could not provide."

"Hang it," Cadogan grumbled. "What do they expect us to do, give them the land for nothing?"

"Exactly," Patrick said. "Ireland for the Irish is Mr. Parnell's fondest desire."

The earl sat back and lit his cigar. "Well, gentlemen, while I have been reducing my rents, I hear St. John Standon has been increasing his, and those who cannot pay will be evicted soon. His master has been most displeased with the recent reduction in his income."

Patrick quirked one brow. "Not enough money for the duke's horseless carriage?"

The earl smiled. "Apparently not. My friends in London keep me abreast of matters there, and according to them, the duke is reaching a critical stage in his outlandish invention's development. He needs a major infusion of capital right away, and expects his Irish estate to provide it."

"And if Standon can't?" Patrick asked, leaning forward on the edge of his chair.

"Who knows? Perhaps the duke will find himself another estate agent."

That surprised Cadogan. "As little use as I have for the bastard, I can't see the duke doing that. Standons have always served as estate agents for their family. Standon may not own it outright, but Drumlow is the only home he's ever known.''

''Well, this duke isn't like his father,'' Nayland said. ''He's not a loyal or sentimental man. Or a patient one, for that matter.''

Patrick's smile was smug and self-satisfied. ''I must say, gentlemen, the thought of seeing St. John Standon lose everything he holds most dear quite appeals to me. Revenge at last.''

Lord Nayland drained his glass and refilled it. ''Who knows if that will happen? But I would say Standon has more pressing problems.''

''Such as?'' Cadogan asked.

''Incurring the wrath of his tenants and perhaps even Captain Moonlight.'' Nayland looked at them. ''So far, the moonlighters have only gone after land grabbers with their tactics, but I heard just yesterday that a landlord in Skibbereen was murdered.''

Cadogan slapped his hand down on the table, causing the crystal and silver to jump. ''I knew it! Just like the Ribbonmen.''

''Still, gentlemen, I think we should all take precautions when we go riding out.''

''Who knows?'' Cadogan said with a chuckle. ''Perhaps our tenants will practice Mr. Parnell's social ostracism on us landlords.''

They all laughed at that, then went to join the ladies.

But Cadogan was closer to the truth than even he supposed, for a mere three days after Parnell's speech in Ennis, tenants of one Captain Charles Cunningham Boycott of Lough Mask House, County Mayo, began shunning the estate agent.

His household servants refused to tend his house, and his grooms left his stables. By the beginning of October, all of Ireland had heard of Captain Boycott and what was happening to him.

The moment Margaret arrived at Ballymere, she flung herself off Bramble and scanned the ruins for any sign of Terrence, but he was nowhere to be found.

She swore under her breath and began walking around

the castle, the weeds catching at her skirt like greedy fingers.

It was becoming increasingly difficult for Margaret and Terrence to meet, what with Uncle Cadogan insisting she ride accompanied by a groom now, and Terrence's family questioning his disappearances from the farm for long periods of time. And there was the matter of Fenella. . . .

Suddenly she saw her one true love slowly climbing up the hill, and her heart beat faster. It had been nearly two weeks since she had last beheld his rough, handsome face and felt his warm embrace. Too long. . . .

She couldn't wait any longer. Margaret ran to him and flung herself into his arms, showering his face with ardent kisses.

Much to her hurt surprise, he pushed her away.

Terrence glanced around. "Not here, alanna, not in the open where anyone may see us."

"Forgive me for my impetuosity, Terrence, but I have been laboring under the impression that you would be pleased to see me."

He flashed that heartbreaking grin at her even as he reached for her hand and pulled her inside the castle. "I can always tell when yer mad at me, alanna. Ye use those long words I don't understand."

Then he was kissing her, and she soon forgot everything else in the sweep of passion.

When he finally released her, he said, "Now, what did ye want to see me about, aside from the fact ye long for me kisses."

"It's Fenella Considine. She keeps badgering me to tell Uncle Cadogan about us. She says she can't keep our secret any longer because she feels she's being dishonest with my uncle."

"An' ye think she'll tell 'im herself?"

"She's threatened to." Margaret hesitated. "There is a way we can stop her."

"An' how's that?"

"We could marry right away and immigrate to America or Australia as we planned. By the time Uncle Cadogan realizes what's happened, it will be too late."

Terrence shook his head, and softened the blow by

kissing her briefly on the mouth. "I can't marry ye just now, alanna. With all these troubles, me father needs me right now. I can't just go runnin' out on 'im. Ye know that."

"But when will we marry?" Margaret demanded.

"As soon as these troubles are over, alanna. I promise." Then he took her face in his callused hands and kissed the objections out of her until she was ready to believe once again anything that he told her.

"What about Fenella?" she asked.

"I think it's time Miss Considine was taught a lesson."

"A lesson? What do you mean, Terrence?"

"I'll just show her that she can't trifle with the likes of the Sheely himself."

Fear welled up in Margaret's breast. "You won't hurt her?"

"I'm not a violent man, alanna. All I'm goin' to do is have a little talk with 'er and see that we reach an understandin'."

Margaret glanced around. "I really must be going before I am missed."

As she turned to go, he reached for her and kissed her one last time.

The barn was quiet except for the low murmurings of the men talking among themselves.

One man guffawed loudly. ". . . an' I'd sell me own mother to see O'Day's face when he walked out o' his cottage this mornin' and fell right into his own grave."

Another chimed in, "Arragh, after all the trouble we had diggin' it for 'im, too!"

A third added, "I don't think he'll be too quick to pay his rent after that little warnin' from Captain Moonlight himself."

"An' if he does, we'll just shoot 'im in the knees. Then everyone will be reminded of what he did every time he goes limpin' into Mallow."

Suddenly all chatter dwindled and died as their leader strode in and moved to the center of the barn. He looked around. "One of our band has requested something special of us.

"As ye know, Fenella Considine has ignored all our attempts to make 'er see the error of 'er ways, even after we burned 'er house. Stubborn woman she is, an insult to Irish womanhood. She defies us by stayin' with the Quinns. Arragh, we can't have that, now, can we?"

The only response from the other men in the room was a nervous shuffling of feet. None of them liked punishing the women, even though they realized it was sometimes a necessity for Holy Ireland's cause.

"What are ye goin' to do to 'er?" one brave soul asked.

"Clip 'er," their leader replied without hesitation, "so all who look upon 'er will know her for the traitor she is."

An audible sigh of relief traveled around the room. Cutting a woman's hair off was certainly preferable to carding, and usually more devastating to the victim's vanity.

"I need three or four men to volunteer for this job," the leader said. "Mind you, it's goin' to be risky, as it's got to be done during the day."

The men exchanged nervous glances. All of Captain Moonlight's work had been done at night, under the cover of darkness to ensure their anonymity and ease of escape.

"Why can't we clip 'er at night?" one of them asked.

The leader shot him a supercilious look. "Arragh, are ye goin' to be the one who slips into Rookforest to do it? Don't be daft, man! Daylight is better, 'cause the lady has been seen ridin' around the demesne every day around one o'clock. Sometimes Quinn is with her, sometimes not. And here's what we have to do. . . ."

After their leader finished outlining his plan, there was less resistance among the other men. Three volunteered immediately; then they all left to return to their homes and families.

The following afternoon at one o'clock, Fenella mounted Shamrock and went for her daily ride around the demesne. Cadogan was busy with some legal work, so he couldn't accompany her this time.

Even though it was a brisk, cloudy October day, Fenella felt warm with contentment as she walked her horse past the house and beneath the silver beech trees that rustled and whispered in the breeze. She hadn't known such contentment since her engagement to William, and it was all because of Patrick. Ever since they had shared all their secrets with each other, they had become friends. Well, not all of her secrets, Fenella amended silently.

Fenella shifted uncomfortably in the saddle as she recalled Cynara's words to her that day at Drumlow: "Could it be that you fancy Patrick for yourself?"

Cynara was right. Fenella did want Patrick for herself.

She couldn't stop thinking about him. She remembered his sweet kisses most of all, the sensuous way his warm, smooth lips pressed against hers, eliciting a response from her effortlessly. And how could she forget the way he held her, his body strong and unyielding against hers?

She had one advantage over Cynara, and only one: Patrick and Fenella's bond went beyond mere physical attraction. They had sensed in each other kindred spirits. Prison had scarred him as much as the second sight had scarred her, giving them an experience beyond ordinary mortals, making them different, setting them apart. If only Fenella could use that to her advantage.

She sighed as she turned Shamrock and headed for the farthest fringes of the demesne. "You're dreaming, girl," she said aloud. "Men like Patrick Quinn don't marry penniless doctors' daughters. They marry women of their own class."

Fenella was so wrapped up in her own thoughts that she failed to notice the man lying on the ground until she was almost on top of him.

With a squeak of surprise she reined in Shamrock too quickly, causing the normally placid horse to fling back her head in alarm and sidestep. When Fenella finally got her under control, she studied the man who was lying facedown beside a screen of shrubbery, his right arm flung over his face.

Fenella hesitated, wondering what to do. This area was in a secluded part of the demesne, with both the main gate and the house out of sight. No one would hear her if she called for help. She would have to ride back and bring someone with her.

Without warning, the man sprang to life, leaping to his

feet with the litheness of a lion and grabbing for Shamrock's reins. To Fenella's astonishment, he was masked.

Momentarily stunned, she just sat there, unable to even
think or move. Her hesitancy was all the time her assailant needed.

"Get 'er, men!" he growled.

At his signal, three other men, also masked, came
crashing through the shrubbery to surround Shamrock,
barring Fenella's escape.

"Wh-what do you want?" she cried, sawing on the
reins and kicking her frightened horse in an attempt to
break through the circle and flee.

"We want you!"

Then several pairs of rough hands were clawing at her,
clutching her skirt and trying to pull her from the saddle.
Fenella dropped the reins and flailed at them with her
fists, trying to beat them off, but one of the men just
caught her wrists while another reached up and grabbed
her around the waist.

Fenella took a deep breath and opened her mouth to
scream, but at just that moment she was flung to the
ground. The force of the fall knocked the wind right out
of her. She lay there, momentarily stunned, her wits scattered like fallen leaves.

They're going to rape me, she thought. Why didn't the
sight warn me of this?

Panic surged and flowed through her veins like boiling
water, giving her strength she never knew she possessed.

"Leave me alone!" she shrieked.

Rolling over, she fought them with all the fury of a
spitting, scratching wildcat, but there were just too many
of them.

"Cadogan Quinn will kill you for this!" she cried.

The men only laughed.

"Turn 'er over and let's be done with it," one of the
men ordered, and Fenella felt herself rolled back onto
her stomach. A heavy knee was pressed into the center
of her back, pinioning her to the ground as she gasped
in pain. She squeezed her eyes shut and prayed they would
be done quickly.

To her astonishment, she didn't feel her skirts lifted or

her drawers pulled down. One of her assailants was yanking out her hairpins.

"Scream again and I'll kill ye," a disembodied voice said.

But when Fenella heard the first ominous snip-snip of shears and felt her hair pulled, she ignored their threats and screamed anyway.

Patrick, riding through the demesne in search of Fenella, pulled Gallowglass up short and listened. There it was again, a sound like a faint scream coming from near the far side of the property.

He dug his heels into his horse's sides and went charging across the lawn in the direction of the scream. Within seconds he saw them, the masked men grouped around another man holding something on the ground. When he saw another man holding Shamrock, Patrick knew their victim was Fenella.

White-hot rage clouded his mind, and without thinking, he whipped Gallowglass into a gallop as he roared, "No!"

Four heads turned in unison. Before Patrick could blink, all the men were running, crashing through the bushes as fast as they could, vanishing as quickly as marsh gas.

For a split second Patrick almost charged after them, his blood lust high. Then reason asserted itself. He was outnumbered four to one, and there was no telling if they were armed. No, he had best tend to Fenella.

He was out of the saddle before Gallowglass even stopped, rushing to Fenella's side. She lay there so still, he feared she was dead.

"Fenella!" He knelt down beside her. "Are you all right? Did they hurt you?"

She stirred. And then he saw what they had done to her.

As Fenella raised her head, hanks of her freshly cut hair fell to the ground.

"My hair!" she cried, sitting bolt upright. Her hands patted her head as if searching for what was no longer there, and feeling nothing but short fuzz, she screamed, a long, drawn-out wail of disbelief and denial. Then, whimpering and desperate, she began gathering up the long clumps of hair and clutched them to her bosom in a pathetic gesture of possessiveness.

"Fenella, don't . . ." Patrick said gently, but she didn't hear him. She just sat there, eyes glazed with shock, hugging what was left of her beautiful long hair.

Thank God they didn't rape her, Patrick thought as he drew her to him. She was shivering so badly he could hear her teeth chattering, so he put his arms around her and hugged her with all his might.

He remembered with crystal clarity that day the prison barber had shorn him. In his most terrifying nightmares, he could still hear the snip-snip of the shears as they crawled across his scalp, shearing away his dignity by altering his appearance so drastically. He had tolerated it because he had no choice. What must it have been like for Fenella to be held down and butchered this way?

He had to get her back to the house.

"Fenella," he said, rising, "you've got to come with me."

But she just sat there, rocking back and forth, seeing and hearing nothing in her own little world, so he forcibly urged her to her feet. Then he put his arm around her waist and started leading her back to the house.

She collapsed halfway there, so Patrick was forced to carry her. Since she weighed less than a wolfhound, she was no burden. But to hear her whimpering mindlessly like a wounded animal was almost more than he could bear.

"Mrs. Ryan, come quickly!" Patrick bellowed as he swept into the foyer with the semiconscious Fenella in his arms.

The housekeeper came at once. "By the Holy, Master Patrick! Whatever happened to Miss Fenella?"

"Moonlighters attacked her and cut off her hair," he said without stopping, hurrying up the stairs.

"Oh, the poor child! She's not hurt otherwise?"

"I can't tell. Send someone at once for the doctor, then join me in Fenella's room. Hurry!"

No sooner did Patrick set Fenella on her bed than Margaret came bursting into the bedroom.

"Patrick, what happened? Mrs. Ryan said Fenella was

attacked and . . ." Margaret's voice died as her gaze rested on Fenella and looked away.

"Captain Moonlight's handiwork," Patrick said bitterly. "And they're so very brave. It took not one, but four of them to subdue one defenseless woman. Courageous of them, don't you think?"

"But why Fenella?" Margaret asked. "She's never done them any harm."

Suddenly Margaret thought of her conversation with Terrence, when she had complained that Fenella was going to inform on them. Terrence had said he was going to do something about that, but surely he hadn't meant clipping Fenella like this? Not her Terrence.

Patrick interrupted her thoughts by saying, "Evidently they think her a traitor, that's why they did this to her." He whirled around. "Where in the hell is Mrs. Ryan?"

"Don't ye go cursin' at me, Patrick Quinn," the housekeeper replied as she came sweeping into the room and went right over to the bed. She shook her head as she peered at Fenella lying there, her eyes wide and vacant, her closed fist still clutching her hair. Then Mrs. Ryan waved her hands at Patrick. "Now, off with ye. There's women's work to be done here. Mistress Margaret, I'm going to need yer help undressin' her and getting her to bed."

"And I'll tell Father what happened," Patrick said.

He turned on his heel and left the women to their task.

Patrick found his father in his study, his head bent over his accounts.

"Father," he began, "Fenella was just attacked by moonlighters."

"What!" Cadogan pushed away from the desk and bounded to his feet, his face crimson with fury. "Is she all right? Did they hurt her?" Then he started charging across the room, heading for the door. "I've got to go to her."

Patrick put out his hands to restrain him. "Father, please . . . They cut off her hair, but she's all right. Mrs. Ryan and Meggie are with her now and the doctor's been sent for. There's nothing you can do right now except calm yourself."

"They clipped her? The bastards!" He staggered over

to the decanter of brandy and splashed a generous measure in a glass. "Is that all they did to her?"

Patrick nodded.

Cadogan tossed down his drink. "Thank God they didn't . . ."

"They didn't. At least, I don't think so. But she's had a terrible shock."

Cadogan put down his glass, his mouth set in a determined line. "What are you standing around for? Let's get some of the men together and find the bastards responsible for this . . . this outrage. When I catch them, they'll rue the day they were born."

"Father, they ran when I accosted them, and by this time I'm sure they're halfway to Mallow. Besides, they were masked. They could be any of a hundred people."

Cadogan ran his hand through his hair, helpless frustration emanating from him in palpable waves. "Tell me exactly what happened," he said as he went to pour himself another drink.

After Patrick told him, Cadogan's nostrils flared and his eyes narrowed into slits, making him look even more bull-like. "You mean those brazen bastards actually came onto Rookforest land in broad daylight to attack Fenella? God damn them to hell!"

"They hid behind shrubbery in a remote corner of the demesne, well beyond the notice of the gatekeeper," Patrick said.

"Why did they single Fenella out?" Cadogan demanded. "That gentle little thing wouldn't harm a fly. She's never spoken out against the moonlighters, though we all have cause."

Patrick shrugged. "Perhaps they object to her friendship with our family. They consider her a traitor and meted out a traitor's punishment."

"Poor Fenella . . ." Cadogan muttered, his face suddenly bleak and ravaged. "It's my fault. I should have protected her. I never should have let her go out riding by herself today."

"Now, stop this at once!" Patrick put his hand on his father's shoulder and shook him. "Who would have thought they would dare to attack her on Rookforest land, right under our noses? No, Father, you must stop blaming yourself. What are we all supposed to do, spend every waking hour locked in our rooms for fear of Captain Moonlight?"

Cadogan sighed, his mindless rage subsiding as logic took its place. "Hang it, you're right. But if a man can't protect his home and family . . ."

I've never seen him so furious, Patrick thought. He's already thinking of Fenella as his wife.

Cadogan lowered his head and his voice was soft and deadly. "They are going to pay for this, Patrick, and pay dearly, the lot of them."

"But you have no idea who they are."

"Oh, but I will. One way or another, I'll learn who these cowards are, and when I do, they'll wish they had never heard of Cadogan Quinn. Now, if you'll excuse me, I've got to go up to Fenella."

And without another word, he strode from the study.

Fenella awoke to soothing, comforting warmth and a sense of peace and security. She found herself in bed, in her nightgown, with the sheet and coverlet pulled up and tucked beneath her chin. She looked around the room. Even though the curtains were drawn, she could tell it was daylight outside. She stretched, wondering why her shoulders and legs ached so.

And then it all came back to her in a blinding rush, the attack and its aftermath, shattering her peace and security like a stone against glass.

Her hand flew up to her right shoulder and groped for the long, thick plait that usually hung there. Nothing. Then her frantic, searching fingers patted her head and encountered the soft fabric of an old-fashioned nightcap. But she was not fooled for an instant. She yanked it off and continued her explorations.

All that was left of her thick, heavy hair was a pelt as short as a wolfhound's coat.

Tears of loss began streaming down her cheeks. Her beautiful hair, her crowning glory, the one aspect of her appearance she was actually proud of, was gone. It would be months, perhaps years, before she felt it rest heavily on her shoulders again after she brushed it out for bed.

She threw the covers back and forced herself to sit up.

Taking a deep, shuddering breath, Fenella rose and headed for the mirror.

Just before she reached it, she stopped, afraid of what she would see reflected in the glass. But she knew she had to go on. She boldly stepped in front of the mirror.

"I look like a little boy!" she wailed at her reflection.

"And a right handsome lad at that," a familiar voice came from the doorway, and she turned in time to see Mrs. Ryan come bustling in with a tray. "Now, back into bed with ye before the master himself has me hide. The doctor said he wanted ye to rest for as long as ye liked."

When the dejected Fenella was back in bed, the house-keeper wagged a stern finger at her. "Now, we'll not be havin' any more tears from ye, Miss Fenella. Mind ye, I'm not tryin' to make light o' what happened to yer lovely hair, but yer lucky those unholy fiends didn't do worse to ye."

Fenella shuddered as she recalled rough hands pushing her down brutally, taking liberties with her person even as they held her still. "I know that, Mrs. Ryan."

"So I'll not have ye feelin' sorry for yerself. Now, eat yer breakfast like the good colleen ye are."

Fenella managed a brave smile and began eating her eggs, though they tasted flat on her tongue.

Mrs. Ryan beamed at her. "I'll tell the masters and mistress ye are up. The lot o' them are most anxious to see ye."

But Fenella was not particularly anxious to see anyone in her present state. Yet she knew she couldn't avoid Cadogan, Patrick, and Margaret forever.

Several minutes later, the three of them came filing in. Fenella scanned their faces for any sign of revulsion, but all she saw there was concern and sympathy.

"Fenella . . ." Cadogan rushed to her bedside, grasped her hand, and leaned over to kiss her cheek. "Are you all right?"

She tried to speak, but the words stuck in her throat, so she just nodded as Patrick and Margaret gathered around her bedside.

"They'll pay for this," Cadogan said, clenching his jaw. "I'll find out who did this to you, and so help me God, I'll make them wish they were never born!"

When Margaret came around the bed, Fenella suddenly remembered the threat she had made that evening in the garden. Fenella shivered uncontrollably. Was Terrence Sheely responsible for this? Had she been clipped as a warning not to betray him and Margaret to Cadogan? Fenella could not meet Margaret's gaze.

Margaret said, "I can trim your hair, if you like, to make it more even. And who knows? Perhaps you'll set a fashion for short hair and every woman in Mallow will follow suit."

Fenella said nothing.

"You're plucky, Fenella," Patrick said softly from the foot of the bed. "You'll weather this as you've weathered other adversities." She knew from the look in his eyes that he wasn't speaking only of her encounter with the moonlighters.

"Thank you for rescuing me," she said to him.

His eyes darkened and his smile died. "I wish I could have prevented it from happening."

Cadogan said, "What's done is done. We can't change it. But we can damn well make sure it never happens again." He looked down at Fenella and patted her hand again. "We'll go now and leave you to your rest."

Then they each said something solicitous and left.

After breakfast, Fenella decided she was through wallowing in self-pity. She would wash, dress, and go downstairs as if nothing had happened. But her resolve soon faltered when Brigid, the maid, came to help her dress. Though she smiled and chatted pleasantly, Brigid could not keep her face from registering horror when she first set eyes on Fenella, and she could never manage to keep her gaze firmly fixed on Fenella's face for more than a second.

The other servants were no different.

Finally Fenella locked herself in her bedroom and refused to come out, even for dinner.

"Fenella, open the door."

"Go away, Patrick."

"Not until I tell you something. If you don't unlock the door, I'll get the key from Mrs. Ryan and let myself in."

Fenella sniffed into her handkerchief. "That would be most improper of you," she said primly, "a bachelor gentleman entering a spinster's bedchamber."

"I realize that." He sounded as though he were smiling. "But occasionally the end justifies the means. Please. Open the door. I think I have a solution to your problem."

That intrigued her.

Fenella rose and reluctantly unlocked the door, to find Patrick standing there in his evening clothes, a lamp in one hand.

"I know it's silly of me," she said, sniffing, "but I was very vain about my hair. It was my best feature, you see, and now it's gone."

"It will grow back," he said gently. "And as for its being your best feature, that is debatable."

The look he gave her silenced Fenella for a moment. When she regained her voice, she said, "Knowing that doesn't make me feel any better now, when everyone is staring at me as though I'm . . . I'm some changeling left on the doorstep."

"As I said, I think I have the solution. Come with me."

Before Fenella could protest, he grasped her hand and started striding down the hall, pulling her in his wake.

"Where are we going?"

"To the attic."

Fenella fell silent as she followed him down the hall to the closed door that led up to the attic. Patrick opened it and started up the stairs slowly, the light from the lamp casting flickering shadows on the narrow staircase.

"Here we are," Patrick said when they emerged. "Eerie, isn't it?"

Fenella found herself in a cavernous room smelling of dust and stale air that must have been a century old. Boxes and trunks were everywhere, some stacked with neat precision and others piled haphazardly, but all filled with the mementos of entire lives lived out in this house. She sneezed in spite of herself.

Patrick started weaving his way past boxes piled high, and trunks, taking special care to brush away the cobwebs hanging down like gossamer curtains.

"What are you looking for?" Fenella demanded, following cautiously in his wake, brushing at the cobwebs he had missed.

"My grandmother's trunks," he replied, his voice echoing back.

"Why would you need your grandmother's trunks?"

"You'll see. I just hope I can find them in all this."

Fenella hurried to catch up with him, her curiosity aroused.

Suddenly Patrick found them. With a cry of triumph he set his lamp down in a safe place and knelt before a huge brass-bound trunk. Fenella stood behind him and watched as he lifted the lid cautiously and began rummaging through the trunk's contents.

From her vantage point over his shoulder, Fenella peered into the trunk and saw what looked like clothes carefully wrapped and folded so they would last another hundred years.

"Your grandmother's clothes?" she asked.

"Yes. When she was young, she was quite a belle of the Regency *ton* and she and my grandfather spent every season in London. They would return to Rookforest in the winter."

Fenella frowned. "That is all very interesting, but what does your grandmother have to do with me?"

Patrick didn't reply at first, just kept rummaging. Finally he found what he was looking for. While Fenella watched, he began unwrapping several layers of dry, crackling paper from some object.

He spoke as he unwrapped. "My grandmother was very fond of wearing turbans," he explained, as one such piece of millinery emerged. "And, since you feel so awkward about appearing in public with your hair in its present state, I thought you might like to cover it with one of Granna's turbans." Patrick handed it to her. "I realize it's not all the fashion in ladies' millinery, but . . ."

Fenella sank to her knees beside him, turning the turban in her hands. Even after sixty or seventy years, the bronze-colored damask was well-preserved, with no signs of mildew or rot, and its jaunty velvet cord tassel was still a burnished gold. It even still shimmered softly in her hands.

"Put it on," Patrick said.

Fenella placed the turban on her head, tucking in any stray hairs carefully. "How do I look?"

"Like a sultan in skirts."

Well, I feel quite ridiculous, like I'm dressed for a costume ball, she said to herself. But she couldn't bring herself to say it to Patrick.

"Thank you, Patrick," she said softly. "This is very thoughtful of you."

Fenella extended her hand and placed it on his cheek, which felt hard and smooth beneath the side whiskers. Patrick's cool eyes warmed suddenly as his gaze traveled down to her lips in blatant inquiry. Fenella leaned forward and kissed him.

She had intended it to be only a brief kiss of gratitude, much the same as the kiss he had given her the day she had told him about her visit with Cynara. But all the events of late had put such a strain on her, that when she felt Patrick's mouth respond beneath her own, Fenella weakened.

She leaned toward him, her hand sliding from his cheek to the back of his neck, so she could hold him in place while she kissed him with as much feeling and passion as she could muster. Her heart leapt with joy when he didn't pull away, but turned to her, slipped his arms about her, and drew her to him.

Fenella realized the pair of them were a sight, kneeling together among the trunks and dust, but she didn't care. Patrick was returning her kiss with vigor, and she was going to enjoy it.

His mouth was soft and moist against hers, his lips moving over hers with a tentative, tender probing, as if to gauge her response. When Fenella leaned forward, eager for more, he responded by deepening his kiss, making it more demanding.

A little whimper of pleasure escaped from Fenella, and the passionate sound seemed to excite Patrick, for he groaned. The tip of his tongue sought to possess her mouth, and Fenella did not draw away as she had that time in the library.

When he filled her mouth, the shock of it caused her to shudder and pull away, but he held her fast, unwilling to release her. Fenella relented, letting herself be surrounded by the rising sensations, reveling in and welcoming them with the heart of a wanton.

As her senses reeled under his sweet assault, Fenella yearned for his fingers to undo the buttons running down the back of her dress. She wanted him to pull her bodice down and shower sweet kisses on her bare shoulders and breasts until she became delirious with pleasure. She wanted—

Suddenly Patrick pulled away, gasping for breath.

Fenella's eyes flew open to find him staring at her, surprise and delight in his eyes' pale depths.

"Ah, Fenella . . ." he whispered, his breath a warm sigh against her cheek.

She blushed. "I . . . I'm sorry. I didn't mean—"

"Yes, you did. And so did I."

Fenella stared at him in surprise, not knowing quite what to say. She had half-expected rejection, not an admission of mutual guilt.

He tapped the turban's tassel with his forefinger, causing it to swing against her cheek. "Sweet Fenella. . . . You never cease to surprise me."

Without another word, he rose to his feet, brushed the dust from his knees, then extended his hand to help her up.

Fenella said nothing, though there was much she wanted to say to Patrick, and much she wanted him to say to her. She wanted to ask him how he felt about her, but he was turning away from her to go rummaging through more trunks.

When he had collected several more turbans, they left the attic with their treasures, and Fenella went back to her room with only the memory of Patrick's kiss to sustain her.

14

FROM THE DRAWING-ROOM window seat, Fenella watched Cadogan mount his chestnut hunter. She didn't notice the murderous glint in his eyes or the rigidity of his jaw as he settled himself in the saddle and gathered the reins. She didn't even notice his expression softening when he looked at her long and hard before turning his horse and riding down the drive. She was thinking about his son.

Fenella smiled as she touched the brown silk turban she was wearing. She knew it looked out-of-place with her dress, with its fitted bodice and natural waist, but at least the turban hid the remnants of her ravaged hair. Patrick had been so considerate to offer it to her.

Her smile faded as she recalled Patrick's kiss in the attic. He had responded to her as a man responded to a woman he was attracted to. She hadn't imagined it. She wasn't worldly or particularly knowledgeable about men, having known the love of only one in her entire life, but she trusted her instincts. As improbable as it seemed, could Patrick possibly find her desirable?

You're wading way out of your depth, Fenella, she warned herself.

She was so deep in thought that she failed to notice Patrick standing in the doorway, watching her silently.

She looks so pensive, he said to himself. I wonder what she's thinking.

He found himself hoping she was thinking of last night in the attic, just as he was.

The depths of his own feelings astounded him. Of all the women in the world, Fenella Considine was the least likely one he would seek out. Yet her particular appeal was insidious and that much more dangerous. She was not a woman of bright, glittering surfaces that attracted with brilliant plumage, but of complex depths that became apparent only after long exposure. Familiarity bred admiration in this case.

He had sensed that last night, when she had surprised him with the kiss in the attic, a kiss that had blossomed into something more. Unless he had lost his ability to judge women, Patrick was certain that Fenella had been on the verge of yielding to him last night. He could have taken her right there amidst the trunks and the dust, and she would have welcomed it.

Suddenly a vision of Cynara crowded his thoughts, her loveliness shimmering before him as entrancing as a siren's song. Now she wanted him. A goal he had once thought unattainable, a goal he had once sacrificed his life for, was finally within his grasp. All he had to do was reach for it. Cynara could be his.

He sighed as the confusion returned a hundredfold.

Fenella heard him and looked up. "Patrick. I didn't see you standing there."

She watched as he crossed the room, moving with the litheness of a cat, his stride light but sure. He looked especially handsome this morning, wearing a dark blue coat that deepened the color of his eyes and showed off his broad shoulders to perfection.

He's too handsome for me, she thought with dismay. Even if I could win him, I could never hold a man like that.

When he reached the window seat, he sat down beside her. "Is something the matter? You looked sad just then."

Handsome and always perceptive, Fenella thought. He reads my mind as effortlessly as I can sometimes read the future.

"I was just thinking of my hair," she lied, touching the turban self-consciously.

"Your hair will grow back. And in the meantime, your turban looks quite stylish. I heard one of the maids remarking on it just a few moments ago."

"Thank you for finding the turbans for me."

Patrick's eyes hardened. "I wish we could find the men who did this to you."

Fenella thought of Terrence Sheely. "Do you think you will?"

He shook his head. "Constable Treherne wasn't hopeful. If they were moonlighters—and I'm certain they were—no one will speak against them for fear of vicious reprisals. The most we can hope for is that someone will turn informer. My father is posting a reward, you know, for information leading to the men's arrest."

"I didn't know that. If I may be so bold, how much is he offering?"

"Fifty pounds."

Fenella's eyes widened. "Fifty pounds? That is a huge sum of money for your father to spend just for that, Patrick."

"He was outraged by what happened to you, Fenella. He's determined to bring those men to justice. And if money will do it . . ."

And what about you, Patrick? she thought. What would you give to bring my assailants to justice?

"Fifty pounds could pay a farmer's rent for several years," she mused, "or feed his family for a long time. That is quite an inducement for someone to come forward."

She also realized it was a true measure of Cadogan's esteem for her, because he was a man of deeds, not words.

"My father hopes it will be sufficient." Patrick looked around the drawing room. "Speaking of my father, I haven't seen him today. Do you know where he is?"

Fenella replied, "I saw him riding down the drive just before you came in."

Now Patrick rose. "He's probably gone to talk to Treherne about the reward."

So, he wasn't going to say a word about what happened between them last night. Fenella felt a fresh surge of disappointment.

To her surprise, Patrick suddenly reached for her hand and brought it to his lips, his eyes warm as they bored into hers. As he held her hand for a moment longer than was proper, his thumb caressing the knuckles, he murmured, "I have no regrets about what happened last night, Fenella. And you shouldn't either."

She looked away and cursed the blush that sprang unbidden to her cheeks. "I don't."

He grinned. "Good."

Then he turned and walked away.

Later that morning, Fenella found herself summoned to Cadogan's study along with Patrick and Margaret.

As she seated herself next to Margaret in a second chair brought in just for the occasion, Fenella thought Cadogan looked unusually grave, his blue eyes as implacable as an executioner's and his lips pursed into a thin line.

While Patrick stood by the windows, Cadogan stood behind his desk, hooked his thumbs in his waistcoat's pockets, and addressed them with a curious formality.

"I've asked you all to come here because there is something of great importance I must share with you." He looked directly at Fenella. "I have promised myself that I shall find the men responsible for the attack on you and bring them to justice. To accomplish that task, I've offered a reward for information leading to their arrest."

Patrick said impatiently, "I've already told Fenella that, Father."

Cadogan scanned their faces before clearing his throat. "I've also informed my tenants that if the culprits aren't turned over to the police within two weeks, I shall begin evicting one family per week until someone comes forward with the information."

No one spoke. Not a chair creaked, not a skirt rustled in the astonished silence.

Patrick was the first to grasp the enormity of the situation. "Father, you can't punish all of your tenants for something the moonlighters did!"

Cadogan scowled and lowered his head like a charging bull. "Hang it, I can do whatever I damn well please with my land. Half of my tenants are probably moonlighters as it is, and if the other half are innocent, they damn well know who's guilty. If they want to save their farms, they can come forward and tell me what I need to know."

Now Fenella rose. "Please, Cadogan, you mustn't do this on my account."

He looked at her without really seeing her. "Oh, but I must, Fenella. It's the only thing I could think of to do that would bring these people to their senses."

"But to punish many for the misdeeds of a few . . ."

Margaret added, "I agree with Fenella and Pat, Uncle. It's sheer madness. Such a vengeful act won't accomplish anything. It will just make the farmers hate us and resist us all the more."

"Or they will want to save their own skins and turn in the men who attacked Fenella," Cadogan said stubbornly.

Patrick ran his hand through his hair, tousling it. "Please, Father, I urge you to reconsider. No good can come of this, especially in these volatile times. We're sitting on a powder keg as it is."

"Someone hurt Fenella and someone will pay."

Patrick turned crimson. "And what happens if the moonlighters start retaliating? They were brazen enough to attack Fenella in broad daylight. What if they try to harm Margaret or Fenella again, or any of the house servants?" A blue vein stood out on his forehead and his voice rose. "This could mean war, Father! Are you prepared for it?"

Cadogan grew livid, his nostrils flaring. "Hang it, they caught me off guard once. Do you think I'd let them catch me napping a second time? Besides, these moonlighters are cowards, the lot of 'em. I've nothing to fear from them. They wouldn't dare attack me."

Three voices rose in dissent, but Cadogan silenced them by raising his hand. "It's already been done. My tenants were informed this morning. I am not turning back now, no matter what any of you say."

Without another word, he turned and marched out of the room.

As soon as the door closed, Margaret tossed her head. "He mustn't do this! For God's sake, Patrick! Can't you do something to stop him?"

Fenella glanced sharply at Margaret. If it hadn't been for you and your lover, none of this would be happening, she said to herself. But she kept silent. She couldn't prove anything, so what was the use of making accusations? It was her word against Margaret's.

Patrick stood there staring at the door, a dazed look on his face. "I can't do anything, Meggie, not when he gets that bellicose gleam in his eye. He's a stubborn man, especially when he knows he's right. Then nothing anyone can do or say can change his mind. You know that as well as I."

"Perhaps I can," Fenella said, rising. "I seem to be the cause of this, so perhaps I can make him listen to reason."

"I doubt it," Patrick said, "but by all means try."

After Fenella left to go find Cadogan, Margaret and Patrick fell silent, she staring down at her hands, and Patrick leaning against the edge of his father's desk, his brow wrinkled in thought.

Finally Margaret looked up at him. "Uncle is doing this to avenge Fenella, isn't he?"

Patrick nodded. "This is his way of showing her he loves her."

"Wouldn't it be simpler just to tell her?"

"You know that's not Father's way."

Margaret felt light-headed. "Oh, dear God! He's going to ruin people's lives, endanger us, and risk all he's worked his whole life for, just to avenge her."

She thought of Terrence. What would happen if her uncle evicted the Sheelys? A dark, uncertain future loomed before her, and Margaret suddenly felt cold all over.

"Troy fell because of a woman," Patrick said. "I suppose Rookforest could fall as well."

"One can hardly call Fenella Considine a Helen, Patrick," Margaret said with some asperity. "And besides, you're taking this all rather well."

"I'm not," he snapped. "I'm just as furious as you are with him. But I won't accomplish anything by butting heads with Father once he's made up his mind."

Margaret knotted her fingers together. "I hope Fenella can persuade him to stop this madness."

"I wouldn't count on it," Patrick glumly replied.

Fenella found Cadogan in the library, a glass of whiskey in his hand as he stared out the window.

At first she said nothing, just watched him for a moment, trying to assess his mood and how she could approach him. With his feet planted firmly apart and one arm behind his back, Cadogan resembled a general surveying his troops just out of sight. The lines around his eyes and mouth seemed deeper to Fenella, making him look battle-weary, but there was still a self-satisfied air about him, as though he had fought the battle well in spite of overwhelming odds.

Fenella entered the library and closed the door behind her. "Cadogan?" she said softly.

He turned to her and smiled. "Come to make me change my mind, Fenella?"

"Yes."

"You're wasting your time."

"I don't think so. My father always said you were a fair and reasonable man, so I'm counting on that to work in my favor."

Cadogan raised one brow. "Did Liam say that about me?"

"Often. Those were the characteristics he most admired in you."

He sipped his drink. "I am a fair, reasonable man. But hang it, Fenella, there comes a time in a man's life when he's got to protect those people he l . . . cares about, and he's got to take a stand. The moonlighters invaded my home and attacked you. What kind of man would I be if I didn't try to make them pay?"

"I'm not going to argue with you, Cadogan. I'm going to ask you—no, beg you—not to threaten your tenants with eviction." She placed her hand on his arm and looked earnestly into his eyes. "Please. For my sake."

He took a deep breath and let it out with a weary sigh. "I can't, Fenella, even for you."

She withdrew her hand. "In that case, I shall have to leave Rookforest."

Much to her chagrin, her pronouncement didn't move him as she had hoped it would. Cadogan merely smiled.

"Where would you go? To that uncle of yours in London?"

"Yes."

"Even if you were to leave, my dear," he said, using an endearment for the first time since she had known him, "you would not keep me from doing what I must do. So you may as well stop making empty threats. They don't become you."

Fenella turned away, feeling suddenly foolish. She had used the threat to leave as an attempt to exert her power over him, the way beautiful women did, and she had failed miserably. Men bowed to the threats of a Cynara Eastbrook, not a Fenella Considine.

Behind her, he said, "If you are serious about leaving, I won't stop you. But I hope you will stay at Rookforest. If Patrick is right and this means war, I would like to have you here."

With the battle lost, she accepted defeat gracefully. "You know me too well, Cadogan. I could never leave you and Patrick and Margaret." Especially Patrick. Not now.

Suddenly some of the tension fled from his face, easing those tired lines and making him look years younger.

"Someone will come forward," he said confidently, "before I even have to evict another tenant. Captain Moonlight will be brought to justice. You'll see that I'm right."

But Cadogan was wrong.

Nearly two weeks passed without anyone coming forward to claim the reward or volunteering information that would save his farm.

All of Mallow was rife with rumor concerning Cadogan Quinn's transformation from a sympathetic landlord to one who rivaled St. John Standon for sheer heartlessness. Most of the blame focused on Fenella. What had she done to earn the enmity of the moonlighters? they wondered aloud to each other. And why had she stayed so long at Rookforest? others asked themselves. But there was no information forthcoming from Rookforest.

The good citizens gossiped and waited for Sunday church services, but they were doomed to disappointment. Dozens of pairs of curious eyes stared and gaped at Fenella in her turban when she and the Quinns walked down the aisle and entered their pew. When the service was over, the quartet hurried out the side door, with Patrick and Cadogan guarding Fenella on either side and

Margaret marching behind resolutely. They left curious, unsatisfied townspeople in their wake.

Speculation about Cadogan Quinn even overshadowed Captain Boycott's situation at Lough Mask. His social ostracism was so complete that laborers were being brought in from all over Ireland to help harvest crops that would have otherwise rotted in the ground. Many were putting the blame squarely on Parnell's shoulders and demanding his arrest. But such news hardly made a ripple in Mallow these days.

Everyone engaged in speculation concerning who would be the first to be evicted from Quinn land, and whether Captain Moonlight would retaliate.

The barn was bitterly cold tonight, though the men assembled there hardly noticed, for they had their patriotic fervor to warm their blood.

Their leader said, "Are we all in agreement, lads?" as he held up a piece of paper for all to see. On it was a coffin, crudely drawn, but its message and intent clear.

A unanimous cheer rose and echoed through the empty building.

The man who had objected so vehemently to Liam Considine's assassination now raised his fist and cried, "Death to Cadogan Quinn! Long live Captain Moonlight!"

Their leader smiled, a wolfish baring of teeth. "This will be tacked to his gate tomorrow mornin' so he'll be sure to see it as he rides out to evict one of our own."

"Who's it to be?" someone asked nervously.

"Don't know," another replied. "I heard himself will draw lots."

A third man shook his head. "We nivver should've attacked Miss Considine. That's what turned Quinn against us, attackin' the woman on his own land. Offended the man's pride, it did, attackin' the woman on his own land."

"She was a traitor, like 'er father, and had to be punished," the leader growled. "She's lucky we didn't slit 'er throat." He looked around the barn. "Mind ye, since we clipped 'er, how many others have turned informer?" When no one answered, he said, "None. No one turned informer on Captain Moonlight, not even fer fifty pieces of gold.''

Murmurs of assent rippled through the gathering, and their strength and power grew.

One dissenting voice said, ''Aye, but how long can we hold out once Quinn starts evictin' us? What will we do to feed our starvin' families? Where will we go? There's just so much a body can stand.''

The leader's voice turned to steel as he waved the piece of paper in the air. ''He'll be dead before the week is out. An' without a landlord, there will be no more evictions, I'll promise ye that.''

''What about his son? 'E's not gonna take too kindly to us killin' 'is father.''

Their leader smiled. ''He'll listen to reason. An' if he doesn't, he'll follow his father right to the grave.''

In the drawing room, Fenella sat close to the fire, but even its heat couldn't warm her. She shivered uncontrollably and gathered her shawl more closely around her.

What a perisher of a day for an eviction, she thought as she looked out the window at a raw, blustery October day. The sky was the color of blackberries and a fine mist was falling.

Today a family, husband, wife, and children, would be turned out of the only home they had ever known for refusing to name Fenella's attackers. She felt partially to blame. She could still feel the accusing stares of all the townspeople in church, hear the angry whispers behind her back, see the sour faces glaring at her.

She sighed, leaned back in her chair, and closed her eyes.

''You're not to blame, you know.''

She opened her eyes as she turned in her seat to see Patrick come striding into the room. How uncanny that she with second sight could never read his mind, but he always seemed to know what she was thinking.

''But he's doing this to avenge me, and I feel responsible.''

He stood before the fire and extended his hands to warm them. ''What a perisher of a day this is. Cold and dank.'' Then he said, ''It's not your fault. Father would have done the same if Meggie or I was attacked.''

Fenella cast a worried look at the rain, which had suddenly turned from a fine drizzle into a downpour, the wind lashing the nearly bare trees into a frenzy. ''But to turn people out of their home on such a day. Couldn't you persuade him to wait a day or two?''

''I tried,'' came a voice from the doorway, ''but it's no use.''

Lord Nayland came toward them, wiping the rain from his spectacles with a handkerchief and nearly tripping over a footstool he couldn't see. ''His mind is made up. The eviction will proceed.''

Patrick extended his hand. ''Good of you to come on such a day, Nayland. Brandy?''

''Yes, please.'' Nayland put his spectacles back on and studied Fenella's turban. He smiled. ''Most ingenious.''

She smiled back. ''It's preferable to resembling a little boy.''

While Patrick went over to the decanter to pour, the earl stood with his back toward the fire. ''The other landowners and agents in the area are divided on the issue. Some say Cadogan is foolhardy, while others applaud his courage for taking a stand against the moonlighters.''

''And what does Saintly Standon think?'' Patrick asked, handing the earl a glass.

''Oh, he's positively gloating,'' Nayland replied. ''He's telling everyone who'll listen what a hypocrite Cadogan Quinn is.''

Patrick scowled, his fingers tightening on the glass he held. ''That's one more score we have to settle.''

Before anyone could comment, Margaret came sweeping into the room in a dress of warm gold that brightened the gloomy day. She hadn't bothered to put up her hair today, so it tumbled down her shoulders in wild abandon, giving her the look of a Gypsy queen.

She took one look at Lord Nayland, eyeing her appreciatively, and sniffed disdainfully. ''And what are you doing up and about on such a miserable day, my lord? I would have thought you'd be locked away in your library, wearing out your eyes.''

The earl chuckled indulgently, for Margaret's barbs

never seemed to sting him. "After I'm through wearing out my eyes, Miss Atkinson, the mere sight of you restores my vision. That's the reason I braved the elements today."

Margaret rewarded his fulsome teasing with a haughty glare, then addressed Patrick. "I know it's pointless to ask if Uncle is going through with the eviction."

"He is, that's why we're here," Patrick replied.

"This is madness!" She hurried over to the brandy decanter, poured herself a generous measure, and swallowed it neatly, causing Lord Nayland to stare goggle-eyed at her.

Before anyone could say another word, Cadogan himself appeared in the doorway. "Ah, so you've decided to join us, Nayland," he said, stuffing a piece of paper into the pocket of his ulster. "Good man."

Fenella just sat there, debating whether to make one last plea; then she decided against it. She could tell by the morose expression on Cadogan's face that he really didn't want to evict anyone, but she knew him well enough to realize he was a man of principle. To back down now would be to show one and all that his threats were merely threats without substance, like milkweeds blowing in the wind.

"Who's it to be?" Patrick asked, setting his glass down on the mantel.

"The Grogans," his father replied.

Margaret started. "The Grogans! But, Uncle, they were just married two months ago. Surely you don't mean to—"

"Hang it, Margaret, I do mean to evict them," he snapped. "It will be no hardship for the Grogan and his bride to go live with her parents until someone comes forward with information about the moonlighters. Then, when this is over, the Grogans can move back into a newer and larger cottage for their pains."

So, of all the tenants on the Rookforest estate, Cadogan had chosen the ones with the least to lose.

"Your bark is worse than your bite, Father," Patrick said.

Cadogan grumbled something in reply, then motioned

for the men to follow him as he turned on his heel. "Let's get this over with," he said.

The men returned later that afternoon, at four o'clock, their clothing spattered with mud, their faces streaked with water and dirt.

Cadogan said nothing to either Fenella or Margaret, just climbed the stairs wearily, leaving Patrick and Lord Nayland to relate what had happened. There had been resistance. Several policemen barely escaped being doused with scalding water, while Patrick and the earl had been pelted with mud and stones. This information earned Nayland a glance from Margaret, but no offers of sympathy.

But in the end, might prevailed. The young Grogans were evicted as an object lesson to those who would defy Cadogan Quinn in his quest for justice.

"They hate us now," Patrick said, passing his hand before his eyes wearily. "They hate us as much as they hate Standon. We've become the enemy."

"Surely not," Margaret commented hopefully.

"Oh, yes. You could see it in their eyes, hear it in their voices. Cold, implacable hatred."

"Surely someone will come forward now," Fenella said.

"We shall see. It's Captain Moonlight's move," Patrick said.

The ominous words felt like cold fingers on the back of Fenella's neck, and she shuddered.

A day passed, then another. Still no one came forward to inform on Captain Moonlight.

With each passing day, Fenella noticed that Cadogan was becoming increasingly pensive and morose. She knew the prospect of another eviction was tearing at his insides, but he was a stubborn man and would not give in.

Everyone in Rookforest was on pins and needles wondering how the moonlighters would retaliate. Fenella and Margaret were warned not to go walking or riding alone, even on the estate, and Patrick and Cadogan had taken to arming themselves with revolvers.

Then came the day Fenella saw the banshee and heard it wail.

Friday dawned cold but sunny, a welcome change from all the rain of the previous days. Fenella felt her spirits rise just looking at the sun bathing the demesne in its warmth.

But by late afternoon the clouds had rolled in, darkening the landscape ominously and putting a chill into the air.

As the shadows lengthened, Fenella felt inordinately chilly. A draft played about her ankles, and little shivers went shooting up her arms. She decided to go upstairs to her room to find a warmer shawl.

The moment she walked into her bedroom, she felt it, the faint sense of uneasiness stirring in the back of her mind. And when the scar on her wrist began throbbing like an aching tooth, she knew what was coming next.

A strangled cry of denial caught in her throat as the dizziness spun her around with such force that Fenella thought she was going to be physically ill. Her brain seemed to burn in her skull like the fires of hell.

It's never been this bad before, was her last conscious thought as her bedroom faded away.

It was the middle of the night and Fenella was floating above Rookforest. She could see the house beneath her, all silver in the moonlight.

Why am I here? she asked herself. What shall I see this time?

She heard it first, the chilling, high-pitched keening sound of mourners at a wake, coming from the grove of silver beech trees at the back of the house. As Fenella listened and watched, a tall, slender figure of a woman dressed in silvery raiment came gliding through the trees, clapping its hands as it wailed. But the specter's most unusual feature was its hair, so long that it flowed like a waterfall, at least a yard of it on the ground.

Fenella felt no fear as she watched the apparition glide about, circling the house, clapping her hands, and wailing most piteously. The fear would come later. All she could do now was observe and wait for the vision to play itself out.

The apparition floated past and turned to look at Fenella. But before Fenella could see its face, she blinked.

When she opened her eyes again, she found herself back in her room, the weak late-afternoon light banishing the blackness. She moaned and sat up, cradling her aching, spinning head in her hands, unwilling to believe what she had just heard. But she knew denial was fruitless.

She had heard the wailing of the banshee, and one of the Quinns would die.

Patrick! Fenella hauled herself to her feet with the aid of the bedpost, and stood there on weak, wobbly legs. Then she went lurching and staggering toward the door. She stood there for a second, clutching the doorjamb for support, waiting for her head to clear, when Patrick suddenly appeared walking down the hall.

His brow was furrowed with worry. "Fenella, have you seen Mr. O'Malley anywhere? He's been missing since yesterday, and I—" Patrick stopped and stared at her, grasping her arms when she almost fell. "What's wrong?"

"I . . . I just had another vision." She clutched at Patrick's lapels in desperation. "I saw the banshee and heard it wail. Just now, in my room."

He turned white. "What did you say?"

"You heard me. I said I heard the banshee wail. And you know as well as I what that means!"

"That's nonsense, Fenella," he said with a nervous laugh. "Irish superstition. You only heard the wind. It's been rising all day and—"

"Patrick!" Stung by his denial, she shook him in her desperation. "I know what I heard. You know for yourself my visions don't lie."

He just stared at her, his intellect warring with his intuition. Finally he ran his hand through his hair and said, "I know they don't, Fenella, but I pray to God this one is wrong. Tell me exactly what happened." And he drew her into the bedroom lest they be seen and overheard by some servant passing by.

Her voice shaking and hesitant, Fenella told him what had happened when she returned to her bedroom for a shawl. "The sound was horrible, just horrible!" She burst into tears.

Patrick took her in his arms and held her until her tears subsided.

"What are we going to do?" Fenella asked when she drew away.

His brow furrowed. "According to what I remember of the legend, the banshee appears the night before someone in the family is to die. So since your vision occurred today, I'm assuming that the death will occur tonight."

Fenella nodded.

"Well, then, we shall try to cheat death. Margaret, my father, and I will stay here tonight and be on our guard."

Suddenly Fenella felt faint. "Oh, my God! Where is your father?"

"He went into Mallow, to the office," Patrick said. "Don't worry, Fenella. He'll be safe in town."

Panic coursed through her. "Please see that he's safe, Patrick. Take some men with you and bring him home. I won't rest easy until I know that Cadogan is home safe and sound."

He nodded. As he left the bedroom, he turned and said, "It could still have been just the wind."

"I pray it was, Patrick," she replied.

Patrick galloped out of Rookforest as if the devil himself were chasing him, but in fact, he was being followed by two of the grooms, each armed with a rifle. Patrick himself carried a revolver. He was taking no chances.

He scanned the horizon with impatient eyes. It would be dark soon, and he didn't want his father riding home alone in the dark.

Patrick shivered as the wind whipped the tears from his eyes and tore through his woolen coat. He had put on a brave facade for Fenella back at the house when she told him of her vision, but in reality, he was more frightened than he had ever been in his life.

Though he resisted believing her, he knew her visions were real. Hadn't the woman in the blue shawl proven it to him that day at the Finnerty's eviction?

If Fenella said she heard the banshee wail, she heard it.

Patrick set his spurs to Gallowglass, urging the horse to run even faster. At the same time, he scanned every hill and hedgerow for signs of an assassin lying in wait. After all, he was just as much a Quinn as his father. He could be the one slated to die tonight.

I pray to God she just heard the wind, he said to himself as Mallow came into view.

Minutes later, Patrick and his men were riding down the street when he noticed a throng of people gathered near the Quinn's estate office. There was a man lying on the ground. Patrick slowed Gallowglass to a walk, trying to postpone the inevitable.

He knew it was his father and that Cadogan was dead.

The onlookers heard him coming and stood back respectfully, staring up at him out of silent, shifting eyes.

Patrick halted his horse a few feet away and looked down at his father, lying facedown in the street, one arm flung up as if to break his fall or ward off an assassin. He was so still.

Patrick forced himself to drag his gaze away and look at each and every man in turn. "How did it happen?" His voice sounded loud, aggressive. "Did anyone see how it happened?"

One man raised his hand and stepped forward.

"Who are you?" Patrick snapped irrationally, for he knew.

"Sheely, yer honor. Terrence Sheely. I was just coming out of the public house down the street when I saw a man walkin' with yer father. I didn't pay them any mind at all. Then I heard a shot and saw yer father fall. The other man ran off just as soon as it happened."

Cadogan Quinn murdered in broad daylight, right in the street, his life's blood spilling out onto the cobblestones from a gunshot wound in the right side.

"Did you see his face?" Patrick rasped.

"No, yer honor. He was too quick fer me. I went to see if I could help yer father, but I was too late. He was already gone."

All of those present crossed themselves and bowed their heads.

Hypocrites, Patrick thought, ignorant hypocrites. All of you wanted to see him dead so you could steal his land.

His throat suddenly constricted, and he had to clear it

several times before he could say, "Did anyone else see anything?"

"Just Sheely tryin' to help yer father," a faceless voice replied from the crowd.

The grief threatened to overwhelm Patrick, but he ruthlessly suppressed it. He would not give these people the satisfaction of seeing him break down and weep for his father.

He dismounted and strode forward. The onlookers respectfully stepped out of his way so he could kneel. Patrick almost broke down then. His father, so vital and alive, now lying dead in the street, his shocked eyes staring sightlessly toward eternity.

He turned Cadogan over on his back and closed his eyes so he looked as though he were merely sleeping. Then Patrick stood and, in spite of the cold, stripped off his coat so he could cover his father's face and shield it from the curious and those who had secretly come to gloat.

Suddenly several constables appeared.

Patrick heard himself tell one of his men to fetch a wagon, but it was as though someone else were speaking with his voice and he was just observing from a long way off. So much to be done. He was so very tired.

How am I ever going to tell Margaret and Fenella? he thought.

But Fenella already knew something tragic had happened.

She had spent the time praying that Cadogan and Patrick would return safely, but as the hours dragged by with no sign of them, her optimism dwindled into bleak raw fear.

Finally, when only Patrick came through the front door at seven o'clock that night, Fenella knew instinctively that the banshee had wailed for Cadogan.

She stood there in silence, staring at Patrick, willing him to break into a grin and reassure her that everything was all right. But he didn't. He just stood there silently, his eyes tired and sad and devoid of inner fire.

"Cadogan . . . ?" Fenella asked, her voice breaking.

Patrick took a deep breath. "Someone shot him as he left the office. He's dead."

"No!" came a shriek, and Fenella turned to see Margaret come running down the stairs. She grabbed Patrick by the arms. "What are you saying? Uncle can't be dead! He can't be!"

"I'm sorry, Meggie," he said wearily, "but it's true."

"How? Did anyone see who did it?" she demanded.

"Come into the drawing room and I'll tell you." He turned to Fenella. "Would you please have Mrs. Ryan join us?"

Minutes later, they all assembled in the drawing room. Margaret was weeping openly, and a grim-faced Mrs. Ryan went to comfort her. Fenella was still too numb for tears.

Controlling his emotions as best he could, Patrick told them what had happened in Mallow. Then he reached into his pocket and pulled out a sheet of paper, unfolded it, and smoothed out the wrinkles before he handed it to Fenella first.

It was a drawing of a coffin with Cadogan's name written beneath it in a childish scrawl.

"What is it?" she asked as she passed it to Mrs. Ryan.

"A warning from Captain Moonlight that he was marked for death," Patrick replied. "Evidently my father had found it tacked to the front gate several days ago, but kept it a secret from everyone." Patrick's jaw worked and his eyes grew unnaturally bright. "I don't know why he did this, because if he had told someone, perhaps we could have taken precautions and prevented his death today."

"Arragh, Master Patrick," Mrs. Ryan said, "there's nothin' ye could have done. There's no escapin' their vengance."

"They're not invincible, Mrs. Ryan," he said. "They're only men. And they will all pay dearly for my father's death."

Without another word, Patrick whirled on his heel and stormed out of the room to be alone with his grief.

15

IT WAS PAST midnight before Fenella retired, and even then, she couldn't sleep.

Unlike Margaret, who had spent the last few hours sobbing and wailing over her uncle's sudden and tragic death, Fenella was quiet, her emotions locked tight inside her and bound by excruciating guilt.

She lay on her back, staring at the ceiling, feeling like the fabled Cassandra, her dire prophecies never to be believed. In Fenella's case, she saw a future that could not be changed. Well, she had been able to save Cadogan from a scalding at the Finnertys' eviction, but to what end? To have him meet a worse fate at an assassin's hands?

I'm Jonah, she said to herself. I don't belong with decent people. I may as well find myself a cottage in some godforsaken place like Connemara and live alone. Alone. People will say I'm a witch and give me wide berth. Children will throw stones at me and call me names. In time, I'll go mad. It's what I deserve.

Rolling onto her side, she cradled her head on her arm and thought of Patrick. She had wanted to go to him, to hold him in her arms and share his pain, but he had locked himself in his room right after he left her and Margaret in the drawing room. She didn't think it was her place to intrude on his grief. And he had not sought her for comfort. That made her feel lonelier than ever.

Fenella sat up in bed and pressed the heels of her hands into her eyes, trying to relieve the ache of pent-up, unshed tears. Then she lit a candle to banish the blackness encroaching on her heart.

Suddenly the unmistakable sound of the doorknob

turning caused her to start. As she watched, the door opened slowly to reveal Patrick.

He looked bereft and abandoned, like a child spending his first day at boarding school. Yet there was a touching hopefulness about him as well.

Fenella flung back the covers, rose, and padded across the room on bare feet. "Patrick?"

He shook his head as he closed the door softly behind him. "I couldn't sleep."

"That's understandable, under the circumstances."

Fenella was on the verge of asking him what he wanted when Patrick's expression changed. His dazed, vacant eyes suddenly blazed with desire as he raked Fenella up and down. That quick appraisal made her feel naked even though she was wearing a modest white flannel night shift that came up to her chin and covered her wrists and ankles.

Her pulse quickened as she realized the danger she was in. She and Patrick were alone in her room past midnight in defiance of all propriety. She remembered what had happened whenever she and William were alone.

Fenella moistened her dry lips. "What do you want, Patrick? Why have you come?"

He walked toward her. Then he reached out and cupped her face with an unsteady hand. "It's been such hell, Fenella, for days, and now"—his eyes watered and his voice broke—"my father's dead."

His fingers felt like ice against her skin. "I know how you feel, Patrick, and I'm so very sorry. I'd do anything to bring Cadogan back and spare you such pain."

"Then let me share your bed tonight. Let me love you, Fenella. Please."

She caught her breath, unable to believe she had heard him correctly.

"I can see that I've shocked you. You've never been married, but I suspect you're not an innocent schoolgirl, either. After what happened in the attic, surely you must have sensed it would eventually come to this between us."

She thought of William's fate and she knew she mustn't succumb to Patrick's request. "Patrick," she said gently, "it's late. Perhaps you'd better go back to your own room before you do something we shall both regret."

His hand fell away from her cheek and he shook his head as if to clear it, his sigh echoing in the room. "I'm sorry. You're right, of course. What was I thinking of, trying to force my attentions on you, a guest in my house? You're an honorable, respectable woman who probably doesn't have the slightest idea what I'm talking about, and I'm acting more like a rutting boar than a gentleman. Forgive me for my atrocious behavior, Fenella. It won't happen again."

As he turned to go, looking so forlorn, Fenella caught his hand. "Patrick. Wait."

He turned and looked at her quizzically.

She decided it was time to tell him her second secret.

"But I'm not as respectable as you may think," Fenella said softly, "and I understand what you mean quite well." She took a deep breath for courage. "You see, my fiancé and I were lovers." She hesitated. "In every sense of the word."

Patrick's eyes widened as comprehension dawned. "You were his mistress?"

"Yes. William seduced me and I . . . No, that's not fair to his memory. We seduced each other. And even though we both knew it was sinful to . . . to become lovers out of wedlock, we couldn't help ourselves. We loved each other so much, and it didn't seem wrong. After all, we planned to marry."

Fenella felt her face grow warm under Patrick's unceasing scrutiny, but she plunged on. "And then William died." She caught at a bit of the flannel and twisted it. "Don't you see? We were punished for what we had done."

Patrick was at her side in two strides, taking her in his arms. "Fenella, why didn't you tell me this sooner?"

"Because I thought you'd lose all respect for me," she replied, burying her face against his shoulder. "I was afraid you'd think me a . . . fallen woman."

"I could never think ill of you." Then he held her at arm's length so he could look at her. "You weren't responsible for William's death, so stop blaming yourself.

You have been blaming yourself all this time, haven't you?''

She nodded.

"Well, stop it this instant. William died of pneumonia, not the wrath of God.''

"Then why did he come to me in a dream?'' she demanded, her voice anguished. ''Why did he curse me with these damned visions?'' She turned away from Patrick and rubbed her arms, for she felt oh so cold.

"Fenella—''

She whirled around. ''Don't you see? Everything I love dies. William, my father, your father . . . And if you stay with me tonight, you'll die too!''

"I'll risk it.''

"Patrick, please don't make light of this. This is not a laughing matter.''

"I'm not. Whatever you may think, you're not cursed. Everything that happened is circumstance or fate, nothing more.'' He looked at her long and hard. ''Fenella, please let me stay. Let me prove to you that it's all in your mind.''

"But I'm so frightened.''

"Then you need me even more tonight, just as much as I need you.''

And she did need him, more than she thought she could ever need another human being.

"Stay with me, then, if you dare.''

Her words were both a surrender and a challenge. Patrick felt a flame melting the ice of desolation encasing his heart. He took her cold hands in his and brought them to his lips to warm her fingers, which betrayed her nervousness by trembling just a little.

He dropped her hands, but still held them. ''Come to me, Fenella,'' he whispered.

She obeyed without hesitation, slipping her arms about his waist and drawing him against her so that her full breasts were crushed enticingly against his chest and her thigh was nestled against his own.

Then she waited patiently for his kiss, her face inches from his own. He could see her eyes darting from his forehead, across his eyes, and down to his chin as if she were reading a map. Finally she smiled, a slow, seductive smile of acceptance and encouragement that pleased him.

Once again, he wondered fleetingly how he had ever thought her plain. Tonight, with soft candlelight illuminating her, she was beautiful.

Patrick reached for her lips with his own, and kissed her slowly, gently at first. Fenella's lips were so soft and yielding beneath his own, responding and following his lead. He gently parted them with the tip of his tongue and felt her stiffen momentarily at the intrusion. But she responded, willingly accepting his tongue's sweet invasion.

When he had her as breathless as he was, he drew away and began raining kisses across her forehead, against her eyelids, and then her cheeks. She murmured his name and hugged him closer to her.

He shifted her slightly to the left and was delighted when a small frown of annoyance appeared between her brows.

Patrick nuzzled her ear and whispered, "I only wanted to free my arm so I could do this . . ." He began unbuttoning the tiny buttons on the high neck of her night shift.

Fenella's sigh was ragged with anticipation. As Patrick gradually freed one button after another, Fenella felt the garment begin to open. First her neck was exposed to Patrick's teasing fingers and questioning lips, then her collarbone. He only paused to dip his tongue into the hollow of her throat before continuing with those buttons. When Fenella felt his long, elegant fingers brush the tops of her breasts, she held her breath until the blood began crashing against her temples.

She half-expected him to pull the garment open and dive for her breasts as William was apt to do, but Patrick would not be rushed. Her breath came out in a swoosh and her eyes flew open in surprise when he cupped her right breast through the night shift and began caressing it. Her knees began trembling uncontrollably as wave after wave of pleasure rocked her, forcing her to lean against Patrick lest she collapse. All of her doubts and misgivings melted away.

His cheek was hard against hers, his lips soft against

her ear. "Bare your breasts to me, Fenella," he whispered.

She gasped, her neck and face flushing crimson at his bold, shocking command, but she wanted to please him tonight. Fenella slipped her hand beneath the soft fabric and pushed the night shift off one shoulder, then the other.

What if he finds me repulsive? she thought as she shrugged her breasts out of the garment and gathered it at her waist.

Patrick swallowed hard. Her ivory breasts were full and round, their crests tipped with pale rose. He wanted to rest his head upon them and forget all the horrors of tonight.

"You're beautiful," he said.

Fenella's smile was shaky with relief. She couldn't resist saying, "So my tavern-wench attributes please you?"

He grinned as he reached out to tease one nipple. "Oh, yes. But I want to see all of you."

Fenella held her breath and released the night shift. It fell over her hips in a soft rustle, slid down her legs, and gathered in a puddle at her feet. She resisted the impulse to cower in embarrassment. She held herself straight and proud, her arms at her sides as though she were a great courtesan displaying herself for her master.

Patrick gazed at her in wonder. Who would have guessed that beneath all of Fenella's drab brown dresses as impenetrable as metal lurked such a perfectly made form? He wanted to take her right there, to feel those strong, slender limbs wrapped around him, giving him pleasure. But he restrained himself. There was time enough.

"Where have you been hiding . . . all this?" he asked.

Fenella blushed, then smiled. "Your turn, Patrick. Undress for me."

Patrick undressed quickly, with the confidence of a man who knew his body was pleasing to women. When his shirt and trousers had joined Fenella's night shift on the floor, he stood there in silence, awaiting her verdict.

Fenella swallowed hard as her eyes drank in Patrick's body. He was all muscle, and broader and heavier than

William in every respect. And he paid her the ultimate compliment of being so obviously aroused by her.

"You're very handsome," she said shyly, dragging her gaze up to his face.

"I'm glad you approve."

He effortlessly swung her in his arms and walked over to the bed, gently setting her down as if she were his most precious possession. When he went to blow out the candle by her bedside, she surprised him by staying his hand.

"Leave it on."

"I think you're more vixen than spinster." He slid into bed beside her.

As Patrick began making love slowly and tentatively, he felt as though he were getting to know Fenella all over again. He learned to his delight that her breasts were as sensitive as he had supposed, requiring much attention, and if he dragged his lower lip lightly up her spine, she would shudder and groan with rapture. And though she might be prim and secretive by day, in bed she held nothing of herself back, hid nothing. Every caress elicited an appreciative moan of pleasure or a high-pitched cry of delight that increased Patrick's ardor.

He found himself irrationally jealous of William, who had known Fenella first.

It was never this way with William, Fenella thought as she writhed beneath Patrick.

He was a skilled and patient lover, mastering her as if she were a puppet beneath his sure hand. He coaxed pleasure out of places she never knew existed, reducing her to his whimpering slave.

When she could stand no more torment, he finally possessed her, fitting her as perfectly as a sword to its scabbard. And as they moved together in an ageless rhythm, rising higher and higher, Fenella felt all of her disappointments and tragedies burned away in the fire of Patrick's love.

Later, they lay together in the darkness, Fenella's head pillowed on Patrick's shoulder, her arm flung across his waist. Their cooling flesh was still moist, and the musky scent of lovemaking surrounded them.

Patrick kissed the top of her head. "You know, you never cease to surprise me."

Fenella smiled as she snuggled closer. "Do I?"

"Often. Just when I think I know you, you do something quite unexpected."

"Because I asked you to stay with me?"

He nodded. "But now I'm the one who's feeling guilty."

Fenella placed her fingertips against his lips. "Hush, Patrick. No more talk of guilt or tomorrow or consequences. The present is all that matters. We were both suffering so much, and we needed each other tonight. We each gave and we each received something in return. Neither of us is to blame."

But even as she said the words, she knew she would feel differently when reality intruded on the little insulated world they had just created for themselves. Already she was thinking of tomorrows, and a tomorrow without Patrick suddenly seemed intolerable. She forced the thought out of her mind.

"Thank you, Fenella," he murmured, before drifting off to sleep.

Fenella gently brushed his lips with her own, closed her eyes, and slept.

She was awakened hours later by Patrick whispering her name.

When she opened her eyes, he kissed her. Then he said, "It's almost dawn. I think I should get back to my own room before one of the maids catches me here." Seeing her puzzled look, he added, "I didn't want you to awaken and find me gone with no explanation."

When she murmured a sleepy response, he chuckled and said, "Go back to sleep."

Then the bed sagged as he sat up, and he was gone.

Tomorrow came too quickly for Fenella.

When she next opened her eyes, weak, watery gray light was filtering in through the curtains. She made a face and rolled over. It was too early and too dark out to wake up just yet.

Then she realized she was naked beneath the covers, and why: she and Patrick had become lovers last night.

A slow smile curved her lips. And it had been wonderful. But that was last night and this was the following morning.

She remembered how it had been after the first time she and William had been intimate in her father's house when the doctor had been away in Dublin. Oh, the passion of the moment had been grand, but then came its aftermath, the guilt slicing as sharp as a razor across the conscience, the awkwardness of facing each other over breakfast the following morning, the necessity of living one's life as if nothing had changed when everything had. Something that had appeared glorious and golden under cover of darkness suddenly turned as tawdry as tinsel in the harsh light of day.

Her heart heavy, Fenella retrieved her night shift, then summoned a maid to help her dress in deepest mourning for Cadogan.

When Fenella walked into the dining room, she hesitated, for Patrick was there, filling his plate from the covered dishes on the sideboard.

He turned and saw her. However, unlike William, Patrick's eyes lit up at the sight of her and his smile was one of genuine pleasure.

"Good morning," he said, a teasing sparkle in his voice. "Sleep well?"

Fenella smiled back as her awkwardness vanished. Everything is going to be all right this time, she thought. "Very well indeed."

Patrick set down his heaping plate and held her chair for her. "May I get you something?"

"Bacon and eggs, please."

Before he did her bidding, he leaned forward and whispered in her ear, "No regrets?"

"No regrets."

"Good. Neither have I."

After he served her and sat down to eat his huge breakfast, Patrick reached out and covered her hand with his own. "Thank you, Fenella. It's going to be so much easier for me to face what has to be done now."

She knew he was referring to his father's death and the

upcoming funeral, so she just nodded sympathetically. Then she said, "Have you found Mr. O'Malley yet?"

He shook his head sadly. "I think he must have wandered away and become cats' meat."

"Oh, Patrick, I'm so sorry. I know how attached you were to him."

"Silly to be concerned over a pet mouse when my father has just been murdered, but I grew quite attached to the little creature in prison. He seemed human for all the companionship and comfort he brought me during the most dark and trying times."

"Perhaps he'll reappear yet."

"Trust you to be so optimistic, but no, I think he's gone for good. I doubt if I'll ever find him. That chapter of my life is closed."

Before they could discuss the mouse's disappearance further, Margaret glided into the room, a somber wraith swathed from head to hem in stiff black bombazine. Her eyes were red and swollen from crying, and her lovely face ravaged with sorrow, a potent reminder that Cadogan was gone and the future had to be faced.

It was finally over.

Patrick watched in stone-faced silence as the gravediggers began shoveling dirt over his father's coffin as Cadogan was laid to rest beside his ancestors in the Quinn family plot. No, he took that back. He was on the verge of a new beginning. He was the master of Rookforest now, and the awesome responsibility weighed heavily on his shoulders.

Suddenly he felt someone gently squeeze his hand and he looked down to see Fenella standing beside him, her face soft with sympathy.

"Patrick," she said, "it's time to go."

He nodded, took one last look, and turned to go. Before Fenella could withdraw her hand, he drew her arm through his, not caring who noticed or disapproved. He needed her by his side today.

"It was a beautiful service," Fenella said, "and so many people . . ."

They had come from far and wide to pay homage to Cadogan Quinn, mostly members of the landowning class or their agents. No tenants had attended, not a one to curry favor with the new master of Rookforest. Perhaps they felt they were gaining the upper hand with Parnell's support and didn't need to.

Patrick glanced at Fenella. "I don't think I could have endured it without you by my side."

"You would have done just fine." Then she added, "Poor Margaret. She is taking Cadogan's death so hard."

"When her own father died, he became a second father to her. As much as Meggie always liked defying him, she loved my father."

"Look at poor Lord Nayland following her like a devoted puppy. All he wants to do is comfort her, and Margaret refuses to allow him anywhere near her."

Patrick saw that Fenella spoke the truth. Margaret was hurrying her pace out of the graveyard, and the earl was quickening his steps to catch up. When he reached her and tried to take her arm, she brushed him off. His hand fell to his side lamely.

By this time, all of the carriages had driven off except the Quinns' and another parked out of the way, near the church entrance. Just as Patrick and Fenella approached their carriage, the door to the second carriage opened and Cynara disembarked.

Patrick stopped and stared at her as she came gliding across the churchyard toward him. She was dressed in black as she had been that day she had come into church on her brother's arm. When she lifted her veil, she was just as beautiful as ever.

Patrick felt Fenella's hand stiffen on his arm as Cynara approached them boldly.

"Patrick," Cynara said, "I'd like to speak to you, if I may." Only then did she spare Fenella a frosty glance. "Alone."

"Good morning, Lady Eastbrook," Fenella said. "What a pleasure it is to see you again."

"And you, Miss Considine." Her tight smile belied the warmth of her words. "Patrick?"

Before he could excuse himself, Fenella released him. "I'll be waiting in the carriage." She went to join Margaret and Lord Nayland, already waiting inside the Quinn vehicle.

Patrick looked down at Cynara. The blackness of her mourning dress turned her violet eyes to the color of amethysts.

"Yes, Cynara? What do you wish to speak to me about?"

Her pouting lips parted as she leaned toward him. "Walk with me, Patrick. What I have to say to you is very personal and I don't wish anyone to overhear."

He knew he should refuse her request, but he couldn't. Vivid, joyous memories assailed him, pulling him like an undertow back toward the past.

"Very well."

As he started forward, Cynara rested her hand on his sleeve, and he had no alternative but to offer her his arm. Her hand was as light as gossamer, her touch still capable of clearing his mind of all rational thought.

"I risked a great deal by coming here today," she said in her husky voice. "St. John has forbidden me to even speak to you, but I had to come to offer you my sympathies on your father's death."

He glanced back at her carriage. "I hope you've bribed your coachman well, or at least sworn him to secrecy, or your brother will know where you've been."

"The driver has promised he will say nothing." They reached the far churchyard, and Cynara stopped. "Patrick, I . . . I want us to be friends again."

He clenched his jaw. "I don't know if that can be possible, Cynara. Too much has happened between us for even a simple friendship."

But even as he rebuffed her, he felt his blood stir as he caught a faint whiff of her intoxicating perfume. She was standing so close he could have kissed her without any effort, if he chose to.

"If you could just find it in your heart to forgive me, Patrick, I know we could recapture what we once had."

"I wasn't aware that we had anything worth recapturing," he said wryly.

She wants you back, Fenella had said.

"You know we did."

He tried to conjure an image of Fenella as she had been last night, naked and moaning in his arms, but the vision that came to mind had Cynara's face. It was a mockery, and Patrick shut his eyes to banish it.

"It's over between us, Cynara." But even the words sounded stilted and unconvincing to his own ears.

Her smile was slow and seductive. "Is it, Patrick? Are you sure?" She grew bold. "Forget the past. We can have a glittering future together, one bright with promise, if only you'll forgive me. I want you, Patrick, as badly as you want me. I'm yours for the taking."

As Cynara waited expectantly for his answer, the occupants of the Quinn carriage were waiting for Patrick.

Margaret sniffed and dabbed at her red, swollen eyes with her handkerchief as she stared out the window at Patrick and Cynara.

"What's that witch doing here?" she muttered, her hazel eyes ablaze with anger. "She never cared for Uncle Cadogan, and everybody knows it."

Fenella said nothing. Actually, she found Cynara's performance fascinating to watch. The woman used every opportunity to touch Patrick, resting her hand on his arm, drawing closer and closer to him with every step so that her skirts brushed his leg, her lovely oval face always turned toward his, all the better to display her beauty. Always touching, always enticing. Tiring of the spectacle, Fenella turned away from the window.

Admit it, you're jealous of her, she said to herself. She is so beautiful, what man could resist her? All she has to do is crook her little finger and Patrick will go running to her. You may have comforted him with your body last night, but it's Cynara he wants to spend his life with.

Lord Nayland removed his spectacles and began cleaning them with his handkerchief. "I suspect Lady Eastbrook is using her wiles to ensnare him, but you needn't worry, ladies. Contrary to what you may think of our sex, we are not that susceptible to feminine guile."

Margaret's muffled snort of laughter earned her a rare look of reproof from the adoring earl.

He added, "Especially Patrick."

But somehow, Fenella didn't find that reassuring, especially when Patrick returned to the carriage and sat there in brooding silence all the way back to Rookforest.

* * *

Margaret reined in Bramble and looked over her shoulder. Satisfied that no one was following her, she continued her slow canter across the fields.

It was the perfect time to slip away for a tryst with Terrence. Ever since her uncle had been buried yesterday, Patrick was too busy getting estate matters in order to notice her whereabouts. Even eagle-eyed Fenella hadn't said a word when Margaret left the house without an explanation.

She shivered in the saddle, her warm breath forming a cloud of vapor in the chilly air. She wouldn't be able to stay long this time, so she and Terrence would have to make the best of it.

There was the cottage, a thin line of blue smoke swirling from the chimney as a prearranged signal that Terrence was there, waiting for her in their new trysting place. Margaret smiled in anticipation and spurred Bramble into a gallop.

No sooner did she ride into the yard and slide off her horse than the cottage door swung open and her love was standing there, filling the doorway.

To Margaret's chagrin, Terrence didn't run out to meet her and sweep her into his arms after their long absence. Instead, he kept looking around furtively and motioning to her. "Come inside, alanna. Quick, now, before someone sees ye."

Only when they were safe inside, with the door closed behind them, did he grin and take her in his arms. "Alanna, alanna . . ."

"I've missed you so," Margaret said, kissing him, reveling in the feel of his hungry mouth beneath her own.

Terrence grinned when they parted, and ran his rough fingers through her hair, his roguish eyes sparkling. "An' I've missed ye as well."

Then Margaret waited, but Terrence said not one word of condolence about her Uncle Cadogan, especially since he had witnessed what happened that evening in Mallow.

"We buried my uncle yesterday," she finally said, hoping he would take her hint.

Terrence turned away and made a great pretense of putting another block of peat in the hearth. "Och, and what a sad thing that was, him killed in cold blood like that.''

"I was told you saw the man who did it."

Terrence rose, brushing one hand against the other. "I only saw 'im runnin' away. He was gone before anyone could catch 'im."

Margaret nodded, suddenly blinded by tears.

Terrence came over and stood before her, not a hint of softness in his craggy face. "I know he was yer uncle, alanna, but there were many who hated Cadogan Quinn for evictin' the Grogans and anyone else who wouldn't turn informer."

"He was more than my uncle," she corrected him, bristling. "He was more like a father to me, and he only wanted the names of the men who attacked Fenella Considine, that's all. There was no reason for anyone to kill him!"

Terrence raised his square jaw stubbornly. "Ye don't understand. Some would think betrayin' yer own was cause enough to kill a man."

Margaret took a deep breath and blurted out, "Terrence, did you have Fenella clipped?"

He stared at her, his expression unreadable for just a second; then it changed to one of outrage. "Alanna, how can ye accuse me of such a heartless crime? Ye wound me deeply with yer doubt."

"Well, you did say you were going to persuade her to keep silent."

"Alanna, ye do offend me. I said I was only going to have a little talk with 'er, that's all. An' I haven't even had the chance to do that. No, it's innocent I am of clipping Fenella Considine."

Since Terrence had never lied to her, Margaret raised her hands and placed them on his shoulders. "I'm sorry if I hurt you, my darling, but I had to be sure in case Fenella makes any wild accusations against us."

He grinned at that and his mouth swooped down to claim her own.

But even as Margaret responded to his kiss, a vague dissatisfaction kept plaguing her. Something was just not the same between them. She couldn't understand why their relationship had suddenly changed, but the thought terrified her.

When they parted, Terrence said, "So, yer cousin is the new master of Rookforest."

This annoyed Margaret, for she wanted to discuss their future together, not Patrick. But she said, "Yes, he is. The lawyers will read Uncle's will tomorrow, but it's only a formality. Patrick is the heir."

"And what would himself be plannin' to do about the evictions, now that 'is father's gone?" He crossed himself.

The question took Margaret aback. She stared at Terrence and was alarmed to find him regarding her with great anticipation in his eyes. But with blinding clarity she realized it was her answer he was waiting for, not her fervid embraces.

Was that all he wanted after all, information about Rookforest?

"I don't know," she replied truthfully. "Patrick hasn't confided in me."

He must have sensed her annoyance, for he grinned that heartbreaking smile of his. "An' will himself have any objection to our marryin'?"

Hope flared in Margaret's heart, bewildering her. She did love him so!

She stepped forward eagerly. "You mean to ask Patrick for my hand in marriage? And we'll immigrate to a new life together?"

"Alanna!" he said in aggrieved tones. "Did ye doubt me? It's what I've wanted above all else, to leave this accursed barren land and make a new life, with ye by my side."

"Oh, Terrence!" She flung herself into his arms and hugged him for dear life. "I want you so much!"

"Do ye, alanna? Do ye want me?"

Margaret stopped. There was something different about the way he was looking at her now, some change in his expression. Gone was the light bantering of their stolen kisses and embraces at the ruins. Terrence was serious.

"I want to love ye, alanna, as a man loves a woman," he whispered hoarsely. "Right here. Now. I can't wait any longer for ye, me love."

This was crazy. Margaret caught her breath, unable to believe what he was saying to her. She had been begging him to love her ever since she had made up her mind to marry him, but until this moment he had been the reluctant one, always stopping her when she would have gone too far.

If Margaret and Terrence became lovers, Patrick would have to let them marry. He would have no choice.

"Oh, yes, Terrence! Yes!"

"Alanna ye've made me a happy man." And without another word, he swung her into his arms and carried her across the dirt floor to a pallet of straw, where he set her down gently, as if he were a fine gentleman with his lady.

"I wish I had time to do this proper," he muttered, glancing at the door as if he expected someone to come bursting through at any moment.

Margaret just lay there, unable to comprehend what he meant. Then Terrence was lying beside her, his breath hot on her face, his rough, blunt fingers undoing the buttons down her riding habit. She swallowed hard, her heart thudding and her face growing warm as his hand found her breast. No man had ever touched her there before, and the sensation was rather alarming.

She tried to push his hand away. "Terrence, I . . ."

But this seemed to anger him, for he stopped his groping and glared down at her. "I thought ye said ye wanted me to love ye?"

"I . . . I do, but —"

"Then let a man do what he's supposed to."

When his questing fingers squeezed her nipple, Margaret's back arched in response and a small groan escaped her lips.

So this is what it is like, she thought with delight as another spasm of pleasure shook her. I am lying with my lover, listening to his endearments.

"Damned corset," Terrence growled, his breathing labored.

Without warning, his hand was beneath her skirts, pushing them up about her waist, baring her booted legs to the chill of the cottage. Margaret flushed in embarrassment, uncertain that this was supposed to happen next, but she trusted Terrence. Besides, she dared not voice her ignorance and incur his wrath again.

Then Terrence was on top of her, heavy and panting into her face, pinning her down so she couldn't move, his knee parting her thighs.

"Terrence, stop! You're hurting me!"

"I can't now, me love. It'll be better, you'll see."

Then he was hammering against her, and she was being ripped apart. A scream of terror and pain rose in her throat, but Terrence was ready for her and his mouth came down on hers to muffle the sound. Before she could take another breath, he gave several more quick thrusts, shuddered, and sagged against her.

He smells like a cow, Margaret thought as he hauled himself off her and adjusted his clothing. Then he smiled down at her as if he had just given her a gift as rare as the crown jewels.

"Ye'd best be up and away now, alanna," he said, sniffling and wiping his nose with his sleeve, "before himself comes lookin' for ye."

Then he was gone.

Margaret lay on the straw pallet to gather her wits about her. She had expected to feel wonderful after Terrence made love to her, but she only felt hollow inside and humiliated.

Well, you got what you wanted, Margaret Atkinson.

Then why wasn't she contented?

She sat up stiffly, the ache between her legs a potent reminder of her folly. She knew there would be blood, but her maid needn't see it. No one need ever know how stupid she had been.

She shook out her skirts so no telltale straw clung to the heavy wool, then buttoned her bodice with trembling, hesitant fingers. Then those same fingers, steadier now, raked through her hair. When she was satisfied that she looked as she had when she went riding out of Rookforest an hour ago, she strode from the cottage and mounted Bramble.

She decided she never wanted to see Terrence Sheely again. And no one would ever know what happened to her today.

16

DURING THE WEEK after Cadogan's funeral, Fenella saw little of Patrick. He arose early every morning before anyone else, so that by the time Fenella came downstairs, she ate breakfast alone. Patrick stayed out all day "on estate business," as he told Margaret, and when he finally joined them for dinner, he was so tired, he barely said two words to them before excusing himself and retiring early.

And he never came to Fenella's room after that one night.

Fenella tried to assuage the hurt of Patrick's sudden lack of interest by reminding herself she had promised not to think of tomorrows. She had to accept that night of passion for what it was, merely a momentary source of comfort for both of them. She had no right to change the rules at this late date and make further demands of him.

But now that she knew she loved him, she wanted more than Patrick was prepared to give. She wanted tomorrows, but he didn't. All he had wanted was a woman's soft and yielding body to momentarily ease his pain, not a lifetime with Fenella.

She was stung by his sudden indifference, but she said nothing to him. Fenella had too much pride to wheedle or whine for something not freely given.

It was Margaret who reminded her that her situation at Rookforest had changed.

On a rare sunny afternoon in late October, Fenella was in the library reading when Margaret came into the room with her nose buried in a copy of the *Dublin Daily Express*.

Margaret glanced up, saw Fenella sitting there, and said, "Have you read the newspaper today?"

Fenella marked her place with her finger and shook her head. "No, I haven't."

Though she still wondered if Margaret and Terrence were to blame for her being clipped, Fenella tried to hide her true feelings and be cordial at all times.

"Well, you should," Margaret went on. If she had noticed a subtle cooling in Fenella's attitude toward her, she never remarked upon it. "There's an interesting article about that Captain Boycott of Lough Mask House. It's reprinted from the *London Daily News* and it's entitled 'The Isolation of Captain Boycott.' "

As Margaret seated herself at the reading table and began scanning the newspaper with rapt interest, Fenella said, "What does it say?"

"The poor man . . . ," Margaret began. "All of his servants have run off, so he's forced to run his estate and harvest his crops all by himself. The local blacksmith refuses to shoe his horses and the shopkeepers won't do business with him. Captain Boycott has had supplies shipped in from neighboring towns. He's even applied for constabulary protection."

Fenella shook her head. "Terrible."

"I'll have to show this to Patrick," Margaret said, folding the newspaper. "If this is what Parnell is recommending, any landlord could find himself the victim of this social ostracism."

Fenella raised her brows at that. "Do you think the townspeople of Mallow would really ostracize your family?"

Margaret shrugged as she rose from the reading table and walked over to the window. "Who knows? I suppose it's possible, though I would be hard pressed to think of Mrs. Ryan and any of the other household staff deserting us. But perhaps the farmers would refuse to harvest the crops."

Fenella set her book aside, suddenly tiring of reading. "Still, Patrick has reinstated the Grogans in their farm, and he's promised not to evict any more farmers because of what was done to me. That should show them he's trying to be fair."

"Ah, but he's doubled the reward for information about the men who attacked you," Margaret reminded her. "That's enough to anger Captain Moonlight." Then she lapsed into thoughtful silence.

Fenella studied Margaret standing before the window, her hands clasped behind her back, her coloring too vivid and alive for the somber black of mourning. But ever since Cadogan's tragic death, Fenella had noticed the sudden change in Margaret. She was more subdued, like a banked fire. A certain sadness was to be expected, for Margaret had worshiped her uncle, but the change went deeper than that. It was as though Margaret had suddenly grown overnight from a headstrong girl to a mature young woman.

Suddenly Margaret said wistfully, "I wonder what shall become of us."

"We'll have to hope that sanity prevails," Fenella replied.

"I wasn't referring to Ireland in general, I meant us. You and me."

Fenella gave her a puzzled look. "I don't understand."

"Now that Uncle Cadogan is gone and Patrick is the master of Rookforest, I wonder what shall become of us? You certainly can't remain here, living under the same roof as a bachelor gentleman. How improper! What would people think?"

Fenella thought she detected a faint note of mockery in Margaret's voice, but she chose to ignore it. Instead, she said, "You're right, of course. I'm sure I'll have no alternative but to make other arrangements for myself now."

"At least you have somewhere to go."

Fenella rose to her feet, aghast. "Surely you can't believe Patrick would cast you out. Rookforest is your home. I'm sure he'll let you remain here for as long as you like."

"I don't doubt that. I was just wondering if he will press me to accept Lord Nayland's suit, just as Uncle Cadogan did. He admires Nayland a great deal, you know."

"He will no doubt allow you to choose your own husband, Margaret, provided he is not Terrence Sheely."

Fenella waited for a second, then added, "You are planning to tell him, aren't you?"

Margaret didn't even look at Fenella, she just kept staring out the window. "There's no need now. Terrence and I have broken off. I shan't be seeing him ever again." Then she turned and gave Fenella a wry smile. "Don't worry, Fenella. There will be no more secret trysts at Ballymere. You needn't have to worry that by keeping my secret, you will be betraying anyone."

Fenella couldn't believe that the Margaret who stood before her now with eyes as dry as an empty glass was the same young woman who had so often pleaded with her not to betray her and Terrence.

"I realize it's none of my affair, Margaret," she said, "but may I ask why you have broken off with young Sheely? You seemed so much in love."

Something like acute disillusionment flickered in those empty hazel depths, then was gone as Margaret shrugged and looked away. "I finally realized that you were right. Terrence is a farmer and I am a lady. The difference in our backgrounds would have been insurmountable."

Fenella was overcome with relief, yet a certain uneasiness as well. For someone who had just broken off with the man she had so passionately defended, Margaret was just too cool and composed. Fenella suspected there was more to it than met the eye, but she refrained from speaking her mind.

Instead, she went over to Margaret and placed a reassuring hand on her arm. "I think it's for the best, Margaret."

"Oh, I realize that now," she agreed, her voice trembling slightly. Then she brightened. "November's Eve will soon be upon us. Perhaps I should set the table as the Irish girls do and wait for the *fetch* of my future lover to come through the window and dine. Mrs. Ryan told me that story once. Have you ever heard of it?"

Fenella nodded. "Yes, I have, though I think you should place your trust in yourself to attract a suitable husband, not superstition."

Margaret smiled, and her eyes sparkled with amusement for the first time in days. "Dear Fenella, always so practical and sensible."

If I'm so practical and sensible, Fenella thought, why do I yearn for your cousin to come to my bed every night? Why am I making myself suffer so by wanting what I cannot have?

But before Fenella could reply, Margaret suddenly turned and bolted from the library. Fenella decided it would be best not to follow her with unwanted confidences. She had her own feelings for Patrick to contend with.

Later that night, Fenella rolled over on her side and closed her eyes, but sleep eluded her.

Her thoughts kept returning to dinner, when she had asked Patrick if she could possibly talk with him in private after the meal was over. Much to her chagrin, he was brusque with her, saying that he had legal papers to study and he couldn't possibly spare her the time.

Rebuffed, Fenella had all she could do to keep herself from bursting into tears right at the table. Only her pride kept her there, making strained, inconsequential small talk with Patrick and Margaret.

In his defense, she had to say he did look exhausted, with great dark circles beneath his eyes. Managing the estate in these unsettled times had taken its toll. No wonder he was brusque and preoccupied.

But even those excuses sounded lame to her own ears. She felt as discarded as an old pair of shoes.

Finally she dozed.

Sometime later, a drowsy Fenella was awakened from a fitful sleep when she heard the mattress creak and sag as though a great weight were being lowered upon it. Then she felt an iron band being tightened across her waist, and she was being drawn against and fitted to something quite solid and unyielding, yet warm.

It took her three seconds after regaining her faculties to recognize the solid feel of Patrick's body against her own, her soft backside curved into his hard, lean hips, her back against his naked torso. In spite of the trousers he had on, Fenella could feel his blatant arousal.

"Patrick?" she muttered, still groggy with sleep.

She felt the rumbling chuckled start deep within his chest, then the warm tickle of his lips against her ear.

"Who else would it be?" he whispered. "Have you another lover that I don't know about?"

Fenella's eyes flew open and she stiffened in his arms. "I'm just surprised to see you here."

He grew so very still, his breathing stopped. Then he released Fenella and rolled away from her. She felt his absence at once as the bed sagged again. She rolled over, intending to pull him back, but he rose in one fluid motion.

Suddenly a match flared, illuminating Patrick in the darkness as he lit the candle by her bedside. He stood there for a long time, looking down at her out of narrowed eyes, his thoughts hooded, his face half-hidden by the feeble light of the candle.

Just as Fenella looked away, he dropped down onto the edge of the bed, lifted her chin with his fingers, and turned her face to look at him.

"Why would you say such a thing to me?" he murmured, his pale blue eyes filled with hurt and surprise.

Fenella felt her cheeks grow warm under his scrutiny, and she tried to look away, but couldn't. "I thought you came to me that night because you needed comforting, not because you wanted me."

Comprehension flared in the depths of his eyes, and he released her long enough to run his hand through his hair.

Patrick smiled at her. "You thought I only wanted you that one time, for physical release, nothing more?"

"Didn't you?"

"My sweet, adorable Fenella . . . if physical release were all I wanted, I would have gone to a whore in Mallow that night and paid to use her body." He studied her silently again. "I came to you that night because I wanted you and needed much more than a willing body. And I'm here now because I want you."

Confusing emotions warred within her. "But . . . but you've practically ignored me all week."

He reached for her, and she went willingly into his arms, wanting so much to believe him. "You're right. I have been beastly to you lately, and for that I humbly apologize and beg your forgiveness. But since my father died, Rookforest needs tending, and I want so badly to succeed at it as Father would have expected me to. I'm afraid it's eclipsed all else, and I have ignored you shamefully.''

Fenella sighed shakily, perilously close to tears. "I . . . I was so afraid you didn't want me.''

He dislodged himself gently so he could look at her. "But I do want you, Fenella. So much.''

She hesitated, waiting for him to say he loved her, for she would not be the first to confess her true feelings for him. If she bared her soul and Patrick did not reciprocate, she would face humiliation and more pain than she could bear. Fenella had learned not to beg for what wasn't freely given.

He mistook her silence for rejection, for his face suddenly turned bleak. "If you don't want me tonight, please tell me, and I'll go back to my room. You owe me nothing, Fenella.''

Ah, but I do, she thought sadly.

"I want you, Patrick,'' she whispered, placing her hands on his shoulders. If only for tonight.

A spark of desire kindled his eyes as he traced the line of her cheek with the back of his fingers. "You are so beautiful.''

She smiled dryly. "And I think you need to borrow Lord Nayland's spectacles.''

Patrick didn't laugh. He grew very still and scowled down at her. "Why do you always belittle yourself so?''

His unexpected anger disconcerted her momentarily. When she recovered herself, she said, "I'm only being realistic. I know I'm no beauty. Men have never written sonnets in praise of my oval face or flocked to my door to court me.''

"Then they're fools.''

"And you're a kind man to say so, Patrick Quinn.''

"I merely speak the truth.''

To convince her, he drew her face to his and sought her mouth with his own. He teased her at first, pressing his lips against hers lightly, then harder, until she let out the breath she had been holding and moved instinctively nearer to him, her aroused breasts brushing against his chest through the material of her night shift. Patrick kissed her deeply, urging her lips to part, which they did willingly. The moment his questing tongue invaded her mouth for a delicious prelude to intimacy, he felt her shudder and stiffen momentarily as she always did in token resistance. Then she relaxed and touched his tongue with her own in tacit agreement of her surrender.

When he had tasted his fill of her, he released her just long enough to kiss that stubborn chin and murmur, "I think we'd be much more comfortable if we took off our clothes, don't you?"

He rolled off the bed and made short shrift of his trousers' buttons, all the while never taking his eyes off Fenella. He enjoyed watching her undress, but this time she moved too quickly. She sat up, raised her arms to grasp the back of her night shift, then pulled the voluminous flannel garment over her head in one quick, fluid motion. She was naked in an instant. As he let his trousers fall to the floor, he decided he would have to teach her the art of tantalizing and inciting a lover with leisurely undressing, the gradual exposure of long creamy legs, followed by her rounded backside, the gentle curve of her back and shoulders, and ultimately her breasts.

But there was another lesson she had to learn, so when he slid into bed beside her, he turned her so her back was toward him, and she was nestled against him once more. Then he slid his hands beneath her arms so he could cup and squeeze her warm, heavy breasts while his lips and hot breath teased her sensitive ears.

The hiss of her sharp intake of breath spurred Patrick on, and he toyed with her erect nipples until Fenella was moaning in his arms. When he sensed she was ready, his hand trailed down her flat belly until his fingers found the soft folds of her womanhood.

The moment he touched her there, Fenella went wild in his arms, seeking to twist around to face him, but Patrick held her fast against his teasing fingers.

"Shhh, Fenella. Lie still. You're always giving. Now it's time you learned how to take."

She fell still and did as he bade her. Patrick increased his tempo, delighting in Fenella's uninhibited response. She was panting now, her fingers clenching at the sheets, the pleasant musky scent of her arousal like a sweet perfume to Patrick's nostrils.

Suddenly she flung her head back against his shoulder and her back arched away from him.

"Patrick!" she cried as spasm after spasm gripped her and she shuddered from the force of it.

Finally she sagged against him, spent at last.

Patrick only chuckled diabolically. "Oh, no, my dear. I'm only just beginning."

With a whimper of resistance, a sated Fenella tried to push him away, but he would not be denied. Murmuring sweet endearments, he knelt between her parted thighs and possessed her slowly, reveling in the slick tightness of her that threatened to unman him before he was ready. As Fenella sighed and accommodated herself to him, he began loving her slowly and exquisitely until she once again knew ecstasy in his arms.

Later, as they lay there exhausted, their limbs entwined as if they couldn't bear to be parted, Patrick kissed the top of her head and murmured, "Sweet Fenella. You are an apt pupil."

She grinned sleepily. "And you, sir, are an excellent teacher."

"Ah, but there is much you have yet to learn."

She nuzzled his cheek with the tip of her nose. "If they are anything like these last lessons . . ."

"I can promise you they are, only much, much better."

Suddenly Patrick grew serious. "Fenella, may I ask you something?"

She caught his change of mood at once and raised her head to look at him. "Of course. What is it?"

"What would you have done if I had kidnapped you and taken you to Ostend?"

"I would have been flattered," she replied without hesitation.

Her answer so astonished him that Patrick propped himself up on one elbow and stared down at her. "You would?"

She nodded. "I must admit that when my father first told me what you had done to warrant being sent to prison, I condemned you roundly. I know how I would have felt if some man abducted me from William. I probably would have conked you over the head with a wine bottle and summoned the police as well.

"But now that I know you, I would have been flattered that you wanted me enough to take such desperate measures."

"Well, Cynara certainly wasn't flattered."

"Ah, but that's because she was so used to masculine attention, she could pick and choose. I, on the other hand, am—"

"Hush," Patrick admonished her, placing his fingertips against her lips to silence her. "I warned you that I will not tolerate you belittling yourself ever again. Agreed?"

Fenella nodded happily, and he released her.

Patrick grew serious once again. "Thank you for saying that."

"You needn't thank me. I only spoke the truth."

"And now I think it's time for your next lesson."

She paid him the highest compliment by going willingly into his arms. Even though he loved her a bit more roughly this time, Fenella matched his ardor and didn't shrink away, even when her eyes widened with surprise when he made certain requests of her. Her trust humbled him.

By the time they finished, each knew every inch of the other's body.

Exhausted at long last, they slept just as the clock was striking two in the morning.

"Good morning to ye, miss, though it's fair closer to noon than mornin'. It's time to be up and about."

At the sound of Brigid's light, chirping voice, Fenella opened one bleary eye and looked around to see the little maid bustling about, flinging the curtains aside to let in the daylight.

"What time is it exactly?" Fenella asked.

"Eleven o'clock, miss. Master Patrick asked me to wake you and ask if ye'd like to go into Mallow with him."

So, even after a rigorous night, he had risen before her. Fenella smiled to herself lazily.

There were several items she would be needing after

last night, so she said, "Tell Master Patrick I will join him shortly."

"Very good, miss."

Just as Brigid strode by the bed, she noticed something lying on the floor and knelt on one knee to pick it up. When the maid rose with her cheeks flaming, Fenella suddenly realized that she was naked beneath the covers, and the object Brigid had retrieved was none other than Fenella's rumpled night shift.

Without so much as a telltale glance at Fenella, Brigid draped the garment over the foot of the bed and went sailing out of the room, the tails of her cap flying out behind her.

When the door closed, Fenella muttered, "Well, there'll be gossip in the servants' hall tonight."

But she honestly didn't care if the world knew the master of Rookforest was sleeping with his houseguest. As she stretched languorously, her body still pleasantly sore from the rigors of Patrick's lovemaking, Fenella felt content and satisfied, both physically and emotionally.

He had wanted her and had come to her. And just before he left her at the crack of dawn, he whispered, "Until tomorrow night."

Now was the time to consider consequences.

Fenella sat up, one hand resting on her abdomen thoughtfully. She did not want a child to result from her illicit union with Patrick, no matter how much she loved him. Fenella had been fortunate. William, always pragmatic, had explained the preventive properties of sponge and vinegar to her, then insisted she use them before he bedded her. He went to his grave childless, a testament to the efficacy of the method.

Now Fenella felt the first stirrings of fear and worry. What if she were already carrying Patrick's child? They had been intimate twice already, and once was enough to produce such tangible results. Then she recalled her father once telling her that some women had difficulty conceiving, though one would never know it by the way many farmers' wives presented their husbands with a lusty addition every year.

She prayed it was not too late, for she would not hold Patrick against his will just for the sake of a child. He was an honorable man and Fenella was certain he would stand by her if she were ever in such a situation. Still, she didn't want to place him in such a position.

As she rose and washed, she knew what she would buy in Mallow.

The dining room was empty save for Patrick.

The moment Fenella entered, he was on his feet and striding toward her, a roguish smile twisting his lips.

Fenella returned his smile. "Good morn—"

Patrick's kiss cut off her greeting as he slid one arm around her waist and crushed her to him in a fierce hug that took her breath away. Fenella melted against him, losing herself in the warmth of his mouth. But when he raised one hand and cupped her breast possessively, she struggled to free herself.

"Patrick, the servants!" She was half-laughing, half-gasping for breath as she pushed him away. "Brigid already caught me naked in bed this morning and is probably spreading tales downstairs right as I speak. What if one of the footmen were to walk in on us and caught you . . ." Her voice trailed off as she blushed.

"They won't," he replied as he effortlessly subdued her and drew her into his arms again, where he proceeded to trail hot kisses down her neck. "I told them we would be eating alone." He stopped long enough to grin at her. "I could feast on your lovely body forever. Your neck is especially tasty, and . . ." His eyes trailed down to her breasts, making her blush even harder.

"Please, Patrick," she murmured, placing her hands on his chest to keep him at bay. "Such talk is . . . un-seemly during the day."

"Oh, I see. My passion flower blossoms only at night." He grasped her hand and nipped at the fleshy part of her thumb. "But by the light of day, she turns into a plaster rose, so stiff and cold."

"Now you mock me."

"Just a little. And just to tease you into being a bit more lighthearted."

Fenella sighed. "I am being priggish again, aren't I?"

He nodded with mock solemnity. "Just a bit. And it

doesn't suit you. I much prefer the wanton wench who turns into a passion flower for me.''

She reached up to cradle his face in her hands. ''I much prefer her too.''

''Besides,'' he added, ''I like to see you laugh. Lord knows, both of us have had enough tragedy in our lives to warrant a little laughter.''

Before Fenella could grow morose thinking of her father and Cadogan, Patrick grasped her hands in his and kissed her palms. ''I am a demonstrative man, Fenella. I have never been one to hide my feelings, no matter what the dictates of propriety. I would suggest you get used to my . . . er, demonstrations of affection, for I assure you, they will be frequent and in the most unconventional of places.'' Then he wiggled his eyebrows comically and twirled an imaginary mustache while leering at her.

''Oh, dear,'' she murmured in mock dismay. ''And where shall they be, I wonder? Church on Sunday? At the dinner table? Walking down Mallow's main street?''

Patrick sobered instantly. ''I hadn't thought of that one.''

They both burst out laughing just as there came a knock at the door. Immediately they sprang apart and adjusted their countenances just as the door opened to admit the butler.

''Sir, the carriage has been brought round.''

''Tell the driver to wait, Bell. We haven't yet dined.'' Patrick stared at Fenella's neck pointedly when he said the word ''dined.''

She tried to smother the giggle welling up within her, but she couldn't. Fenella burst out laughing once again and hurried to take her chair.

Patrick's antic mood continued all during the carriage ride to Mallow.

He put her at ease with his outrageous teasing and ribald comments, and soon she was laughing uninhibitedly at his sallies, with nary a trace of a blush.

Patrick was a different person when he laughed. He looked so young and carefree that Fenella found herself hard pressed to recall the bitter, surly man who had stopped at her cottage that windy night in April. Convict Number Twenty-six seemed like a vanquished nightmare.

She recalled what Patrick had said to her in the dining room just before they left. With Ireland in its present state of unrest, with Captain Moonlight terrorizing the countryside, they had precious little to laugh at. When the opportunity came to indulge themselves in a little levity, they had to seize it, for who knew what tomorrow would bring?

When they arrived in Mallow, Fenella braced herself for the surreptitious stares and inquisitive looks she knew her turban would garner her. Everyone knew she had been clipped by Captain Moonlight for associating with the Quinns, but she was not going to give anyone the satisfaction of seeing the results of this handiwork.

But with Patrick at her side, Fenella felt safe.

Let them smirk and stare, she said to herself. I am with Patrick and no one can harm me.

They patronized several shops, with Fenella taking great care to buy her vinegar in one place and the sponge in another. Patrick's only comment was, "Are you taking over Mrs. Ryan's housekeeping duties?" causing Fenella to suppress a laugh once again.

So their spirits were high and their mood convivial as they finished their errands and returned to the carriage.

Just as Patrick was about to hand her into the carriage, Fenella remembered that she wanted a bit of lace.

"I'll dash into FitzRoy's around the corner and be right out," she told Patrick. "I won't tarry. You needn't accompany me."

"I'll be waiting," he replied, and tipped his hat to her as a sop to propriety.

The moment Fenella rounded the corner, she stopped dead in her tracks, for there was St. John Standon just coming out of FitzRoy's. Before she could turn and flee, he saw her.

"Why, Miss Considine . . ." he murmured smoothly, doffing his hat to her. "What a pleasure it is to see you again."

Her smile was polite but cool. "Mr. Standon."

As she tried to brush past him, he deliberately stepped in front of her, blocking her way. "Oh, please don't be so hasty to avoid me, Miss Considine, especially when I'm trying so hard to be neighborly.''

"I don't believe we have anything to say to each other, Mr. Standon.''

His smile was falsely brilliant. "But we do. You see, Miss Considine, I have heard some vile rumors being circulated about you, and I have found them to be most upsetting.''

"I never put much stock in rumors, sir,'' Fenella said, "and you shouldn't either. Now, if you will excuse me . . .''

Before Fenella could brush past him, he grasped her hand and drew her arm through his, holding it there so forcefully, Fenella would have had to struggle to free herself, thus creating a scene.

"Let go of me,'' she muttered through clenched teeth.

St. John Standon only tightened his hold and drew her aside. "I think you will find this rumor most interesting.''

"I doubt that.''

He ignored her protestations. "The good citizens of Mallow have been wondering why a spinster such as yourself continues to remain under the same roof as an unmarried gentleman.''

Fenella just glared at him in stony silence.

"You're causing tongues to wag furiously, Miss Considine.''

Out of the corner of her eye Fenella saw she and Standon were starting to attract the curious looks of passersby.

"Release me at once, Mr. Standon,'' she said, "or I shall scream and cause you untold embarrassment for molesting me.''

He grinned slyly. "It's Quinn who does the molesting, not I. You must be his mistress, or else you would deny it.'' Then he released her.

Without dignifying his accusation with a reply, Fenella turned and began walking away on legs as heavy as bronze.

Suddenly Fenella felt her turban yanked off her head, just as an impatient Patrick rounded the corner in search of her. With a startled cry, her hands flew to her head,

and she whirled around to find St. John Standon dangling
the turban from his fingers and laughing at his own malicious prank. Several other people nearby gaffawed, and
Fenella felt hot tears of humiliation well up in her eyes.

Standon's smile died, however, as he looked over Fenella's shoulder and came face-to-face with Patrick.

Without warning, Patrick hurled himself at Standon,
landing a blow to his jaw that sent him reeling back
against the shop front.

"I'm not weak and defenseless this time, Standon,"
he growled, waiting for the other man to shake his head
and recover himself. "And I'm going to enjoy this."

With a bellow of rage, Standon launched himself at
Patrick, catching him around the middle and toppling him
into the street, scattering onlookers as both men fell and
rolled, pummeling each other with their fists.

Fenella stood on the sidelines, her turban forgotten as
she watched Patrick battle his old enemy. She felt every
blow, heard every grunt and groan Patrick made as he
fought to throw the heavier man off him. When Standon
managed to get his hands around Patrick's throat, Fenella
almost ran to his aid, but she held herself back. This was
Patrick's fight, and he was fighting for her. He wouldn't
thank her for interfering.

Patrick's fist shot out, clipping Standon on the chin and
breaking the man's stranglehold. He toppled off Patrick
with a grunt of pain, then crawled on his hands and knees
just out of Patrick's reach. Both man managed to rise at
the same time.

Standon's fist shot out before Patrick had fully regained
his balance, catching him near the eye. Patrick staggered
back, his arms flailing for balance, but he did not fall.
Recovering himself, he circled Standon warily, elated to
see his opponent's handsome face bruised and bloody.

"It's not as easy to beat me this time, is it, Standon?"
he jeered.

Standon swore and swung, but Patrick was ready for
him. He saw his opening and took it, jamming his fist
into Standon's midsection, and when the man doubled
over with a sharp "woof" of agony, Patrick followed
through with another blow to the jaw.

Standon fell to the cobblestones. The crowd cheered. But Patrick had eyes only for Fenella.

Towering above the prone body of his vanquished foe as if he were offering a sacrifice to Fenella, Patrick stared at her, his breath coming in short, hard gasps. Then he extended his hand to her and Fenella came forward to take it, not caring if the whole world saw her.

She put her arm through his and together they returned to the carriage.

Once inside, when he and Fenella were seated next to each other and the vehicle began moving, Patrick reached out and wiped away a tear with his thumb.

"I'm sorry," he said thickly, for his jaw felt as if he had been kicked by a horse. "I should have prevented him from doing that to you."

Fenella withdrew a lace-edged handkerchief from within her sleeve and began dabbing at the corner of his mouth. "I'll survive, Patrick." Her eyes darkened with worry. "But you . . . Perhaps we should stop at the dispensary and let the doctor dress those cuts."

Patrick could only stare at her with wonder. Here was Fenella, white-faced and teary-eyed from that cruel, humiliating episode, and all she could concern herself with was his welfare.

At that moment, a fierce possessiveness flowed through his veins. He wanted to wipe away all the humiliation and hurt she had ever suffered at the hands of insensitive, uncaring people, and protect her with his life. He wanted to make her laugh again so her dark eyes would sparkle with mirth.

I love her, he thought, startled by the depth of his feeling for a woman he had once scorned.

But even as that astounding thought penetrated his brain, a tempting vision of Cynara flitted across his consciousness, her beauty beguiling him as always.

Confused, Patrick shook his head to clear it.

"Patrick, are you all right?" Fenella's alarm was palpable. "Perhaps we should stop at the dispensary after all."

"No, I'm fine, Fenella, really. All I need is some cold compresses when we return to Rookforest, and I'll be fine tomorrow."

She look skeptical. "Really?"

He patted her hand and tried to smile, but the pain was too great. "Really. You needn't worry about me."

She took his hand and brought his skinned knuckles to her lips for a gentle kiss. "Thank you, Patrick."

He smiled through the pain, wishing he could defend her always.

17

SEVERAL DAYS LATER, Fenella was having luncheon with Patrick and Margaret in the dining room when Lord Nayland was announced.

Margaret was the first to greet him. "Good morning, Lionel."

The earl stopped so fast he swayed on tiptoes for a moment, his astonished reaction comical to observe. "Lionel? I beg your pardon, Miss Atkinson, but did I just hear you address me by my Christian name?"

Margaret set down her teacup. "Lest you think your hearing has grown as weak as your vision, yes, I did address you by your Christian name."

After exchanging hasty greetings with Fenella and Patrick, Nayland strode over to Margaret. "And dare I hope you will grant me the honor of calling you Margaret, Miss Atkinson?"

"You may."

He sank down into the nearest chair and gazed raptly at her. "Forgive me for asking Miss . . . Margaret, but are you ill? Suffering from a delusionary fever of the brain, perhaps?"

Margaret sighed. "No, Lionel, I am just weary of sparring with you, that's all."

"Oh, dear, that's disappointing news. I had grown to enjoy our little verbal matches. They add such excitement to my dull, bookish existence, a bit of pepper to my custard, as it were."

Patrick interceded. "It's good to see you again, Nayland. Why don't you take a plate and join us for luncheon?"

"Don't mind if I do." Nayland rose and went over to the sideboard. As he filled his plate, he glanced over at

Patrick. "I can see by those colorful decorations to your face that the rumors about your fighting Saintly Standon are true."

"The bruises were worse yesterday," Fenella said. "His eye was closed shut and his jaw had blossomed into the most striking combination of purple and yellow."

"Standon got the worst of it," Patrick said with supreme relish. "I wasn't still weak from the hardships of prison this time, and I think he was quite astonished by his defeat."

Nayland seated himself next to Margaret. "I heard he's not going to press charges against you."

"He wouldn't dare," Patrick said. "There were too many witnesses who saw him provoke me this time."

The earl said to Fenella, "I also heard what a cruel, thoughtless thing he did to you. It must have been most humiliating."

"I suspect he thought he was being amusing, the way schoolboys often are when they pull the wings off flies," she replied. She could still see all those people staring when Standon yanked off her turban, still hear their outraged mutterings about "traitor" and "clipped."

Patrick reached out across the table and covered her hand with his own. "He paid dearly."

"Standon's paying in other ways as well," Nayland said. "He evicted three more tenants yesterday in an especially violent confrontation. Several constables were attacked and beaten with clubs, and two farmers were shot, though not seriously." He shook his head. "Standon is about as popular a land agent as Captain Boycott."

Margaret said, "I have heard that a relief fund has been established to aid the Boycotts. They're asking for volunteers to go to Mayo and help harvest his crops before they all rot in the fields."

"And where will these volunteers come from?" Patrick wanted to know.

"Loyal Irishmen and even men from England," Margaret said, "where support is greatest for Boycott and feeling runs high against Parnell and the Land Leaguers. At least, that's what the papers have written."

"The Land Leaguers and Captain Moonlight won't be pleased," Fenella said, finishing the last of her tea.

Patrick regarded the earl speculatively. "Tell me, Nayland, what is my standing in the community? You seem to know the mood of the countryside better than anyone else. How am I regarded by my tenants and the good citizens of Mallow?"

Margaret looked annoyed. "You make him sound like such an old gossip, Patrick."

Nayland's pale brows rose almost to his receding hairline. "Are my ears deceiving me? Did Miss . . . Margaret actually defend me just then?"

Margaret appeared surprised herself, but she recovered her wits nicely. "Do forgive me for my lapse, Lionel. It was the effects of brain fever, nothing more. I shan't do it again, I promise."

Fenella thought the earl looked delighted with the change in Margaret.

But he grew serious once again. "What you say is true, Patrick. People have always been quick to confide in me for some strange reason I have never been able to fathom. Despite my noble lineage, this homely visage seems to inspire trust in others."

Margaret coughed into her napkin, earning her a quick grin from the earl and a scowl of disapproval from her cousin.

"As I was saying," Nayland continued, "I do hear snippets of information from time to time. I know that Standon is feared and hated, but that is common knowledge. The Quinns of Rookforest were always held in high regard until your father began evicting tenants indiscriminately, if you'll forgive me for saying so. Now that that practice has ceased, the tenants are feeling more favorable toward you once again."

Then Nayland grinned boyishly. "And I, of course, am the most well-loved of all for my exemplary fairness and generosity."

Margaret scoffed openly at that, while Fenella couldn't help smiling at the earl's easygoing, self-deprecating manner.

Then Nayland's smile died. "But in all seriousness, I believe matters are going to become worse, and soon all landlords, no matter how well-favored, are going to be all tarred with the same brush.''

Patrick drummed his fingers against the table. ''The tenants want the land for themselves free and clear, and no matter how much their rents are lowered or even abolished altogether, they won't be satisfied.''

Nayland nodded. ''That seems to be the way of it.''

''The enemy is at the gates,'' Patrick said.

Fenella felt a shiver of foreboding run up her arms, yet the mark on her wrist remained still.

She prayed Patrick was wrong.

The cold winter rain was falling steadily, but Fenella didn't care. She was safe and warm in the study, reading a book quietly while Patrick sat at the desk—his desk now—and wrote out new rental agreements.

Fenella found herself glancing up at Patrick quite often, for though his beloved face was bruised and battered at the moment, it never ceased to delight her, especially when she contrasted those serene features with the way they had looked last night. Vivid images exploded through her mind. Finely arched brows coming together in a frown of rapt concentration . . . pale eyes darkening with sublime passion . . . shapely lips parting to cry out her name at his moment of ecstasy.

She looked away hastily as the room suddenly seemed too warm, and tried to concentrate on her book, but she couldn't. Patrick possessed her mind now just as surely as he had possessed her body last night.

The printed page blurred before her eyes as her mind wandered again.

Patrick had taken her for his mistress and had fought for her honor in Mallow, but not once in all that time had he told her he loved her.

Suddenly fresh doubts assailed her. What if all he wanted was for her to be his mistress, nothing more? Ah, but now she was thinking of tomorrows again, and she had promised herself she wouldn't do that.

''Why the forlorn sigh?''

The sound of Patrick's voice snapped her out of her reverie, and she looked up to see him regarding her with a gentle smile on his face.

"Did I just sigh? I must have come to a moving passage in my book."

"Come, Fenella, don't dissemble with me. You know I can read you like that book you're holding in your lap. What's troubling you? And don't tell me nothing, because I won't believe it."

Should I tell him? she asked herself. Should I tell him I love him and risk the heartbreak of hearing from his own lips that he doesn't love me in return?

"Nothing is troubling me, Patrick. I was just thinking of Margaret and Lord Nayland this morning. She seems to have changed her opinion of him. They actually appeared to get along together."

Patrick smiled, successfully diverted. "Yes, it would seem that way. I wonder why the sudden change in my wild Meggie?"

Fenella thought of Terrence Sheely, but she held her tongue. That secret would always be between her and Margaret. Instead, she said, "Perhaps she has come to see the earl's finer qualities."

"As I came to see yours?" he inquired gently.

"I would hope so," she replied with a smile.

Patrick nodded as he rose and stretched his cramped body. "I'm relieved. I would be pleased to see Margaret and Nayland make a match of it. They are well-suited to each other. And I know it is what my father would have wished for her, to be settled with a fine man."

And what about us? Fenella asked herself. Are we suited to each other?

Just at that moment there came a knock on the study door, and when Patrick bade them enter, the butler appeared.

"Constable Treherne to see you, sir."

"Show him in, Bell."

A moment later the constable walked through the door, eyed Patrick's bruised face, and said, "So it's true, then."

"Constable," Patrick said smoothly, extending his hand. "I assume St. John Standon has pressed charges against me for our little, er, difference of opinion in Mallow the other day, and that you are here to arrest me."

The policeman's eyes popped open wide. "No, sir, not

at all. No charges have been brought against ye. I've come to see ye on another matter." Then he nodded at Fenella. "Something to do with Miss Considine."

"Me?" Fenella laughed nervously. "Why, constable, to the best of my knowledge, I've not broken any laws."

The constable shifted his weight from one foot to the other nervously. "Not you, miss, but perhaps yer father."

Fenella glanced at Patrick in alarm. "My father? What do you mean? He's been dead for these four months now. How could he have possibly broken any laws?"

Patrick indicated a chair and the constable seated himself. He cleared his throat as if he dreaded what he was about to say. "I don't know of any other way to say this than to come right out with it. It seems Dr. Considine was a moonlighter, miss."

Shock immobilized Fenella for a moment. "I beg your pardon?"

"Yer father was a moonlighter."

Fenella jumped to her feet. "That is absurd! My father would have never been involved with those . . . those fiends! He never would have maimed cattle or burned down houses or carded defenseless women. He was a doctor sworn to save lives, not to injure people."

She whirled away and crossed her arms, lest she strike the policeman in her rage.

Behind her, she heard Patrick said coldly, "And I suppose you have proof of Dr. Considine's involvement with the moonlighters, constable?"

"Aye, that I do. Sworn testimony, as a matter of fact. Can't find more proof than that."

Fenella spun around. "Then whoever made that statement is a liar and you're more the fool for believing him!"

The policeman turned crimson and glared at Fenella. "Now, I know how upset ye are at the news, miss, but there's no call for ye to insult meself."

Fenella did not apologize, just stood there with arms tightly crossed and lips pursed.

Patrick said, "Perhaps you should start from the beginning, constable. How did you learn of Dr. Considine's alleged involvement with these men?"

Treherne settled himself in his chair as if he had a long story to tell.

"An informer told us that Captain Moonlight would be makin' a raid on the MacConnell farm because the man was to be punished for bein' a land grabber. So I took me men and set a trap for 'em. In the scuffle, we managed to nab one of 'em, though the rest of 'em got clean away."

"Who is this man?" Patrick asked.

"Galty Garroty's son."

Fenella sank back down into her chair. "Jamser? Jamser Garroty?"

"Himself."

"And what did young Jamser have to say for himself?" Patrick asked, flicking a concerned glance at Fenella, sitting on the edge of her chair. "Did he inform on the others?"

"I wish he had!" Treherne exclaimed. "But he refuses to betray his friends. All he would say was that Dr. Considine was a moonlighter and that he was murdered because he went against them."

"Murdered?" Patrick echoed, looking at Fenella.

Suddenly Fenella felt the room shrink as the walls closed in around her as tightly as a matchbox, robbing her of breath. She swayed in her seat and would have fallen forward onto the floor if Patrick hadn't rushed to her side and steadied her.

"I'm . . . I'm all right," she murmured, fighting to clear the swirling mists from her mind. When Patrick released her, she said to the policeman, "My father was murdered?"

Treherne nodded gravely. "According to Jamser Garroty, the moonlighters had been watching yer house at night. When they saw yer father leave, they followed him. When he got to the bridge, he was struck on the head and his clothes doused with whiskey before they threw him over. Thought they'd make it look like an accident, they did. Fooled me right enough."

"But why?" Fenella moaned helplessly.

"Because he was against the moonlighters' methods. It was one thing to dig an empty grave before a land grabber's door. Yer father thought that was harmless. But

when they started cardin' women or shootin' men in the
knees and crippling them for life, yer father didn't like
that, and let 'em all have the edge of his tongue. According to Jamser, they were afraid he'd turn informer on the
lot of them.''

Fenella sat back in her chair, still unable to believe
what she had just been told.

Treherne cleared his throat. "I am here today, Miss
Considine, to ask you if you had any knowledge of your
father's activities.''

"That's absurd!" Patrick growled, placing a protective
hand on Fenella's shoulder. "Any fool can see that this
news has come as a great shock to her.''

"I don't mean to insult the lady," Treherne replied.
"I'm just doing me job.''

Fenella rested her aching head against her fingertips.
"I can't help you, constable. If my father was a moonlighter, he kept that secret well hidden from me.''

"I don't mean to press you, miss," Treherne said, "but
please think back carefully. Were there any nights yer
father came home late, or went off for hours at a time?''

"Liam Considine was a doctor, for God's sake," Patrick said. "Of course there were times when he wasn't
at home. He had patients to tend to.''

"Aside from those times," Treherne said.

Fenella was silent for a moment as she tried to gather
her scattered wits about her. But she was in such turmoil,
she couldn't think clearly.

After several minutes, she just shook her head. "I'm
sorry, constable. I can't seem to recall any such instances.''

Something like disbelief flared in the policeman's eyes
for just a second. Then he shrugged and rose. "If you
should happen to remember some bit of information that
would be helpful to us . . .''

"Miss Considine will be sure to tell you," Patrick replied. Then he added, "What will happen to Garroty
now?''

"He'll rot in jail for a while as an incentive to inform
on his fellow moonlighters, then he'll go to trial. If it's
proven he murdered Dr. Considine, he'll hang.''

Fenella shuddered.

Patrick said, "I suppose the news of Dr. Considine's involvement with the moonlighters has spread through Mallow?"

"I wouldn't know that, sir."

"Very well. Good day to you, Constable Treherne."

Thus dismissed, the policeman wished Fenella a good day and left.

She made no reply. She just sat there, unable to perceive her surroundings through the cloud of disbelief and doubt that surrounded her like a thick cloak.

Patrick knelt by her chair and clasped her hands in his. "I'm sorry," he said gently, his eyes mirroring the concern and helplessness he felt. "I know this must come as a great shock to you."

"My father a moonlighter," she said, shaking her head. "I can't believe it."

"Jamser's obviously lying," Patrick said. "He needed someone to blame, and he came up with your father, a dead man who can't defend himself."

Fenella clutched at his hands, trying to absorb his strength. "But I think he's telling the truth."

Patrick's eyes widened. "Why would you think that?"

"Because now that I think back on it, there were several times when my father wasn't home, and when he did return, he didn't give very convincing reasons for his absences."

"Tell me what they were."

Fenella stared at the ceiling as if to collect her thoughts.

"The first occurred the night we met," she began. "If you'll recall, I was waiting for my father to come home from delivering the O'Hara baby. Well, he didn't come home until nearly midnight."

"Perhaps the delivery took longer than he anticipated. What was so odd about that?"

"Nothing, except for the fact that he told me the O'Hara baby was born at ten o'clock that night. When we later went to call upon the O'Haras at their farm, Mrs. O'Hara told me the baby had been born at three o'clock in the afternoon."

The silence in the study was deafening.

Fenella swallowed hard. "So, where was my father

between the time of the birth and the time he arrived home? And why did he lie to me?''

"I see," Patrick said, swinging to his feet. "Very suspicious indeed." He was silent for a moment. "And did you confront your father about the discrepancy?''

She shook her head. "No, I'm afraid I didn't. I dismissed it as something inconsequential. I thought perhaps my father had gone to the public house with some friends and didn't want me to know about it." A bitter smile twisted her mouth. "Some friends."

Patrick was frowning, deep in thought as he braced himself against the edge of the desk. "Were there any other such instances that you can recall?''

Fenella nodded. "One night, a man came to the door very late, long after we had retired. I remember it distinctly because whoever it was knocked on the door so loudly, it awakened me. When I went to my father's room, I saw that he was gone.''

"Perhaps he went to treat a patient."

"I thought so too, at first. And then I discovered he hadn't taken his medical bag with him."

"I see. And did you mention this to him the following morning?''

"Yes, I did. And he told me this particular patient didn't need a treatment that would require his medical bag. I didn't stop to think that if this patient's affliction wasn't serious, my father needn't have been summoned in the middle of the night to treat him.''

"Point well taken."

"And now I remember how furious he was when the Heanys were carded. I've never seen him so angry over anything.''

"Perhaps that is why the other moonlighters distrusted him and feared he would inform on them. He disapproved of their methods, as Constable Treherne said.''

Fenella rose now and began wringing her hands. "I've been so stupid . . . so blind! Why didn't I see something was amiss? Why didn't I press him for answers?" She turned to Patrick, her face crumpling with guilt. "Perhaps he'd still be alive today.''

He went to her at once and took her in his arms. "Hush, Fenella. You mustn't blame yourself. There's nothing you could have done. People who want to keep secrets from someone else often go to diabolic lengths to practice their deception. No matter what your accusations, your father would have dismissed them with a convincing excuse.'' He held her at arm's length and gave her a little shake. ''So don't blame yourself for something your father did. I won't hear of it.''

''But, Patrick—''

''I said I won't hear of it. Your father chose to become a moonlighter for reasons of his own that died with him. He knew the type of people he was dealing with, and I'm sure he knew the risks involved. Men often do strange things in the name of patriotism. His death was tragic and senseless, but, as cruel as this may sound, he brought it upon himself. You were not to blame in any way, so stop it this instant.''

Fenella gazed into his eyes and saw the tender concern written there, as well as fierce insistence.

Her smile was bittersweet. ''Easier said than done, I'm afraid.''

He wiped away a stray tear with the ball of his thumb. ''You're not afraid of anything, Fenella. You are brave and strong, and you'll surmount this tragedy.''

I'm not as brave as you think, Patrick, she said to herself. If I were, I'd tell you how much I love you and damn the consequences.

She slipped her arms around his waist and hugged him for dear life. ''Patrick, I don't know what I'd do without you.'' As soon as the words inadvertently popped out of her mouth, Fenella realized the implications of what she had said and froze, waiting for his rejection.

He held her tightly, his cheek pressed against the top of her head, but said nothing.

She sighed. She couldn't do without him, but he obviously could do without her.

It was so cold and rainy outside that for a moment Fenella contemplated returning the covered inside car back to the stables and abandoning the raw, wet weather for the warmth and dryness of the drawing room.

But she couldn't. There was something she had to do that just couldn't wait. Her contentment rested on it.

Even though her breath was turning to smoky vapor and her fingers were stiff with cold despite Margaret's castoff gloves, she brought the reins down smartly on the horse's rump and started through the demesne. Once she passed through Rookforest's gates, she turned the inside car down the road to Mallow.

She shivered, thankful for the car's roof that protected her from the driving rain now pelting the horse's hide and turning the landscape gray and dreary.

"Forgive me," she said aloud to the horse, now slogging his way through the rutted, muddy road. "But this is something I must do."

So she drove resolutely along, praying that one of the car's two wheels wouldn't become stuck, and soon she came to her destination.

Fenella turned the car down the drive until she came to what was left of the Considine cottage.

The moment she halted the horse before the blackened stone ruin, the rain slowed from a drenching downpour to a gentle, merciful drizzle. Fenella just sat there for a moment, trying to picture her home as it had once been, whole and filled with warmth and love that transcended mere walls. But it was well nigh impossible now.

There was very little of the physical house left standing. The ravenous flames had devoured every scrap of wood, from the beams in the roof to the windowsills, and what it couldn't destroy, it desecrated by blackening with thick, omnipresent soot. Part of the stone walls were still standing, but other parts were falling into ruin where enterprising farmers had pried the stones loose from their mortar and hauled them away for their own cottages, the final indignation.

Fenella had to blink back tears. This was all that was left of her past life, a gutted pile of rubble standing in a charred, blackened heap.

Ireland demands so much of its people, she thought. And for what?

Taking a deep breath, she turned the inside car around and drove away without a backward glance, for she still had one more stop to make.

Fifteen minutes later, she was standing before her father's grave.

"Father, why didn't you tell me?" she asked, staring down at the rain-streaked headstone.

There was no response, only the monotonous drip-drip-drip of water pattering against dry leaves.

Question after unanswered question reverberated through her mind. Did he lie because he wanted to protect her? Did he fear she would disapprove of his being a moonlighter? Did he think she would betray him if she knew?

Fenella shivered as a rivulet of rain slithered beneath the collar of her ulster and ran down her back. Why had her father, a man dedicated to healing the sick, become a lawless moonlighter?

She thought she knew the answer to that. No matter how friendly he had been with the Quinns and other landowners, Liam Considine had always sympathized with the plight of the farmer. To him, they weren't ignorant, superstitious peasants, but Ireland's true nobility. Perhaps he thought he was doing the right thing by joining Captain Moonlight, and when he saw his mistake, it was too late for him to extricate himself. He had paid for it with his life.

Murder . . .

Fenella shuddered as a fresh barrage of rain began to fall, driving against her face so that raindrops mingled with her own tears. She tried not to think about the night her father died, but horrible, haunting thoughts forced their way to the surface. She hoped his death was quick and that he did not suffer or realize that the cause he had served ultimately betrayed him. That would have been the ultimate insult.

Turning up the collar of her ulster, she trudged through the sodden graveyard, climbed into the inside car, and started back to Rookforest.

When she walked in the door, there was Patrick pacing impatiently in the foyer. He wordlessly held out his arms to her, and Fenella went to him, grateful for the strength and warmth of his arms around her. Then he divested her of the soaked ulster and ruined bonnet and took her to the library, where he wrapped her shivering body in a warm woolen lap rug, seated her before a roaring fire, and pressed a generous glass of brandy into her hands.

They sat there in silence with their thoughts.

* * *

Later that night, when Patrick came to Fenella's room, all he did was hold her tightly against him and stroke her back.

Outside, the rain had stopped, but the wind was rising again, heavy gusts rattling the windows. Inside, the room was cold, but Fenella felt warm and safe cradled by Patrick's body.

"You've had quite a shock today," he murmured, brushing her hair with his lips.

"My father a moonlighter . . ." Fenella shook her head. "And I never even suspected."

"He hid his secret life well."

"That he did. I just wish he had trusted me enough to tell me."

"Perhaps he wanted to protect you, or feared your disapproval."

She raised herself on one elbow. "I do disapprove of their tactics, but perhaps if Father had confided in me, I would have understood." Fenella fell back against the pillows. "But of course he wouldn't confide in me. After all, I am a mere woman, put on earth to keep his house and darn his socks. Heaven forbid I should have an independent thought of my own."

"Hush," Patrick said softly. "It's too late now for bitterness."

'I can't help the way I feel," she said, her voice rising. "Did my father once think of my welfare when he went off gallivanting with these men? Did he ever stop to think of what I would do without him if he were arrested or killed?" She shook her head. "First William, and now my father . . ."

Patrick cradled her face with one hand and gazed deeply into her eyes. "You're not alone, Fenella. You have me."

But for how long, Patrick? she asked him in silent appeal. Tell me exactly how long I will have you? Another week? A month? A year, if I'm lucky?

He kissed her then, a leisurely exploration of her mouth with his own. Fenella closed her eyes and abandoned herself to the heaviness of his lips pressing against her own, and the delicious way her insides melted.

When they parted, she said, "I don't know what I'd do without you, Patrick."

He just smiled and kissed her again.

Then he said, "Even if your father had confided in you, there's nothing you could have done, Fenella. These men would have stopped at nothing to silence him if they feared he would turn informer on them. That's how they keep their power, through fear and intimidation. They demand unswerving loyalty from their members, and once your father appeared disgruntled with their methods, they branded him a traitor."

He caressed her cheek with the backs of his fingers and smiled down at her gently. "If they hadn't killed him that night, Fenella, they would have found another opportunity. Make no mistake about that. And perhaps you would have died as well."

She shivered. "Do you know what I find so frightening about this?"

"What?"

"That someone I know, someone I pass on the streets of Mallow and wish good day, could have killed my father. Perhaps it was Galty Garroty or one of Francis Finnerty's turnip-brained sons. Or it could have been Tim O'Hara, whose son was delivered by my father."

"That is a frightening thought. But that's what a conflict like this does to people. It turns brother against brother, neighbor against neighbor, friends into enemies. No one is above suspicion."

Fenella sighed and nestled closer to him. "I hope they catch this murderer before more innocent people are killed."

Suddenly Patrick stiffened beside her and turned his body toward the door.

"What is it?" Fenella whispered.

He scowled. "I thought I heard a floorboard creak outside the door."

Fenella's heart stopped, then started with a rush. "Do you think one of the servants is spying on us?"

"Let them spy and gossip," Patrick replied, turning toward her again with a glint of pure possessiveness in his eyes. "Let the world know I am Fenella Considine's lover. I am the master here, and I may take whomever I please to my bed.''

Whenever he spoke that way about her, hope and happiness flooded Fenella's heart like the warm rays of the noonday sun.

She smiled up at him. "But we're not in your bed, we're in mine."

He grinned wolfishly. "Yours, mine . . . what does it matter?''

Then he took her in his arms and banished her fears in the passion of his lovemaking.

The following morning dawned clear and cold, with pale hoarfrost icing each blade of grass with its ghostly glaze.

Fenella washed and dressed quickly, then went downstairs to breakfast. The moment she saw Margaret's pinched, bellicose expression, Fenella knew something was wrong.

"Good morning, Margaret," she said cheerily.

"You're Patrick's mistress, aren't you?''

Fenella froze in the shock for a moment, the bald accusation hanging in the air like an upraised sword over her head. She turned toward the sideboard to hide her face, crimson with guilt and embarrassment. "Margaret Atkinson, such language for a young lady. Mrs. Ryan will wash your mouth out with soap if she catches you talking that way.''

"Ailagh has heard much worst from my lips," Margaret said. "Stop trying to evade me, Fenella.''

"I'm sure I don't know what you're talking about," she said, wishing her hand wouldn't tremble so as she reached for a plate.

"Don't lie to me, Fenella," Margaret said with an exaggerated sigh. "You're not very good at it, for one thing, and for another, I heard the both of you in your room last night.''

Fenella returned to her seat, confident her emotions were under control now. "Spying, were you? I'm ashamed of you.''

"The end justified the means. You see, I first overheard Brigid tell another one of the maids that she caught you naked in bed one morning, your nightgown crumpled on the floor. Most unseemly for a lady, don't you think?''

Fenella said nothing, just seated herself and made a great pretense of shaking out her napkin.

Margaret went on with, ''Brigid thought it most peculiar, but then I began thinking that perhaps you had had a nocturnal visitor. So I began watching Patrick's room. I thought it most odd that he had suddenly taken to sleeping with his bedroom door closed, as he's always kept it open. One of the more bizarre effects of his imprisonment, you understand.''

Margaret affixed Fenella with a cold hazel stare. ''Last night I went to Patrick's room. And do you know what I discovered?''

''Enlighten me.''

''His bed was empty. Then I went to your room, and do you know what I discovered there?'' Before Fenella could reply, she said, ''I heard voices, and one of them was decidedly my cousin's.''

Fenella poured herself a cup of steaming tea. ''Whether or not I am Patrick's mistress, it's none of your concern, Margaret.''

''Oh, I quite agree,'' she said with surprising blandness. ''Whom my cousin chooses to sleep with is his own concern. I just don't want to see you succumb to false expectations.''

Fenella hesitated, caught off balance. ''What do you mean?''

Margaret's lovely face softened with pity. ''He'll never marry you, you know. Oh, he may enjoy you as his mistress, but when he tires of you . . .'' She shrugged.

''Thank you for the warning,'' Fenella said stiffly.

''I'm not being frank in order to hurt you,'' Margaret said gently, ''but you see, now our situations are reversed. Now you are in love with a man not of your class, and I must give you the same sage advice you once gave me about Terrence Sheely.''

Stung, Fenella stared down at her plate.

''You're a doctor's daughter, Fenella, and Patrick is a wealthy, prominent landowner. When he marries, he will

doubtless choose the daughter of another wealthy landowner. This is the way marriages are arranged among
the wealthy and privileged. And you do not fit in.''

Without another word, Margaret rose and left the dining room.

Fenella just sat there staring at her unwanted breakfast,
her heart filled with misgivings and uncertainties. When
she was with Patrick, lying in his arms, she felt confident
that he loved her even though he hadn't said the words.
But when someone like Margaret made such cutting
statements, Fenella was assailed by fresh doubts.

She sighed and rose, leaving her breakfast untouched.

Patrick leaned against the paddock fence and watched
a half-dozen long-legged thoroughbreds race and gambol
about. The crisp, frosty air was making the sleek animals
frisky, and they bucked and kicked up their heels as they
worked off their high spirits.

Satisfied that the horses were fit and well-cared-for,
Patrick turned away and started back to the house. All
he could think about was Fenella's warm bed and how he
had hated to leave it this morning.

Just as he rounded a corner of the stables, he was startled to see Margaret come down the path toward him.
She was bundled up against the cold in a heavy woolen
coat, and a stylish fur hat graced her head. When she saw
him, she waved.

''And what are you doing out on such a cold day, my
wild Meggie-of-the-moor?'' he asked when she came up
to him and slipped her arm through his.

''Oh, I might ask you that same question,'' she replied.

''I came out to see the horses.''

Margaret raised her brows. ''You left Fenella Considine's bed just to see the horses?''

Patrick stopped, dropped her arm, and glared down at
her. ''What did you say?''

''Don't look as though you could cheerfully strangle
me, Pat. I know you and Fenella are lovers.''

''So, Margaret Atkinson, you've been snooping. I
ought to take you over my knee and warm my hand on
your backside for that.''

She tossed her head. "I'm shaking in my boots, Pat."

He glared down at her. "How did you find out?"

When Margaret told him, he swore under his breath. "Damn you, Margaret. I don't appreciate being spied upon. I know you're a member of the family, and quite advanced for your age, but that doesn't give you any right to spy on me like some curious chambermaid. Whom I choose to sleep with is my own concern, not yours."

She listened to his scolding with great equanimity. When he was through, she said, "You can take Captain Moonlight to bed for all I care, but I am concerned about Fenella."

Patrick stared at her. "Why should you be concerned about Fenella? She is a grown woman. She wanted me as much as I wanted her. I am not forcing myself upon her, if that's what you mean."

"At the risk of sounding like some elderly maiden aunt, what are your intentions toward the lady, Cousin Pat? Do you intend to keep her as your mistress until you're both old and gray? Do you intend to marry her?"

At the word "marry," Patrick glanced at her sharply. Then Margaret stopped and faced him squarely. "Do you even love her, or is it simply lust?"

His eyes narrowed. "I can't believe I'm hearing this. Father was much too lenient in your upbringing, Meggie, my girl. You're much too forward for a girl of eighteen."

"Woman of eighteen," she corrected him with a stubborn outthrusting of her chin.

"Pardon me."

"You haven't answered my question."

Patrick looked away, suddenly feeling uncomfortable under his cousin's steady scrutiny. "I haven't really thought about a future with Fenella. And as to loving her . . ." He shrugged. "Sometimes I think I do, but then I'm not certain."

"Well, I would suggest you give the matter a few moments' thought," Margaret said. "Fenella and I have had our differences in the past, but I like her and I would hate to see her hurt by anyone, especially you, after all she's been through."

"Now you do sound as stodgy as a maiden aunt," Patrick grumbled.

"It's not my fault that I'm wise beyond my years," she retorted with a quicksilver grin. Then she became sober. "Please consider what I've said."

"I will."

Patrick stopped and stared at the house looming before them, suddenly needing to be alone. "I think I'll go for a ride. Gallowglass needs the exercise."

Margaret nodded and placed a hand on his arm. Then she strode off down the path alone.

Patrick rode his black stallion hard across the fields, letting the wind whip tears from his eyes.

His discussion with Margaret had disturbed him, forcing him to confront matters he would have rather not faced. But he knew he had to. It wasn't fair to Fenella.

Did he love her? In all honesty, he wasn't sure. He enjoyed her company, her laughter, and her ready wit. She really listened to him, and seemed as comfortable with long silences as she was with endless conversation. And he certainly enjoyed her expertise in bed, for she was a passionate and surprisingly uninhibited woman for the sheltered life she had led. He was drawn to her, but did he love her and want to spend the rest of his life with her?

"Gallowglass, my boy, I honestly don't know."

Part of his indecision was based on the fact that he had loved only one woman in his life, Cynara. He had never considered loving anyone else, even when she had betrayed him. She exerted such a powerful, irrational hold on him, even now.

As he galloped across another field, Patrick realized he wasn't being fair to Fenella, but he knew how women were. Despite her constant assurances that they shouldn't think of tomorrows or consequences, he knew she would eventually. After all, she was a woman. She would accept the role of mistress only so long, and then desire that of wife. They all did.

What woman could possibly compete with Cynara? She possessed his thoughts again, her dusky beauty tantalizing him, beckoning to him.

Suddenly Patrick reined in Gallowglass on a hilltop to

get his bearings. He sucked in his breath when he saw where he was.

There, below him, was Drumlow. Patrick turned his horse around and rode for home.

18

FENELLA, MARGARET, AND PATRICK were sitting in the drawing room when Lord Nayland came bursting in upon them with a shocking announcement.

"Standon is being boycotted."

"And good morning to you, Lionel," Margaret said blithely. "How good of you to knock."

Patrick folded the copy of the *Dublin Daily Express* he had been reading and set it aside. "Ignore my cousin, Nayland. You know you're always welcome here, even if you don't knock first." He gave Margaret a level look. "In fact, I've come to think of you as a member of the family."

Margaret glared back at him, tossed her head, and said to the earl, "Your spectacles are fogging, Lionel. You'd best wipe them before you go crashing into the furniture and injuring yourself."

Nayland wished Fenella a good morning, then removed his spectacles and did as Margaret suggested while striding over to the fire. "Forgive me for bursting in on you like this," he said, putting his spectacles back on and proceeding to warm his hands, "but I had to come as soon as I heard. Standon is being boycotted."

"Boycotted?" Patrick frowned. "What does Standon have to do with Captain Boycott?"

"Our illustrious captain has just lent his name to a new word in the English language. They're now referring to social ostracism as a boycott, and people who are ostracized as being boycotted."

Fenella set down her embroidery. "You mean to say that what is happening to Captain Boycott will now happen to the Standons?"

"Exactly," Nayland replied.

"Why?" Margaret asked.

"In retaliation for exorbitant rents and the frequency of his evictions," the earl explained. "The tenants and shopkeepers of Mallow have all banded together and refuse to serve the Standons or sell them any goods. In fact, all of their servants left yesterday—the guards at the gate, the household staff, and even the stableboys. Rats leaving the sinking ship."

Fenella thought of that day she had visited Cynara at Drumlow and the sullen nursemaid who had been reluctantly taking care of little Louisa.

"Everyone?" she said in disbelief.

"Everyone," Nayland replied. "The house is empty save for Standon, his sister, and the child."

"Who will take care of the child now?" Fenella asked.

"Her mother, I would assume," Patrick replied.

Margaret smiled maliciously as she rose. "What an interesting picture, a Cynara without her handmaidens to do her bidding. Who will draw her bath and dress her hair? Who will clean and mend her fine gowns?"

They all fell silent as they pondered the prospect of the lovely and pampered Cynara being forced to perform the tasks of her lady's maid.

Sufficiently warmed by the fire, Nayland seated himself across from Patrick. "The situation is far graver than that. It's a question of daily survival. Who is going to light the fires in the morning, cook their meals, sweep the floors?"

Margaret's eyes widened in mock horror. "I must say the thought of seeing the proud, vain Marchioness of Eastbrook down on her hands and knees, scrubbing floors, gives me great satisfaction after all she's done to this family."

Patrick added, "Standon has an enviable stable. Without men to muck out stalls and feed the horses, those fine animals will all sicken and die."

Nayland sighed. "That's why social ostracism is so effective. We landlords take our servants for granted. They perform those tasks that we consider beneath us, and we often treat them as though they were invisible, without feelings of their own. But take them away, and we soon find out how dependent we are upon them."

"Saintly Standon is certainly finding out," Patrick commented.

Margaret chuckled and turned to Fenella. "Shall we pay a call on Cynara and gloat over her misfortune?"

"I wouldn't be too quick to gloat, Meggie," Patrick said reproachfully. "For all you know, we could be next."

That sober pronouncement wiped the smile off Margaret's face quickly. "What do you mean?"

The earl said, "He means that Rookforest or Devinstown could be the next to be boycotted. Our servants could leave us to cook our own meals and sweep the floors."

"They wouldn't dare! Mrs. Ryan and the staff are loyal to us because we treat them so well."

"Perhaps not," Patrick said. "If they had to choose between us and Ireland, who knows which they'd choose?"

Nayland gave Margaret a teasing smile. "Don't worry. I would gladly lay down my life to spare you the indignities of cooking or scrubbing floors."

"Why, thank you. I shall remember your kind offer should the need arise."

She was so serious, the earl burst out laughing. "Why, I believe you would."

Fenella said, "So what are the Standons going to do without servants?"

"More important," Patrick said, "what are they going to do without food and other basic necessities of life we all take for granted? If the shopkeepers of Mallow won't sell to them . . ." He shrugged.

"I imagine Standon will have supplies carted in from Fermoy," the earl said. "Shopkeepers there have no ax to grind with him."

"But those shipments may be intercepted on the road by moonlighters," Patrick said. "That's what happened to Boycott when he tried it."

Fenella frowned. "But why would the shopkeepers be a party to this? Isn't Standon's money as good as the next man's?"

"But the shopkeepers' livelihood is closely tied to the farmers'," Nayland explained. "And if the main source of his income tells him to boycott someone, he's got to do it or face an even greater loss of revenue. The farmers could boycott him, and then who would buy the shop-keeper's goods?''

Fenella shook her head. "The whole situation is fright-ening." She looked first at Nayland, then at Patrick. "Where will it all end? In more violence? In revolu-tion?''

The men stared at her thoughtfully.

"We don't know," Patrick replied.

"There is talk of arresting Parnell and the other Land Leaguers on charges of sedition," Nayland said.

"What good would that do?" Margaret wanted to know.

"The Land League would be dissolved."

"And Captain Moonlight?" Fenella demanded. "Would the moonlighters disband as well, and return peace and tranquillity to the countryside?''

"We don't know that for sure," Patrick said, "but I seriously doubt it. They want the land."

Fenella tried to fight down the rising panic. "So much violence . . . First my father, then Cadogan. Where will it all end?''

No one answered her.

After luncheon, Fenella was left to her own devices. Lord Nayland and Margaret had gone out riding, and Patrick rode off to Mallow, though he had invited Fenella to accompany him. She had refused, pleading a head-ache, but in reality, she wanted to be alone.

As she sat by herself in the drawing room, staring out the tall windows at the cloud-studded sky, her shawl wrapped around her to chase away the chill, Fenella found herself thinking of the odd, unsettled turn her life had taken ever since William's death. One calamity had fol-lowed another in rapid succession.

She absently rubbed her wrist. The one beacon of hope in all the senseless death and violence was Patrick. He had sheltered her and protected her during her blackest hours of despair. Just being with him gave her strength and hope. She felt more secure with him than she had with anyone else.

And when he came to her room at night, loving her with such wanton intensity, she responded with all of her being.

She loved him.

Fenella had thought she loved William until she got to know Patrick Quinn, and he made her realize what her love for William had been lacking. That first love had been true, she realized now, but it lacked depth and dimension. It was rather like being satisfied with drinking only water and then discovering champagne.

Fenella sighed and pulled her shawl more tightly about her. Having once tasted champagne, she knew she'd never be satisfied with water again. And the thought of losing Patrick tormented her.

She had seen the look that passed across his face so fleetingly when Margaret painted such a vivid picture of Cynara as housemaid.

"If he didn't care for her," she mused aloud, "he would have been indifferent. But he wasn't. He looked visibly shaken by the news."

If that were the case, how could she fight such a formidable opponent as Cynara?

"You don't stand a ghost of a chance."

Without warning, an object came hurling at the window. As it hit the glass with a distinct thump, Fenella started and jumped to her feet with a shriek, fearing moonlighters were attacking Rookforest with stones. But when the glass didn't break, she overcame her fear and went to the window to see what it was.

She looked around, dreading what she would see. Then her gaze fell on the ground beneath the windowsill. There was a small brown bird, lying there so still.

Fenella knew what had happened. Seeking warmth and shelter from the winter winds, the bird had flown toward the window, only to be stopped short by the thick, transparent glass.

A dry smile played about Fenella's mouth. "You're just like that bird, Fenella Considine. You come up against obstacles and they thwart you. You just don't fight. Perhaps it's time you stood up for yourself and started fighting for what you want."

But even as she uttered the words, a cold despair started

forming around her heart. She was not accustomed to getting what she wanted. Always there were outside forces conspiring to keep her from achieving her heart's desire, making her a victim of circumstances beyond her control.

What if she told Patrick that she loved him? Would he tell her that he loved her in return? She was so reluctant to risk even saying those words, afraid of learning she was good enough to be his mistress but only Cynara was good enough to be his wife.

Fenella turned and left the room.

Patrick was surprised to find Mallow bustling on this brisk November day. Even though dark, glowering storm clouds were scudding swiftly across the sky, threatening to change the weather at any moment, there was no rain falling, at least for the time being.

As Patrick rode down the main street, he noticed St. John Standon up ahead of him, farther down the road. Standon halted his white horse before the fishmonger's shop and dismounted. He looked around for some obliging boy to hold his horse while he went inside, but all those he summoned with an imperious gesture refused with vehement shakes of their heads before going on.

From where he stood watching, Patrick couldn't see Standon's face very clearly, but he could tell by the way the man flung down the reins and stormed inside that he was in a foul mood.

No sooner had the shop door closed behind Standon than several mischievous boys banded together and ran up to his horse, shouting and waving their arms. The skittish animal bolted at once, running down the street at a full gallop, the reins dragging on the ground.

Patrick smiled to himself. As uncharitable as such feelings were, he found he enjoyed seeing Standon tormented by the very same people he had abused for so long.

"You're getting your comeuppance at long last, Standon," he murmured to himself. "Couldn't happen to a nicer fellow."

A moment later, the shop door opened and a furious, empty-handed Standon stalked out, muttering under his breath. He stopped in his tracks and first looked down the street, then in the opposite direction for his horse.

He still stands as proudly as if he's the uncrowned king of Ireland, Patrick thought to himself. Arrogant bastard.

The urge to add to Standon's misery was one Patrick couldn't resist. He rode down to where Standon stood and said, "Looking for your horse, Standon?"

The handsome face was livid with fury. "Go to hell, Quinn."

Patrick raised his brows. "Such language, and me trying so hard to be helpful."

Without a word, Standon turned and started down the street in search of his horse.

Patrick followed on horseback at a leisurely walk, keeping in step. "Some boys chased him away, so I'm afraid he'll be halfway to Drumlow by now. But then, it's a fine day for a walk. I'm sure you'll catch him in an hour or two."

Standon said nothing, but Patrick could see he was seething inside. Then Standon turned sharply and walked into Jasper's dry-goods shop.

Patrick swung down out of the saddle, and suddenly a boy appeared out of nowhere to take Gallowglass's reins. Patrick paid the lad a penny and went inside Jasper's.

The small shop wasn't crowded. Three farmers in rough homespun were at the counter, and an elderly woman was perusing the stores of tea, as was St. John Standon, who seemed oblivious of the baleful stares and silences.

Standon selected a box of tea and walked over to the counter to pay for it.

"How much, Jasper?" he growled at the proprietor, a burly man with the jowls and bellicose face of a bulldog.

"Your trade is no longer welcome here, Mr. Standon," Jasper said without smiling, his jowls shaking.

Blue eyes flashing, Standon slapped some coins down on the counter. "Isn't my money good enough for you, Jasper?"

"Not anymore," the proprietor replied, making no move to take the coins. "I'll not sell you so much as a needle and thread, and you know why."

"There's your money," Standon said. "I've paid for this tea, and I'm taking it."

As Standon reached for the box, Jasper's beefy hand shot out and closed around the other man's wrist. Out of the corner of his eye Patrick could see one of the men move toward the door and another position himself almost behind Standon.

They look as though they're itching for him to start something, Patrick thought.

"You take that without payin' for it," Jasper said, his voice a low and menacing growl, "and I'll have ye arrested for stealin' it."

One of the men laughed at that, causing Standon's face to turn a murderous shade of crimson as he whirled around to glare at his tormentor. The other man returned his stare boldly, as if to tell him he had only contempt for the great St. John Standon.

Then he wrenched his hand free and swept his coins off the counter.

"Just you wait, Samuel Jasper," he uttered between clenched teeth. "When this is over and we landlords are done with the likes of you, you'll come begging me to buy a box of your miserable tea. And then I'll have the last laugh, just you wait and see."

He turned and started for the door, only to stop when he reached it. "I have a long memory, Jasper. I always reward my friends and punish my enemies. Ask Quinn there. He'll tell you what happens to those who cross St. John Standon."

Then he squared his shoulders and walked out of the shop as if he owned it.

When the door closed behind Standon, Patrick said to Jasper, "Is my money still good here?"

The proprietor beamed. "Yer money is always good in Jasper's, Mr. Quinn."

"Fine. I'll take the box of tea you wouldn't sell to Standon."

When Patrick was back outside, he mounted his horse and went after Standon, who was striding purposefully up the street. His entire being radiated impotent rage, from his balled fists to the lowered set of his head.

"Standon," Patrick called.

When Standon looked up, Patrick tossed him the box of tea. "A small gift for Cynara with my compliments."

Standon caught the box deftly, then dashed it to the cobblestones and ground it into the street with his heel, crashing the box and spilling tea leaves in all directions. "That's what my sister and I think of your gifts, Quinn. She didn't want you four years ago, and she doesn't want your charity now."

Then he started walking and kept on going without a backward glance at Patrick.

In the days to follow, Patrick couldn't stop thinking of Cynara and what was happening to her at Drumlow.

Standon's ostracism in Mallow that day had made a profound impression on Patrick. He had sensed that Jasper was reluctant to antagonize the powerful land agent, but at the same time, he was pleased with himself for having done so. And when all the shopkeepers and farmers stood united, they made a formidable opponent indeed.

During the first week of the Standon boycott, many rumors found their way to Rookforest, usually through Lord Nayland. He told Patrick that many people now traveled through Drumlow land as if it were public property, leaving gates open behind them so livestock would escape and trample the fields. One or two men had remained loyal to their employer, so they were able to see that no vandalism was done to the house itself. And even though Standon had been importing supplies from Fermoy without much difficulty, there were no household servants to cook or clean.

After neither St. John nor Cynara had appeared in church that Sunday, Patrick's conscience began to bother him. Even though St. John had behaved abominably toward him and was his sworn and despised enemy, Patrick couldn't help but feel sorry for him.

The following Monday, he decided to call on Cynara at Drumlow.

The late-November day dawned clear and cold, though by the time Patrick started for Drumlow, he could see threatening clouds begin to gather in the distance. A half-hour later, when he reined in Gallowglass on the hill overlooking the Standons' house, the skies had turned a flat, leaden gray that presaged a storm.

He pulled up his collar against the wind and sat there for a moment regarding Drumlow below him for any sign of habitation. There was none. No guards stood at the gates, which had been left wide open as if in invitation to anyone, rich man or poor, who happened by.

Patrick smiled dryly as he urged his mount down the hill. "I'll wager Standon didn't leave those gates open on purpose," he muttered to himself.

Aside from the yawning gates, other results of the boycott soon became apparent as Patrick walked his horse slowly through the demesne. Blown down by the harsh winds, bare fallen branches were scattered everywhere, waiting to be picked up by groundsmen who were no longer there. The gravel drive was littered with horse dung and deeply pitted with hoofprints, since there was no one to sweep it smooth. The shrubs near the house were straggly and untrimmed, giving Drumlow a decidedly seedy, unkempt air, as though it were uninhabited and on the verge of falling into ruin.

Patrick halted his horse before the entrance, but just sat there in silence for a moment. No footman hurried through those imposing iron-bound doors to take his horse. The doors remained closed as if fearful of revealing what was inside.

He dismounted and tied his horse to the post, then trotted up the steps, his footsteps the only sound. He rang the bell once, then waited. As he expected, no butler opened the door to admit him, so after what Patrick considered a decent interval, he tried the door. Much to his surprise, it was unlocked, so he let himself in without stopping to think what he would do if St. John himself were on the other side.

He stepped into the foyer and hesitated, giving his eyes time to accustom themselves to the darkness.

"Is anyone here?" he called, his voice echoing eerily through the hall.

No one answered.

He waited and listened for footsteps, an answering

voice, anything that would tell him there was human habitation in this cold, cavernous house. There was nothing.

"Cynara? Standon?" he called, taking a few tentative steps through the foyer, but still there was no response.

Well, Patrick decided, I'll just look around until I find someone.

If the care of the grounds had suffered because of the boycott, the house had fared the worst. As Patrick slowly made his way through the foyer, he noticed that all of the furniture was covered with a gray layer of undisturbed dust that made him sneeze several times. There was dirt on the rugs and in corners, begging for the energy and thoroughness of Mrs. Ryan and a good housemaid's mop and dustcloth.

Patrick went from room to room, opening doors as he looked for any sign of Cynara or her brother, but all he saw were appalling signs of the boycott's effect on the household. No fires burned in the grates to chase the chill from these freezing, empty rooms. Patrick shivered. It was almost as cold in here as it was outside.

When he came to the dining room, he wrinkled his nose in disgust. There, on a beautiful mahogany table now smudged and dulled with many fingerprints and spills, sat unwashed china and cutlery haphazardly piled high, the remaining scraps of rotting food emitting a foul odor. He thought about what Meggie had said about Cynara lowering herself to wash dishes like a common scullery maid. Evidently that hadn't happened.

Nayland was right, Patrick thought to himself as he closed the door behind him. We landlords may be the ruling class, but take away those people we depend on to wash our dishes and cook our food, and we become nothing more than animals wallowing in our own filth.

Patrick quickly glanced through the other rooms on the ground floor and found most of them in the same deplorable condition. He debated going upstairs, then decided against it, for all he needed was for St. John Standon to catch him prowling about the upstairs bedchambers.

"Then he'd probably accuse me of trying to rape his sister," Patrick muttered.

Just as he was turning to leave, he heard a faint cry.

He hesitated and listened, trying to determine where the sound was coming from.

There it was again, louder this time, the high-pitched wail of a child in distress. It was coming from an open door at the end of the hall that led to the kitchens below.

Patrick went through the green baize door and started quietly down the stairs, deciding it was more prudent than announcing his presence, for he didn't know whom or what he would find there.

He stopped halfway down the stairs, appalled and saddened by the sight that greeted his eyes.

The first thing he noticed was the child sitting in the middle of the kitchen floor and crying its eyes out, its tears leaving streaks down its dirty face. Then he noticed Cynara standing at the huge black cast-iron stove, her back toward him. She appeared to be trying to stir something in a large steaming pot, and by the looks of it, she was having a frustrating time.

"Louisa!" she shouted, whirling around. "Will you stop that crying before I—"

She looked up and noticed Patrick standing there.

He just stared at her, unable to believe that the beautiful Cynara he had loved with all of his soul, the woman he had gone to prison for, was the same woman standing before him. Her black hair, so thick and lustrous, now hung down to her shoulders in lank hanks, a few wisps sticking to her hot, perspiring cheeks. The dress she wore was wrinkled, spattered and spotted with cooking grease. The elegant marchioness looked like a common scullery maid, and not a particularly efficient one at that.

"Go away!" she shrieked. "Get out of here!"

Without warning, she flung a heavy wooden spoon right at him, but it fell short, hitting several steps below where Patrick stood, and clattered to the floor.

"I said get out of here, damn you!"

"I came to see if there was anything I could do to help," Patrick said kindly as he started down the stairs. The little girl had grown quiet, and now watched him approach with wide-eyed interest.

Cynara snapped, "Help? Don't make me laugh, Patrick. You came here to gloat, to revel in our misery."

Suddenly her anger changed to abject mortification as

she realized what a pitiable figure she must be presenting
to him. Her violet eyes widened in horror and her pale
cheeks turned crimson with shame. She turned away from
him, her hands busily smoothing and patting at her hair,
trying desperately to put it in some semblance of order,
but failing.

"Is this your daughter?" Patrick asked, kneeling on
one knee beside the child, who was smiling up at him
shyly, blissfully unaware of how she looked.

"Yes," Cynara replied.

"What is her name?"

"Louisa, as I'm sure the virtuous Miss Considine has
already told you."

He ignored the spite in her voice. "She's a lovely little
girl. I imagine she takes her fair coloring from her father?"

When Cynara didn't reply, Patrick looked up at her
straight back, and noticed that it was shaking. He rose
and went to stand behind her.

"Cynara," he murmured, placing a tentative hand on
her shoulder, "I'm not here to gloat. I honestly came to
see if I could help you."

She turned slowly, and he could see she was crying,
those great violet eyes like shimmering crystals.

"Hush," he said, trying to draw her into his arms, but
she resisted.

"No, Patrick, you mustn't touch me," she whimpered,
trying to push herself away. "I look like a witch."

He held her anyway. "Do you think that matters to me,
how you look?"

"Oh, Patrick," she wailed, surrendering and burying
her face in his shoulder, "it's been a living nightmare
here since this boycott began and the servants left."

"I know, I know." He stroked her back, soothing her
as she sobbed.

He only meant to comfort her, nothing more, because
his relationship with Fenella and four years of prison
stood between them now. But as he held Cynara in his
arms, her breasts pressed provocatively against his chest
and her slight frame trembling against his, Patrick felt
his resolve wavering. Even as disheveled and unkempt as

Cynara was, her presence still tantalized him, exerted a pull as strong as ever.

He sternly reminded himself why he had come, and gently put her away from him on the pretext of retrieving a handkerchief for her.

Cynara took it and dabbed at her eyes. "Thank you."

He looked at the pot boiling on the stove and gave her a teasing smile. "So, you've become a cook, have you?"

Fenella would have laughed at his gentle sally, but Cynara just glared at him through her tears.

"It's not in the least amusing, Patrick Quinn. I've been trying my best since the cook and all the other servants left, but it hasn't been easy. In fact, it's been hell."

Suddenly her daughter began whimpering, and Cynara went to her at once and picked her up. "There, there, Lou-Lou. Mama's here. Everything is going to be all right. Just don't cry, my precious."

She turned to Patrick. "It's been especially difficult for little Louisa. She needs her mama's constant attention, someone to brush her hair and wash her little dresses when they're dirty. Yet how can I attend her when I must be downstairs maid and cook?" Fierce maternal anger darkened Cynara's face. "It breaks my heart when I see her like this, as dirty and ragged as some peasant's child in a miserable hovel.

"I've begged St. John to send us to Dublin, at least until this is over, but he won't, not even for little Louisa's sake. He says my place is here, with him. He wants me to be as miserable as he is."

Patrick said, "Has your brother tried to hire more servants from Cork city or even Dublin? Perhaps they would come, if he paid them enough."

"I don't know what St. John has done. He never confides estate matters to me. You know that."

"Have you been able to get food?"

"St. John has it shipped in from Fermoy, but what good does it do? Half of it spoils because there's no one to cook it." She glared at the pot as though it were a living, breathing person she could strangle gleefully. "I try, but the results are barely edible, unless St. John shoots a pheasant or woodcock and we roast it."

She set down her daughter and began crying again,

throwing up her hands in frustration. "I'm a lady. I shouldn't have to draw my own bath and carry heavy cans of hot water up three flights of stairs until my back aches. I shouldn't have to dress myself, or clean my own gowns when they're dirty." Her voice rose almost to a wail of protest and outrage. "I just shouldn't have to do such menial work!"

He almost reminded her that her servants had done such menial work every day of their lives, but he thought better of it.

"Please calm yourself, Cynara," Patrick said soothingly, trying to resist taking her into his arms again. "I know this has been difficult for you."

"How can you possibly know the hell I'm going through?" she snapped. "How can you possibly know what it's like to have your life so disrupted you feel as though you're living in another world?"

He stared at her in disbelief. Could she really be so self-absorbed and insensitive as to forget the four years he had spent in prison living in just such another world, a world she would never know or even comprehend?

A retort was on the tip of his tongue, but he bit it back. He shouldn't judge poor Cynara too harshly. She was a lady, born and bred to a life of gentility and ease, to have others take care of her and cater to her every whim. She could no more be expected to cook and clean than she could sprout wings and fly to the moon.

Cynara sank down into a nearby chair wearily, her head drooping in defeat as she buried her face in her hands. "Damn every one of those servants for leaving us," she moaned through her tears. "It's their fault this is happening to us. Just wait until they come crawling back for their old positions. It will be my supreme pleasure to tell the lot of them to go to hell!"

Then she started sobbing, upsetting the child, who started crying as well.

Patrick walked over to Cynara and placed a hand on her shoulder. "I promised to help, and I will. I'm going to find your brother. Perhaps we can work this out between us."

She caught at his hand and stared up at him beseechingly out of melting violet eyes. "Please help me, Patrick. I don't know how I can endure much more of this."

He smiled down at her and left the kitchen in search of St. John.

St. John found Patrick first.

Patrick was just emerging from the kitchen when he heard someone behind him shout, "You!" He stepped aside quickly just in time to see St. John go lunging past.

"I didn't come here to fight you again," Patrick said as his old enemy whirled around with murder in his eyes, "but I will if you force me."

St. John hesitated and stared malevolently at him, his nostrils flared and his eyes narrowed in hatred. "What are you doing here in my house, Quinn? You're trespassing. I could shoot you where you stand and still be within my rights."

"I heard you had been boycotted and I came here to see if I could help."

"Help us? You?" Standon's sharp bark of laughter rang through the foyer. "What do you take me for, a fool?"

"I take you for what you are, Standon, a petty, jealous, and vindictive man, but there's no reason why your sister and her child should suffer for your shortcomings."

"Ah, so that's it. Cynara's behind your sudden mood of generosity. I should have known." St. John flexed his fingers. "Come, then, Quinn. Out with it. Tell me just how you plan to 'help' us."

"If you won't send her to Dublin, at least let me take Cynara and the child back to Rookforest with me."

St. John just stared at him, dumbfounded for a second. Then he burst out laughing.

"So that's it." He shook his head in wonder. "You're still trying to get under my sister's skirts and you'll try anything to do it."

"Your mind always was in the gutter, Standon," Patrick snapped, trying to restrain himself. "I have no designs on Cynara. What happened between us is in the past, where it belongs."

"If you think that, you're deluding yourself. You've always wanted my sister, and you always will, no matter how many Fenella Considines come along. Don't deny it.''

"You're wrong. I am only thinking of the child. At least at Rookforest she could be cared for properly, and Cynara wouldn't be reduced to performing the duties of a scullery maid.''

"No,'' he said. "My sister stays here with me.''

"Dammit, man! Think of someone else besides yourself for once!''

Standon smiled slowly and maliciously. "Give it up, Quinn. You'll never have her as long as I'm alive.''

Patrick fought down the impulse to hit Standon in the face again. "You don't care that your little niece suffers?''

"My chief concern, as always, is seeing that you don't get what you want.''

Patrick shrugged. "Suit yourself. It's on your conscience, not mine.''

"Oh, my conscience is always clear. Servants will be arriving from Dublin tomorrow, so you needn't concern yourself, Quinn. Our household will be back in order in no time. I'll beat this boycott if it's the last thing I ever do.''

Without another word, Patrick strode past Standon and out to where his horse waited, and left for home.

"I went to Drumlow today,'' Patrick announced at the dinner table that night.

Fenella was so startled, she spilled a spoonful of soup on the tablecloth. "Sorry,'' she murmured, and proceeded to blot it up with her napkin in order to hide her own confusion.

Margaret looked at her cousin as if he were mad. "You did *what?*''

"I said I went to Drumlow today.''

"Whatever for?'' she asked incredulously.

"I wanted to see if I could help in any way.''

"Help the Standons? But why? Have you gone mad, Pat?''

"Now, now, Meggie, don't look at me like that. Much as I have no use for St. John, we landlords have to stick together in times like these.''

Margaret looked at Fenella. "I cannot believe I'm hearing this. He has gone mad."

Fenella remained silent, not knowing what to say.

"I assure you my concern was purely charitable. No matter what the Standons have done to me, there is a child living at Drumlow now, and she shouldn't be made to suffer."

"How is Louisa?" Fenella asked.

Patrick looked at her, approval in the depths of his eyes. "The poor mite was in dire need of a nursemaid, I'm afraid. She looked rather dirty and disheveled, as did Cynara."

Margaret smiled gleefully. "And how was the lady of the manor? Up to her dimpled elbows in soapy water, I trust, her delicate fingernails broken from scrubbing floors?"

"As a matter of fact, she was in the kitchen, cooking."

"Cooking?" Margaret let out an unladylike whoop of laughter. "Trying to poison her brother, I would assume."

Patrick gave her a sharp, reproachful glance, but Margaret was unrepentant. "I won't be a hypocrite, Pat. I've never had any use for the Standons after the hell they put you through. I can't pretend I'm sorry for them now that they're finally getting what they deserve, so don't expect me to. That would be asking too much."

Fenella said, "How has the boycott affected them?"

"As one might expect," he replied, then proceeded to relate the conditions of the grounds and the appalling ones in the house.

"In fact, the house was so filthy I offered to take in Cynara and her daughter until the boycott was over."

Fenella sat there in stunned silence, unable to believe what Patrick had just said. Cynara here at Rookforest, under the same roof as Patrick . . .

Margaret slammed her spoon down on the table with a crash. "You did what?"

"I invited her to stay with us at Rookforest," Patrick replied insouciantly, "but her brother wouldn't hear of it."

Fenella gave great attention to her soup so she wouldn't have to endure Margaret's pitying glance.

"Inviting that woman into this house?" Margaret screeched. "You deserve to be horsewhipped."

"I was only thinking of her daughter," Patrick replied defensively. "A child shouldn't have to suffer for the mistakes of its elders. Here she would have Mrs. Ryan and all the maids to dote on her."

Fenella felt treacherous tears sting the backs of her eyes. Patrick had invited Cynara to stay at Rookforest without any concern for Fenella's feelings. Did he plan to keep two mistresses under the same roof?

Her eyes were swimming now, and her lower lip was beginning to tremble with the force of keeping her emotions bottled up inside. She knew if she didn't leave, she'd break down right at the table and humiliate herself.

"Excuse me," she murmured as she rose, flung down her napkin, and blindly fled from the room.

Just as she was going through the door, she heard Margaret say, "Patrick Quinn, you are nothing but a thickheaded clod. Don't you realize what you've done?"

Fenella didn't linger to hear Patrick's reply.

The moment her bedchamber door was closed and locked behind her, Fenella gave vent to her feelings and let the tears flow unchecked.

Heartrending sobs were torn from her throat as she flung herself down on her bed and buried her face in her pillow, the same pillow where Patrick's head had rested next to hers night after night.

How could he do this to me? she asked herself, feeling the sharp sting of betrayal as sharply as a knife through the heart. Don't I mean anything to him? Or will Cynara always possess his heart?

As Fenella lay there weeping, all of her grand, selfless plans not to impose upon Patrick suddenly turned to dust. She just couldn't surrender him to Cynara without a fight. She loved him too much. And she couldn't pretend Patrick's announcement tonight hadn't devastated her, because it had.

She took a deep breath, sat up, and dried her tears with the back of her hand. She was through holding her feelings back because she feared Patrick would reject her. She might have been accursed with second sight, but she couldn't let it keep her from fighting for what she wanted.

Fenella felt like that little brown bird that had killed itself by flying into the window the other day. But unlike that bird, she was determined to pick herself up and persevere.

Suddenly there came a soft knock at the door.

When Fenella opened it, she saw Patrick standing there, his face grave.

"Come in," she said without smiling, standing aside so he could enter. After closing the door, she turned to face him, waiting for him to make the first move.

"I'm sorry." His voice was low. "I didn't mean to hurt you."

"Well, you did."

That took him aback, for he looked stricken by her response. He ran his hand through his hair.

"You must let me explain. I only invited Cynara and her daughter to stay at Rookforest out of charity, nothing more. If you could have seen what a pitiable state the both of them were in, you would have done the same, Fenella. I know you would."

"This is your house, Patrick. You may invite whomever you please to stay here." Fenella took a deep breath and prayed for courage. "But if Cynara moves in here for whatever reason, then I shall leave."

She held her breath, waiting for his response to see if her risk had been worth it.

Patrick took a tentative step forward. "You can't mean that."

"But I do. I may be a spinster past her prime, but I do have some pride. I couldn't stay in the same house with Cynara, seeing the two of you together. That would be asking the impossible of me, I'm afraid."

She was silent for a moment as she marshaled her courage once again. "I love you too much to share you with another woman, Patrick."

She watched his face carefully to gauge the reaction her declaration was having on him, half-fearing what it would be.

Suddenly his face lit up, and all the lines of strain

about his mouth melted away. His pale blue eyes softened and darkened, and a smile that was both relieved and pleased twisted his mouth.

"Fenella!" he murmured huskily, reaching for her and pulling her against him tightly, so she couldn't escape his fervent embrace. "I need you so much!"

Fenella, one cheek pressed against his, sadly dislodged herself and placed her hands against his chest to ward him off. "You may need me, Patrick, but do you love me?"

She stared deeply into his eyes, searching for her answer, and a lump formed in her throat when she saw the hesitancy written there.

"I care for you very much. Surely you must know that."

She had risked all and lost.

Fenella stepped back away from his disconcerting touch before her resolve had time to weaken. "That's not what I asked you."

He stared at her, his brow furrowed with uncertainty. "I don't mean to hurt you, Fenella, but I don't know if I love you in the way you deserve to be loved."

"I don't understand."

He walked over to the bed and leaned against the bedpost heavily. "I know that I enjoy being with you, and the thought of never seeing you again would make my life empty and joyless. I know that I want to protect you and keep you from harm, and I feel flattered that you entrusted me with your secret."

His face clouded and he looked away. "But even if what I feel for you is love, I can't give myself to you completely."

"Because some part of you still loves Cynara," she finished for him.

He sighed. "You know me better than I know myself."

"But I thought you insisted it was over between you."

"That's what I've been telling myself," he said, smiling dryly, "because I've wanted so desperately for it to be true." Patrick shrugged helplessly. "I can't explain why I feel the way I do. There's no rhyme or reason for it, considering the stormy past we share. I may be mad, or just obsessed. All I know is that I still feel something for that woman, and I can't let go of it, no matter how hard I try.''

Fenella turned away from him so he couldn't see her eyes brighten with misery.

"How can I give you only a part of myself, Fenella?" he asked. "What kind of life would we have together, knowing I can't come to you as a whole man?"

She wanted to tell him she would take any little piece of himself that he chose to give her, but she had too much pride for that.

She cleared her throat. "So will you ask Cynara to marry you? She's made it plain that she wants you."

He flung up his hands. "I don't know if I even want that."

"You can't have both of us. You know you must choose."

"I know. I just pray to God I make the right choice."

"So do I, Patrick, so do I."

He looked at her for the longest time. "You won't go, will you, Fenella? You will at least give me time to make up my mind?"

"I'll stay—at least for a little while." Her gaze slid over to the bed. "But from now on, I'll have to sleep alone."

"I understand," he said softly, but there was a bleakness to his voice that tugged at Fenella's heart.

As he turned to go, and hesitated with one backward glance, her strength almost crumbled. But she knew if she gave in now, she truly would be lost.

She watched Patrick go through the door; then she closed it behind him with a decisive click.

19

A WEEK LATER, Margaret awoke feeling strange.

As she sat up in bed, she suddenly felt dizzy and was forced to lie back for several minutes before the disconcerting feeling passed. When she sat back up a second time, she felt fine.

"Just a little indigestion," she mumbled to herself as she rose from her warm bed to wash. "I shouldn't have eaten so much at supper last night."

Shivering, she splashed cold water hurriedly on her face, then rang for her maid to bring her her ritual morning cup of tea. While she sat at her dressing table and began unplaiting her hair, she thought of Patrick and Fenella.

She shook her head at her own reflection.

How can Patrick be so stupid? she thought. Even a blind man can see how much Fenella loves him. I know her. We may have had our differences in the past, but she's not the kind of woman who would sleep with a man she didn't love. Not like me.

Her wide hazel eyes stared back at her accusingly, but Margaret ignored their message.

And what does the clod do? she went on thinking. He invites that cold, heartless bitch to come live here at Rookforest, that's what he does. All in the name of charity. Since when did that woman ever have a charitable thought for anyone except herself? Fenella's worth thirty of Cynara, and my stupid cousin hasn't realized it yet.

Margaret picked up her silver-backed brush and began brushing her hair with long, strong strokes, momentarily distracted by the play of red-gold light in its auburn depths, the soft crackling sound it made, as if it were alive.

She had observed Fenella all week and felt so sorry for her. Fenella tried so hard to keep up a brave front, conversing politely at mealtimes, trying to pretend that her heart wasn't breaking, but Margaret noticed the deep, abiding sadness in Fenella's great brown eyes whenever her longing gaze happened to light on Patrick.

And Patrick?

To his credit, he wasn't faring much better. Deep shadows, the likes of which Margaret hadn't seen since he first returned to Ireland from prison, now underscored his eyes. When he looked Fenella's way, those eyes were also filled with anguish and unfulfilled longing.

Margaret set down her brush and shook out her hair until it tumbled past her shoulders.

"If they're so miserable apart," she demanded of her reflection, "why aren't they together?"

She knew Patrick was no longer going to Fenella's room every night because, curious, she had taken to spying again when the house was asleep for the night. Sometimes she heard muffled sobs coming from Fenella's room, and one time the sounds of Patrick pacing the floor sent her scurrying back to her own room before he caught her listening.

Whatever had been said between them, whatever arrangement they had made between themselves, was never discussed with Margaret. But at least Fenella hadn't packed her bags and left in a huff over the Cynara incident, and that gave Margaret hope that a reconciliation could be effected between the two.

She shook her head. "Why isn't love ever easy?" she asked her reflection. "Why must such a noble emotion cause such pain and heartache?"

A loud knock on the door banished Margaret's reverie, and she called out for her maid to enter and prepare her for the day ahead.

When Margaret entered the dining room for breakfast, she found only Patrick there, a revolver beside his plate.

"Good morning, Pat," she said, her brows raised in surprise. "Is it really necessary to bear arms at the breakfast table?"

He looked up at her over a plate piled high with food.

"It will be, from now on. I've just received word that moonlighters killed a land agent near Fermoy just as he was sitting down to dinner with his family."

"What?" Margaret sank down into the nearest chair and stared at him out of shocked eyes. "They broke into his house?"

Patrick nodded gravely. "In broad daylight. They shot him right in front of his wife and two daughters, then the murdering cowards ran."

"Does anyone have any idea who these men can be?"

"Not a clue, I'm afraid."

"How horrible for those poor people!"

"This is a time of madness for Ireland. That's why I've decided to have my revolver by my side," he said, "even at the breakfast table."

"But surely you don't think anyone would try to break into Rookforest, do you?"

Patrick shrugged. "They came on our land to clip Fenella, didn't they? I can't take any chances, Meggie. I don't want any harm to come to you or Fenella."

Margaret looked around the room. "Where is she, by the way?"

"I don't know. Perhaps she just wanted to sleep late this morning." He glanced toward the windows. "I took one look outside and wanted to crawl back under the covers myself."

Margaret walked over to the window and looked out with the delight of a child. "Why, it's snowing!"

"Just when I wanted to go out," Patrick grumbled.

"To see Cynara again."

He sighed. "No, Meggie, not to see Cynara again."

"Good." She tossed her head and went to the sideboard. "You're showing some good sense at last."

"Enough!" Patrick cried, slamming his palm down on the table in a gesture curiously reminiscent of his late father. "I've grown weary of your sarcastic comments, Meggie, my girl. You're becoming tiresome, and if you persist, I shall be forced to pay Nayland a princely sum to take you off my hands."

She flashed him a teasing smile. "I'm shaking in my shoes, cousin."

"You should. You may have half the men of Cork eating out of your hand, but I am not one of them. When I say I wish no more discussion of Cynara, I mean it!''

Seeing that he was serious, Margaret quietly took her meager breakfast and seated herself at Patrick's left.

''I just wish to say one thing, and then I'll never mention Cynara's name again, I promise.''

''Margaret . . .''

''Please, Pat. Just let me ask you one question, and I'll stop badgering you. I promise.''

His sigh was an exaggerated sound of surrender.

Margaret said, ''What is this hold that Cynara has over you? Why does everyone else see her for what she is, yet you don't?''

Patrick looked away. ''I don't know what you're talking about, Meggie.''

She sat back in exasperation. ''Stubborn as the day is long. Forgive me for even asking. I'll not trouble you again.''

Suddenly the dining-room door opened, and Fenella hesitated in the doorway. ''Am I interrupting anything?'' she asked.

Margaret shook her head. ''Do come in. Patrick and I weren't discussing anything of importance, were we, cousin?''

He flashed her a warning look, then said, ''No, we weren't. Come in, Fenella, and join us for breakfast.''

As Fenella wished them good morning and started for the sideboard, she too noticed Patrick's revolver, and a look of distress passed over her face.

''Patrick, why have you taken to carrying guns with you?'' she asked.

''Because it's necessary,'' he replied, then explained what had happened to the land agent just the day before.

Fenella looked as though she had just lost her appetite. ''Dear Lord . . . to kill a man in his own home, in front of his wife and family.'' She shook her head. ''When will these moonlighters be brought to justice?''

''I'm afraid I don't have the answer to that,'' Patrick said. ''But under the circumstances, we should all be prepared for the unexpected.''

Fenella rose and rubbed her arms as she walked over

to the windows and looked out at the sprinkling of newly fallen snow.

"Christmas is only three weeks away," she mused as if she were alone in the room. Then she turned to them, her eyes sad. "But it doesn't feel that way, does it, with so much misery in Ireland?"

"And Uncle Cadogan gone," Margaret said softly, suddenly missing him afresh.

"Not to mention your father, Fenella," Patrick added.

They all fell silent, each with his own thoughts of loved ones gone and the upcoming holiday, usually such a festive time.

Fenella turned. "Do forgive me for sounding so melancholy. It was seeing the fresh snow that made me think of Christmas."

But Margaret wasn't fooled. Christmas was not responsible for Fenella's pensive, melancholy state.

Suddenly, from the window, Fenella said, "Why, here comes Lord Nayland, riding as though Captain Moonlight were chasing him."

"Lionel?" Margaret jumped up from her seat and went to join Fenella by the window. "Whatever is he doing calling so early in the morning?" She turned back to Patrick. "Cousin, you'll have to speak to him about these unorthodox calling hours of his."

But even as she said the words, Margaret couldn't help but steal another glance at Nayland galloping down the drive. He almost looked like a gallant knight of old, astride his huge gray charger with steam coming from its distended nostrils like some fire-breathing dragon. Nayland sat the animal as though he were glued to the saddle, the picture of mastery and control, his flawless horsemanship winning Margaret's reluctant admiration once again.

I can't understand, she thought to herself as she watched him rein in his horse and dismount in one smooth motion, why a man who rides like a centaur prefers his musty old library to the excitement of the hunting field.

Moments later, a breathless Nayland strode into the dining room, his pale cheeks ruddy from the cold, his blue eyes shining with excitement.

"Good morning, everyone," he said, whipping off his spectacles and wiping the fog from the lenses with his handkerchief. "Do forgive me for calling so early."

After everyone greeted him, Margaret said, "This is becoming a habit with you, Lionel."

When his spectacles were back on, he grinned at her. "A not unpleasant habit, I trust."

Suddenly, much to her chagrin, Margaret felt her heart begin to beat just a little faster at the gentle caress in his voice.

She quickly turned away to hide the blush that rose unbidden to her cheeks. "Tea, Lionel?"

"Thank you, that would be splendid." He clapped his hands together as if to warm them. "It's a perisher of a day out there."

As Margaret turned around and handed him his cup, she smiled sweetly. "Then why did you brave it to come here?"

"I wish I could say it was solely to see you again, Margaret," he said, "but that would be a falsehood." He began rummaging in his coat pocket, and drew out a piece of paper. "I came because this was tacked to my gate."

Since Margaret was standing the closest to him, she took the proffered paper and opened it. The moment she saw the crude drawing of a coffin and the words "Lord Nayland" scrawled beneath it in a childish hand, she knew that Lionel had been targeted for assassination by Captain Moonlight. He would die as surely as Uncle Cadogan had.

Margaret looked up at him in alarm, a warning on the tip of her tongue. But the words seemed to thicken, like treacle, and became stuck in her throat. Then she felt that morning's light-headedness return, and she watched Lionel's surprised face spin away and dissolve into nothingness as the room grew blessedly dark.

Margaret first returned to consciousness by hearing a disembodied voice say, "She's only fainted."

Then came the sharp odor of smelling salts and Margaret was wide-awake again, staring up at four anxious faces floating above her.

"W-what happened?" she mumbled, taking a deep breath to clear her mind.

"You fainted," Fenella said. "Don't try to sit up just yet. Lie there for a moment and get your strength back."

Margaret did as she was told. Then she remembered the missive of doom, and she felt the overwhelming panic rise within her again.

She sat up, her eyes searching for Lionel.

"I'm here, Margaret," he said, coming around the divan to kneel by her side and take her hand.

Her fingers bit into his. "Do you know what that paper means?" she cried, her voice rising. "They're going to kill you, Lionel. The moonlighters are going to stalk you like they did Uncle Cadogan and they're going to—"

"Why, Margaret," he began with unabashed delight, "one would think that you were truly worried about me and that your tender concern caused you to swoon."

His teasing was just what she needed to regain her strength and her tongue. "My swoon was caused by a tightly laced corset, nothing more," she retorted.

Lionel looked crestfallen.

"I am worried about you, Lionel," Margaret added. "I'm worried that you'll provide Captain Moonlight with the easiest target he's ever had!"

Lord Nayland rose to his feet and addressed Patrick and Fenella. "It is my pleasure to announce that our Margaret has returned to us, tart tongue and all."

She sat up and swung her legs over the side of the divan. For a moment, her head swam; then she was fine.

"I'm serious, Lionel!" she cried. "This is no time for levity."

"She's right, Nayland," Patrick said. "My father received such a *billet-doux* from the moonlighters, and you saw what happened to him. You must take precautions."

The earl shook his head indulgently. "Why does everyone assume that because I am a bookish sort, I'm incapable of defending myself?"

When no one answered, he continued with, "I am taking this threat quite seriously. I have no intention of becoming a sitting duck for anyone. As soon as this piece of paper was brought to me this morning, I applied to

Constable Treherne for police protection. Two of his men will be moving into Devinstown to guard me, and several more will set up camp outside in the demesne.

"I plan never to go out alone or unarmed." He glanced at Patrick's revolver on the table. "I can see you have arrived at the same decision."

"After what happened to that land agent in Fermoy . . ."

Nayland nodded. Then he smiled and looked down at Margaret as if they were the only two people in the room. "So, as you can see, my friends, I do not plan to become another one of Captain Moonlight's victims."

She opened her mouth to say something, but the strength and determination in his pleasant, gentle voice gave her pause. Margaret felt as though she were looking at a Lord Nayland she hadn't dreamed existed, a man of courage and strength beneath that veneer of bookishness and conviviality. He was a man of action as well as of the intellect. She wondered why she had never seen that side of him before.

Now Fenella was saying, "I wonder why you have been singled out this time, Lord Nayland? Surely Captain Moonlight has no quarrel with you."

He sighed and ran his hand through his fine blond hair. "I must confess that puzzled me as well, Fenella. Everyone knows I am a model landlord, so they have no cause to target such a paragon for assassination."

Margaret didn't scoff at him this time.

Patrick said, "Perhaps their aim is to rid Mallow of all landlords, no matter how fair."

"Ireland for the Irish," Fenella murmured.

"Precisely."

"Whatever their reasons," Margaret said, "we must all be careful."

Everyone agreed.

Fenella stood at one of the library windows, watching Patrick trudge down to the stables through the light dusting of snow that covered the ground like sugar, making Holy Ireland look pristine and new again. She watched his familiar, beloved figure move with a hesitant grace lest he slip on the slick path, and she wanted to rap on the glass to catch his attention, and motion for him to join her inside, where a fire was burning in the grate, so warm, so welcoming. She wanted to fling herself into his arms again, feeling him clasp her so close he took her breath away. But she knew that wouldn't happen. There was a distance between them now as palpable as the window glass separating them. She watched him disappear beyond the line of bare beech trees until only his tracks were left to show he had passed that way.

She didn't turn away from the window. She just stood there staring after him.

Fenella didn't know how long she could remain in this limbo of indecision, not knowing whether Patrick would choose her or Cynara. And would she even care once the choice was made?

I'm becoming cynical, she said to herself. Of course I care which of us he chooses. But I wish he'd decide soon. The longer he takes, the more the distance between us grows and the less sure I am of his love for me.

Fenella was trying to be understanding. She tried to understand his obsession with this woman who, to Fenella, had only beauty to recommend her. She tried to understand how a man might be blind to all else. And she tried to understand how a man might cling to a youthful obsession. But she was finding it extremely difficult.

She sighed and turned away from the window. Well, Patrick isn't perfect, she reminded herself, and neither am I. We all have our own ghosts to live with. Cynara is his, the sight is mine.

Fenella sat down before the fire, picked up her book, and pretended to read. But her heart was on the stable path with Patrick. She suspected it always would be with him, no matter who won or lost.

At dinner that night, Patrick had an announcement to make.

"Nayland is giving a Christmas ball."

Margaret stopped eating her roast woodcock and pursed her lips in disapproval. "A ball? With all the violence going on? It seems rather insensitive to have such festivities when the whole country is in such turmoil."

"That doesn't sound like Lord Nayland," Fenella said.

"He said he wanted to give the ball as a gesture of solidarity among the gentry and to defy the moonlighters," Patrick explained.

"That's uncharacteristically courageous of him," Margaret muttered.

"He's invited us, by the way, and told me he is depending on our attendance."

"Well, I don't think we ought to go," Margaret said huffily. "After all, we're in mourning for Uncle Cadogan, and I don't think he would wish us to go."

"I can't disagree with you more," Patrick said. "Father might have been a most conventional man, but he would have loved thumbing his nose at his murderers even more." He turned to Fenella. "Would you go, Fenella?"

She started. "I didn't know I was included in the invitation."

"Of course you are." His pale blue eyes held hers. "And I would be honored if you would agree to go with me."

The softness in his voice made the hope rise in her heart, and her pulse quickened of its own volition.

Before Fenella could reply, Margaret said, "I don't think any of us should go. No matter what Lionel's intentions, I don't think it would be seemly."

Patrick looked put out with her. "Well, Meggie-of-the-moor, if you really have such strong convictions about it, you may stay home. But I fully intend to take Fenella."

Margaret looked at Fenella. "You really want to go, after what happened to your father as well?"

The thought that Patrick could even want her to attend such a public event was enough to convince Fenella. But she said, "My father did not believe in the customary year of mourning. He always said that he knew that I loved him and I didn't have to prove it by wearing black after he was gone. So I think he would have wanted me to go." She turned to Patrick. "And I would be honored to accompany you."

"Who else will be there?" Margaret wanted to know.

"Nayland has invited practically all of Mallow," Patrick replied. "It promises to be the social event—the only social event, I might add—of the season."

Margaret's smile was bright and malicious. "How wonderful it will be to see all of those fine, upstanding neighbors who have snubbed us since your release from prison."

"All the more reason to attend, Meggie, so show them we don't care a fig for their grandiose airs."

"Now, that's your most persuasive argument yet, cousin," Margaret said stoutly. "I surrender, Pat. I shall go to the ball with you and Fenella." A devilish twinkle shone in her eyes. "We'll need new ball gowns, of course. Something stylish, from Dublin perhaps."

He grinned and shook his head. "I'm afraid the limited skills of our own Mrs. Burrage will have to do."

Margaret sighed and rolled her eyes to the ceiling. "If you insist . . ."

Fenella felt herself coloring. "I . . . I can't afford a new dress. Perhaps one of Margaret's old ones, cut down . . ."

"Nonsense," Patrick said. "You will have a new gown to wear. I'll not have you going dressed as a governess or some poor relation in someone else's castoffs."

Even as the possessiveness of his tone pleased her, Fenella was insulted by the implication, that she was his kept woman who needed to be outfitted in exchange for her favors.

"Your gown will be an early Christmas present from me," Margaret said.

That generous offer took Fenella aback. "Oh, but I couldn't possibly—"

"Oh, but yes, you can," Margaret said. "And I'll not take no for an answer. The generous dress allowance that my equally generous cousin here gives me will certainly be sufficient for new ball gowns." Before Fenella could utter another protest, Margaret added, "I insist, and I shall be mortally offended if you don't accept my gift."

Fenella surrendered. "Put that way, I have no alternative but to accept. Thank you, Margaret."

"You're most welcome, Fenella."

Later that night, Fenella sat in the drawing room, alone by the soft glow of lamplight, picking out simple melodies on the piano, little songs she had learned as a child.

Outside, she could hear the wild wind sighing so mournfully, as if lamenting Ireland's woes, but even that haunting, melancholy sound couldn't damper her elation.

Patrick had invited her to the Christmas ball.

Surely that is a good omen, she said to herself as her fingers moved over the keys with stately grace if not consummate skill. He didn't ask Cynara to accompany him, he asked me.

Margaret had told her that Lord Nayland felt obligated to invite the Standons to his ball, since they were gentry, no matter how disliked. And, with her new Dublin servants to restore her life to some semblance of luxury, Cynara had accepted the invitation wholeheartedly.

But even the thought that Cynara would surely be there as well couldn't curb Fenella's optimism that matters between her and Patrick were closer to being resolved. Tonight she felt as though Cynara posed no threat to her at all.

She heard the drawing-room door open, but she didn't need to turn in her seat to know it was Patrick. She always knew whenever he was close, and it was something more than the confident sound of his footsteps, something instinctive inside of her that responded to him.

"That's lovely," he said, coming to stand behind her.

She could see his fractured reflection in the tall window, which, when backed by blackest opaque night, became a mirror. Patrick looked the epitome of the country gentleman tonight in his evening attire, but his long, unruly hair sweeping across his brow and onto his collar made him resemble one of the early Irish warrior kings, a half-civilized man who lived by the might of the sword rather than laws. The image was so vivid, Fenella lost her place and her fingers almost stumbled on the keys.

"Oh, I know I'm not as skilled at the piano as Lord Nayland," she said without looking up, "but I enjoy making noise with the instrument now and then."

"Well, it's still lovely noise."

She ended the piece, covered the ivory keys, and turned to face him. When she looked into his eyes, she sensed that there was a little less distance between them now, and that gladdened her.

He extended his hand to her, and she took it, trying to

ignore the strength and warmth in those fingers and failing.

As she rose, he said, "Thank you for agreeing to come to the ball with me."

"I'm looking forward to it."

He seemed surprised. "Are you?"

"Yes, very much."

"Even knowing the way part of me still feels about Cynara?"

Fenella looked away as she seated herself on the divan. "Some women would think me foolish, I suppose. But I love you, Patrick." She tried not to sound hungry and desperate. "I agreed to give you time to reach your decision, and I can't see why I shouldn't enjoy your company in the interim."

But please don't ask to share my bed tonight, she pleaded to him silently. If you did, I wouldn't have the strength to refuse you.

He shook his head in wonder, and all he said was, "You are a remarkable woman, Fenella. I'm not quite sure I deserve you, whatever the outcome of this muddle."

"Don't put me on pedestals, Patrick!" she said shortly. "Don't make me into something I'm not, some sort of saint, because I'm not. Far from it. I would do anything short of murder to win you from Cynara."

The vehemence of her confession startled even her.

He smiled at her. "I believe you would."

"But it's not up to me, is it?"

"No," he said gently, the torment and confusion plain in his eyes. "I wish it were, but this is one decision that must be mine, and mine alone."

Then he bid her good night and left her alone with her dreams, fears, and the sighing night wind.

"Fenella, you're beautiful," Margaret said.

"It's the dress," Fenella replied, smoothing the skirt of heavy shot silk and delighting in the ball gown's rich rustle. "I feel rather like a woodcock who finds itself magically transformed into a peacock."

"Now, now, I'll not tolerate your disparaging yourself." Margaret shook her head. "It's more than just the dress. It's you. You look . . ." She fumbled for the right word, then found it in triumph: "Radiant!"

Fenella stared at her reflection in Margaret's full-length cheval glass, unable to believe that the radiant young woman standing there was really her.

Fenella had never possessed such a beautiful dress in her entire life.

It had taken a week to make it. For a simple village seamstress, Mrs. Burrage was a wizard at accentuating her customers' attributes. She cut the neckline low, despite Fenella's protests that she was indecently exposing too much bosom, then she added a sash to the waist, making Fenella's waist look even narrower. Knowing instinctively that Fenella was too strong-featured to be overpowered by ruffles and furbelows, Mrs. Burrage wisely left the gown unadorned except for the train sweeping out behind her. The gown's charm lay in its utter simplicity.

Now Fenella was dumbfounded by the transformation in herself. The gown's color, a warm, rich garnet, seemed to shimmer with a life of its own, giving her skin a lively glow. It even warmed her deep brown eyes with reddish lights.

Margaret, inspired by a portrait of her Granna, the belle of the Regency *ton,* had had her maid dress Fenella's short hair into clusters of curls that framed her face attractively.

"You look beautiful," Margaret insisted, standing back to admire her handiwork for the twentieth time.

"I feel like a princess," Fenella said in wonder, studying herself again.

"You look like one, and I say that sincerely." Then Margaret cleared her throat. "Before we go downstairs to Patrick, there's something I've got to say to you."

"Yes, Margaret, what is it?"

"I just want to say how ashamed I am for all of the hurtful, unkind things I've said about you." She looked as sheepish as a child caught with its hand in the biscuit barrel. "I hope you'll accept my apology, Fenella. I've come to admire and like you a great deal since you've come to Rookforest."

Fenella reached out and hugged her. "Apology accepted, Margaret.'' When they parted, she smiled. ''And I'll have you know that I like you a great deal too.''

Margaret shook out her skirts one last time. ''Come. Let's not keep Patrick waiting.''

As Fenella stood at the head of the stairs, she felt butterflies fluttering in her stomach. What would Patrick think of her in all her finery? She didn't have long to wait for her answer.

Patrick stood at the foot of the staircase, gazing up at her as if he were spellbound, his eyes filled, not with astonishment, but with flattering pleasure. And his eyes stayed riveted on Fenella as she gathered her skirts and came gliding down the stairs.

When she reached him, he took her hand and drew it to his lips for a lingering kiss, his smoldering eyes holding hers compellingly.

''You are beautiful.''

He said it with such conviction that Fenella could have wept.

Instead, she squeezed his fingers in return and murmured, ''Thank you.''

Still gazing at Fenella, Patrick said, ''And you look lovely tonight as well, wild Meggie-of-the-moor.''

''How can you tell?'' Margaret retorted with feigned asperity. ''You haven't torn your eyes away from Fenella long enough to spare me a glance.''

He did so, then murmured, ''Nayland will be pleased,'' before he returned his attention to Fenella.

Then the butler announced the carriage was waiting. Patrick assisted the ladies with their wraps and they left for the ball.

As the carriage sped toward Devinstown, Patrick decided Margaret was right: he couldn't tear his eyes away from Fenella.

In the feeble light cast by the outside carriage lamps, she reminded him of some noblewoman painted by a Renaissance master, unadorned, yet beautiful in her strength and simplicity. She radiated a certain glow tonight, a confidence that he hadn't seen before, and it made her beautiful.

He knew that he wanted her again, but there was Cynara, always Cynara, intruding on his peace of mind, pulling him in an opposite direction.

He sighed. But the end to his torment was near at hand. After weeks of thinking, analyzing, warring with his emotions, he knew he was on the verge of making a decision. When he saw Cynara tonight, he would know.

Margaret interrupted his thoughts by glaring distastefully at the pistol he held between his knees. "Can't you put that thing away?"

Patrick shook his head. "Not with Captain Moonlight on the prowl."

"But the drivers are armed," Margaret pointed out. "What more do we need?"

"I'd rather err on the side of caution, Meggie."

They drove on in silence until they reached the gates of Devinstown.

Patrick looked out the window. "I can see Nayland wasn't kidding when he said he was calling out the dragoons. They're billeted all over the grounds. See their tents and campfires?"

Both Fenella and Margaret craned their necks to see.

When they sat back, Fenella said, "I certainly feel safer knowing there are soldiers guarding us tonight."

"The moonlighters wouldn't dare attack tonight," Margaret said, then added an unsure, "would they?"

"They shot my father right in the streets of Mallow," Patrick said coldly, his blood stirring at the memory, "and they've killed people in their own homes. I think it's safe to assume they might attack Devinstown tonight, or landlords on their way home."

Both Margaret and Fenella shuddered.

But all thoughts of dragoons and moonlighters were quickly forgotten as their carriage joined the long line of other carriages waiting to deposit their passengers at the front door.

As Patrick stepped out and handed Fenella down, she caught the infectious excitement and enthusiasm in the air. All around her, horses were snorting and stamping impatiently, their harnesses jingling festively, while throngs of richly dressed guests chatted among themselves and called out to old friends, their jocular voices sounding sharp and crisp in the cold night air. Warm, welcoming light poured out from every window in Devinstown, surrounding them like a warm embrace, and as Fenella mounted the steps, her arm tucked possessively through Patrick's, she found it difficult to believe that there was a troubled world outside these gates.

She was forcibly reminded of that world, however, when she entered the foyer and spied the dozens of revolvers piled on the hall table. She shivered as Patrick removed her wrap. Evidently every other guest had had the same idea as Patrick, who also left his revolver among the others.

But Fenella didn't have too much time to contemplate the dark side to the festivities, for the foyer was filling fast with guests, and Patrick was busy acknowledging greetings from those very same neighbors who had been snubbing him since his return to Ireland.

Hypocrites, she thought. Here they are, smiling, shaking his hand, slapping him on the back, and not six months ago they were averting their eyes and scurrying away from him like beetles on the streets of Mallow. Perhaps I'm too hard on them. I should let bygones be bygones, as Patrick is doing.

It didn't take Fenella long to realize that she herself was the object of surreptitious stares and whispers from members of the gentry she knew through her late father. And then she realized why.

Here she was, nothing but a dispensary doctor's daughter, attending the Earl of Nayland's Christmas ball.

But as Patrick offered her his arm, Fenella realized that what these people thought didn't matter. Lord Nayland had invited her, and Patrick asked her to accompany him. She belonged here as much as anyone else, perhaps more, since she was Lord Nayland's friend.

Now the earl himself was coming toward them, a wide smile on his face.

"Good evening," he said, bowing. "Fenella, you look enchanting, and, Margaret, you are . . ." His voice dropped as he reached for her hand and kissed it. "Words fail me."

The teasing light was back in her hazel eyes. "For a man who professes to read so much, that does astound me, Lionel."

He sighed. "It's because I haven't opened a book since he day I met you."

"Liar." But Margaret looked quite pleased nonethe-less.

The earl said, "If you'll excuse us, Patrick, I'd like to borrow your cousin for a few minutes and introduce her o some friends of mine from Dublin."

"She's all yours," Patrick replied, giving his cousin a knowing look.

After Margaret and the earl left them, Patrick said to Fenella, "Come, I'd like to introduce you to several peo-ple as well, since everyone seems to have conveniently forgotten I once served a prison term."

As Fenella took his proffered arm and followed him into the ballroom, where all the guests were gathering, she felt a surge of triumph. Patrick was introducing her to old friends as if she were his equal.

But her triumph was short-lived.

Cynara and St. John had arrived.

Fenella knew the exact moment her enemy entered the ballroom, for that was the moment conversation ceased with the abruptness of a door slamming shut.

Fenella refused to pay Cynara tribute by turning and gawking at her, as everyone else in the room seemed to be doing. All she had to do was listen to what those around her were saying.

"Och, what a beauty she is!"

"That dress she's wearing must have come from Paris. I've never seen anything like it, even in London."

"And look at those sapphires around her neck . . . they must have cost a king's ransom."

"Saintly Standon never paid for them, I'll be bound. He's as tight as a vise."

Then Fenella risked a glance at Patrick, and her heart sank. He was regarding Cynara with something like hun-ger in his eyes.

Fenella pursed her lips in determination. She might have lost Patrick forever, but she was not going to make Cynara's victory an easy one.

Patrick stared down into Cynara's upturned face as he whirled her around the dance floor.

As always, whenever he looked at her, he was taken with her beauty. One couldn't help it. Cynara's beauty was such a part of her, the way Fenella's second sight was unique to her.

"What are you thinking?" Cynara asked, her voice dusky, her violet eyes sparkling.

"How beautiful you are."

She smiled but did not thank him, since compliments were her due. "I wouldn't have come tonight if St. John hadn't been able to hire those servants from Dublin to break the boycott." Even her titter was deep and rich. "Can you imagine me coming to this ball looking like I did the day you came to Drumlow and found me in the kitchen?"

"No, Cynara, I honestly can't."

"Don't think of how I looked then, Patrick, I beg of you," she said. "Think of me the way I look now."

"Always."

She frowned, but only for a second, so as not to wrinkle her clear, smooth brow. "Patrick, is something the matter? You seem preoccupied this evening."

He smiled. "Do forgive me. I was thinking about a decision I must make that will affect me for the rest of my life."

"And does that decision concern me?" she asked.

"Yes, it does."

Excitement shimmered in the amethyst depths of her eyes. She moistened her plump lower lip with the tip of her tongue. "Come, let us go to the conservatory, where we can talk privately."

Dancing with Lord Nayland, Fenella missed a step when she saw Patrick and Cynara slip out of the ballroom.

"You love him very much, don't you?" the earl said.

Her eyes following Patrick, Fenella nodded. "I'm in danger of losing him and I just don't know what to do."

"Oh, yes, you do," Nayland said. "You must do what all of us do to win the ones we love. You've got to fight with everything at your disposal, and with gloves off."

"But she's so beautiful," Fenella said hopelessly.

"And you are gentle, kind, loyal, and true."

"I'm afraid those sound more like faults than virtues."

Nayland smiled at that. Then he said, "Let me give you some advice, Fenella. People like us who are not gifted with great physical beauty have to work harder to attract people like Patrick and my Meggie. We have to convince them that we are beautiful inside. But if we are persistent, we can win their hearts through the back door, as it were."

Fenella frowned. "I don't understand."

"Take me, for example. I'm quite an ordinary-looking fellow—no, don't deny it, much as it would flatter me to have you do so—with thinning hair and weak eyes. I am rather bookish, and am not the sort of romantic fellow headstrong women like my Meggie seem to prefer. But I persisted. I charmed her with my voluble wit and showed her other facets of my personality she never dreamed existed. I stole her heart when she least expected it.

"And you must do the same to Patrick. You must fight for him. You must make him realize that Cynara is shallow beneath that veneer of exquisite beauty. But you, on the other hand, are complex and steadfast."

When Fenella hesitated, Nayland said, "I think Patrick realizes it already, but it wouldn't hurt to help him along." He stopped in the middle of the waltz. "Courage, Fenella. Go find him. Now."

"Thank you, Lord Nayland," Fenella said, and she did just that.

The conservatory, located at the other end of the house, away from the heat and noise of the ballroom, was quiet and dark, except for the feeble light of a lamp on a nearby table.

Patrick let Cynara draw him into the hot, glass-enclosed room, where exotic tropical plants towered above them as if they were in a jungle. Heady, sweet scents mingled with Cynara's own spicy perfume, filling Patrick's nostrils. But his head was surprisingly clear tonight.

And then Cynara kissed him.

She entwined herself around his neck and pulled his head down to her waiting mouth. He responded by slipping his arms around her waist and crushing her to him, feeling her pliant body respond to his with an eagerness he had only dreamed about. He kissed her long and hard, his just reward for all he had endured because of her. He felt her lips part beneath his own, but before she could claim his mouth with her tongue, Patrick pulled away.

"Don't, Patrick," she whispered, still clinging to him. "You know you want me as much as I want you. We can be married, if that's what you want. It's what I've wanted, all along, for years."

"But what about your brother? Surely he would object."

Cynara's soft gaze hardened. "He will have nothing to say in the matter this time. I'm tired of being treated as his slave." Her smile was beguiling. "Besides, he is no match for you. You will see to it that he doesn't stand in my way this time, won't you?"

And she kissed him again.

Fenella stopped at the conservatory door, unable to believe her eyes. There was Patrick, holding Cynara in his arms and kissing her.

At that moment, Fenella faced her moment of truth. She would know in the space of a heartbeat if she had lost Patrick forever.

She stepped forward boldly. "There you are, Patrick. I've been looking all over for you. You promised me the next dance. Have you forgotten?" Her voice sounded strong and confident.

Patrick started as Cynara jumped back out of his arms and turned to glare at Fenella. Then Cynara did something that made up his mind for him once and for all.

She cast a contemptuous glance at Fenella, and her lip curled ever so slightly in perfect imitation of her brother. Then, ignoring Fenella as if she did not exist, Cynara looked up at Patrick and said, "Come, Patrick. I believe the next dance is ours. And all of them for the rest of our lives."

Fenella's heart was hammering against her ribs so loudly, she felt as though it could be heard all the way to the ballroom.

Please, Patrick, she begged him silently with her eyes.

"I'm sorry, Cynara," Patrick said. "I promised the

next dance to Fenella. And all of them for the rest of our lives.''

When Fenella saw him leave Cynara's side without a backward glance and come walking toward her, she could have shouted for joy. But she restrained herself and hoped her wide, triumphant smile spoke eloquently enough as Patrick crooked his arm and slipped hers through it.

Fenella had no desire to see Cynara's reaction, so she looked into Patrick's eyes, and found them regarding her with a tenderness that took her breath away. But even more important, the troubled shadows she had seen there had disappeared.

Patrick had made his choice tonight, and she had won.

By the time the laughing, high-spirited revelers entered Rookforest's foyer, it was three o'clock the following morning. The house was hushed, for all the servants had gone to bed hours ago, and dark, save for a solitary lamp Mrs. Ryan had left burning on the hall table.

"Shall we have sherry in the drawing room?" Patrick whispered.

"Not for me," Margaret replied, stifling a yawn. "Lionel kept me dancing, and now I'm so tired I could sleep for a week. So if you two will excuse me, I'm off to bed.''

Then she lit a candle, bade them good night, and started up the stairs.

"And you, Fenella?"

"I'd love some sherry, thank you.''

As Patrick took her wrap, his hands lingering on her shoulders in a brief caress, Fenella shivered, but more in anticipation than from the chill of the foyer.

"Wasn't the ball wonderful?" she murmured. "I still feel as though I'm dancing on air.''

It had been a magical, enchanting evening, especially after Fenella and Patrick had left the conservatory together. After they returned to the ballroom, neither of them spoke of the incident or its significance. She suspected—she hoped—that would come later, in the privacy of her bedchamber. But for the rest of the evening, she was content to let explanations remain unsaid, and abandoned herself to the merrymaking.

As she danced and later dined with Patrick on a delicious buffet supper, Fenella couldn't help but steal a glance or two at Cynara, and she was surprised to see her rival dancing and laughing and flirting with a dozen men as if she hadn't a care in the world. She was either a consummate actress, or not as concerned for Patrick as she claimed.

Once inside the drawing room, Patrick went to pour the sherry.

"I think Margaret enjoyed herself tonight," he said conversationally.

"I think she did too," Fenella replied, seating herself on the divan. "She and Lord Nayland danced so often together, I thought tongues were going to start wagging."

"Almost as often as we did." He crossed the room and handed her a glass of sherry. "To us."

Fenella touched her glass to his with a soft clink. "To us."

When he seated himself beside her, Fenella said softly, "What made you reject Cynara tonight?"

Patrick was silent for a moment, as if collecting his thoughts.

"I think the seeds of my disillusionment were sown the day I went to visit Drumlow to offer the Standons assistance during the boycott. There was Cynara, whining and blaming her circumstances on others. And then I thought of you."

Fenella raised her brows. "Me?"

Patrick smiled and nodded. "You would have made the best of the situation with courage and strength."

He sipped his sherry. "And as I thought about it, I realized that whenever I thought of Cynara, I thought only of her beauty, not the woman inside.

"Then I found myself comparing her to you over and over again." He smiled and shook his head. "Cynara just couldn't stand up to the scrutiny."

Absurdly pleased, Fenella still couldn't resist saying, "But everyone else saw right through her."

He smiled wryly. "So why couldn't I? Because I had lived with the myth for so long, I hated to part with it. She had been my first love, my only love, and she was so different in those early days. More carefree and light-hearted somehow. Even when she betrayed me that night in Ostend, I blamed that betrayal on her brother.''

Fenella placed a comforting hand on his arm.

"I don't think she really ever loved me," he said softly, staring into the depths of his sherry glass. "Cynara is just as ambitious as St. John. She wants a man who can provide a luxurious life for her and her daughter, and is willing to sell herself to the highest bidder. When unpleasantness strikes, she doesn't have the fortitude to weather it.''

"Oh, Patrick, I don't think that's true.''

He looked up at her. "But it is. Just before we left, I went to find Cynara, to say good-bye to her once and for all. I found her kissing Pryce Vernham in the conservatory.'' His laugh was self-deprecating. "Her broken heart certainly mended itself rather quickly. I suspect the banns will be read for their wedding soon. Young Pryce always did fancy Cynara, almost as much as I did.''

Fenella shook her head. "I feel so sorry for her.''

Patrick didn't look surprised. "I know you do. That's one of the many things I love about you, Fenella.''

He set down his sherry glass, then leaned forward to kiss her. It was a mere brushing of the lips, but oh, what sweet promise it held.

When they parted, Patrick stifled a yawn. "I think it's time we retired." He looked at her expectantly, but said nothing, waiting for her to make the first move.

Fenella took a deep breath. "Patrick, I don't want to sleep alone anymore.''

Fires of desire burned fiercely in his eyes. "Neither do I.''

Fenella rose and extended her hand to him. Patrick placed his hand in hers, and together they went upstairs.

20

FENELLA STOOD in the drawing room and looked out over the demesne, glad for a bit of sun to brighten the dreary mid-January day. She watched as several sea gulls, blown inland by some gale at sea, wheeled through the air in confusion, swooped down, then climbed again when they could find no food, their haunting, disappointed cries making Fenella feel melancholy.

She didn't know why she should feel so discontented, as though a black cloud were weighing down her spirit, because she had much to be thankful for. It was now 1881, a new year full of hope and promise, like blank pages of a diary awaiting new entries. Her hair was growing out and now reached to her earlobes, and she hadn't had a vision in weeks. But most of all, she had vanquished Cynara Eastbrook, and Patrick was hers, totally and unconditionally.

Fenella moved away from the window and went over to the fireplace. Perhaps there was just too much sadness abroad in the land, smothering the joy that should have been hers. With both her father and Cadogan gone, Christmas had been unusually somber and subdued. No holly garlands had graced the stairs, no gifts had been exchanged, because as Patrick said, they had nothing to celebrate this year.

She sighed as she rubbed her wrist absently. Perhaps it was the new year's uncertainty as well as its promise that made her uneasy. Ireland remained unsettled, with Captain Moonlight still on the rampage. No one knew what would happen next. Fenella knew that she could have a vision at any time. She wondered what her horrible gift would show her in the months to come.

What she needed was Patrick's company. Being with

him was always a soothing balm to her troubled spirit. He would listen attentively, consider her thoughts, then cajole her out of a black mood in minutes.

Smiling, she turned and left the drawing room to find him.

Just as Fenella entered the foyer, she noticed the gatekeeper talking in hushed, urgent tones to Mrs. Ryan, who was staring at a piece of paper in her hand. When the housekeeper turned as white as her hair and crossed herself, Fenella knew that something was dreadfully wrong.

"Mrs. Ryan, what is it?" she demanded.

The housekeeper started, and Fenella had never seen her look so flustered. "It . . . it's for the master himself."

"May I see what it is?" Fenella asked, extending her hand.

For a moment, Mrs. Ryan gave her a look that plainly stated she had overstepped her authority. "It's for the master."

"If you won't show it to me, then let us find Patrick together. I believe he is in his study."

Then Fenella stepped aside so the housekeeper could precede her down the hall.

Patrick was in the study, his head bent over some papers strewn about his desk. He didn't even look up when Fenella and Mrs. Ryan entered.

"Patrick," Fenella said, "Mrs. Ryan wishes to speak to you."

He looked up and smiled briefly. "Yes, Mrs. Ryan, what is it?"

The housekeeper came forward and handed the paper to him. "Reynolds found this tacked to the gate, Master Patrick."

Fenella watched Patrick's face carefully for any clue as to what the message contained. As he took the paper, he looked mildly curious, and when he opened it, his expression registered surprise. He sat way back in his swivel chair and stared at the paper for a moment; then his brows came together in a furious scowl, and raw anger darkened his eyes.

"What is it, Patrick?" Fenella asked, her heart beating faster.

He turned the paper around so she could see the crude drawing of a coffin with his own name scribbled beneath it.

"Another message from our esteemed friend Captain Moonlight," Patrick said, his voice flat and emotionless. "It would appear I've been slated for assassination, just like my father."

Fenella's hand flew to her throat as cold, unreasoning fear flowed through her veins. She stared at the death threat, unable to tear her eyes away from the drawing. She felt light-headed, and fearing another vision, she staggered back.

"Fenella?" Patrick said sharply, rising to his feet and easing her into a chair.

Dear God, please don't let me have another vision, she said to herself. Please don't let me foretell Patrick's death this time.

She held her breath and waited for the inevitable, but seconds passed and nothing happened.

Trembling with relief, she murmured, "I . . . I'm all right."

The tension drained out of Patrick's face and he patted her arm.

Fenella looked up at him and grasped his hand for dear life, seeking his strength. "Why you? Captain Moonlight has no reason to single you out."

"I am a landlord," he said, returning the pressure of her fingers. "That's reason enough."

Mrs. Ryan spoke up. "We belowstairs have heard gossip in Mallow, Master Patrick."

"What do the good people say about me, Mrs. Ryan?"

"There's much black talk of how ye tried to break the boycott against Saintly Standon by offerin' him yer own servants. That didna please Captain Moonlight."

"So I'm to be punished, is that it?"

The housekeeper nodded gravely. "Och, it would appear so."

Patrick released Fenella's hand and went around to his desk. "Well, I have a message of my own for the moonlighters."

As Fenella and Mrs. Ryan watched, Patrick rummaged through the drawers until he found a blank sheet of paper. Then he took his pen and proceeded to write something on it. When he finished, he held up the results of his handiwork for Fenella and Mrs. Ryan to see.

In retaliation, Patrick had drawn a crude stick figure of a man swinging from a gallows. Beneath it, he had written "Captain Moonlight."

"I think that message makes my intentions clear, don't you, ladies?"

Then he rose and handed the drawing to Mrs. Ryan. "Have Reynolds tack this to the front gate. I want to make sure that these moonlighters know what will happen to them if they dare try to harm me or my family."

Mrs. Ryan smiled as she took the paper and turned to do his bidding.

"And, Mrs. Ryan?"

She stopped and turned back. "Aye, Master Patrick?"

"I want all of the servants to know what I've done, so please make sure this incident becomes common knowledge belowstairs. And I would also encourage them to gossip to their hearts' content whenever they go into Mallow." Patrick's eyes hardened. "I want Captain Moonlight to get my message."

"Aye, Master Patrick."

Once the door closed on Mrs. Ryan's retreating figure and Fenella was alone with Patrick, she felt icy fingers of fear race down her spine, causing the fine hairs on the nape of her neck to rise like hackles.

"Patrick, do you think it's wise of you to antagonize Captain Moonlight?"

"Someone has to stand up to them."

He looked so defiant, so invincible, that Fenella rushed into his arms, needing to hold him close. "I'm so afraid."

Patrick made a soft sound of reassurance as he held her tightly against him. "There's no need. I'm not about to let these cowards murder me as they murdered my father."

Fenella hugged him for dear life, clinging to their moment together as if it were their last. It was inconceivable to her that the heart beating so strongly against her ear could ever be stilled, or those hard arms lose their strength to the finality of death. But that's what she had thought of her father and Cadogan, and she had learned a bitter lesson about the fragility of human existence not once, but twice.

"Patrick, if I ever lost you, I would die."

He reached down and lifted her chin with his fingers, so that she had to look up at him. "Hush, Fenella. Let's have no more talk of losing anyone or dying. You're not going to lose me."

"But . . . but they killed our fathers. What makes you think they can't kill you?"

"Because I'm not going to let them." Patrick gently put her from him and seated her in a chair. "If Jamser Garroty is to be believed, your father was a moonlighter himself. He never dreamed his compatriots would turn against him, so they caught him unprepared. My father— God rest his soul—foolishly ignored their warning and rode into Mallow alone. If you'll recall, he never even told anyone he had received their death threat tacked to the front gate."

"That's true," Fenella admitted.

"And consider Nayland. He received a similar notice from the moonlighters, yet he's still among us." Patrick's eyes sparkled. "Now, why do you suppose that is?"

"He carries arms?"

Patrick nodded. "He took a leaf from Saintly Standon's book. Not only does Nayland carry a revolver, he takes two armed guards with him whenever he goes out. Men guard his gates, and the dragoons are billeted in his demesne to protect him."

Now Fenella understood. "Since he's so well-armed, the moonlighters have no opportunity to murder him."

"Exactly. Their method of assassination depends on getting their target alone, like your father or mine. The odds are distinctly not in their favor when they're facing three armed men to their one."

"And you intend to do the same?" she asked hopefully.

Patrick smiled and nodded. "Guards, dragoons . . . as much protection as I need. Rookforest may soon resemble an armed camp, but I fully intend to survive, so I can see that my father's murderers are brought to justice."

Fenella smiled tremulously. "I was so worried, Patrick."

He smiled a lopsided grin. "You needn't worry, Fenella. I fully intend to beat the moonlighters at their own game. However, if you should see my *fetch* or hear the banshee wail again, I would appreciate your telling me."

Without warning, Fenella felt an abrupt chill envelop her, as if a door or window had been opened somewhere, letting in a sudden draft of icy air to embrace her. Before she had time to shiver, the sensation was gone so fast, she thought she had imagined it.

She didn't return his smile. "Don't even jest about such things, Patrick."

His smile died and he extended his arms to her. When she was nestled against his broad chest once again, he murmured into her ear, "I would never jest about your visions, Fenella. I have a healthy respect for your powers, but to be forewarned is to be forearmed."

"Let's just pray it never happens," she said.

Because she knew that even a man as determined and defiant as Patrick couldn't change his ultimate destiny.

Though she tried her best to conceal her fears from Patrick, Fenella became even more insecure in the ensuing weeks.

Rookforest, with its high stone wall and deep demesne, had ceased to be a safe haven for her. Each time she saw the revolver lying next to Patrick's dinner plate, every time she looked out the drawing-room window and saw tents and dragoons, she was forcibly reminded that there were cunning, ruthless, desperate men out there who wanted her love dead.

Her only solace came each night in Patrick's arms, when they made fierce, passionate love to each other as they fought to reaffirm life and stave off any fears of death. But morning always came too soon for Fenella. She dreaded the start of each new day because she always wondered if Patrick would live through it to see another nightfall in her arms.

But when danger struck, it did not come from Captain Moonlight, but a very different and unexpected source.

* * *

One morning in early February, Fenella was just finishing her breakfast when Mrs. Ryan asked if she could speak to her.

Fenella knew better than to insist the housekeeper sit at the table and join her for a cup of tea, so she suggested they go to the drawing room. There Fenella insisted Mrs. Ryan take a seat before the fire.

"Now, Mrs. Ryan, what is it you wish to speak to me about?"

The housekeeper clutched at the arms of her chair. "It's Mistress Margaret, miss. I'm afraid she's feelin' poorly."

Fenella frowned. "I noticed she hasn't come down to breakfast for the past several days. And she does look dreadfully pale. Perhaps we should summon the doctor for her."

Mrs. Ryan screwed up her face as if she were trying to say something, yet couldn't quite get the words out.

"Mrs. Ryan, what is it?"

The housekeeper's jaw worked as though she were a fish out of water, but no words came out. Finally she took a deep breath and blurted out, "Arragh, Miss Considine, I fear the poor child is going to have a baby."

Fenella sat there stunned as a sudden picture of Margaret and Terrence Sheely together at the Ballymere ruins flitted through her thoughts. After what seemed like hours, she found her voice. "Why do you think that, Mrs. Ryan?"

The housekeeper gave her an exasperated look. "I've had enough babies of me own to know the signs, Miss Fenella, and ye bein' a doctor's daughter, I'm sure ye would know them as well."

Fenella's mouth felt dry. "What signs, Mrs. Ryan?"

"She's sick every mornin'. That's why she hasn't been comin' down to breakfast. An' when I bring her a tray, she pushes it away, sayin' the smell o' the food turns her stomach."

"Perhaps there is some other reason," Fenella said. Then she rose, though her knees were trembling so badly she feared she would collapse. "I shall speak to her."

Mrs. Ryan rose to go, her expression bleak. "Arragh, I pray I'm wrong, Miss Fenella. Me poor Meggie. She always was a bit wild, but I pray she hasn't gotten herself into trouble with her headstrong ways.''

So do I, Mrs. Ryan, Fenella said to herself. So do I.

Upstairs, she knocked on Margaret's door, and when she was bidden to enter, she found Margaret still abed in her night shift. Fenella thought she looked peaked, her hazel eyes underscored by shadows.

''Good morning, Margaret,'' Fenella said cheerfully as she closed the door behind her. When Margaret responded rather listlessly, Fenella added, ''Mrs. Ryan tells me that you've been feeling unwell.''

Margaret passed a hand over her forehead. ''I have been feeling out of sorts lately, and I don't know why.'' She sighed wearily. ''I've quite lost my appetite.''

Fenella brought a chair over to Margaret's bedside and sat down. ''And you have no idea why?''

''Cook's cooking must disagree with me.''

Can it be possible she really doesn't know? Fenella asked herself. Did her Aunt Moira or Mrs. Ryan tell her nothing?

''I may know the reason why you're feeling so poorly,'' Fenella said.

''Well, if you do, I wish you'd tell me and not keep me in suspense,'' Margaret replied.

Fenella hesitated. ''Margaret, when you would meet Terrence Sheely at Ballymere, were you ever''—she took a deep breath and plunged on—''lovers?''

Margaret turned chalk white, her hazel eyes wide with outrage. ''How dare you ask me such a personal question!''

''You certainly had no reservations when you accused Patrick and me of being lovers,'' Fenella reminded her, ''so you must forgive me if I return the favor. But I remember you once said to me that you hoped he would seduce you, because then you would know what it really felt like to be a woman.''

Margaret's defiant glare slid away, and she nervously plucked at the coverlet. ''We were lovers only once.''

Fenella felt as though someone had plunged a fist into her midsection. She let out the breath she had been holding with a loud sigh of dismay and sank back in her chair.

"Once is all it takes, Margaret," she said gently, "to get a woman with child."

The look of incredulity on Margaret's face was pitiful to behold. She shook her head as her mouth formed words of denial, but they died on her lips as the full import of Fenella's words sank in. Gradually the anger faded from Margaret's eyes, to be replaced by such a look of bleak despair that Fenella instinctively reached for her hand and held it.

"Is that what's wrong with me?" she asked, her voice as querulous and frightened as a child's. "I'm going to have a baby?"

"Only a doctor can tell for certain," Fenella replied, "but first tell me something."

She asked Margaret another personal question that caused the girl to blush, avert her eyes, and stammer out the answer Fenella had expected but hoped not to hear: Margaret had missed three of her monthly cycles.

"I can't say conclusively, Margaret, but I'm afraid you may be carrying Terrence Sheely's child," she said.

"No!" Margaret cried, flinging off the covers and rising from bed. "I'm not going to have a baby! I can't!"

Suddenly she turned paler, clutched at her midsection, and went staggering over to the washstand, where she retched into the basin.

Fenella looked away helplessly. Even though she had warned Margaret time and time again that nothing good would come of her clandestine meetings with Terrence Sheely, Fenella felt no satisfaction now that the ultimate disaster had befallen the headstrong young woman.

After wiping her perspiring face with a wet cloth, Margaret turned to her. "What do I do next, Fenella?"

Fenella rose. "First you must be examined by a doctor to confirm that you really are with child. Also, Patrick will have to be told."

"No!" Margaret cried wildly. "He must never know!"

"He must. Soon you won't be able to keep the child a secret from anyone."

Margaret began pacing around the room like a cornered tigress. "I . . . I can go away, to London perhaps, or Paris. I can have the child there without anyone ever knowing."

Fenella shook her head. "I doubt if Patrick would send you there without an explanation. Besides, there are other people to consider in this matter."

"There is no one to consider but myself."

"That's where you're wrong. There is the child's father."

"Terrence Sheely?" Margaret scoffed at that. "I never want to see him again, and good riddance!"

The vehemence in Margaret's voice took Fenella aback. She found herself wondering what young Sheely had done to turn Margaret's passion for him into such cold contempt.

"And there is Lord Nayland," Fenella reminded her softly.

"Ah, Lionel . . ." Margaret murmured, and a shadow of a smile passed across her mouth. Then her lips quivered, and she broke down sobbing.

Fenella was at her side in an instant, cradling Margaret in her arms as if she were a child.

Oh, Margaret, she said to herself. What a tangle you've gotten yourself into this time. And no one can extricate you.

When Margaret's sobs subsided and she raised her tearstained face, Fenella said, "Don't worry. Everything will work out."

"But I'm going to have a child. My life will be ruined at eighteen. Ruined!"

She began to sob anew.

There was nothing Fenella could say to comfort her, so she just held Margaret and let her cry.

Margaret stood at her bedroom window and stared out over the bleak February landscape. Spring would be coming soon, but she felt that it would always be winter in her heart.

She was going to have a child.

Ever since Fenella had left an hour ago to await Patrick's return from Mallow, Margaret had thought of nothing else. Even as her mind tried to deny the inevitable, her body spoke the truth. Her missed cycles, the retching every morning, the unaccustomed tightness in her breasts—the evidence was overwhelming, and Margaret had just refused to see it.

As she folded her arms, Margaret's first thoughts were only for herself and her own plight. First she thought of all the physical changes that would inevitably take place in her body, the swollen breasts and belly, the fatigue, and rebellion flared in her heart. Then she thought of how her life would change once the child was born, and she knew real fear.

"I don't want it, and I won't have it," she muttered. "I won't!"

She had overheard the maids talking once and she knew there were evil, sinful ways of getting rid of an unwanted child. And even if she didn't have the stomach to go through with it, the child could always be given away to someone who really wanted it. Then she could go on with her life as though nothing had happened.

Thinking of alternatives appeased her somewhat, easing her sense of hopelessness. Then she thought of the consequences of her stupid, reckless action on others.

Patrick would be disappointed in her, of course, if not outright furious. And Lionel?

Fresh tears welled up in Margaret's eyes and she leaned her forehead against the cold window glass. What would his reaction be when he learned she was carrying another man's child? Hurt? Outrage? Condemnation?

He'll spurn me, and I'll never see him again. But I can't say that I blame him. After all, what man wants another man's bastard?

Now that she was going to lose him forever, she knew that she loved him. With persistence, he had insinuated himself into her heart when she was too preoccupied with Terrence to even realize the gem of a man who was right there on her doorstep.

Her last thought was for Terrence, and it was a fleeting one stripped of all romantic illusion. If she were to confront him with the tangible results of their one afternoon of lovemaking, he would laugh in her face and tell her good riddance. She knew that now. There would be no sympathy, only blame, and all of it hers.

Fenella was right all along. Terrence was only using me. And I was such a fool not to see it.

Suddenly the sound of hoofbeats caught Margaret's attention. She looked down in time to see Patrick come galloping down the drive with his two bodyguards not far behind on his trail.

Margaret knotted her fingers together nervously as she watched the three horsemen disappear behind a screen of beech trees. Fenella had said she would tell him the moment he returned.

Soon Margaret would learn her fate.

"Margaret is *what?*"

Fenella flinched as Patrick's disbelieving voice reverberated through the study, shaking the very walls, but she resisted the impulse to step back, and faced him squarely.

"I said, Margaret is with child. She's going to have a baby."

Patrick's ashen face then turned as black and ominous as a thundercloud, his pale eyes icy with cold, relentless rage. His lips were pursed into a tight line of displeasure, and a muscle jerked in his jaw.

"You're sure of this?" he demanded.

"I'd give anything if I weren't. But the telltale signs are there. All that's needed is a doctor's examination to confirm my suspicions."

Patrick stood there seething. "Was it Nayland? Did he do this to her?" Before Fenella could answer, he began prowling the room like a hunting tiger. "I don't care if he is a peer of the realm. When I get my hands on him I'll—"

"Patrick, it wasn't Nayland."

He stopped. "Who, then?"

"Terrence Sheely."

To Fenella's surprise, Patrick burst out laughing. "Sheely? The farmer's son? You must be mistaken, Fenella. Meggie would never—"

"I'm not mistaken. Farmer's son or not, Sheely and Margaret were lovers."

His face was a mask of disbelief. "Margaret and a farmer's son? When did she have the opportunity for such a liaison?"

"They met at the ruins of Ballymere Castle all during the spring and summer," Fenella said.

"She told you this?"

Feeling drained by the force of her own emotions, Fenella turned from him and took a seat. "No, she didn't. I caught them together once." Before Patrick could comment, she hurried on. "Do you remember the night my father and I came to dinner, and you thought I was ignoring you?"

"Yes. You later told me you were having a vision at the time."

"I had a vision of Margaret and Sheely together at the ruins. The following day, I drove out there to see if my vision had been accurate. I saw them embracing."

Patrick looked down at her, his face inscrutable.

"You've known for all this time that my cousin and this . . . this farmer were having an affair? And you never mentioned it to me or my father?" He slammed his left fist into the palm of his right hand. "Fenella, how could you!"

Fenella just stared at him in disbelief as she suddenly realized he was blaming her for Margaret's predicament.

Patrick ran his hand through his hair. "Why did you keep this to yourself? Couldn't you have at least told my father that Margaret was having these trysts? Didn't you realize that this . . . this bog-trotting peasant would eventually seduce such an innocent as my cousin?"

Fenella rose and clasped her hands together to keep them from shaking.

"I kept it to myself because Margaret made me promise not to tell anyone. She led me to believe she was going to tell your father herself."

"And you believed her, an eighteen-year-old girl? I would have thought you had more sense!"

At Patrick's withering tone, Fenella felt her cheeks turn red. "Margaret also threatened me."

"Margaret? I find that rather difficult to believe."

"Well, it's true. She intimated that Terrence Sheely would harm me if I dared tell anyone about their liaison. With the moonlighters terrorizing the countryside, I was justifiably afraid. Shortly after Margaret made her threat, I was clipped."

If Fenella thought her confession would mollify Patrick, she was mistaken. If anything, he looked even more furious with her.

"Why didn't you tell me this? Didn't you trust me?"

Fenella shrugged helplessly. "I was afraid you'd take Margaret's side over mine. Besides, when I confronted her again about Sheely, she said she had broken off with him, so I didn't see the need in dredging it all up."

"By that time, Sheely had what he wanted," Patrick said between clenched teeth. Then he shook his head. "I'm disappointed in you, Fenella. You've behaved most irresponsibly in this matter."

Anger welled up inside of her. "Just wait one moment, Patrick Quinn. I'll concede that I should have come forward earlier with this information, but I am not totally to blame for Margaret's situation. You know yourself that everyone in this family has always spoiled and indulged Margaret, allowing her to go riding wherever she pleased without a groom. And she herself bears some responsibility for her own actions. She could have stopped seeing Sheely at any time."

"True. But you could have done more to prevent this, Fenella."

"I wasn't aware that I was Margaret's keeper. Who was I to tell her what to do? I am only a doctor's daughter, living in this house through your generosity, while she is gentry."

"You make it sound as though we treated you as some poor relation, afraid to speak her mind for fear of being banished. You are more than that, and you know it," Patrick said softly.

"I can't help it. Rightly or wrongly, there were times when I did feel that way."

"It's a question of trust, Fenella. All you had to do was trust me. I would have confronted Margaret and kept Sheely from harming you. But you didn't. You kept it all to yourself, and Margaret is the one who's suffering now. Margaret is the one whose life will never be the same. And you could have prevented it, damn you, with one word!"

Tears stung Fenella's eyes, but she fought them back. "You're right, of course. I made a serious error in judgment. I should have trusted you, Patrick.'' She took a tentative step forward. "Will you forgive me?"

Instead of extending his arms so she could fly to his embrace, Patrick kept them stiff at his sides. "I don't know, Fenella. Perhaps in time. But right now I'm too angry and confused. My first concern must be Margaret's welfare now, so if you'll excuse me, I'd like to be alone to decide what to do."

Fenella started for the door quickly, to hide her disappointment. "Of course." When she reached the door, she turned. "You won't be too harsh with her, will you? She needs your understanding, not censure."

"I'll try to remember that," he said, then turned his back on her.

Fenella hesitated, then left quietly, for there was nothing left to say.

Once back in her own room, she leaned heavily against the door and closed her eyes.

Patrick is right, she said to herself. There is no excuse for what I did. I should have told Cadogan about Margaret and Sheely, but I didn't. I should have known a willful, headstrong girl like Margaret would get herself into trouble. And because of that, I may lose Patrick forever.

When she opened her eyes, the bedroom swam before them, and she had to wipe away her tears with the back of her hand.

The first thing she noticed was the bed. Would Patrick come to her tonight? Would be come to her ever again?

Fenella sighed. He had been so furious with her, perhaps his rage went beyond forgiveness. She had certainly seen no hint of warmth in the depths of his eyes, only betrayal.

She feared she had lost him forever.

Margaret had just finished dressing and regarding her still-slender figure in the cheval glass when she heard a knock on the door.

It was time to pay the piper.

"Come in, Pat," she said heavily.

The door opened and Patrick stepped into the room. All it took was one look at his drained, bleak face for

Margaret to know there would be no secrets between them now.

Her smile was forced. "Well, Pat, it would appear I've gotten myself into quite a bind this time."

"Yes, Meggie, it would appear so."

The disappointment in his voice nearly broke her heart. Margaret's face crumpled, and the tears started streaming down her cheeks.

Wordlessly Patrick extended his arms to her and she ran to him.

"Oh, Pat, I've been such a fool!" she sobbed into his shoulder.

"Yes, you have," he agreed.

Margaret cried even harder, but when she was finished and drew away, Patrick said, "But what's done is done. We can't change the past no matter how badly we want to. All we can do is accept the situation and try to make the best of it."

She dried her tears. "You surprise me, Pat. I thought you'd be furious with me."

Anger sparked his gaze. "Don't think for a moment that I'm not furious with you, Margaret. It's only at Fenella's urging that I'm not scalding you with my tongue."

"It's what I deserve," she said, turning away.

Behind her, Patrick said, "I understand Fenella knew of these . . . meetings of yours with Sheely."

Margaret whirled around. "Yes, she did. But I made her promise not to tell anyone, so you mustn't blame her."

"Margaret, if she had told Father or me, you wouldn't be in the state you're in."

"It's not her fault," she insisted. "Fenella wanted to tell Uncle Cadogan, but I wouldn't let her. I convinced her I loved Terrence and I played upon her sympathies, making her think we were star-crossed, like Romeo and Juliet. I . . . I even threatened her."

"Margaret—"

"No, Pat! I won't allow you to make excuses for me any longer. I've been headstrong and willful, always wanting everything my own way and never listening to anyone's advice. Fenella tried to make me listen to reason, but I wouldn't. So it's my own fault that I'm with child, no one else's." She tossed her head defiantly. "I'm the one who will have to live with the consequences of my actions."

Patrick regarded her oddly, as if really seeing her for the first time. "I'm very proud of you, my wild Meggie-of-the-moor."

Her smile was bittersweet. "Wild Meggie is no more, Pat. I think I'll just be plain Margaret from now on."

He put his arm around her. "We have to discuss your future."

Margaret took a deep breath and nodded. "It looks very bleak, doesn't it?"

"Not necessarily," Patrick said. "Here's what I think we should do. . . ."

Fenella found Patrick and Margaret waiting for her in the drawing room.

"Mrs. Ryan said you wished to see me," she said, looking at Patrick hopefully.

If his feelings for her had warmed, he showed no sign. All he did was indicate a chair for her.

"Margaret and I have agreed on a course of action," he said, once Fenella was seated, "and we would very much appreciate your help."

"Of course. What do you wish me to do?"

"Marriage to Terrence is out of the question," Margaret said, "so I would appreciate it if you could accompany me to Dublin and stay with me. Patrick is going to rent a town house there for me under an assumed name. First, I shall have a doctor examine me to confirm my condition. If I am with child, I shall remain there until the baby is born, then . . ." Her voice shook. "I shall give it up for adoption and try to go on with my life, if I can."

All those months in Dublin, away from Patrick. Was this to be her punishment?

"So no one is to know?" Fenella asked.

"No one," Patrick said. "Mrs. Ryan has been sworn to secrecy, and not even the dispensary doctor in Mallow will know. Everyone will be told that Margaret has gone to the Continent for a short sojourn."

Fenella looked from Patrick to Margaret. "And what

of Lord Nayland? Won't he wonder what happened to you?"

Margaret's face fell, and she stared down at her hands. "Under the circumstances, I think it best if I forget about Lionel." She raised her chin defiantly. "What right do I have to expect him to forgive my wanton behavior?"

"Why don't you tell him, and let him make that choice for himself?" Fenella suggested. "After all, two people in love can forgive each other anything."

"Almost anything," Patrick said flatly.

"No," Margaret said, "Lionel is so noble, he would want to do what was right. And I can't allow him to sacrifice his life for me."

Patrick looked at her gravely. "Are you sure that's what you want? It's your decision, Margaret."

She said, "When are we leaving for Dublin?"

"The day after tomorrow."

So Patrick was giving her only one more day to be with him, and then Fenella would be banished to Dublin.

Fenella stood at the window and looked out into Fitzwilliam Street at a fine carriage passing by at a leisurely pace.

She certainly couldn't fault the accommodations Patrick had secured for them in Dublin. The red-brick Georgian town house was part of the long row that ran down the length of Fitzwilliam Street, a quiet, private thoroughfare near Marrion Square, seeming as far away from troubled Mallow as America was from Ireland.

Here she and Margaret had been living a discreet, secluded existence for the past three weeks. The servants knew them only as "Mrs. Brown" and "Miss Smith," and they kept to themselves, avoiding their neighbors and seldom going out unless it was for a stroll through the square or the grounds of nearby Trinity College.

Fenella sighed. How was she ever going to endure five more months of being separated from Patrick? A Dublin doctor had confirmed their worst fears that Margaret was indeed with child, so they were going through with Patrick's plan to keep its birth a secret and spare Margaret the shame of an illegitimate child.

Thinking of Patrick made the old longing well up in

Fenella's breast. He had been so cold toward her, so distant, ever since learning of her part in Margaret's deception. No matter how much she tried to justify her actions, he refused to forgive her. He hadn't come to her room those last two nights at Rookforest, and he hadn't even kissed her good-bye at the Mallow train station.

Fenella turned away from the window and took a seat before the fireplace. Suddenly a new fear weighed down her heart like a stone. What if Patrick were so disillusioned with her that he turned to Cynara again? She closed her eyes and tried to shut out the picture of them together in the Devinstown conservatory, Patrick's arms about Cynara and her lovely face turned up for him to kiss.

The frantic sound of someone knocking at the door jarred Fenella out of her pensive mood.

"Who can that be?" she muttered to herself. "No one knows we're in Dublin."

Peering out the door's sidelight to see who was there, Fenella gasped in surprise and pleasure.

There, standing on the stoop and furiously pounding on the door as if seeking to break it down, was none other than Lord Nayland himself.

The moment Fenella opened the door, the earl rushed past her into the foyer and looked around. "Where is she? Is she here? I've got to speak to her at once."

He looked so distracted and desperate that Fenella felt sorry for him.

"Lord Nayland, what a pleasant surprise. May I take your coat and hat?"

"Uh, yes, thank you," he mumbled as he began divesting himself of his garments, but his eyes kept searching for Margaret.

"How did you know where to find us?" Fenella asked, draping his coat over her arm. "Patrick wanted to keep our whereabouts secret, even from you."

"Oh, he told me a tale of her going off on some jaunt to the Continent," Nayland said, jabbing his spectacles up his nose, "but I didn't believe him for a minute. Finally, after I threatened to assist Captain Moonlight by murdering him myself, he told me what he had done with my Margaret."

Fenella almost smiled; then she noticed he was in deadly earnest.

"Patrick told you . . . everything?" she asked, leading him into the drawing room.

"Everything. And it makes no difference whatsoever in my feelings toward Margaret. I just have to let her know before she does something rash that she and I will regret for the rest of our lives. So, my dear Fenella, if you would be so kind as to fetch her, I shall tell her that myself."

"With pleasure, Lord Nayland."

Fenella turned and started up the stairs.

Margaret was roused from her afternoon nap by someone shaking her shoulder. When she opened her eyes, she found Fenella standing there.

"What is it?" she asked, yawning and stretching. She was feeling so lethargic these days.

"You have a visitor downstairs," Fenella replied with a smile.

Margaret sat up at once. "Patrick is here?"

"Not Patrick. Lord Nayland."

Panic coursed through Margaret's veins and she sat up. "Lionel? Here?"

Fenella nodded.

"Oh, dear God! If he's found me, then he must know everything."

"He does. But I wouldn't be concerned, Margaret. Lord Nayland said, and I quote, '. . . it makes no difference whatsoever in my feelings toward Margaret.' "

Margaret clutched at Fenella's hand desperately. "Do you think he really means it, Fenella? Do you think he could possibly still want me after the way I've ruined everything?"

Fenella shrugged. "You'll just have to go downstairs and find out for yourself, now, won't you?"

Margaret rose and went downstairs to face her future.

She found Lionel stalking back and forth in the drawing room, glaring at the carpet and muttering to himself like one demented. His fair thinning hair was standing out every which way, as though he had been pulling it

out. Before Margaret could announce her presence, he
stopped his pacing and looked up at her.

For the space of a heartbeat they stared at each other
wordlessly. Margaret searched his face for any sign of
contempt, anger, or bitterness, but she saw only relief
and a desperate hunger that equaled her own.

Still, she waited, lingering in the doorway, allowing
him to make the first move, for only then would she know
his true feelings.

"Margaret." He said her name as lovingly as a caress,
then crossed the room in three strides to stand before her.
He grasped her by the shoulders. "Why didn't you tell
me? Why didn't you trust me?"

There was such plaintive appeal in his voice that she
had to dislodge herself and turn away under the pretext
of closing the drawing-room door.

When she turned back, she said, "What was there to
say, Lionel? I am a fallen woman. I am carrying another
man's child."

"I don't care about that, Margaret. I love you."

Even as her heart leapt with joy, Margaret shook her
head. "You've been burying your head in those books
too long, Lionel. The reality of the situation is—"

"Oh, stop it, Margaret!" he snapped with uncharac-
teristic ire, his eyes flashing blue fire behind his spectacles. "I'm not some fuzzy-brained scholar who lives in
a utopian world of theories. I'm a practical man. I know
the reality of your situation full well, and I've moved
heaven and earth to come here to tell you that it doesn't
matter one whit to me."

"But it's got to matter to you, Lionel! There's so much
at stake."

He shook his head vehemently. "All that matters to
me is that you'll agree to marry me."

Margaret stared at him. "Marry you?"

"Yes, marry me. Today, tomorrow, next week. Is that
so abhorrent to you?"

"No," she said weakly. "Not at all."

He grinned. "Splendid. I'll obtain a special license
and—"

"But what about the child?" she cried in exasperation.

"If you'll be so kind as to stop interrupting me, I have

got it all worked out with my customary efficiency. After we are married, we shall go to Italy, where I shall rent a charming villa in Florence, or Rome, if you prefer. We shall stay there until several months after the baby is born. I believe with a large enough bribe, I can have some corruptible official change the child's birth certificate so there will be no question of his legitimacy.

"When we return to Ireland, everyone will assume the child was conceived on our wedding night and praise me for the virile fellow I am."

As Margaret realized the enormity of what he was proposing and the greatness of his gift to her, she suddenly felt weak and sank down into a nearby chair.

"Lionel," she began, her voice shaking with emotion, "you would do that for me? Raise Terrence Sheely's child as your own?"

"Of course. Am I not making myself perfectly clear?"

"But what if it's a boy? You'd claim an Irish peasant farmer's bastard son as your heir?"

Lionel knelt down by her chair and took her hand in his. "Margaret," he began gently and with infinite patience, "how many times do I have to tell you that I love you, and would do anything for you, including laying down my own life? The most important thing in the world to me is that I have you for my wife. And I promise to raise the child as if it were my own, because you're forgetting that it has your blood as well as Sheely's." He smiled. "How could I not love a child that was part of you?"

"But what if we were to have other children?"

"I'd rather fancy a brood of four myself, if you are agreeable. And I promise to treat them all equally and not play favorites."

Margaret sighed, wanting to believe him, yet fearing for her firstborn's future, for she was beginning to love it already.

"Please, Margaret. Say you'll marry me. It will be wonderful, I promise you."

She took a deep breath. "Yes, Lionel, I'll marry you."

He beamed down at her and extended his hand so she could take it and rise. Then he whipped off his spectacles and set them aside.

"I won't be needing these for what I have in mind," he murmured thickly.

Lionel reached out, drawing his thumb lightly across Margaret's cheek, then slipped his hand around the back of her head to hold it still. Margaret stared at him in wonder as his eyes darkened with passion and his gaze traveled down to her lips. He moved toward her slowly, stretching out the moment. When his lips pressed against hers, she felt as though fireworks were exploding in her brain. He kissed her thoroughly, possessively, with a consummate skill that left her breathless and quite delighted. Terrence's kisses had never been like this.

When they parted, a bemused Margaret murmured, "Why, Lionel, you do surprise me."

He grinned, making Margaret realize what a handsome man he really was. "I wasn't born with my nose buried in a book, contrary to what you may think. I have taken the time to perfect other . . . talents. And I'll have you know I'm quite adept." He hesitated, then added, "At least that's what I've been told."

What had Uncle Cadogan once told her about Lionel, after she had claimed he was a man who had no fire in him? "I wouldn't judge by appearances, if I were you," were her uncle's exact words. "The earl just may surprise you in that area."

So he had. . . .

Margaret moistened her lips and took a step toward him. "Will you provide references, my lord?"

"Do I need them, vixen?"

"On second thought," she murmured, winding her arms about his neck, "they would only make me jealous."

Lionel laughed, and then he kissed her again.

Much later, as Fenella was showing Lord Nayland out, she couldn't resist asking, "And how is Patrick? Is he well?"

The earl smiled the smile of a contented man. "He is fine. Captain Moonlight is finding him impossible to kill."

"You don't know how relieved I am to hear you say that."

Nayland studied her for a moment. "You know, Fenella, you shouldn't be here playing nursemaid to my Margaret. You should be back at Rookforest, with Patrick."

"He doesn't want me there," she said, turning away.

"Hang what he wants," Nayland said vehemently. "What do you want, Fenella?"

She turned back to face him. "To be with Patrick, of course."

"Then go to him."

"He's probably gone back to Cynara by now."

The earl shook his head. "I have it on the best authority he hasn't been anywhere near Drumlow." He hesitated, then added, "Courage, Fenella. Fight for him as you did the night of my ball. You won then, didn't you? What makes you think you wouldn't win this time?" Before Fenella could answer, he bade her good day, bowed, and went out the door.

As Fenella watched the earl skip down the steps, she thought to herself: I am so tired of being afraid. Afraid no man would want me because of my second sight. Afraid to compete with a beauty like Cynara Eastbrook. Afraid of Margaret's threats and of Terrence Sheely.

She turned and went back into the house, her step firm with resolve. Lord Nayland was right. If she wanted Patrick, she would have to fight for him again.

Tomorrow she would return to Rookforest and demand that Patrick allow her to make amends.

21

As FENELLA was traveling back to Mallow the following day, she had her most terrifying vision of all.

She was alone when it happened, sitting in a first-class compartment on a Great Southern Railway train and idly watching the scenery fly by her window. As she sat there, her thoughts were not focused on mountains and rolling green hills, but on Patrick, and then she wished the train would go even faster so she could be with him again.

She was halfway to Mallow when it happened.

The scar on her wrist began to throb with such violent intensity that it took Fenella's breath away.

"No!" she gasped as she braced herself in her seat. "Please, dear God, no!"

Her entreaties were fruitless. She waited in resignation for the light-headedness. When the dizziness hit her with gale force, it was so tremendous Fenella felt as though the railway compartment were being whirled around like a spinning top. She thrust out her arms to regain her balance, but the whirling motion made her feel like retching. She squeezed her eyes shut to make the feeling stop.

When she opened her eyes, the railway compartment had disappeared.

She found herself floating high above the countryside, once again a spectator to someone else's future. Fenella made note of her surroundings, the gently sloping hills, the road bordered by high hedgerows, the crossroads, with its sign where the roads intersected. She knew where she was now. She was at the crossroads between Drumlow and Rookforest.

As she waited for something to happen, she sensed

movement in the hedgerows. Turning her full attention in that direction, she saw a figure wearing a shapeless black coat and a wide-brimmed hat standing behind the thick hedge. Fenella couldn't tell if it were a man or a woman, only that he or she was peering through the vegetation and staring intently at the empty road beyond.

Then Fenella saw the person stick a rifle through the bushes. At that moment she knew she was watching an assassin waiting for his target.

Suddenly, for the first time while having a vision, Fenella wasn't a dispassionate observer. She herself was racked by strong emotions of terror and impending doom. Even when she had seen the banshee the night of Cadogan's death, she had never felt such strong emotions. She struggled to end the vision, but she knew her efforts were futile.

The vision had to run its course. She would watch someone be murdered and, as always, be helpless to prevent it.

She waited. The man in the hedgerow waited. Seconds dragged into minutes, minutes into hours.

And then Fenella saw the intended victim.

He was alone, cantering his tall black horse slowly down the road, but was still too far away for Fenella to discern his identity.

The assassin saw him too. Fenella watched as he steadied the rifle and lowered his head to take aim.

Her gaze flew back to the man on horseback, and her heart stopped when she saw who it was.

"Patrick!"

Fenella's loud, desolate scream reverberated through the countryside like a gunshot, but neither Patrick nor the man in the hedgerow heard it.

Patrick kept riding closer, inexorably closer, blissfully unaware that he was riding to his doom.

Suddenly there came the harsh bark of gunfire. Patrick stiffened in the saddle, an expression of astonishment on his face as his head jerked around toward the sound. His right hand started to come up to his chest, and then he was tilting out of the saddle and falling. His body hit the hard earth like a sack of potatoes and lay there splayed across the road, unmoving, a bloodstain blossoming across his chest like a bright red rose.

He was dead.

Fenella closed her eyes, unable to endure any more. When she opened them, the country road had vanished. She was back in the railway compartment, facing empty seats.

She sat there in stunned silence, sucking in great gulps of air through her open mouth as she tried to stem the rising panic. It was only then that she realized her cheeks were slick with her own tears.

Her greatest fear had come true: she had witnessed Patrick's death and there was nothing she could do to stop it.

Trembling, she staggered to her feet and reached for the compartment door. She had to do something. She had to go to the conductor and tell him to make the train go faster. She had to reach Mallow in time to warn Patrick.

Her hand fell away.

What am I thinking of? she asked herself. They will think me mad if I do that.

She sank back down into her seat, feeling a great aching loneliness in her chest where her heart should have been. He was going to die without her ever seeing him again to tell him how much she loved him.

Dry, agonized sobs racked her body, tearing her apart. Then the tears came afresh, and Fenella let them fall.

She didn't know how long she had spent crying when the sound of her compartment door opening caused her to pull herself together.

"Anything wrong here, miss?" the conductor asked, an expression of concern on his kindly face.

"N-no, thank you," she murmured, sniffing into her handkerchief. "I'm fine. I just received a bit of bad news before I left Dublin, that's all."

"Well, there's always hope for a better day, eh, miss?"

He left without waiting for her reply.

Fenella glared after him, hating the man for his cheerfulness when her world was falling apart around her.

Hope? There was no hope. Her visions never could be changed.

And then Fenella thought about her first vision, the little girl in Mallow she had saved from being run over by a wagon. She had changed someone's destiny then. And she had warned Patrick that his father would be scalded if he went to the Finnertys' door.

Suddenly, elusive hope filled her afresh. If she had been able to save that little girl and warn Cadogan, why not Patrick?

Fenella dried her eyes and sat up straight, her mind working furiously. The fact that she had had the vision didn't mean that Patrick was dead yet. It was an event that would happen in the future, not right away. Perhaps she still had time to warn him. Perhaps she still had time to alter his destiny as she had that little girl's.

She would fight the ultimate battle for him.

Fenella pressed her fingertips to her forehead as if she could physically coax the answers out of her brain. She didn't know when the assassination would take place. It could happen tomorrow or even this afternoon. So her most prudent course of action would be to ride to the crossroads as soon as she arrived in Mallow, then on to Rookforest. If Patrick were still alive, she could tell him about her vision and he could take his own precautions to see that it never came true.

Fenella sat back in her seat and tried to focus on the tranquil countryside slipping by. But the rhythm of the rails seemed to say: Patrick is dead . . . Patrick is dead.

She prayed they lied.

Patrick halted his horse atop the hill overlooking Drumlow and waited for his two armed guards to catch up.

He thought of the message he had received from Cynara just that morning requesting that he see her. He would have thought that after the night of the Christmas ball, when he had rejected her in favor of Fenella, Cynara would never want to see him again.

Well, he thought as he spurred his horse forward, I'll never understand women.

He thought about Fenella, away in Dublin these last few weeks, and a wave of longing washed over him. He missed her. True, he had been furious with her for not telling him about Margaret and Terrence Sheely, but now that his anger had run its course, trickling away to nothingness, he wanted her here again, by his side.

He would go to Dublin tomorrow and surprise her, he decided as he and his guards rode through the Drumlow demesne. He would reconcile with Fenella and ask her to come home with him, telling her that he loved and needed her. Besides, he had much news to tell both her and Margaret about Terrence Sheely.

Margaret . . . Patrick shook his head. He wondered how she would accept the shocking truth about the father of her unborn child?

When he rode up to that formidable front door, Patrick told his guards to wait while he dismounted and handed the reins to the footman who materialized out of nowhere.

Then he went inside to find Cynara.

She was waiting for him in that dark, somber drawing room.

"Patrick," she said, rising from the divan and gliding over to him. "How good of you to answer my summons so quickly."

She was as breathtaking as always in a morning gown of pale lavender, her glossy black hair dressed just perfectly, with not a hair out of place. But ever since the Christmas ball, Cynara's beauty no longer moved him, seeming too perfect somehow, like a hothouse flower.

"You did ask me to come at eleven," he said.

Suddenly he just wanted to be away from here, out of this oppressive house and on the next train to Dublin and Fenella.

"Please sit down, and I'll tell you," she said in her dusky voice.

"I'd rather stand, thank you."

Something like annoyance flared in the depths of her eyes. "So impatient to leave when you've only just arrived? I should be insulted that you find my company boring."

"I have much work awaiting me at Rookforest."

"I see. Well, I shan't keep you, then." She hesitated. "I asked you here this morning to say good-bye, Patrick."

His brows rose in surprise. "You're leaving Drumlow?"

"Yes. I'm getting married."

Then Cynara waited while she stared at Patrick expectantly to see just what effect her words would have on him.

And, much to his delight, they had no effect at all.

"Congratulations," he said. "Who is the lucky man?"

"Pryce Vernham."

"An excellent catch . . . handsome and wealthy. And are you madly in love with him?"

Some indefinable emotion flared within the depths of Cynara's amethyst eyes. "Don't be absurd. He is a means to an end, a means of providing me and my daughter with a secure life, and a means of getting away from my brother. Especially now."

Patrick frowned. "Especially now? What do you mean?"

"You haven't heard? My brother's employer, the profligate duke, has dismissed him as land agent for his estates. He claims St. John has been unable to make enough money from the farmers, and must be dismissed. St. John must vacate Drumlow by the end of the month so the new land agent can take over."

Patrick felt as though he had been felled by a rock.

"The duke is turning St. John out of his home?" he asked incredulously.

"Not his home any longer," Cynara said without a trace of pity.

Patrick rubbed his jaw. "But Standons have lived at Drumlow for decades. Where will he go? What will he do now?"

"I don't know, and I don't care."

Suddenly furious with her, Patrick said, "That's rather callous of you, isn't it, Cynara? After all, he is your brother."

Her eyes narrowed, spite hardening her beauty. "My

brother has never cared for my feelings, so why should I care about his now? All he's ever done is use me as a pawn to advance himself.''

Patrick raised his brows. "But isn't that what you're doing to poor Vernham, using him as your pawn?"

"It's not the same at all," Cynara snapped.

He stared at her long and hard. Cynara had never loved him. He realized that now. She had only wanted to ensnare him to secure her own future and that of her child. And he had almost fallen for her.

She stepped forward and placed a hand on his arm. "Patrick, I needn't marry Vernham. We can still be together, you and I. You have but to say you want me . . .''

She placed her hands on his chest and stepped closer before he had a chance to draw away. The spicy, exotic scent of her perfume filled his nostrils as she entwined her arms around his neck and pressed herself against him like a cat waiting to be stroked and petted.

Patrick reached up, caught her arms, and firmly dislodged her. Then he stepped back out of her grasp.

"No, thank you, Cynara," he said, trying to keep the disgust out of his voice. "I'm in love with Fenella Considine and plan to marry her." If she'll have me, he added silently to himself.

"Are you really? That does surprise me. She's so . . . so common.''

The cold contempt in her voice angered Patrick. "Oh, no, I'm afraid it is you who are common, my dear. Fenella is quite uncommon, and I was a fool for not appreciating her virtues sooner.''

Cynara's lip curled, but before she could say another word, Patrick bowed and wished her good day before starting for the door. Just as he reached it, he turned. His thoughts flew back to the night he had asked Fenella what she would have done if he had kidnapped her.

"Fenella would have been flattered, you know," he said. "She would have hit me with the bottle, but she would have been flattered that I abducted her.''

Vexation furrowed Cynara's smooth brow. "Whatever are you talking about?''

"Nothing you would understand.''

Then he left.

When Patrick stepped outside, he was startled to see that his two guards were not there.

"Where have my men gone?" he asked the footman who was holding his horse.

"They rode off, yer honor. The master himself said he saw some strange men on the estate. Yer men went riding off in case they be moonlighters."

Patrick stood there for a moment wondering what to do. Should he wait for his guards to return and escort him back to Rookforest? Or should he ride on ahead?

Suddenly he wanted to be alone. Seeing Cynara for the last time and seeing a lifelong dream destroyed had made him melancholy. He mounted Gallowglass.

"When my men return," he said to the footman, "tell them I've already returned to Rookforest."

"But the moonlighters, yer honor . . ."

He patted the revolver at his side. "It's broad daylight. I've nothing to fear from them."

Patrick turned his horse and rode off.

Fenella eyed the sleepy-looking bay gelding with disdain.

"It doesn't look very fast," she said to the livery-stable owner.

"Looks can be deceivin', miss," he said, stroking the horse's neck lovingly. "Cromwell 'ere can run as fast as the wind. Besides, he's the only horse I've got. Take 'im or leave 'im."

Fenella sighed. She didn't have time to find another horse. The moment the train had pulled in to Mallow station, she had disdained hiring a cart, figuring that horseback would be quicker. The sooner she reached the crossroads, the better.

"I'll take him. If you would be so kind as to put a sidesaddle on him . . ."

Five minutes later, Fenella went cantering out of the stableyard.

As she went clattering through the cobbled streets of Mallow, she ignored the startled stares of pedestrians and concentrated on staying aboard Cromwell, who had the roughest gait of any horse Fenella had ever ridden. Each time she bounced in the saddle, she feared she would lose her seat and go tumbling to the ground, but she gritted her teeth and hung on for dear life while trying to remember everything Cadogan had taught her about riding.

Soon she left the town limits of Mallow. Her thighs were beginning to ache from the effort of staying in the saddle, and her fingers felt stiff on the reins. Fenella hung on, not even daring to wipe away the tears being whipped from her eyes.

When she passed the burnt-out ruin of her former house, relief swept through her like fire because she knew it wouldn't be long before she came to the crossroads.

She was going to save Patrick. She just knew it.

And then disaster struck.

About a mile from the crossroads, Cromwell began slowing down. His canter turned into a trot, then a sedate walk. To Fenella's chagrin, he stopped altogether and just stood there in the middle of the road.

"Go, Cromwell!" Fenella commanded, kicking him in the ribs with her heels.

Cromwell grunted and shook his head, but didn't budge.

"You're worse than a donkey! If you don't move this instant, I'm going to sell you to the knacker."

The insults were to no avail, and neither was a painful slap on the rump with the ends of the reins. Cromwell merely whinnied, strolled over to the side of the road, and lowered his head so he could graze.

"I should have known better than to trust a horse named Cromwell," Fenella sputtered.

But indignation soon gave way to panic as she realized she would never reach the crossroads or Rookforest in time.

I've got to try, she muttered to herself.

Sliding down off Cromwell, she spared the gelding one venomous look, then started down the road. Fenella prayed that someone would come along soon and she could get a ride to Rookforest.

But today of all days, not a horseman, not a carriage, not a tinker and his donkey were on the road.

She hurried along, walking fast, taking as long a stride

as she could, hampered as she was by her narrow skirts. Sometimes she even tried running, though the stays of her corset crushed her ribs like steel fingers, squeezing the air out of her lungs so she kept gasping.

And then she saw it, the final hill before the crossroads. Fenella paused for a moment, ostensibly to catch her breath, but in reality to prepare herself for what she might find when she topped the rise.

She listened. All was still, except for the sighing of the wind.

Taking another deep breath and praying she wouldn't swoon, she started up the hill. When she reached the top, her worst fears were realized.

She felt as though she were back in the train, having the vision. She saw the crossroads below. To her left was the hedgerow, and in the exact spot she had foreseen crouched the sinister figure in black, his rifle ready.

And there, slowly cantering down the road, came Patrick, blissfully unaware that he was riding to his ultimate destruction.

But right at that moment in time, Patrick was still alive. She wasn't too late to intervene and save him.

With her last ounce of strength, Fenella hurled herself down the hill, screaming, "No, Patrick! Go back!" at the top of her lungs as she waved her arms frantically above her head in warning.

Patrick reined in his horse just as the crack of rifle fire split the air.

Fenella stopped her headlong charge as if she had come up against a stone wall. She watched in horror as Gallowglass screamed and reared into the air, then dropped his head and collapsed into the road. Patrick was flung out of the saddle and went rolling onto the grass, where he lay still.

He's dead, Fenella's benumbed brain told her. I couldn't save him. He's dead.

When she heard the whine of a bullet perilously close to her ear, she realized Patrick's assassin was now shooting at her.

"Fenella, get over here!"

Patrick's voice roused her from her lethargy. Her eyes widened in disbelief when she saw that Patrick was very much alive and lying behind the lifeless Gallowglass, using the animal as a shield.

Fenella ran to him just as another bullet went whizzing past.

As Patrick pulled her down beside him, Fenella babbled, "You're alive."

"Later," he snapped, his cold, fierce eyes on the hedgerow where their assailant was hiding. "Keep your head down and don't say another word."

Fenella obeyed him and fell silent. She could hear her own heart booming as she crouched behind the dead horse. Poor Gallowglass. He had caught the bullet meant for Patrick.

Another shot exploded the stillness. Patrick ducked his head and pressed Fenella's down. Fenella squeezed her eyes shut and held her breath, tasting fear on her tongue.

Patrick whispered, "I'm going to run for that break in the hedge. You stay here."

Before Fenella could protest, he sprang to his feet and was darting across the road, first to the left, then to the right in a winding serpentine. Two more shots rang out, but they missed the elusive Patrick. As Fenella peered over the horse's saddle, she saw Patrick slip through the hedge and disappear.

One more gunshot, then silence.

Fenella crouched there, her heart pounding out of control as she waited to see who would emerge from behind the hedge, Patrick or the assailant. She knew if Patrick had been killed, she would also die, for the man she had seen in her vision could not afford to leave any witnesses to his crime.

Suddenly the familiar sound of Patrick's voice calling her name made her sigh with relief.

As she sprang to her feet, she heard him add, "Come see who our erstwhile assassin is."

Gathering her skirts, she scampered across the road to the break in the hedge. As she emerged, she saw Patrick standing there with his revolver pointed at someone.

Then she saw their would-be assassin.

"Mr. Standon!"

There was St. John Standon not twelve feet away,

standing awkwardly as he cradled his left arm, which bore a bullet wound up near the shoulder. His handsome face was twisted savagely with a mixture of pain, humiliation, and the desperation of a cornered animal.

He glared at Fenella with such hatred in his eyes that she found herself edging closer to Patrick.

"It's all your fault," Standon said between clenched teeth. "If you hadn't warned him, he'd be dead now."

"Lucky for me she did," Patrick said, his gaze never wavering for a second.

"I thought you were a moonlighter, Mr. Standon," Fenella said.

Patrick said, "I suspect that's what he wanted everyone to think, right, Standon? It's common knowledge that Captain Moonlight had me targeted for assassination. Once my body was found at the crossroads, everyone would assume he committed the crime, not the fine, upstanding St. John Standon."

Standon said nothing.

"Tell me," Patrick went on, "did you have your sister invite me to Drumlow today because you knew I would return to Rookforest by this road?"

"I admit to nothing," Standon muttered.

Patrick shrugged. "As you wish. But it's not difficult to piece together. You lured away my guards by telling them there were moonlighters on your property, and then you took a chance that I would be so upset by your sister's news that I would ride off alone."

Fenella glanced at Patrick. What was this about his going to Drumlow and Cynara's upsetting news? But that would have to wait.

"Why did you want to kill Patrick?" she demanded of Standon, who was busy stanching his wound with a handkerchief. "I know you hated him, but to try to kill him . . . ?"

White-faced and shaking, Standon took a step toward her, only to be stopped by Patrick's, "Stay where you are."

Standon stopped. "Because of him, my employer has dismissed me. He's turned me out of my home as if I were a stray dog."

"Now how does it feel," Patrick said coldly, "to be evicted, just as you've evicted so many others without a thought for their welfare?"

Fenella was aghast. "The Duke of Carbury has dismissed you as his estate agent? Well, that's hardly Patrick's fault!"

"Everything is his fault!" Standon cried.

Patrick shrugged. "Believe what you like. It's of no consequence to me. Only one question remains: what are we to do with you?"

Standon fell silent, his eyes never leaving Patrick's face.

Patrick smiled slowly, savoring the moment of his revenge. "You know, Standon, I could shoot you where you stand and it would be self-defense. No jury in the world would convict me for that."

"Patrick, you wouldn't!" Fenella cried in alarm.

"Why shouldn't I? He just tried to murder me. And before that, he had me sentenced to hell on earth for four years. Why should I show him any mercy after what he's done to me?"

"Because you're not a murderer, Patrick Quinn."

He did risk a quick glance at her then. "You have such faith in me, such trust."

"I do. I always have."

Suddenly Patrick took a deep shuddering breath. Fenella was right. In spite of all the anguish St. John Standon had caused him he couldn't murder him in cold blood, for that would make him no better than his enemy. And suddenly Patrick knew just how to achieve a vengeance more horrible than death.

"I'm going to give you a choice, Standon. I'll give you your freedom, if you'll agree to leave Ireland, never to return. You may go to England, America . . . the choice is yours. Or, if you prefer, I'll turn you over to Constable Treherne on a charge of attempted murder. Of course, you'll be tried and serve a prison term that's likely to be much longer than my paltry four years, but your fate is in your own hands."

Patrick smiled ruthlessly. "I wonder how you'll like prison, Standon?"

"Damn you to hell, Quinn!"

"Come, come, Standon. Make your choice before you bleed to death."

Suddenly proud Standon's shoulders slumped, and the fight seemed to drain out of him. "I'll leave," he muttered.

"Wise choice," Patrick said.

The sound of hoofbeats distracted him momentarily, and Patrick turned to see his two guards come riding up on lathered horses, their rifles drawn and their faces set with a mixture of remorse and reproach.

"Trouble, Mr. Quinn?" one of them asked as he reined in his horse and eyed Standon warily.

"Yes, but as you can see, I've taken care of it," Patrick replied.

"Ye should have waited for us, sir," the other guard said. "When we didn't see any sign of moonlighters on Drumlow land, we feared something was amiss. Then when they told us ye had already gone back to Rookforest alone, we came ridin' after ye as fast as we could."

"We were all duped by Mr. Standon here," Patrick said, slipping his revolver back into its holster, "but luckily, his ruse failed, thanks to Miss Considine." He smiled at Fenella, then turned back to his men.

"I want you two to escort Mr. Standon here to the dispensary and see that his wound is cared for. Then I want you to return to Drumlow and wait while he packs a bag. You are then to accompany him to Cork and see that he boards the next packet to England."

"Today, sir?"

"Immediately."

Standon stared at him in disbelief. "You can't send me packing as if I were some cotter! I'll need time to put my affairs in order."

Patrick's voice hardened to steel. "I'm a trusting man, Standon, but I'm not a fool. I'll not rest easy until I know you're off Irish soil for good, so you'll agree to my terms or face Treherne. What's it to be?"

"Do I have a choice?" Standon asked bitterly.

"No, but then, you never gave me one either."

Head bowed in resignation, Standon started hobbling toward his horse, while the guards urged theirs forward to accompany him.

When Standon was mounted, Patrick looked up at him. "Just remember never to return, because you owe me your life now. And if you try to harm me or a member of my family ever again, I shall come after you no matter where you try to hide. And the next time, I won't be merciful."

Standon looked over at Fenella, a puzzled expression on his face. "Tell me one thing, Miss Considine. How did you know I was waiting for Quinn?"

Panic coursed through Fenella. She couldn't tell him that she had had a vision. Then her terrible secret would become common knowledge.

Thinking fast, she replied, "When I returned from Dublin, I was told Patrick had gone to Drumlow to meet with Cynara. I was so jealous, I had to go riding after him. I saw you from the hill and yelled out a warning to Patrick."

Standon gave her an odd look, then touched his heel to his horse's ribs and started off without a backward glance, the two men riding on either side.

Fenella and Patrick stood there in silence, watching Standon slowly ride away and out of their lives forever.

Patrick turned to Fenella, his pale blue eyes filled with deep emotion. "Thank you for saving my life."

Before Fenella could say a word, he reached for her, cradling her face in his hands tenderly, gazing deeply into her eyes as he stroked her cheeks with his thumbs. Then he lowered his head and reached for her mouth hungrily with his own.

The moment his warm, pliant lips touched hers, Fenella went into his arms and clung to him as though she were drowning and he was her salvation. She had missed him so, fearing she would never see him again, or feel his strong arms holding her in just this way, encircling her with his love.

She returned his kiss with a passionate one of her own, claiming his mouth with her tongue and reveling in the shocks of delight such sweet intimate possession always sent through her. She belonged to him, and he belonged to her. They would never be separated again.

When they finally drew apart, breathless and shaken, they stared at each other rapturously.

"I was coming back to you when I had a vision on the train," Fenella said. "In it, I saw you die."

She burst into tears and had to cling to him for support. "Oh, Patrick, I was so afraid I wouldn't get here in time to save you."

"Hush, Fenella," he crooned, stroking her hair as he held her tightly against him. "But you did save me."

She pulled away from him so she could look into his eyes. "Usually I am too late, and my visions foretell the future. I couldn't save my father or Cadogan."

"But you saved me," he reminded her yet again.

"Thank God! I don't know what I would do without you."

He smiled down at her, draped his arm around her shoulders, and led her through the hedge's opening. When his eyes lit on his dead horse, his smile died. "Poor Gallowglass. If I hadn't reined him in when I did, that bullet would have killed me instead."

Fenella patted Patrick's arm. "He gave his life for his master."

Patrick knelt down and stroked the fallen animal's neck in a fond last farewell. Then he rose and looked up and down the road.

"Shall we stand here and wait for a passing carriage, or should we start walking?"

"Let's start walking," Fenella replied. "Perhaps we'll find my rented hack, a pernicious beast with the apt name of Cromwell."

Patrick grinned at that. "Did he throw you just as you were riding to my rescue?"

"No, he merely stopped, began grazing, and ignored me, which was even more humiliating."

Patrick burst out laughing. "How unchivalrous of him! He did that because he knew he could get away with it."

Fenella gave him an indignant look.

Patrick leaned over and planted a quick kiss on the top of her head. "Have I ever told you how adorable you look when you become indignant?"

"No, but I enjoy each and every compliment you give me."

As they walked in search of Cromwell, Patrick grew somber, as if a black cloud had suddenly blotted away his sunny mood.

"Jamser Garroty finally loosened his tongue," Patrick said. "He informed on the moonlighters and their leader."

Fenella stopped dead in her tracks. "He did? Who is it?"

"Terrence Sheely."

She stared at Patrick, unable to believe her own ears. "Terrence Sheely?" She shook her head. "Poor Margaret . . ."

Patrick's jaw hardened. "Young Garroty also revealed that Sheely was responsible for the deaths of your father and mine."

For a moment Fenella was too shocked to even think or feel. Then it hit her with the force of a storm, ripping the grief out of her anew. She doubled over in pain as a wild, desolate cry of denial and anguish escaped her lips.

Patrick took her in his arms and held her as though he'd never let her go.

"Why?" Fenella wailed as tears coursed down her face. "Why did they kill them?"

"I talked to Sheely in jail. He told me your father had to be executed because they were afraid he would inform on them. By the way, young Jamser spoke out against it. And they killed my father because he was evicting tenants and offering a reward for the names of the men who clipped you." Patrick took a deep breath before continuing. "Sheely and his men also put the dead rook on your doorstep and vandalized your garden because of your friendship with us Quinns."

Fenella shook her head. "I don't understand. Wasn't Terrence Sheely the one who tried to help your father the night he was shot?"

"A ruse," Patrick replied bitterly. "Sheely walked up behind him and engaged him in conversation. Then he shot him, and pretended to go to his aid. When people came running into the street, all they saw was Terrence

Sheely bending over my father, ostensibly trying to save his life." Patrick ran his hand through his hair, tousling it. "I'm told that's how moonlighters assassinate someone without drawing suspicion on themselves."

Fenella shook her head. "Cold, murdering bastards . . ."

"All one can say in their defense is that they believed their cause was just."

Fenella looked up at him. "Did you tell him about his child?"

Patrick shook his head with grim determination. "Perhaps I should let him go to the gallows knowing he'll never see it, but somehow, I don't think it would matter to him. And he's caused Margaret enough pain. The cocky bastard did tell me he never loved her. He only wanted to know what it felt like to bed a lady. I hit him then. It took two guards to pull me off."

Suddenly the sound of hoofbeats distracted them momentarily, and they turned to see a fine carriage drawn by two matching bays coming down the road toward them.

"Ah, perhaps we can prevail upon these good people to give us a ride back to Rookforest," Patrick said. As the carriage slowed and drew to a halt, he looked down at Fenella with an inscrutable expression in his eyes. "We have much to discuss later, Fenella."

She smiled and nodded.

Later, back at Rookforest, secure behind the locked door of Patrick's bedchamber, Fenella lay naked in her lover's arms, her warm, silken body blissfully languid and replete after their leisurely lovemaking.

"Mmm," she murmured, rubbing her face against his shoulder and breathing deeply the scents of heather and moist skin. "There's something sinful about making love in the middle of the day. Whatever will the servants think?"

Patrick smiled slowly. "Let them think what they please. I am the master of Rookforest and may do as I wish."

"So you have said on numerous occasions."

Suddenly Fenella's light, teasing mood vanished, and

Patrick sensed the change in her at once. He looked at her quizzically. "Is something wrong?"

Fenella's gaze fell away. "Why did you go to Drumlow to see Cynara?"

"She summoned me, and I, being the gentleman that I am, couldn't refuse a lady's request."

"Oh? Why did she wish to see you?"

One corner of Patrick's mouth rose in a roguish smile; then he leaned forward until his lips were almost touching her ear. "She wanted to tell me she was getting married again, and to offer me my last chance to be the lucky groom."

Fenella pulled away to gape at him. "She's going to marry again?"

He nodded. "She plans to marry Pryce Vernham, the man she flirted with at Nayland's ball."

Suddenly Patrick rolled away from her, rose, and strode across the room to the window, where he stood staring out at nothing in particular.

Fenella watched him, delighting in the smooth, sensuous way he walked, the taut muscles of his lean body rippling with every step. As he stood in the cool light of afternoon, the planes of his face illuminated, she felt desire stir within her all over again.

He looked at Fenella with such intensity that she felt a blush rise to her cheeks.

"I want you to know that even before I went to Drumlow today, I was certain that any feelings I once had for Cynara were dead. Any illusions I had about her had been stripped away long ago."

"Don't be too harsh on her," Fenella said. "She must do what she has to to survive in this world, as must we all."

Patrick strode back and stood at the bedside, looking down at Fenella expectantly. "That is the last time I shall ever mention her name. She was a part of my past, a very painful past, and now it's time for me to look toward the future"—his eyes were bright with promise—"with you."

Fenella's heart leapt with joy as she extended her hands toward him, and he took them, clasping them almost painfully.

"Fenella, will you marry me?"

She glanced at the scar and shivered. "Are you sure you want me, Patrick, knowing of my supernatural powers as you do?"

"Yes."

She smiled up at him, relieved. "No hesitation or reservations?"

"None. I want you for my wife, just as you are. As simple as that."

"And I want you for my husband," Fenella said softly, drawing him down by her side. "I think I've wanted you from the first moment we met."

That brought a teasing smile to his lips. "Considering what a surly brute I was, I doubt that, my love."

"But I came to love that surly brute."

Patrick took her in his arms. "No hesitation or reservations?"

"None, my love."

Fenella stared down at the gold band gracing her left hand, still unable to believe that just moments ago she had become Mrs. Patrick Quinn.

As the carriage made its way toward Devinstown, where Lord Nayland and the new Lady Nayland were giving a wedding reception in their honor before departing for Italy, Fenella kept looking up at Patrick seated across from her. He looked so handsome in his formal attire, yet there was still something as wild and untamed as the Irish night about him.

"And what might you be starin' at, Mrs. Quinn?" His pale blue eyes sparkled with mischief.

"My handsome husband, Mr. Quinn." With a sigh, Fenella smoothed the creamy satin skirt of her wedding dress. "I still can't quite believe you're mine, Patrick."

He leaned forward, took her left hand, and brought it to his lips. "And I can't quite believe you're mine, Fenella Quinn."

Suddenly Patrick glanced down at her wrist, a puzzled frown on his face. "Fenella, your scar is gone."

"What?" Her eyes widened in disbelief, but as she

pushed the cuff of her gown up, she realized Patrick spoke the truth.

"It's disappeared. Gone." She stared at her wrist in wonder. The flesh was as smooth and unmarred as the day she was born. "Patrick, what can this mean?"

"Perhaps it means you no longer have the gift of second sight."

She stared at him, bewildered and confused. "I . . . I don't understand. I truly did have second sight. I didn't imagine it."

"We both know that."

"Then why is it suddenly being taken away, if that is what has happened?"

A teasing smile tugged at his mouth. "You sound almost regretful."

"I'm not," Fenella said vehemently. "It's caused nothing but untold heartache for me, and I'm glad to be free of such a curse." She frowned. "But why was it ever given to me in the first place, if only to be taken from me now?"

Patrick stared out the carriage window, his brow furrowed thoughtfully. He said, "Perhaps William gave it to you so you would one day find happiness for yourself. Once you achieved that by marrying me, you didn't need the sight any longer."

Fenella rubbed her wrist, and nodded. "I think you're right. The power is gone. I can sense it. The sight has left me. Now that I have fulfilled my own destiny, I no longer need it."

Patrick said, "Now we're both free. I am free of my past and the need to avenge myself on St. John Standon, and you are free of the burden of knowing others' future. So now we can face our own great unknown future together like anyone else."

She smiled at him, her heart overflowing with a love unlike any she had ever known. Fenella uttered a silent prayer of thanks to William.

Patrick looked out the window at the soft green hills of the troubled but beautiful land they called home.

"Ireland will always be a land of magic and madness,'' he said. He looked at Fenella's wrist. ''For you, the magic has gone.''

Fenella smiled as she shook her head. ''Oh, no, I beg to differ with you, Patrick. The magic is just beginning.''

About the Author

Leslie O'Grady was born and raised in Connecticut, where she lives with her husband, Michael. A graduate of Central Connecticut State University, she worked as a public-relations writer for a television station and a hospital before retiring to write fiction full-time. When not writing, Ms. O'Grady enjoys movies, museums, and collecting books about nineteenth-century England and Art Nouveau. Her other novels include *Passion's Fortune*, *The Second Sister*, *Wildwinds*, and *Sapphire and Silk* (also available from New American Library).

There's an epidemic with 27 million victims. And no visible symptoms.

It's an epidemic of people who can't read.

Believe it or not, 27 million Americans are functionally illiterate, about one adult in five.

The solution to this problem is you... when you join the fight against illiteracy. So call the Coalition for Literacy at toll-free **1-800-228-8813** and volunteer.

Volunteer Against Illiteracy. The only degree you need is a degree of caring.